THE DUKE LEGACY

D. W. Duke

iUniverse LLC
Bloomington

THE DUKE LEGACY

iUniverse books may be ordered through booksellers or by contacting:

iUniverse
1663 Liberty Drive
Bloomington, IN 47403
www.iuniverse.com
1-800-Authors (1-800-288-4677)

Because of the dynamic nature of the Internet, any web addresses or links contained in this book may have changed since publication and may no longer be valid. The views expressed in this work are solely those of the author and do not necessarily reflect the views of the publisher, and the publisher hereby disclaims any responsibility for them.

Front cover design by Sean Means, great-great-great-grandson of Washington Duke. Front cover photograph by Duke Photography, Duke University. Back cover photograph by Michael Elderman.

Any people depicted in stock imagery provided by Thinkstock are models, and such images are being used for illustrative purposes only. Certain stock imagery © Thinkstock.

ISBN: 978-1-4917-2620-4 (sc)
ISBN: 978-1-4917-2621-1 (hc)
ISBN: 978-1-4917-2622-8 (e)

Library of Congress Control Number: 2014903348

Printed in the United States of America.

iUniverse rev. date: 3/19/2014

The Duke Legacy is dedicated to my father, Jewel Eugene Duke.

Contents

Part 1
The Early Years

Part 2
The Story of Doris Duke

Part 3
The Legacy Continues (Featured Stories)

Preface

On October 29, 1993, newspapers around the world announced that Doris Duke, the richest woman in the world, had died.[1] Her estate was officially estimated at $1.2 billion, though other sources valued her estate at more than twice that amount. Despite her wealth, happiness eluded her. In her loneliness, she fell victim to some of the worst elements of human greed and lust for power. The controversy surrounding her death has never been officially concluded, and certain aspects will forever remain a mystery. This book, in part, is an attempt to understand this woman and the world in which she lived. It was a world created a century before her time, when her ancestors made a conscious choice to forgo the luxury of the city for the more family-centered life of the countryside. In exploring the accumulation of the Duke fortune, we will come to understand the sequence of events that later led to Doris Duke's untimely end. Along the way we will meet other members of this prominent family and follow their journeys to lives lived very differently from both their ancestors and their descendants.[2]

Many volumes have been written about this family, and many

---

1   Eric Pace, "Doris Duke, 80, Heiress Whose Great Wealth Couldn't Buy Happiness, Is Dead," *New York Times*, October 29, 1993; "Doris Duke, the Richest Girl In The World," *Harper's Bazaar*, 2013 Hearst communications, accessed September 16, 2013, http://www.harpersbazaar.com/magazine/feature-articles/doris-duke-richest-girl-in-the-world-0912#slide-1.

2   For a partial genealogy chart of Washington Duke's descendants, please see appendix D.

more could be written. With this volume, I hope to fill in some of the gaps between what is widely known and what is preserved in family folklore, letters, court documents, and other records. I supplement the documentation with interviews on occasion.

The Duke Legacy examines the lives of these family members and the manner in which they interacted with each other and with others. How did they address important issues such as slavery and gender discrimination? What was their perception of the rights of human beings, and who were human beings in their eyes? Did the definition of "human being" include African Americans who had been relegated to an inferior position by the colonial government and subsequently the constitutional government of the United States? How did they view Native Americans in the structure of humanity? Our story begins with Washington Duke, the patriarch who laid the foundation for the multibillion Duke financial empire.

Most of what I know about Washington Duke's younger years I heard from stories my grandmother Sarah Taylor Duke told me.[3] These are stories she told over a period of many years as I was

---

3   My ancestor, William Duke, is said to have been the uncle of Washington Duke. He was one of three brothers, William Duke, Henry Duke Jr., and Taylor Duke. Taylor was the father of Washington. William's son, Mordecai, was a wagon maker and a farmer. Mordecai and his son William P. Duke would travel several times each year from Woodbury, Tennessee, to North Carolina to buy metal parts for the wagons from a blacksmith in Durham. When they traveled they would stop to see Washington's family and would usually stay with them for several weeks.

William P. Duke was born in 1819, a year before Washington, and died in 1912 at the age of ninety-two. He spent a great deal of time with Washington on their visits to Durham and thus was a personal witness to many of the events described in this book. He heard firsthand accounts of others. Sarah Taylor Duke's father died when she was a toddler, and her mother married William A. Duke, the grandson of William P. Duke. So she was raised in the home where William P. Duke also lived. He passed much of this information on to his son William M. Duke, who told it to Sarah, who was born in 1901 and died in 1987. Thus, Sarah heard stories about Washington Duke from her great-grandfather and after his death from her grandfather. She in turn passed this information on to me.

growing up. They covered events from the time he worked against the law to free a slave to the time he was tricked into using a moose to pull his plow. Washington was a complicated man, and I wanted to know more about him—not just him, but his descendants too, who built a family fortune and brought the Duke name to international prominence. So I dug into old correspondences, family records, university archives, deeds, wills, military records, and any other relevant documents I could find and became a bit of a historian and genealogist. In the process, I came to understand that the Duke legacy is more than just an inheritance. It is a view of the world formed in the crucible of dark moments of the nation and of individual lives.

For most of my life, these stories were simply great stories about Washington Duke that had been personally witnessed by my fourth-generation great-grandfather William P. Duke, and told to his son and my grandmother Sarah Duke. Later in life, I realized that much of this information was simply not known to others, not even some of Washington's direct descendants. Given his impact in the lives of so many persons, it seemed unfortunate that more was not known about him. As I shared some of this information with others, I was encouraged to document these accounts in a publication. One person to whom I am particularly grateful for this encouragement is the Honorable Judge Elwood Rich (ret.), a Duke University graduate of 1943, to whom a tribute is provided in appendix C of this book.

For over twenty years I have continued my genealogy and family history research, which became exponentially efficient with the invention of the Internet. Eventually I became the administrator for the Duke Family DNA Research Project for Family Tree DNA. I also began hiring other genealogists to assist in the research and to help fine-tune data, locate missing pieces, and solve puzzles. Previous genealogists have attempted to unravel the complicated Duke family genealogy with mixed results. Early genealogists worked without modern communication techniques. DNA analysis has been one of the most significant breakthroughs in genealogy research.[4] However, DNA analysis is not without limitation in that it may not reveal the identity of ancestral family members in cases of half siblings, adoption, or infidelity and thus can also be misleading.

As time passed, I began working on this book between other publications while maintaining a busy law practice. Occasionally I would discuss these stories with Duke family members and others who had connections with the Duke family or Duke University. I was repeatedly encouraged to write this book by many of these individuals. In the early part of this century I began to take the idea of writing the book seriously.

While I realized that I possessed information about Washington Duke that was not widely known, in time I also learned that some of the information I possessed conflicted with information that had been published about Washington. For example, it has been published that he once purchased and owned a slave. In contrast, the information I learned as a child was that he never owned a slave but rather purchased a slave so he could immediately set her free. It is also published that he once hired a slave from a slave owner and

---

4   The most recent Duke family genealogist of note was Evelyn Duke Brandenberger. Brandenberger spent fifty years researching every family in the United States with the surname Duke. She was working without Internet, a form of modern communication that we today take for granted. If she needed to research the line of Henry Duke, Oglethorpe County, Georgia, 1779, she literally had to travel to Oglethorpe County, find and search the appropriate records, and then document her findings. Such an event could take months and sometimes years. Genealogists had a network that allowed them to share information to lessen the need for personal travel, but even then, if a particular line had not been researched, it could require months, or even years, of travel and investigation. With modern communication techniques we can often accomplish the same research in a matter of minutes. In referencing Brandenberger, we quickly discovered that her writings contain a number of significant errors, but the data collection was excellent for her day. She gathered deeds, land grants, military records, prison records, estate documents, letters, and any documentation of relationship. For this work, we are deeply indebted to her and duly note her research herein.

the slave escaped while in his custody. In contrast, the information I previously learned was that he once helped in the escape of a slave who was his childhood friend. Through research, I discovered that his childhood friend had the same name as the slave who escaped while in his custody. In time the pieces of the puzzle began to fall into place. Taking the bits of information from the stories I learned about Washington from my grandmother, I was often able to find documents in the archives at Duke University and elsewhere that confirmed the information I had been told as a child.

Finally, around 2003 I began working on this book. I have attempted to report the stories as accurately and clearly as I could recall them, with the caveat that I heard most of them many years before I reduced them to writing. More recent events in the Duke family were much easier to research, often because interviews of eyewitnesses were possible, and in some instances the matters occurred during my lifetime and were reported in the news. With the stories about Washington, I went to great lengths to tie them to events I could confirm or document elsewhere and sometimes to customs as they existed in those days. I have not reported all of the stories I have heard about Washington and his descendants but have focused on the stories that would be of the greatest interest to others, and I have created a storyline in third-person narration, in the form of a novel, to provide the greatest interest to the reader. I have at all times tried to remain as true to the actual events as I believe they most likely occurred. It is important to understand that what I am giving here is my opinion of what actually transpired based on an analysis of the data. Others might disagree with some of my conclusions.

This book, then, is the Duke legacy as I have come to understand it. I am presenting it to you as I have learned it. I will retell the stories I learned as a child, though sadly Sarah Taylor Duke, who told them to me, is no longer with us. Where possible I will include footnotes to identify letters, public records, publications, and court documents to demonstrate the history as it can be known; but I will occasionally exercise writer's prerogative to bring the story to life and to fill in the gaps, though less frequently than one might expect. Where the account is based on folklore as opposed to historical documentation, I will so indicate. This type of novel is commonly called historical fiction. While it is based upon factual events and dates, details provided in dialogue or other forms of expression, such as action, are added to make the story more interesting and enjoyable.

The Duke Legacy is divided into three parts. Part 1 addresses the early years of the legacy and the formation of the Duke financial empire. Part 2 is the story of Doris Duke, and part 3 includes featured articles about members of the Duke family and Duke University.

If this book seems a hagiography of Washington, then so be it. Everything I have learned about this man has caused me to respect him and his family all the more. He was a man who did not shy away from confrontation when he faced injustice; nor did he shy away from hard work—he built his own house, after all, and how many of us can say that today?

Acknowledgments

While numerous individuals provided important information and materials for this book, I would especially like to thank the following persons for their contributions:

Raymond Cooper (of Cannon County Historical
Society, descendant of William P. Duke)
Elizabeth Dunn (research services librarian at Duke University);
Chris Johnson (of Single Oak Law Offices,
attorney, friend, and consultant);
Brian Kramer (of Brian J. Kramer, PC,
personal attorney of Sean Means);
Don Howarth (of Howarth and Smith, personal
attorney of the late Doris Duke);
Amy McDonald (reference archivist at Duke University);
The Honorable Judge Elwood Rich, retired (Duke BA '43);
Diane L. Richard (president, Mosaic Research and
Project Management, Genealogy, Raleigh, NC);
Suzelle Smith (of Howarth and Smith, personal
attorney of the late Doris Duke);
Steven Spile (of Spile, Leff & Goor, LLP,
attorney, friend, and consultant);
The late Sarah Taylor Duke (my grandmother, whose
Duke family stories I heard as a child caused me to
become a Duke family historian and genealogist).

Part 1

The Early Years

Introduction

Grandma's Stories

It seems that everyone in the Duke family has heard stories about Washington Duke. They have heard that he was kind to everyone and that he respected all persons regardless of race, gender, or financial status. He was always trying to find a way to help others. From the Duke Memorial Methodist Church he cofounded in 1885, to Duke University, named after him in 1924, his generosity and kindness became a lasting symbol throughout the Carolinas, where he lived out his days. In some ways the area where he lived was much different than it is today. In other ways, it was much the same. But the Duke name is recognized far beyond the borders of North Carolina and is today known throughout the world because of the generosity of Washington and his descendants.

I recall that as a boy, several times per month, we would pile into our white Cadillac Fleetwood and endure the tortuous one-hour drive from Ft. Wayne to Pennville, Indiana, to visit my father's family on Uncle Neil's farm. As children we hated the drive, which seemed to last forever, but we loved the destination. My father had six living brothers and one sister. This meant there were cousins everywhere.

Uncle Neil's farm was on a gravel road seven miles from Pennville. My grandparents, Thomas and Sarah Duke, had moved their family from Cannon County, Tennessee, to Indiana in the

1940s, and most of my uncles bought farms. Uncle Neil's farm sat back from the road on a five-acre lawn. On the farm was a small lake, well stocked with bass and bluegill, where we would often fish when we visited. Lily pads floated at the edge of the lake, where the cattails grew. The farmhouse, built in the 1800s, had been remodeled to provide modern amenities. The parlor was toward the front of the house and had a front door that opened to the large lawn, though it was seldom used. I enjoyed our visits to Uncle Neil's farm, which had become a central meeting place for the Duke family.

On a typical Sunday afternoon, in the parlor of Uncle Neil's farmhouse, there would be at least three guitars passing from one person to the next as everyone took turns playing a song. My cousin Nancy and my sister Julie both studied classical piano, so there was often a clash between the guitars playing country-western, folk, or rock, and the pianos playing classical and pop. As the guitar-versus-piano feud raged throughout the day, the aunts and uncles would gather in a separate room with my grandparents to talk about the immediate family. They would generally talk about a cousin or a family friend. As the afternoon neared evening the conversation would turn to religion and politics. After Grandpa Duke died in 1965, Grandma would usually sit in a rocker in the corner of the room, look around at her children and grandchildren, and listen to the conversations, always with a smile on her face. All the time I was growing up, I never saw her without a smile and I never heard her say a cross word to or about anyone. If a person made eye contact with her, she would chuckle and say "Well," as if she had something to say, but she would not continue unless asked a question.

Occasionally the family would talk about Washington Duke and his brother John. Ironically, I seemed to be the only person interested in the family history, so the conversations did not last long. In contrast to most of my cousins, I was fascinated by the stories about Washington's family. I always wanted to hear more of them. I enjoyed hearing about the rugged world in which they lived and how Washington built the family fortune with nothing but two blind mules and a wagonload of tobacco. So I was the one who would sit next to Grandma and ask her questions throughout the afternoon as others talked about politics, religion, or something that happened on one of my uncle's farms. It seemed there was always something happening on one of the farms, from a dog losing a leg through a fight with a combine to a cow getting loose and trampling a neighbor's corn.

Grandma had so many stories that I could not begin to enumerate all of them, and unfortunately, I did not begin to write them down until over a decade after she died. It seemed there was no need. She knew them by heart and she knew our family genealogy and connections like a road map, even before genealogy was a popular interest. She could recite names and events as if she had written a book on the topic. I knew that she could only have learned them by observation and by what she had been told by eyewitnesses. She did not ever travel outside of the Portland and Pennville area, and there were no libraries in that part of Indiana that would have contained the information she accumulated. No one else in the family had much interest in these matters, so I knew that what she told me was based on her own personal knowledge and not something she had read in a book. The Internet had not yet been invented.

"Grandma, would you tell me about Washington Duke again?" I would often ask.

She would chuckle and then begin with something like this: "Well, as you know, Washington was born on a cold December day in 1820, about a year after your ancestor William P. Duke[5] was born. William was your grandpa's great-grandpa, so this was a long time ago. William and his son always talked about their cousin Washington. I remember that they were so happy when Washington's businesses became successful. William used to say, 'If any cousin deserves to be

---

5   William P. Duke was the grandson of William Duke, said to have been Taylor Duke's brother. Taylor Duke was the father of Washington Duke.

blessed with fortune, it is Washington. He is as good a man as they come.' He used to tell us so many stories about Washington."

She would continue: "Now, William lived in a big log house that his dad Mordecai built when he moved to Cannon County, Tennessee. William and Mordecai each had a 1200 acre farm adjacent to one another. William's house sat alongside Duke Creek, which ran through his farm. I don't know how big the house was, but I know it was as big as some barns. My dad died when I was a little bitty thing, and I was raised in that house, so I heard Duke stories all the time. There was a fireplace that was so big a person could walk inside of it without ducking his head. They used to throw a giant log in the fireplace and let it smolder for days. It kept the house plenty warm. There were lots of rooms upstairs, and it was one of the few houses near Woodbury with indoor running water. That house burned down when your dad was a boy. A log rolled out of the fireplace one day and caught the house on fire. Everyone was sad because that house had a lot of memories, and all of the important family papers and books were lost in the fire."

"On Mordecai's farm there was a limestone bluff, covered with ivy. That is how the settlement of Ivy Bluff got its name. Mordecai used to allow neighbors to come to his farm and cut limestone from the mountain that they would use to build their fireplaces. Washington's older brother Billy was a traveling minister for the Methodist Episcopal Church. He came to Ivy Bluff several times in the 1840s and established a Methodist Episcopal Church camp. People would come from all around to the revival meetings. Back then they used to meet in Mordecai's farmhouse. Many years later Ivy Bluff Methodist Church was built about a mile from Mordecai's farm. It is still there today."

Grandma would lean back in her chair and look around the room at her children and grandchildren as if she thought they would help her remember the details. Uncle Neil or Uncle Hershel might look at us with a smile and then ask, "Did you get enough to eat?" or "What are you talking about over there?"

Grandma would rock slowly and then continue. "Now, William's dad, Mordecai, had several businesses. He was a wagon maker, a leather tanner, and a farmer. Mordecai and William used to travel to Durham, North Carolina, to buy parts for the wagons they would build.[6] There was a blacksmith in Durham the family had known for decades that made metal wagon parts and would sell them to Mordecai cheaper than anyone else around, so it was worth it to go to Durham to pick up a wagonload of these parts. Durham was about four hundred miles away, so it would take a couple of weeks just to get there.

"Once or twice each year they would travel to Durham for these metal parts, and they would always stop in to see Washington's family. They would usually stay with them for a week or two, pick up the parts, and then come back home. It was while they were visiting that William would spend a lot of time playing with Washington and Washington's brother John. There was a slave boy named Jim who lived on a neighbor's farm. He was a friend of Washington. Back in those days, white kids weren't supposed to play with black kids, but out on the farm no one knew except Washington's parents, and they always said it was a good thing. These boys—William, Washington, John, and Jim—would play together whenever Mordecai took William to Durham for parts. That's how William got all the stories that he would tell us."

Grandma might pause for a few moments as she reflected on the story.

"Washington's mom and dad were Taylor and Dicey. Taylor was your ancestor's brother. Taylor and Dicey always said that there was something unusual about Washington. He wasn't like the other kids. He always wanted to make others happy. At a church

---

6   The parts were for the wheels and the tongues of the wagons. The tongue is the pole on the front of a wagon that hooks onto the yoke to hold the oxen, the mules, or the horses. Most wagon makers in those days used wooden tongues to hold the horses, but Mordecai and William always used metal tongues to achieve a much stronger wagon with a longer life.

picnic, if he noticed that someone didn't have enough food, he would invite them over to share what his family had. That was just his way. This was true from his youngest age. While the other children were concerned about winning a game, he was always more concerned about making sure everyone had a chance to play and that everyone played fair.

"When they were teenagers, Washington and his brother John went to live with their older brother Billy, but John didn't like it there. Billy was hard on him. He made him work long hours and would whip him if he didn't do his chores. So one day John ran away by sneaking out of a bedroom window. He showed up at Mordecai's house near Ivy Bluff and wanted to stay for a while. Mordecai felt sorry for him, so he let him stay. John never went back to North Carolina but instead moved over by Milan, Tennessee, where he lived the rest of his life."

This is how Grandma would tell the stories, and I would listen intently. She knew them so well that it seemed I would always have access to them. It never occurred to me that someday she would not be with us and that the only source of this information might be what she had told me. As the years passed, I grew into adulthood, went to college, and then went on to law school. I would occasionally think about the stories she had told me but was too busy to begin chronicling them. In the early 1990s my father and I began extensive genealogical research of the Duke family for a book I was thinking of writing. We spent many hours in libraries pouring over census records, military records, land records, books, court documents, and anything else that might shed light on the Duke family. It was an arduous task compiling all of this information, and eventually I hired other genealogists and family researchers to assist in the project.

Finally, after twenty years of research and writing, I have finished the compilation of this work, which I am now sharing with you. This is the Duke legacy as it was told to me and as I have found it to exist through my research. This is the story of Washington Duke and his descendants.

1

The Legacy Begins

In the summer of 1826, five-year-old Washington Duke sat in the grass, holding a large, green grasshopper in the palm of his hand. The insect crawled around his thumb, and Washington turned his hand over to watch its progress. Feeling that he could sense the curiosity of this small creature, who appeared to be a gentle giant in his own world, Washington watched the insect walk around his hand unconcerned; he then turned his palm downward, allowing the insect to cross the dorsal surface in an upright position. The grasshopper spat a brown fluid on his hand. "What is that?" he asked Billy,[7] his twenty-three-year-old brother who was sitting next to him. Billy was reading the Bible as they talked. Although the family had a Bible, Billy liked to carry his own so he could study no matter where he was.

"He is spitting tobacco on you," replied Billy. "The grasshopper does that to protect himself from harm. It doesn't hurt people, but it will discourage a field mouse or other small animal."

"Where did he get tobacco?"

---

7   William J. Duke was Billy Duke's true name, but he was more commonly known as Billy, which is the name used most frequently in this book. Billy was the most studious family member and later became ordained as a minister by the Methodist Episcopal Church.

"It isn't real tobacco," Billy said with a laugh. "It's digestive fluid acting upon the plants he has eaten."

"What is it for?"

"The grasshopper does that when he feels threatened. It gives off an odor detectable by small animals. Ordinarily, when a small animal encounters it he will back away from the grasshopper."

Washington put the grasshopper on the ground and then stood up. "I don't want to scare him." Although he could not have known, someday he would become a gentle giant in his own world, much like the grasshopper he so admired as a child.

"It is good that you don't want to scare him. We should be kind to all living things. It says that in the Bible, and even the Eno[8] people say that. We better go to the house for dinner. Mammy is making chicken and dumplings." Billy stood up and reached for Washington's hand.

"I love chicken and dumplings," Washington replied as he and Billy ran to the Duke homestead.

"Wash your hands before you sit at the table," said Washington's father, Taylor, when the boys entered the rustic building they called home. The family home was a wooden structure with five rooms and an oak frame with pine board walls. The family grew produce primarily for their own consumption, and they traded or sold some of the crops at the market in town. The crops consisted of beans, corn, potatoes, tomatoes, onions, peppers, and various fruits. They also grew cotton, some of which was used to make clothing for themselves and some of which was sold at the local market, and they grew tobacco, which they also sold at the local market. In addition, they raised cows and chickens. The cows provided dairy products for the community, and the chickens produced a daily supply of eggs. There were no schools in the area at the time, but

---

8   The Eno people were a small Native American tribe that lived in the area of Hillsboro, North Carolina. See "The Eyewitness Accounts of the Eno and related Indians," *Eno Journal* 4, no. 2 (1976).

Taylor and Dicey successfully taught all of their children mathematics, science, literature, music, and art. The son of Henry Duke, a scholarly man who had left a comfortable position among Virginia high society to raise his family in the wilderness, Taylor was able to keep his children abreast of the latest world events, while providing the rudiments of an education in the backwoods of North Carolina.

Inside the home was a dining table that was large enough to accommodate Washington's family of ten children. At one end of the living room area, which also served as the dining area, was a large fireplace. On each side of the fireplace was a wooden rocking chair; one was for Taylor, and one for Dicey. At various locations around the room there were other rocking chairs, but the children usually sat at the dining table when they studied. A long, soft Georgian couch, which doubled as a daybed, rested against the wall opposite the front door. Next to the door was a gun rack that held several muskets. In a world without modern communication, there was little to do with one's time, especially in the cold winter days, so the family spent most of their time reading.

As they sat at the table, everyone became silent so Taylor could say grace. The handsome deputy sheriff of Orange County, who was also a captain in the North Carolina militia, said, "Creator of the heavens and the earth, we thank Thee for this food we are about to eat and we ask that Thou would bless it for the nourishment of our bodies. Please, bless the hands that prepared it ..." The prayer was interrupted by a loud crash and a rattling sound outside. Boots, the big stray dog with an unfriendly disposition, that had suddenly appeared on the porch one day and stayed, ran out from under the table and began barking ferociously. Taylor jumped from the table and ran toward the door, grabbing his flintlock rifle from the gun rack. As he opened the door, he found himself staring directly into the face of a large black bear that had just knocked over a barrel of walnuts the boys had gathered for the winter. The startled bear jumped from the porch and ran into the woods as quickly as it could, with Boots chasing behind him.

Taylor fired a shot in the air to ensure that the bear would continue running and not turn back.

Dicey, Washington's mother, stood up from the table and walked over to the door. She watched the bear disappear into the woods. "I think you scared the bear more than he scared you."

"Did you hit it?" asked Washington who walked over and looked out the door his father was closing.

"No, son," Taylor replied.

"Why not?" Washington asked with a puzzled expression.

"Because the bear didn't hurt us. He was just looking for food," Taylor said.

"Was it a grizzly bear?" asked Washington's older sister Mary, fearfully.

"No, it was a black bear. The grizzlies are the ones you need to watch out for the most," said Taylor, "but you should try to avoid all bears. Even a black bear can attack if it feels threatened."[9]

This was the wilderness where the Duke family lived. Wild animals were commonplace. Some, such as the rattlesnake, the copperhead, the cottonmouth, the mountain lion, and the bear, were very dangerous, and one needed to exercise caution when going into the woods that surrounded the house.

Washington Duke, son of Taylor Duke and Dicey Jones Duke, was born on December 18, 1820, in Orange County, North Carolina,[10] on his family's farm, which was located twelve miles

---

9   The encounter with the bear is based on a story told by Washington's family.

10   Taylor and Dicey had the following children: William J. Duke (Billy), born in 1803; Mary Duke, born in 1805; Reany Duke, born in 1807; Amelia Duke, born in 1809; Kirkland R. Duke, born in 1812; Malinda Duke, born in 1815; John Taylor Duke, born in 1818; Washington Duke, born in 1820; Doctor Brodie Duke, born in 1823; and Robert Duke, born in 1825. This information was derived from William J. Duke's family Bible.

A number of genealogists (Walter Garland Duke, Evelyn Duke Brandenberger, and others) have maintained that Taylor Duke had children from a prior marriage, even after this claim was rejected by the executors of the estate of James Buchanan Duke. The basis for the claim is, in part, a court proceeding

from a small town called Hillsboro.[11] Washington was very close to his older brother Billy. They would often go into the woods to explore for hours at a time. He was fascinated by wild animals and insects and would study them for hours, asking Billy as many questions as he could contrive, while trying to learn about the animal world. Early in the spring of 1827, on a warm afternoon, Washington and Billy were walking in the woods near a creek that ran near their farm. As they walked, Washington could smell the fresh air and the wonderful aroma of the green forest plants dancing in the wind after a warm rain. He noticed how bright the leaves on the trees seemed with the sun glistening off their wet surfaces. They came to the edge of the creek and sat on a large rock, allowing their feet to dangle in the water. Washington was sitting to the left side of Billy. The clear water flowed quietly over the rocks, making a whispering sound. This was a wonderful time for Washington. He loved these times with Billy.

Suddenly Billy said, "G. W., don't move. Hold perfectly still."

---

between a person named Grief Duke and William J. Duke wherein the court purportedly identified Grief as William Duke's half brother and stated that they were both sons of Taylor Duke. Allegedly, this information was stipulated to by the parties in open court and appears in the court minutes. According to census records, Grief Duke was indeed raised by Taylor Duke and his sister. Washington Duke's niece, Lida Duke Angier, submitted correspondence to the executors of James B. Duke's estate in 1926, saying she had heard that Grief was actually descended from Taylor Duke's brother William Duke. In addition, Benjamin Newton Duke sent a letter to the executors stating that his father, Washington, had never mentioned that he had any half siblings. (See James B. Duke Estate Papers, Correspondence Subseries, David M. Rubenstein Rare Book and Manuscript Library, Duke University.) In an effort to resolve this issue, this author retained researchers to search the Orange County court records and personally communicated with a number of court clerks. Although we have found the case listed in the docket, the actual file is missing. As of the date of this writing, the court clerks are unable to locate the file, and descendants of Grief Duke still maintain that they were wrongfully excluded from the estate of James Buchanan Duke.

11   "Hillsboro" is today spelled "Hillsborough."

Washington became afraid but followed his brother's instruction. Then he saw something that terrified him. A large rattlesnake was slithering out from under the rock on which they were sitting and creeping toward Washington's left side.[12] Billy whispered, "Just hold still. It will be okay."

Terrified, Washington said nothing and moved only his eyes to see the snake better. The rattlesnake locked its eyes on Washington and coiled as if to strike. The snake's stillness, just inches from Washington's left leg, felt menacing. He wondered if he was going to die but trusted his brother and followed his instructions, remaining frozen on the rock.

Billy also remained frozen. The rattlesnake did not move except to wag its split tongue and occasionally shake its rattles while staring at Washington. The sound of the snake's rattles was deafening. After about five minutes, seeing the terrified expression on Washington's face, Billy began to pray softly. "Dear Lord, please protect us from this rattler. You created this creature, you can tell the creature to leave. And please don't let G. W. be afraid."

After what seemed to be an eternity, the rattlesnake slowly began to move away toward the water and then suddenly changed its direction and came back toward Washington. The snake slid under his legs and back under the rock, rubbing against his bare ankles as it passed. Washington could see the bright diamond-shaped markings on the back of the snake. Finally, the rattler disappeared under the rock. When he felt it was safe, Billy slowly lifted his feet out of the water and climbed on top of the rock; he then reached down and lifted Washington up on top of the rock. They looked around to make sure the snake had not come out on the other side. When they were sure it was safe, they jumped from the rock and ran up the hill, away from the water.

---

12   The story of the rattlesnake is fictional and intended to demonstrate the dangers of the environment in which Washington was raised. Rattlesnakes and copperheads were a common danger in North Carolina at the time, as they are to this day.

"Why did that snake stare at me like that?" Washington asked.

"It is hard for snakes to see objects that aren't moving, and they rely upon heat to detect the presence of a person or an animal. Since it's warm out today, he probably didn't know for sure if you were there, and if he did, he didn't even know what you were."

"I was so scared. I thought he was going to bite me. How do you know if a snake has poison?"

"Most the snakes around here that have poison have a head shaped like an arrowhead. If it is far away, you should walk away, but if it is really close, you should hold still like we did a little while ago. God spared us today. We could have been killed."

Still nervous from the incident, Billy picked up Washington and carried him in his arms until they were out of the woods. They didn't return to the woods for several days, and when they did, Washington carried a large stick. "I want to be ready if we see another snake," he told Billy.

Washington would often go outside and play for hours. On these occasions he sometimes came in contact with wild animals. The animals seemed to recognize his gentle spirit and were not usually afraid of him. It was common for other members of the household to come outside and see Washington playing with a raccoon or another undomesticated animal. One day, Dicey went out of the front door of the house only to find Washington playing with a skunk.

Remaining calm and quiet, Dicey said, "Don't make any quick movements or any loud sounds, G. W. You are playing with a baby skunk."

His mother's words startled Washington, who remembered the time his brother had told him not to move to avoid being bitten by the rattlesnake. Washington became afraid. He had seen skunks before but did not know that a skunk could be dangerous. Then he concluded that there was no serious danger since his mother did not seem alarmed, as his brother had seemed when they saw the snake.

A neighbor, Mr. Parker, who had been waiting in the house

for Taylor to come home, heard Dicey's comment and came out to see what was happening. Dicey whispered, "He is playing with a skunk. I don't know if he even knows what it can do."

Mr. Parker laughed. "Oh, that's nothin' to worry about. That one's a baby. His scent glands ain't developed at that age. He can't spray."

They watched for a while. Washington held the skunk like a baby, rocking it in his arms as he had seen his mother do with babies. He touched its nose with his finger and allowed the skunk to lick his fingers.

Washington admired the pretty features of the animal. He liked the sharp contrast between the black and white stripes. He stood up and carried the skunk toward the house so his mother could see it.

"Don't bring it inside," said Dicey. She looked at Mr. Parker. "I know you said he can't spray, but I don't want it to get used to coming around here."

Mr. Parker nodded. "Actually, it might not be a bad idea if I took it away from here and into the woods before it gets accustomed to your yard. He might come around all the time when it gets older. Also, his mother might come looking for him."

"You don't mind? I would really appreciate it," Dicey said.

"Naw, I don't mind."

"Washington, it's time to come in," Dicey said. "Mr. Parker has to take your friend back into the woods."

"But I am playing with him," Washington protested.

"No, you have to come in now."

"Okay," Washington said with a disappointed expression as he sat the skunk on the ground.

Mr. Parker walked over and picked up the skunk and began carrying it into the woods.

"Thanks so much," Dicey said.

"No problem," Mr. Parker replied.

Dicey went back inside and then heard a loud yell from Mr.

Parker which was followed by the sweet, putrid aroma of a skunk. She opened the door to see Mr. Parker standing about forty feet from the house, holding his arms up in the air. His shirt looked wet. "Oh!" he shouted.

"What happened?" Dicey asked.

Mr. Parker replied, "I reckon that skunk ain't as young as I thought."

Washington could see the skunk walking away from Mr. Parker toward the woods. "What happened?" he asked.

Dicey put her hand over her mouth so Mr. Parker could not see her giggling. Then she said, "I have some canned tomatoes you can take with you. They are good for getting the smell of skunk off you."

Finally, Mr. Parker put his hands down, shook his head, and began laughing. "Well, I guess maybe I had that coming. Tomatoes help, but they won't completely kill the odor. You won't be seeing me in church for a few weeks."

Washington asked again, "What happened, Mammy?"

"I will tell you in a little while," Dicey replied as she went in the house to get the canned tomatoes.

Mr. Parker said, "There's a good lesson here for you, G. W. Don't ever think you know everything, because just about the time you think you do, you find out the hard way that you don't."

Dicey carried the jars of tomatoes toward Mr. Parker and set them on the ground about twenty feet from him as she held a white handkerchief over her nose and mouth. She laughed. "Nothing personal, but I think this is as close as I am going to get."

Mr. Parker laughed. "Okay, thanks." He walked forward and picked up the canned tomatoes and turned around to go home.[13]

When Washington became seven years of age, he was given a little more liberty in outdoor activities. He would often walk the neighboring land, exploring the amazing sights of the forest.

---

13   The account of Washington and the skunk is based on family folklore.

He enjoyed this time alone because it allowed him to think about matters without interruption. One summer day as Washington was walking across a field, he came to a wooden fence that surrounded a plantation. On the other side of the fence he saw an African American boy playing in the neighbor's yard. The boy appeared about the same age as Washington. Washington climbed over the fence and walked over to the boy, who looked up with a startled expression and then abruptly stood up.[14]

"What are you doing?" asked Washington, looking at a long, pointed stick in the boy's hand.

"I am hunting a lion," the boy replied.

"A lion? Did you see a mountain lion?"

"Naw, it's a lion from Pappy's home in Africa. Pappy was caught by the traders and brought here on a ship. He taught me things he learned when he was a boy, like how to kill a lion. He said that someday we might go back to Africa and I will need to know how to kill a lion."

"Killing a lion sounds dangerous," replied Washington. "Does your pappy work here?"

"No, my pappy is over by Granville."

"All the way over in Granville? You must not see him very much," Washington said as he sat on the ground.

"I haven't seen Pappy since I was real little," the boy said nervously as he sat down next to Washington. "You best not sit here. We will both get in trouble."

"Why would we get in trouble?" asked Washington.

"Colored folks aren't supposed to talk to white folks. You know that, don't you?"

"That seems like a funny thing to me," replied Washington with a puzzled expression on his face. "Are we really different? You

---

14   The account of Jim in this chapter is based on family folklore. Later Jim's story will be documented by written correspondence.

have two eyes, two ears, one nose, and a mouth. I have two eyes, two ears, one nose, and a mouth."

"Yeah, and the dog has two eyes, two ears, one nose, and a mouth, but that doesn't mean he is one of us," the boy said with a laugh.

"But the dog can't talk to us, and the dog can't think about what he is saying. That makes him different from us, but it makes you and me the same," Washington said, laughing as well. "Do you have to work too?"

"Yep, but sometimes Master Mangum lets me stop working early, like today. You really have to go or I'll get in trouble."

"Okay, I'll leave, but I'll be back so we can talk again. What's your name?"

"My name is Jim," replied the boy.

"I am George Washington Duke. Some people call me Wash, and some people call me G. W."

Jim laughed. "Is it okay if I call you Washtub?"

"I suppose it's okay if you have to," Washington said with a smile.

Every day for weeks Washington came to the fence looking for Jim. One day, when the leaves on the oak trees were beginning to turn brown and reddish orange, Washington saw Jim sitting on the ground at the edge of a cornfield. Washington walked up to him and asked, "Hi, Jim, what are you doin'?"

"I'm just shuckin' corn," Jim replied. "That's my job for today. It's okay for you to talk to me now. Auntie Tilly, who works in the big house, talked to Master Mangum. He said I can talk to you as long as I keep my chores up."

"Can I help shuck the corn?" Washington sat on the ground next to Jim.

"Sure, if you want to." Jim gave Washington a stalk of corn to shuck.

Washington said, "You've shucked a lot of corn. How many ears do you have to shuck today?"

"I have to fill three baskets of corn. I like shuckin' corn. It's easier 'en pickin' cotton."

Washington took a handful of husk and put it on his head and asked, "What do I look like?"

Jim laughed. "You look like a girl."

Washington laughed and then put a handful of husk on Jim's head. "You look like a lion."

"You seen a lion?" Jim asked excitedly.

"Yep, I saw one at the traveling show in Hillsboro. It came all the way from Africa."

"Wow! You saw a real lion from Africa?"

"Sure did. It was huge. It looked like a mountain lion with lots of hair."

"I wish I could see a lion," Jim said.

"Maybe one day you will."

"You boys are really tearin' into that corn. Good job." Startled at the sound of a man's voice, Washington and Jim jumped to their feet and turned to see a tall man standing behind them.

"Thank you, sir," replied Jim, who stood nervously facing Mr. Mangum.

"Who's your friend?" the large man asked with a smile.

"This is George Washington Duke, sir," Jim replied.

"Aren't you Taylor's boy?" Mr. Mangum asked.

"Yes, sir," replied Washington.

"How's your Pappy? I ain't seen him in a good many years. He used to go 'bout with my cousin Chaney. She was a wildcat in those days." He laughed. "She used to go on a journey like she was one of the boys."

Washington and Jim looked at each other and shrugged.

"Tell your Pappy I said hello," Mr. Mangum said.

"I will, sir," Washington replied.

"All right then," Mr. Mangum said. "Jim, I believe your auntie wants you to come and help cut some meat for supper when you finish here. You boys have fun. I'm gonna go back to the barn 'n' finish milkin'."

As Mr. Mangum turned and walked toward the barn, the boys looked at each other and burst into laughter. "What was he sayin' about Chaney Mangum?" Washington asked.

"I don't know, but he called her a wildcat. How can a woman be a wildcat?"

Washington laughed. "I don't know. Maybe she turns into a wildcat after it gets dark."

"The next time you see a wildcat, just say 'Hello, Chaney' and see what it does." The boys laughed again as they sat down to continue shucking the corn. When the three baskets were full of corn, Washington helped Jim carry them to the house.

As fall set in the boys would often meet at the location where Jim was doing his chores so they could talk. In time they were meeting nearly every day so they could laugh and joke. Washington would get up early to do his own chores, and then he would go help Jim with his. After helping Jim with his chores, and spending several hours at play, Washington would go back home and do his own evening chores. One day they were in the barn looking at a large copperhead that had died in the corner under a piece of wood. "What do you suppose killed it?" asked Jim.

"It probably just got too cold and died. Or maybe it was old."

"He was a big one, wasn't he?" Jim said. "Ya think he ever bit anybody?"

"I don't know. Maybe he did."

The boys stood there looking at the snake for a time, and then finally Jim asked, "Wash, how do you know so much? Where'd ya learn all the things ya know?"

"My big brother Billy taught me how to read and write."

"I wish I could read 'n' write," said Jim.

"I could teach you," said Washington.

"No, you can't. We would get in trouble. Slaves ain't allowed to read and write. It's against the law."[15]

"I heard about that law. It's stupid," said Washington. "I will teach you."

"No," protested Jim. "It would be really bad for us. They hang people for teaching a slave to read and write."

"No one will know. I will teach you, and that's the end of it."

Jim grimaced but finally said, "Well I guess you could show me how it works."

---

15   The following act codified common law in North Carolina in 1831.

AN ACT TO PREVENT ALL PERSONS FROM TEACHING SLAVES TO READ OR WRITE, THE USE OF FIGURES EXCEPTED
Whereas the teaching of slaves to read and write, has a tendency to excite dis-satisfaction in their minds, and to produce insurrection and rebellion, to the manifest injury of the citizens of this State:
Therefore,
Be it enacted by the General Assembly of the State of North Carolina, and it is hereby enacted by the authority of the same, That any free person, who shall hereafter teach, or attempt to teach, any slave within the State to read or write, the use of figures excepted, or shall give or sell to such slave or slaves any books or pamphlets, shall be liable to indictment in any court of record in this State having jurisdiction thereof, and upon conviction, shall, at the discretion of the court, if a white man or woman, be fined not less than one hundred dollars, nor more than two hundred dollars, or imprisoned; and if a free person of color, shall be fined, imprisoned, or whipped, at the discretion of the court, not exceeding thirty nine lashes, nor less than twenty lashes. II. *Be it further enacted,* That if any slave shall hereafter teach, or attempt to teach, any other slave to read or write, the use of figures excepted, he or she may be carried before any justice of the peace, and on conviction thereof, shall be sentenced to receive thirty nine lashes on his or her bare back. III. *Be it further enacted,* That the judges of the Superior Courts and the justices of the County Courts shall give this act in charge to the grand juries of their respective counties.

Source: "Act Passed by the General Assembly of the State of North Carolina at the Session of 1830–1831" (Raleigh: 1831).

"First we need to memorize the alphabet," said Washington. "I will teach you a song that was used to teach us the alphabet. My grandma taught it to me." Washington began singing "A, B, C, D, E, F, G ..." but was interrupted by Jim's laughter.

"What are you laughing at?" said Washington, shoving Jim's left shoulder.

"I am laughing at you," replied Jim. "I am laughing because I had no idea you could sing so good."

"Okay, now you try it with me," said Washington, who held up his hands like a conductor's. "A, B, C, D, E, F, G ... Let's just sing that a few times until you have it memorized."

Jim and Washington practiced the alphabet song every day. Within a week Jim had learned the entire alphabet. "Okay, now I am going to teach you what you are singing about," said Washington. He took a piece of chalk and a small chalkboard out of the bag he was carrying. He wrote the letter *a* on the chalkboard and said, "This is the letter *a* that we have been singing."

Washington and Jim became good friends, and Washington secretly taught Jim how to read and write. Many years later Washington would show his friendship in a manner that was very unusual in those days and that put Washington in a great deal of danger.

2

Washington Learns about Hatred

It was the summer of 1833. Twelve-year-old Washington and eleven-year-old Jim decided to go to the "revival show" on a neighbor's farm to hear Washington's brother Billy preach. Mr. Mangum gave Jim permission provided he could remove himself from the plantation without being seen by the other workers. He did not want the other slaves to know that Jim was allowed to leave the property, out of concern that they would also want to leave. The boys decided to make a game of it and for Jim to slip out of the bedroom window while everyone else was asleep. Jim lived in the "big house" with Mr. Mangum and Aunt Tilly because he often helped with house chores. Mr. Mangum's wife had died during childbirth many years earlier, and he had no children of his own. Some thought that perhaps he had subconsciously adopted Jim as a son, and some believed Jim actually was his biological son.

On an August evening, the boys decided to go at 7:30 p.m. since it would be getting dark and the service usually lasted until 9:00 p.m. It was seventy-eight degrees when Washington, his brother John, and their cousin William—visiting from Tennessee—went to pick up Jim. They went to the barn, where they retrieved the hay wagon, which they hitched to two horses; they then left for the Mangum plantation. When they arrived they left the wagon on the road at the end of the long lane leading up to the main house and walked up to the house. It was just getting dark, and the slaves had already gone inside for the night. Washington could smell the fresh-cut hay, which had an aroma he had loved as far back as he could remember. He heard a clanging sound in the barn as Mr. Mangum sat a metal milk bucket on the floor.

Washington looked up and saw Jim peering out of his bedroom window on the second floor. "C'mon, Jim," whispered Washington. Jim carefully leaned out of the window to reach for the tree next to the house. He grabbed a limb, pulled himself to the tree, and began to climb down cautiously. He found a small branch on which he placed both feet and all of his weight. Suddenly, the branch on which he was standing broke with a loud cracking sound, causing him to drop ten feet to the ground. "Are you okay?" Washington asked with concern.

"Ouch," replied Jim as he stood up holding his buttocks. All of the boys suddenly burst into laughter.

"Shh," said John. "Someone will hear us."

"Who?" asked William.

"You sound like an owl," said Washington. All of the boys joined in the muffled laughter. The boys turned and ran from the yard to the lane leading to the road. They jumped onto the wagon and Washington slapped the reins and then said in a loud whisper, "Get up there." The horses launched into a trot.

As the boys reached the farm where the revival was being held, they could smell barbequed beef roasting above the fire. "That smells so good," said Jim.

"That's Billy's hickory barbeque recipe," said Washington.

Washington drove the wagon up the lane toward the large tent set up to serve as a temporary sanctuary. The tent appeared an unnatural monument against the terrain of the farm. Nailed to a tree in front of the tent was a huge sign that read, "Methodist-Episcopal Church Revival. Quakers, Baptists, and Presbyterians Welcome Too." On both sides of the lane, attendees had set up small camps where they were cooking meals. The lane had ruts where the rain had formed puddles and then dried, which caused the wagon to sway and bump. Some people waved as the wagon passed. A big man in bib overalls motioned Washington to pull his wagon next to another wagon. "Evenin', boys," he shouted with a smile.

"Evenin', sir," replied Washington.

"There must be hundreds of people here," John said.

"At least," William replied.

"Do you have revivals like this in Tennessee?" Washington asked William.

"Yeah, but not this big."

The wagon approached the large tent and then stopped. The boys climbed down. Washington hitched the wagon to a post between two other wagons. They walked between the campfires, looking for Billy, and then passed the tent of the Parker family. The Parkers had always wanted to have a boy but had never achieved their goal. Instead, they had nine girls. "Hi, John, G. W.," said one of the girls with a giggle.

"Hi, Betsy," replied John. "What are you doing here?"

"The same thing you are," replied Betsy. "We came to hear Reverend Billy preach."

"Where's your mammy and pappy?" asked John.

"They already went in to get a good bench. Do you want some barbequed ribs?"

"Oh, no thank you," replied John. "We just ate."

As the four boys walked on, William asked John, "What makes you think I didn't want something to eat?"

"Because we ate before we came over here," John replied with a laugh.

The boys walked into the main tent. Washington was immediately overwhelmed by the large number of attendees. It was nearly standing room only. It seemed ten degrees hotter inside the tent than outside. People attempted to cool themselves with cardboard fans, but to little avail.

"This place is packed," Washington shouted over the murmur of voices.

On the platform they could see a large pulpit that looked as if it had come out of a church somewhere. On the front of the pulpit were carved two small crosses and one large cross between them. Below the crosses were carved the letters "IHS." Washington recognized some church elders on the right side of the platform. The tent was very large with a high ceiling and was probably a circus tent that the church had bought for revival meetings.

"Where are we supposed to sit?" John asked.

Washington looked around the tent for empty seats. "I don't know. The only seats left are the front rows, but I don't think we're supposed to sit there. Those seats are for new converts."

"What's a convert?" asked William.

"I think that's someone who used to be a Quaker," Washington replied.

"I don't think we have a choice," John said as the boys made their way down to the very first row. The benches consisted of split oak logs with each end resting on a carved-out stump. The boys sat next to one another on the first bench. In a short time Billy came out onto the platform. The crowd became quiet as they waited for Billy to address them.

"Good evening," Billy shouted.

In unison, the crowd replied, "Good evening, Reverend Billy."

"Did you come here looking for an exciting, rip-roaring, wild experience?" asked Billy as he raised his arm in the air for emphasis.

"Yes," the crowd shouted.

"Then you're in the wrong place." Billy laughed. "Tonight we are going to study the book of Leviticus."

The crowd roared with laughter as Billy continued. "If you have your Bibles, please open them to Leviticus, chapter 12; but before you do, let us stand and bow our heads in a word of prayer."

As Billy said the opening prayer, Washington noticed from the corner of his left eye that Betsy Parker and four of her sisters were approaching from the center aisle. Betsy walked over to Washington and stood next to him. Her sisters all leaned forward and smiled at the four boys. "Why's there a colored boy with you?" asked Betsy in a whisper.

"Why shouldn't there be?" replied Washington. "He is our friend."

"Your friend?" asked Betsy in a puzzled manner.

"He is a great guy. You should give him a chance," replied Washington.

"But he is colored. You aren't supposed to be with colored people unless they're working for you."

"He's our friend, but people will think he is working for us. So there's no problem."

Betsy frowned as she looked at Jim. "What? I don't understand."

"Don't worry; it's fine," Washington replied as the prayer concluded and the crowd became seated.

As he listened to his brother preach, Washington suddenly felt a sting in his left thigh. Looking down, he saw Betsy jabbing a piece of straw into the side of his leg as she looked at him with a grin.

"Oh, so you want to play," Washington whispered with laughter in his voice. He heard a man with a deep voice clear his throat behind them. He turned around to find Betsy's father looking sternly at him. *Why is he looking at me?* he thought. *Betsy is the one who is misbehaving.* Betsy looked straight ahead toward the podium as she pretended to be on her best behavior.

"It would behoove you to behave," Betsy whispered.

Washington laughed and then whispered, "Behoove? Who talks like that?" He reached down as if to tie his shoe and then found a piece of straw on the ground and poked Betsy's ankle with it. He looked up to see her smile as she shuffled her feet slowly, and then he noticed that her father was still looking sternly at him.

After the service, the Parkers walked out into the warm summer evening air. The night was bright in the light of the full moon. "This is almost like daytime," said Sarah Parker in amazement.

Mr. Parker looked at the sky as he stroked his chin. "Your mother and I are going over to the Carrington place for a short visit. You can come if you want, or you can walk home. If you walk home, don't stop along the way. Go straight home." The Parker farm was just across the Eno River[16] and less than a half mile from the location of the revival meeting.

"Okay, we'll go straight home," replied Betsy. After their parents left, the girls went back into the tent to find the Duke boys. When they entered the tent, they saw the boys talking to Reverend Billy. They sat on a bench at the rear of the tent and waited until the boys ended their conversation; they then made their way to one of the tent doors. They ran out of the tent door and over to the boys, who were exiting from a different door.

"Where are you going?" asked Sarah, Betsy's younger sister.

The boys stopped and looked at the five sisters who were running up to them. "We're going to the river for a late-night swim," replied Washington.

"Can we come with you?" asked Betsy.

"No, you can't," said Washington. "We don't wear clothes when we swim."

"That is perfect. We don't either," Sarah said with a laugh.

"Oh no, we can't do that," said Washington, laughing himself. The other boys joined in the laughter.

"Why not?" whispered William to Washington.

"Hey," said Betsy who overheard his comment, "we are not all going swimming together without clothes. Are you two touched by the devil?"

"I was just joking," replied William. "I wouldn't really do that."

"I should hope not," replied Betsy as she looked sternly at Sarah.

---

16   The Eno River is a wide, shallow river that flows for thirty-three miles from Northwest Orange County to Durham, where it connects to Flat River. Because the water cascades over a rocky bed, the water is unusually clear and was a popular swimming location in the 1800s. Today the Eno River State Park serves as a well-known recreation area in North Carolina. "Eno River State Park," North Carolina Division of Parks and Recreation, accessed September 22, 2013, http://www.ncparks.gov/Visit/parks/enri/main.php.

Then she said, "We thought maybe you fellows would like to walk us home tonight, but it sounds like you already have plans."

"Actually, we have the hay wagon and could give you a ride if you like," replied Washington. "We would enjoy taking you home. We can swim later."

"Yes, we would be delighted," said John.

"A hay ride ... That would be fun."

They climbed onto the wagon, and Betsy made her way to the seat next to Washington, who was driving. John, Jim, and William crawled into the back of the wagon with Betsy's four sisters. As the wagon made its way down the lantern-lit lane of the farm, Washington noticed that they seemed to be drawing stares and angry looks. It suddenly occurred to him that the neighbors were troubled that an African American was on a hay wagon with white girls. "Betsy, you should probably switch places with Jim until we are out of this crowded area," said Washington as he motioned for Jim to come up front.

Jim and Betsy switched places, and Jim took the reins. "Thank you for inviting me to come along this evening, G. W."

"This was your idea; how could I not invite you?"

"Thanks just the same," replied Jim, directing the horses down the lane. As the hay wagon made its way onto the dirt road, the teenagers sang and laughed. Jim led everyone in the alphabet song. Finally they came to the Eno River, and Washington said, "Why don't you pull over? We can sit here and talk for a while."

As Jim pulled the wagon off the road, Washington jumped down and said to the passengers, "I thought we could sit by the river for a while if you want to."

"That would be nice," replied Betsy, climbing down from the wagon. "We were supposed to walk straight home, but since we're in the wagon, we have a few minutes to spare."

As she walked along with Washington, Betsy whispered, "It feels strange having a colored boy with us. Where did he come from?"

"He lives on Mr. Mangum's farm. I have known him since I was seven. He is a good friend."

"Washington, we aren't supposed to be friends with the colored folks. You could get into a lot of trouble. It's the law."

"I don't believe in that law," replied Washington. "Jim is the best friend I have."

Betsy didn't say anything. She just looked at Washington inquisitively in the moonlight.

"I think we should swim," shouted Sarah suddenly.

"Sarah, we already talked about that. We can't take off our clothes in mixed company even in the dark," whispered Betsy loudly.

"Who said anything about taking off our clothes?" replied Sarah as she burst into laughter, pushed John into the river, and then jumped in behind him.

"Sarah," Betsy said with a laugh, "are you completely off your rocker?" She looked at Washington. "Are you going to swim?"

"No, I'm not, but I think Jim is," Washington said as he pushed Jim into the river, losing his own balance and falling in with Jim.

"I thought you said you weren't going to swim," William said, laughing hard as he jumped into the river. Soon they were all in the water, swimming about and splashing each other in the bright moonlight.

After about twenty minutes, Betsy asked, "How are we going to explain our wet clothes to Pappy when we get home? He will be mad when he finds out we went into the river."

As they climbed out of the water, they noticed a group of men approaching with lanterns. Behind them was a wagon on which they had arrived. "You kids get up here," shouted one of the men, whom Washington recognized as Stephen Dixon.[17]

As the teenagers climbed up the hill to the road, one of the men said, "There he is. That's the colored boy who was riding in

---

17 This account is based on a story told by William P. Duke to Sarah Taylor Duke, who told it to me. The true name of Stephen Dixon is unknown.

the wagon with the girls. Now he has been swimming with them."
Washington looked at Jim and could see the look of fear in his eyes.

"What's your name, boy?" growled Dixon.

Jim remained silent as he slowly backed away from the group
of men.

"I asked you a question," shouted Dixon. "You answer me or
I will knock those white eyes clean out of your head." Dixon ran
forward and grabbed Jim by the shoulder as Jim started to run away.

"Stop it," shouted Washington. "He didn't hurt anybody."

Dixon turned and said to Washington, "You shut up or you'll
get a beating too!" By then several men had grabbed Jim and were
dragging him toward a tree. Washington and John attempted to
pull the men away from Jim, but they were overtaken by several
other men. They watched in horror as Jim was tied to a tree and his
shirt ripped off his back.

"We're going to teach you a lesson you will never forget," said
one of the men as he pulled a bull whip from the wagon. As he prepared to strike Jim, a shiny black buggy approached with two men
on the front seat. It had a lantern hanging on each side, accenting the
silhouette of the buggy. The driver shouted, "What's going on here?"

Washington recognized the voice of his older brother Billy.
"Billy, they're going to whip Jim," he shouted. "You have to stop
them."

Billy had seen Jim with the boys earlier and knew who
Washington was talking about. "What did he do?" asked Billy.

"He was fraternizin' with white girls and even went swimming
with them," replied Dixon.

"Let him go," said Billy.

"Did you hear what I said?" asked Dixon. "He was sitting with
the Parker girls just like he was a white boy; then he went swimming with them."

"I heard what you said," replied Billy. "Cut him down."

"You might be the preacher in these parts, but you ain't the
law," replied Dixon.

Several of the other men shouted, "That's right. You ain't the law."

"He's not but I am," said Taylor Duke as he jumped down from the buggy. "Anyone who lays a hand on Jim will answer to me. Now cut him down."

Dixon seethed with anger but did as Taylor said. "Sorry, Sheriff," he said with just enough sarcasm for everyone to realize that he was not really sorry. Then he turned to Betsy. "Your father will hear about this. And my guess is that he is not going to take this as lightly as the Dukes."

As the men drove away in the wagon, Taylor looked at the teenagers one at a time and then laughed. "You sure are a fine lot of wet sacks." Everyone laughed in response. "You kids really should know better than to get into a fix like this. I better follow you girls home to keep you from getting a whipping."

"Thank you, Mr. Duke," replied Sarah as she climbed onto the wagon.

When they arrived at the Parker farm, Taylor went up to the door and knocked. As Mr. Parker opened the door, Taylor said, "Hi, George."

Mr. Parker extended his hand to Taylor and then asked, "What's going on?"

"Oh, it seems some of the town boys tried to cause a little trouble tonight. Jim was driving the wagon, but they wanted to cause a ruckus because he was with white kids."

"I saw Jim sitting with your boys tonight, and I knew it wasn't normal, but it didn't bother me," replied Mr. Parker.

"Well, some of the men might try to make an issue with you about it. I wouldn't pay much attention to them. Feel free to tell them to talk to me if they have any complaints."

"I will," replied Mr. Parker. "Thanks for bringing them home. Well, you have a nice evening, and I will see you around."

"All right, see you around," replied Taylor as the Parker girls went into the house.

As they turned to walk back to the wagons, they heard Mr. Parker ask, "How'd you girls get all wet?"

"They'll have to get out of that one on their own," Taylor said. He laughed, and the boys joined in with him.

"What were you kids doing at the river?" asked Billy.

"We weren't doing anything bad," Washington said. "We just stopped by the river and fell in."

"All of you fell in?" asked Taylor.

Washington laughed. "Well, some of us were pushed."

As Washington drove the wagon back to the Mangum place, he noticed how silent Jim had become. He didn't say anything all the way home. He just kept looking at the side of the road, almost as if he were watching for a place to hide in case he had to run again. *It must be really hard*, thought Washington, *to be part of a race of people that is treated as subhuman.*

"You all right, Jim?" asked Washington.

"I'll be okay. I'm just trying to understand everything that happened tonight."

"I've decided that we can't ever understand it. It is the world we were born in. They say that colored people aren't as smart as white folks and that colored people can never learn to read and write because they aren't smart enough. You read and write as well as any white person I know, and you are one of the smartest people I have ever known. I think somebody is lying about colored folks. In fact, I know somebody is lying."

Washington could not understand why everyone seemed to think colored people were so bad. He wondered if it might be something he could not see but that was obvious to everyone else. He wondered if maybe it was true that colored people were inherently evil and subhuman. He wondered if his friendship with Jim was immoral. How could everyone else be so wrong and Washington be right? Even religious leaders and government officials said colored people were evil, subhuman creatures. Washington thought about these things for a time, and then he came to his senses. No matter what people say, he knew Jim was a good person and was not an immoral subhuman creature. As he thought about these things, Washington could feel a little anger swelling up inside of him. Anger was not a common emotion for Washington, and it felt strange. Finally he said, "Jim, I'm going to make you a promise. Someday I'm going to make you a free man. If it takes the rest of my life, I'm going to do whatever it takes to free you from slavery. This is my promise to you, I give you my word."

"There ain't nothin' you can do for me, G. W. Besides, Master Mangum treats me really good. It's just other people who are bad to me. I don't think I will ever go off the plantation again. At least on the plantation I'm safe. Master Mangum keeps us safe."

"That doesn't matter. I'm going to do whatever it takes to get you your freedom. Slavery is evil. No man should ever be owned by another man."

Washington could hear Jim crying softly as they approached the Mangum plantation. "It's okay; I can go up to the house by myself," Jim said.

"Okay, Jim. I'll stop by in the morning and we can fix that broken fence on the south side we talked about yesterday."

"Okay, G. W. I'll see you tomorrow." Jim turned and walked slowly toward the farmhouse with his head down. Then he suddenly turned and said, with a sheepish grin, "The girls have to explain their wet dresses, but I have to explain a torn shirt." Washington laughed and shook his head as he flipped the reins to coax the horses into a trot.

Although the experience that night at the revival meeting awakened both John and Washington to the manner in which African Americans were treated in America, it was not until November of that year that the message truly impacted them with force. As the Thanksgiving holiday was approaching, Taylor asked Billy to take Washington and John on a hunt to get a wild turkey for the dinner they were planning.

Washington was excited as he got up before sunrise and put on his warm clothes. Both Billy and John had a gun, but Washington was not permitted to carry a gun yet. As they left the home, their mother, Dicey, came to the front door from the kitchen where she was preparing breakfast. "You boys be careful now," she said as she kissed Washington on the forehead and gave John a hug.

They had decided to go to the Dixon farm, where they had seen turkey nests earlier in the year. It had been three months since the incident at the Eno River where Dixon had nearly whipped Jim.

"Why are we going to the Dixon farm?" Washington asked.

"Because we had a conflict with Dixon awhile back. We should try to reconcile. It's always better to have good relations with a neighbor. That is better than allowing bad feelings to simmer. Besides, it's the Christian thing to do."

Billy, Washington, and John got into the hay wagon and rode to the Dixon farm, which took about an hour. The farm was laid out with a barn closer to the road than the farmhouse. There was a cow pen on the left side of the lane; it was attached to the barn. Billy said it might seem more peaceable to walk up to the house and to leave the wagon next to the barn, where Dixon had a hitching post. He tied the horses to the post, and they walked along the side of the barn, toward the house. When they neared the edge of the barn, they heard the sound of several people crying. Washington wondered what had happened. As they walked around the corner of the barn and started toward the house, they saw a group of approximately twenty slaves sitting and kneeling on the ground, crying softly. Hanging from a tree with a rope around her neck was a young slave girl who appeared to be about four years of age. Her clothes had been ripped off and her little body was covered with cuts and the marks of a whip. Her tiny feet were still bleeding where they had been cut with a knife. The cuts penetrated to the metatarsus, which was exposed in several locations on each foot. It looked as though someone had tried to cut the bones out of her feet. Her head was tilted slightly in the noose, and her eyes were still open though she was dead. She seemed to be staring directly at Washington. On the ground beneath her were two African American adults, a man and a woman. They were crying bitterly. The woman was holding on to the child's foot, and blood from it was running down her right arm. Steam was rising from the blood on her body, indicating that the body was still warm.[18]

Washington was overcome with grief and fear. He began shaking and fell down on one knee. John vomited.

"What are you boys doing here?" The boys turned around to see the menacing appearance of Stephen Dixon. Dixon had walked up behind them and was staring at them with a bloody knife in his hand that he had used to cut the little girl's feet. At first they did not respond. They did not know how to respond.

"I asked what you're doing here!" shouted Dixon. "And why do you have guns?"

Billy nervously replied, "We came to ask if we could hunt turkeys on your farm. We thought we would bring one back for your family for Thanksgiving."

"I can shoot my own turkeys," said Dixon gruffly. "Run along, boys."

The boys did not move. They were in shock.

Dixon looked at John and Washington, both of whom had begun crying. "You see what we do here to slaves who get out of line. You see her mammy and pappy there next to her on the ground. This morning I made her mammy watch while I whipped her little girl with a whip and then cut her like a pig. Now they have to spend the whole day sitting at her feet."

"What happened?" Billy asked. "What did this little girl do wrong?"

Dixon growled. "She didn't do nothin' wrong. Her brother ran away last week. I know how to keep my slaves in line."

"How could you do something like this?" Billy asked.

---

18   This account is based on an event as told by Washington's family to William P. Duke, though the details and the true name of Stephen Dixon are unknown.

"It is my right under the law, and there ain't nothin' neither you nor your big and almighty pappy can do about it. You go home and tell your pappy I said that." Several more men came up behind Dixon. One had a whip in his hand. "You boys think you're gonna do anything about it? How would you like it if I hung you up and gutted you like I did that little girl?" Dixon asked.

"I would do something about it if I could," Billy said. "Under man's law maybe you are right. But under God's law you have committed murder, and you will answer to God for it someday."

"Well, that day ain't today. Today you are trespassing on my land, and under man's law I have every right to shoot you right here and now where you stand. If you don't get off my land, you and your little brothers will be the ones answering to God today." The men with Dixon began laughing, and one of them slapped Dixon on the back. "You tell 'em, Steve."

Washington and John ran to the wagon and climbed inside. Billy said, "We're leaving." He pulled back the hammer on his flintlock rifle and walked backward toward the wagon, holding his gun ready to shoot in case one of them decided to attack.

Billy climbed onto the wagon, and the boys went straight back to their home without a turkey. They told Taylor everything that had happened. While Billy told the story, Washington could not stop shaking. He could see anger in his father's eyes. His father was always a gentleman, and Washington had never seen him angry before. The more Billy talked, the angrier Taylor became. His father's rage frightened Washington. Suddenly Taylor stood up and grabbed his flintlock rifle, his knife, and his whip, and he then walked swiftly toward the door while putting his hat on his head.

"Taylor, don't go over there," Dicey pleaded as she ran over and took ahold of his arm.

Taylor paused for a moment then said, "Something's gotta be done."

"But you know the law is on his side," Dicey pleaded. "It isn't right, but the law is on his side."

Taylor asked, "Whose law? Any law that allows this evil is an evil law. Besides, that isn't the law. It's illegal to kill a slave except in administering punishment."[19] Then he stormed out the door.

"But they don't enforce that law. It protects slaves," Dicey protested as the door closed behind Taylor.

Billy grabbed his rifle from the gun rack, opened the door, and ran out. "I'm coming with you."

Taylor paused on the porch and looked back at Billy. "You don't need to come with me. I can handle this."

"I want to come. I need to come."

Taylor nodded his head.

After his father and Billy left, Washington sat at the table, staring into the fire. He could not clear his thoughts of the image of the naked, beaten, bloody little girl hanging from the rope. He could not stop thinking how painful it must have been for the little girl's family. His hands were shaking as he tried to become calm, but it was of no use. He began crying. John looked at him, and his mother hugged him to try to comfort him. For many years the image of the little girl dangling in the wind would haunt Washington's dreams, which would become nightmares that even invaded his thoughts while awake. This was an image he would never forget. The look of her parents sitting on the ground, crying bitterly, burned in his thoughts like hot coals. Sometimes he would cry when he thought about it, so he tried not to think about it often.

Taylor and Billy did not return until nearly midnight. The whole family was waiting up for them. When they came through the door, Dicey ran over to them and hugged them. They were dirty and bloody, and their clothes were torn. They put their muskets on the gun rack and sat at the table with blank expressions on their faces. They did not ever say what they did that day. However, Washington later heard from Betsy Parker that Taylor and Billy had gone to the Dixon farm

---

19   See John Spencer Bassett, *Slavery in the State of North Carolina* (Baltimore: The John Hopkins Press, 1899). See also *State v. Boon*, 1 NC 191 (NC Conf. 1801).

with her father and several other men, where they had a confrontation with Dixon and his friends. According to the story, Taylor fought with Dixon with his fists and prevailed so severely that Mr. Dixon was bedridden for nearly six weeks. When he recovered, Taylor arrested him and put him in jail, though he was soon released by the circuit judge. Seven months later, Dixon took ill and died within a matter of days. His wife said that he had never been the same after his fight with Taylor, and she feared there was some serious damage done to his internal organs when they fought. She also said that if there was ever a man so evil he needed dyin', it was her man, Stephen Dixon. She said he was so evil he would make the devil blush. Washington always wondered if Dixon died because he was such an evil man. In time he became convinced that if a person holds enough evil inside, eventually the evil will overtake him and he will die. It must be so, because he saw it time and again throughout his life.

On a cold morning in 1833, Washington stood leaning against a fence with his father, Taylor, and his two brothers, John and Billy, in the field behind the Duke homestead. They had just finished moving a cord of firewood from the barn to the house. All four of them working together were able to complete the task in a few minutes.

After resting by the fence for a time, Taylor and his three sons started walking toward the house. Taylor said, "I forgot something in the barn. Do you boys want to come with me? I might need some help with it."

"Sure," replied Billy as they turned and began walking in the direction of the barn. With each step Washington could hear the snow crunching under their feet. "Why does the snow make that crunching sound when we step on it?"

"Because it's going to freeze; when the snow starts to freeze, it crunches like that," Billy replied. "That is how you can tell it is going to get cold when you are out in the forest in the winter."

As they walked into the barn, Taylor said, "Washington, in the third stall is a very large box of tools. Would you go to the box and bring back a cutter?"

Washington frowned. "A cutter? What kind of cutter?" He walked into the stall to the box that held the tools and opened the lid. Much to his surprise, he found a large Bowie knife inside the toolbox, sitting atop many other tools. "Whose knife is this?" Washington asked.

"It's yours," his father, Taylor, replied.

"It's mine?"

"Yes, today is your birthday. You are thirteen years old now. You are a man," Billy said. "That knife was handmade by Jim Bowie. I bought it from him one day when he was in Hillsboro. Look in the bottom of the tool box."

Washington shuffled the tools around in the toolbox until he reached the bottom. There he found a brand-new Hawken flintlock rifle. "What's this?" he asked.

"That is your new rifle. I bought it from Bowie too. Now that you are a man, you need a rifle and a knife."

"Wow, thank you so much," said Washington.

Later that morning, as the sun was rising in the sky, Washington gave his mother a hug. "Bye, Mammy," he said. "I will be back within three days." It was a tradition in the Duke family that on his thirteenth birthday a son would go on a hunt and spend the night in the forest, not returning until he had a deer, as a symbol of his manhood. It was noteworthy in the town of Hillsboro for a young man to boast of the buck he shot on his first hunt as a man. This was considered a major step of manhood among the merchants and workers. Both Billy and John had been successful on their first hunt. Often this simple feat could lead to romance, since a young man would have thereby demonstrated his ability to provide for a family—something that was a very important consideration for a young woman living in a small town in North Carolina in 1833. Although this tradition is long gone, it was a significant rite of passage when Washington was a boy.

"Be careful, Washington. Remember, if you start to get cold, just come back in," said Billy as he smiled and winked at Taylor.

"I will remember," said Washington. "I will be back before you know it, and I will have a twelve-point buck."

Washington opened the door and walked out of the house and into the cold morning air. In a bundle on his back were several blankets, a flint for starting a fire, a cloth bag full of frozen sweet corn, a pound of salted meat, and a Bible. Over his shoulder was his new Hawken flintlock rifle, and strapped to his belt was his new Bowie knife. His boots, wrapped with warm black bear skin inside and out, complimented his fringed tan coat and reddish-brown coonskin cap that he had pulled down over his ears. He walked into the field behind the house and onto the path that led deep into the forest. He could feel the cold air bite inside his lungs, which made it difficult for him to breathe as he trudged up a snow-covered hill. Washington walked all morning and well into the afternoon, using the sun as his compass. Finally he stopped for a rest along a partially frozen river as the sun reached high overhead. He started a fire for warmth, took a line and a hook from a pouch on his belt and put a piece of jerky on the hook, and then put the hook into the river. He picked up a stick and wrapped the other end of the line around it. He then held the stick in his right hand, allowing the line to fall between his middle two fingers. As he sat on the bank of the river, he saw a rabbit run across the bank on the other side. The curious rabbit seemed content as it stopped and smelled the air to investigate the strange scent of a human.

Washington felt a slight tug on the line, in response to which he gave a slight tug to set the hook. He then felt a harder tug as the fish began to swim and fight. Washington pulled the fish from the water and within minutes was cooking a five-pound bass supported by the long Bowie knife that he held in his hand. *This is a pretty good start*, thought Washington. On a hill a half mile away was Washington's older brother, Billy, who was following covertly to ensure that Washington remained safe. After a hearty lunch of fish and corn, Washington set out to find a deer trail. Several hours later, he located a deer path in the snow. He decided to build a lean-to about fifty feet from the deer path. Washington broke some branches from a tall pine tree and formed a lean-to between two large trees. He started a fire in a hole in the ground next to the lean-to and then sat down on the ground and began to whittle with his new Bowie knife.

As evening approached Washington decided to read by the campfire and then get up early in the morning and build a tree blind from which he could shoot a deer. He always carried a Bible with him, which he read every night before going to sleep. He threw more dry branches on the fire and then placed a number of branches next to the lean-to so he could keep the fire burning all night. Washington lay down on one of the deerskin blankets that he had placed on the snow under the lean-to. He began reading by the fire but soon had fallen asleep. As it became dark he woke several times and placed branches on the fire to keep it burning while, unbeknownst to Washington, his older brother, Billy, observed from afar.

Very early the following morning, just as the sun was beginning to appear in the sky, Billy awoke and looked through his telescope at Washington's camp. He could not believe his eyes. There was a twelve-point whitetail buck, a doe, and a fawn standing next to Washington's lean-to. Washington awoke feeling something cold touching his face. As he opened his eyes he found himself looking directly into the face of the buck, which had pushed its head through the top of the lean-to in order to examine this strange human creature. The deer was sniffing Washington's face with its cold nose. Slowly, Washington reached for his rifle. Then he noticed that the buck seemed unconcerned with his movements. *This is strange,* thought Washington. *Deer always run away when people move.* Washington saw the doe and the fawn standing beside the buck. "What is this? The local trading post?" Washington softly asked the deer family that had invaded his space. "I suppose next you are going to offer to help me build a tree blind."

Instead of reaching for his rifle, Washington slowly reached up and began petting the nose and head of the buck. The buck did not back away even when Washington pulled off his blankets and crawled out of the lean-to. Washington reached into the bag that held the frozen corn and offered some to the fawn. The buck and the doe watched as Washington fed the hungry animal. He then offered some to the buck and the doe, who delightedly ate what they were given.

Later in the afternoon, at the Duke homestead, Taylor was sitting in his wooden rocker by the fireplace, smoking his pipe. Dicey was sitting in her wooden rocker, which was a little smaller than Taylor's rocker and was on the opposite side of the fireplace. She was knitting a scarf for a friend. All of the children were sprawled out on giant bearskin rugs which overlay a deerskin carpet that covered the wooden floor. Suddenly, Billy burst through the door of the house out of breath and gasping for air. "You are not going to believe what is coming up the road!" he shouted.

The entire family rose from their various positions of comfort and assembled around the window. Much to their amazement, Washington was walking up the road wearing his coonskin cap, fringed coat, and bearskin-covered boots with his bundle of blankets and flintlock rifle thrown over his shoulder. Following behind him were a twelve-point whitetail buck, a doe, and a fawn. The entire family began laughing.

Dicey said, "Washington said he was going to be bringing home a twelve-point buck. I guess he knew what he was talking about."

As Washington approached the homestead, the entire family walked out to greet him. The deer family was unconcerned by the sudden appearance of these peaceful friendly humans. "Washington, who are your friends?" asked Dicey. Washington did not reply.

Malinda said, "Oh, they are so beautiful. Why aren't they afraid?"

"For some reason they took to Washington, and I guess they aren't afraid of us either," Billy replied.

"I hope they don't decide to stay around here. They will destroy all of our crops," Taylor said.

"We could eat them if they do," John said, and he then laughed.

"How would you like it if they ate you?" replied Dicey as she laughed and tapped John on the top of his head with her fingers. The children all laughed at this discourse between Dicey and John.

"Well, maybe we could put corn feed out for them and they would leave the crops alone," Reany said.

Taylor laughed. "What's next? Are we going to feed the bears and the rattlesnakes too?"

"Washington, come inside and get warm. You must be freezing," Malinda said. Washington and Malinda began walking toward the house.

"Well, maybe hunting is not going to be your greatest talent, but it seems you will make a really good shepherd," Taylor said with a laugh.

The deer left later that day, but they came back the next day and the day after that. Washington and Malinda always left a small bucket of corn hanging from a tree branch so the smaller animals could not reach it. Before long the deer were coming every day to eat the corn. Soon the fawn had grown into a beautiful doe and had her own fawn, while her own parents gave her siblings. Within a few years the Duke homestead had a dozen deer visiting every day. They found it necessary to put "No Hunting" signs around the farm so neighbors would not shoot the deer as they visited the farm. People from Hillsboro learned not to hunt near the Duke homestead, and the rumor spread that it was God's country.[20]

North Carolina was a slave state in the 1830s. As Washington grew into his teen years, he was deeply troubled by the institution of slavery. As a child he did not understand slavery, but over the

---

20   The account of Washington's first hunt is a re-creation of a story told by his family about the time of the event that was later told to me by Sarah Duke.

years, seeing the manner in which slaves were treated, he came to abhor the institution. Slave owners were notorious for working their slaves beyond reasonable human limits, but even more prevalent, though less known, was the reality that female slaves were exploited sexually. Biracial children often resulted from the relations of slave owners and their slaves, but they were not treated as the children of the slave owners. Instead they found themselves incorporated into the population of slaves on the plantation. Legally, a child born of a female slave was automatically a slave regardless of the status of the father. In many families that had owned slaves for several generations, most of the slaves were actually children or grandchildren of the original plantation owner. The light-skinned females were especially sought after, and many slave owners sold their own biracial daughters and granddaughters into slavery. This was the deep, dark secret of American slavery and was something that Washington knew only too well from listening to traveling slave owners boast about their exploits with the female slaves—something they would never admit in their own hometowns.[21]

On a rainy spring Friday, Washington went into Hillsboro with John and his cousin William from Tennessee to buy supplies. Their heavy boots pounded the wooden planks as they walked on the boardwalk with their hands in the pockets of their bib overalls. With an air of confidence they strode in step three abreast. William asked, "Are there any pretty girls in this town?"

---

21 Mary Boykin Chestnut wrote in her *Diary from Dixie*, March 18, 1861,

"Like the patriarchs of old, our men live all in one house with their wives and their concubines, and the Mulattos one sees in every family exactly resemble the white children, and every lady tells you who is the father of all the Mulatto children in everybody's household, but those in her own, she seems to think drop from the clouds or pretends so to think." See Mary B. Chestnut, *Diary from Dixie*, March 18, 1861, entry (New York: D. Appleton & Company, 1905) (text omitted from censored version).

"Remember the Parker girls? Some of them come in with their dad every Friday afternoon."

William laughed. "So that's why you wanted to come in today."

"Well, sure." Washington laughed and then pointed across the street. "There they are now, going into the general store."

"I get Sarah; you two can have Betsy and Molly," said John.

"Okay," Washington replied.

John laughed again. "I changed my mind. You can have Sarah and Molly; I'll take Betsy."

"I got a better idea," said William. "I get all three of them. You guys can wait in the wagon."

The boys laughed. "Well, you guys better decide or they're gonna be gone," Washington said. They crossed the muddy street and headed for the general store. They entered the store and saw Sarah, Betsy, and Molly standing with their father next to a hopper of potatoes. They strolled gingerly toward the hopper and looked in as if their interest in potatoes exceeded their interest in the girls.

"Hi, G. W.," said Sarah. "Who's your friend?"

"Don't you remember? This is my cousin William from Tennessee. He was with us that night we went for a hayride after the revival show a couple of years back. That was the night those men were going to whip Jim and my dad stopped them."

"Oh yes, I remember. Hi, William. What are you doing here?" Sarah asked.

"I came back to Durham with my dad to buy parts for the wagons."

"Oh, that's right. You make wagons," she replied.

William nodded and then picked up a potato, pretending it was the object of his attention. "Yes, we make wagons."

Washington walked over to the bar to order sassafras tea for his companions. While waiting for the bartender, he overheard an elderly plantation owner from Virginia boasting to the local farmers that he had fathered over forty children through the female slaves he owned. He boasted that he would bind them over to area plantation owners at the age of ten, and then at the age of twenty he would sell them outright to a neighboring plantation owner. That neighbor in turn produced over fifty children through the slave girls. The elderly man laughed that he had a greater progeny than King Solomon and that he made a lot of money and had a lot of fun creating this progeny. Washington was so distraught at hearing these words that he left the tavern feeling ill. How could anyone treat other human beings this way, especially his own flesh and blood?

William saw Washington head rapidly for the door and knew something was wrong. "I'll be right back," he said to John and the Parker girls.

John turned to see what was happening. He saw William follow G. W. out the door, so he followed William. As they walked out onto the boardwalk, they saw a young, pretty slave girl, barely in her teens, trying to cross the muddy street while dragging a heavy bag of grain. Her owner was shouting vulgarities at her and striking her with a hickory stick. The barefoot girl, wearing only a one-piece dress made from a scratchy burlap bag that barely covered her, was slipping and falling in the mud. It was obvious that she could never move the heavy bag across the street and that the slave owner was tormenting her just for amusement. A small crowd of people had gathered around and were laughing at the scene. This event sickened Washington, as he was reminded of the little slave girl he had seen hanged on the Dixon farm a few years earlier.

Though just a teenager himself, Washington walked over to the abusive master, stood between him and the slave girl, and, with his left hand, took a firm hold of the man's right wrist and hand, which was holding the hickory stick, and then stared directly into the man's eyes. Perhaps it was because Washington's father was the highly revered deputy sheriff of Orange County, or perhaps it was simply because the slave owner was startled, but he did not say anything in response to Washington. He just looked down at the muddy street as the crowd became silent and began to disperse, almost as if they were all suddenly ashamed. Washington then walked over to the slave girl, picked up the bag of grain, and carried it for her, getting mud all over his own clothes.

With tears streaming down her cheeks, the young girl followed him to the other side of the street and asked, "Why did you do that for me?"

Washington replied, "Because you don't deserve to be treated this way. This is wrong."

"But that is how they all treat us," she replied.

"That doesn't make it right," Washington said loudly enough for everyone to hear as he lifted the heavy bag into the wagon.

"My name is Caroline," she said. "Please remember me."

"My name is Washington Duke," said Washington as he helped her onto the wagon.

Washington, William, and John went back into the general store to finish their shopping.

"I thought you boys left," Betsy said.

"We did, but we had to come back to get more supplies," replied William.

Washington did not say anything. Now he understood why his father had not spoken when he came home after his fight with Stephen Dixon. Words could not express his emotions. He looked at Betsy and nodded.

When the boys left Hillsboro that day, they talked about what happened and wondered why the farmer let G. W. stop him from striking the slave girl. William said, "You must have startled him. I was really surprised you did that. You really didn't care what happened to you, did you?"

"I just couldn't stand to see what he was doing to that girl. It made me angry."

"Were you going to hit him if he didn't stop?"

"I would if I had to. I decided when they almost whipped Jim at the river that I would never stand and watch something like that happen again. No matter what it means for me, I am not going to let that happen. I made that promise to Jim, and I am going to keep it."

Word of this event spread quickly through the community, and from that time forward, the townspeople were reluctant to discuss slavery around Washington, who soon became known as an abolitionist sympathizer. Washington did not know then that someday Caroline would come back into his life in a very meaningful way.[22]

---

22   This account is based upon an event witnessed by William P. Duke that he passed down through the family. Later we will see written documentation of the identity of Caroline.

3

John Runs Away and
Washington Gets Married

Religion was very important in the lives of North Carolina set-
tlers in the early 1800s. Traveling ministers and evangelists held
campfire meetings throughout the region as they sought converts
to the faith. In these rural areas of North Carolina, there were large
numbers of Methodists, Quakers, and Baptists. Washington's older
brother, Billy, was prominent among the Methodists. Washington
followed in his older brother's footsteps and joined the Methodist
Episcopal Church. The Methodist Episcopal Church in America—
and in particular its affiliated institution, Duke University—bene-
fited greatly from this membership, given that Washington would
become the benefactor who would set the course for his sons, James
Buchanan Duke and Benjamin Newton Duke, to provide millions
of dollars to Duke University, bringing it to the top of the greatest
universities of the world.

Billy married and moved to a region of Orange County called
Bragtown.[23] To assist him in his farming venture, Taylor sent his
sons Washington and John to work for Billy and to live on his farm.
After working there for a time, John concluded that the work was too
hard and decided to run away. Although he asked Washington to go

---

23   "Bragtown" is today spelled "Braggtown."

with him, Washington declined. John and Washington were close, and it was painful for him to see John leave, but he believed it would be wrong to leave his brother Billy and the family. In the middle of the night, John slipped out of a bedroom window. For a few months he worked in the coastal towns of North Carolina as a fisherman and a farm worker, but he found this life miserable. Eventually he decided to find his cousin Mordecai Duke[24] in Tennessee, thinking that perhaps Mordecai would take him in for a while.[25]

Early one summer morning, William P. Duke,[26] Mordecai's eldest son, peered through the front window of the Mordecai Duke oak log farmhouse near Woodbury, in Cannon County, Tennessee. John was walking up the long lane.

"Pappy, there is someone coming up the lane. He looks like he has been walking a long time."

"Who is it?" asked Elizabeth, Mordecai's wife.

"I don't know," William replied as he pulled the curtain back for a better view. "It looks a little like Cousin John from North Carolina."

---

24 Mordecai Duke was said to have been the son of William Duke, who was a brother of Taylor Duke, and thus Mordecai was the first cousin of John Duke and his brother Washington. Contrary to popular assertions by some genealogists, it appears that Taylor had only two brothers, one of whom was named William, and the other is believed by this author to have been Henry Jr. See correspondence from Benjamin Newton Duke and Lida Duke Angier to executors of estate of James Buchanan Duke, *James B. Duke Estate Series,* Inventory of James Buchanan Duke Papers, 1777–1990 and undated, 1924–1925, David M. Rubenstein Rare Book and Manuscript Library, Duke University.

25 According to the information received from my grandmother, John ran away from his brother Billy's home where he was living and went to Tennessee to find his cousin Mordecai, with whom he lived for several years. During this time the Mordecai Duke family was actively involved in the Underground Railroad. This chapter is a re-creation based on this actual event.

26 As explained in the Preface (footnote 3), William P. Duke was born in 1819 and died in 1912 at the age of ninety-two. He was a personal witness to many of the events described in this book and heard firsthand accounts of others. He passed much of this information along to Sarah Taylor Duke, who was born in 1901 and died in 1987. She is my grandmother, who in turn passed this information on to me.

John was thin, underweight, and covered with dust. There were large dark circles around his eyes, and he appeared to be suffering from influenza. He approached the front porch but stopped momentarily in the yard to read a sign that read, "Duke Wagons, by Mordecai Duke." John stepped up on the porch. William and Mordecai were peering through the window. John waved and said, "Mordecai, it's me, Cousin John!"

Mordecai opened the door slowly and then came out and put his arm around the young boy's shoulders to assist him into the house and over to a chair. "John, what are you doing here? You look dead tired. Come in and rest."

"I walked from Bragtown. I couldn't stay at Billy's anymore. He made me work too hard. I had to work from morning till night."

"Taylor is going to be really worried, John. You have to go back," Mordecai replied.

"I can't go back, Mordi, at least not to live. If you could let me stay here for a time, I will work to earn my keep."

Elizabeth said, "Here, have something to eat. I just made some stew." She gave John a bowl of stew and a piece of warm bread. "You look exhausted, John." Elizabeth brushed John's hair with her fingers. "Mordecai, maybe you and William could fetch some water for a bath for John. I will put some more wood in the fire to heat it."

"Please, Beth, could I sleep before I take a bath? I haven't slept in two days."

"Of course," Elizabeth replied. "You can sleep in the spare room upstairs if you don't mind the books and Mordecai's desk. It was your grandfather Henry's library before he passed on. William and Mordecai read in there all the time, but there is a sofa you can sleep on. There are plenty of blankets in the wardrobe."

"It was very dangerous for you to travel so far on foot, John," Mordecai said. "Billy and Taylor must be worried sick." John ate the bowl of stew so fast he did not pause to respond.

"John, you must be starving. When did you eat last?" asked Elizabeth as she placed a second bowl of stew in front of John.

"I ate apples, berries, and nuts that I found along the way, but I haven't had a real meal for about two weeks. I worked for a farmer for a couple of days on the way here. His wife fed me."

"How did you find us?" Mordecai asked.

"It wasn't easy. I remembered that you said you lived near Woodbury. I decided to come here to see if I could stay with you for a while. Would you mind if I went to sleep now? I'm having a really hard time staying awake."

"No, of course not; let me help you to your room," Mordecai replied as he helped John up from his chair and into the spare room. Twelve hours later, in the early evening, John emerged from the spare room ready for a hot bath. The tub was in a room toward the back of the house and was designed to drain out onto the ground beside the house through a pipe in the floor. Mordecai and William carried the hot water from the stove to the tub to make the bath water warm. After John finished his bath, Mordecai gave him some clean clothes to wear. Mordecai, William, and John stayed awake and talked until late that night. Finally Mordecai said, "I suppose you can stay for a spell, but we need to send word to Billy and Taylor. Otherwise they will be worried about you."

It was agreed that John could stay at the Mordecai Duke farm until he decided where he would go. The following day, Mordecai asked a friend who was leaving for North Carolina to stop at Taylor's home to tell him that John was safe and was staying at the Mordecai homestead. The friend agreed and then left for North Carolina. One morning, several weeks later, William got up early to clean the stables. As he entered the stall of Renegade, his father's favorite horse, and began to shovel the manure, there was a scraping sound in the stall immediately adjacent to Renegade's stall. William opened the door of that stall. John was in the stall, shoveling manure into a large bucket. "What are you doing?" William asked.

"I am cleaning the stall," John replied.

"You don't have to do that," William said. "You are a guest in our home."

"I just wanted to help. I don't mind, really. I am glad to help," said John as he dumped a shovel of manure into the bucket. "Do you mind if I ask you something?"

"Sure, you can ask anything," William replied.

"When I was in the tool room looking for a shovel, I noticed a trap door in the floor that went down under the barn into a tunnel. What is that for?"

"It goes up to the house."

"But why do you have a tunnel that goes to the house?" John asked.

"That is to get to the house without being seen."

"But why do you need to do that?"

William paused and leaned against his shovel. "I will tell you something, but you have to promise that you will never tell anyone what I am going to tell you."

John stopped shoveling and looked at William. "I will never tell anyone."

"Do you swear on Grandpa Henry's grave?"

"I swear," John replied.

"Sometimes runaways come here and need a place to hide as they go north. Pappy lets them hide in the barn, and he takes food to them from the house through the tunnel."

"Do you mean you hide runaway slaves?" John asked in a loud whisper.

"Yes, about ten slaves come through here each month, usually two or three families. It's called the Underground Railroad."

"Where do the runaways come from, and how do they get away from the slave owners?"

"They run away in the middle of the night. Usually they travel in boats or rafts on the river so they don't leave tracks and the dogs can't find them."[27]

---

27 According to our family tradition, when a group of slaves was coming through that needed assistance, Mordecai would receive a hand-delivered letter

"Where do the slaves go when they get up north?" John asked.

"They take them to Oberlin College in Ohio. It's a free state."[28]

"That seems dangerous. Would you get in trouble if you got caught helping slaves escape?" John leaned on his shovel looking inquisitively at William.

"It is dangerous. They hanged a white man just outside of Milan last month when they found out he was helping slaves escape."

"That is a good thing Mordi does. I think I would like to help in that business."

That evening, Mordecai, William, and John sat on the front porch of the Tennessee farmhouse. It was a warm evening, and they were enjoying lemonade made of lemons that had been brought up from Florida. Mordecai lit his pipe. The warm air created a pleasant ambiance. A spark in Mordecai's pipe shone bright red when he puffed on it.

"William told me about the runaway slaves," John said to Mordecai. "Could you use any more help?"

Mordecai looked at William uneasily. Then he replied, "Would you like to help? It's very dangerous."

"I would love to help. I have thought about it before, but I didn't know you were involved."

"We're picking up some runaways soon. You could come with us," William said.

"I would like that," replied John.

"The day after tomorrow we are picking up a family of runners

---

from a friend telling him when the slaves were coming. He would pick them up at the river with a hay wagon. Sometimes he would take them back to the barn, where they would stay for a few days. Mordecai and William would take food and water to them through the tunnel. Then, when they were rested, they would take them to the next stop using the hay wagon. There they would meet another driver who would take them farther north in his wagon. Mordecai owned a business making wagons, so it was easy for him to build wagons designed to hide the slaves in the hay. Some of them had a fake floor under which they could hide.

28   In 1803, Ohio became a free state, and Oberlin College, in Oberlin, Ohio, was the headquarters of the Underground Railroad.

coming up from Alabama. They escaped from a plantation where the owner beats the slaves. He kills about two of them every year," said William. "You have to understand it is dangerous. Sometimes they hang the people who are helping the slaves along with the slaves if they get caught. Are you sure you want to come with us?"

"I'm sure."

Two days later, early in the morning, Mordecai, William, and John were loading bales of hay onto the hay wagon to pick up six runaways coming from Alabama. John opened the heavy timber hatch to the hidden chamber under the floor, revealing only twenty inches between the actual floor and the fake floor. "How do they fit in here?" John asked. "What if a woman is pregnant or a man has a big belly?"

Mordecai sat down on a bale of hay at the rear of the wagon next to John. "We haven't had any pregnant women, and we have never seen a slave with a big belly. Most are living on the verge of starvation. They have to crawl in and lie flat on their bellies.

"The wagon is designed to hold seven to ten people depending on their size. Often the runaways are wet because they have just come out of the river and did not have a boat. Heat cannot be used when it is cold because if we were stopped, the heat would be detected. So sometimes the slaves almost freeze just getting to the next station. When it is extremely cold, the slaves are taken to the farm to get warm before going on north."

"Where are the safe houses?"

William said, "There are about forty safe houses between here and Oberlin College. These are houses owned by people who allow their farms to be used for stops in an emergency if we need a place to hide."

"How long does it take to get to Oberlin College?" John asked.

"We can get there in a few days to a week," Mordecai replied. "I built this wagon with the kind of wheels they use in military wagons. Although it's a hay wagon, with those iron spokes and rims and the heavy steel axles packed with grease, this wagon could travel for weeks at a horse's trot or even a canter without sustaining any damage. I keep a spare wheel up by the seat just in case anything ever happens, but I will probably never need it. I also keep a small arsenal of weapons under the seat in case we ever have to defend the runaways."

"I don't think I have ever seen iron rims before. This must be a strong wagon."

Mordecai replied, "It looks like a hay wagon, but the truth is it is the best wagon I have ever built. It would be great for military use. In fact, I got the design from the wagons the Continental Army used to haul armor during the Revolutionary War.[29] The lower floor is a steel plate, to make a smoother ride for the slaves since we often travel at a fast pace. Then beneath the steel plate are the heavy boards, to make it look like a wooden floor. Hopefully, if we are ever stopped by tracking dogs, it will be a little harder for them to pick up the scent under the wagon because of the steel plate."

Later that night, after riding in the wagon much of the day, Mordecai drove the wagon off the main road and across a grassy area next to a stream. They traveled for several miles on a wagon path next to the water and then stopped and backed the wagon down to the bank of Elk River.[30] William was sitting next to Mordecai, and

---

29   The Conestoga wagon, with iron rims, was built by Swiss wagon makers in Lancaster, County Pennsylvania. In 1755 Benjamin Franklin ordered 150 of them to be constructed to serve General Edward Braddock in his campaign against the French. Given the durability of these wagons, they were later used in the Revolutionary War to haul supplies and weapons and, in one instance, $600,000 worth of gold. "Conestoga Wagon Historical Marker," ExplorePAHistory.com, accessed September 22, 2013, http://explorepahistory.com/hmarker.php?markerId=1-A-60.

30   Elk River connects to the Tennessee River in Alabama and was an important tributary for transportation in the Underground Railroad. Traveling by river was the preferred method of travel for runaway slaves since dogs could not track a person traveling by water. Water travel was not without risk, in that the travelers were in open sight of people along the river, so they often hid the slaves in the bottom of the boat and traveled at night.

John was sitting on the other side of William. Mordecai let the rear wheels go into the water and onto a rock bed that had been placed in the water to keep the wagon wheels from sinking in the mud. It was important to get the wagon close enough to the water that the runaways could step from the boat or raft into the wagon without touching the ground. If they touched the ground, the entire mission could be endangered, because the trackers would run along the river with dogs looking for the place where the runaways had come out of the river. The next time a group of runaways came through, they would know exactly where to watch for them.

Mordecai jumped out of the wagon and onto the ground next to the river. He took a lantern with a blue-colored glass globe from the side of the wagon and lit its wick. He put the blue lantern on a tree limb approximately five feet off the ground. He then took a second lantern off the side of the wagon with a red colored glass globe, lit it, and placed it on the limb of another tree on the other side of the wagon, also five feet off the ground. Mordecai then picked up a rifle from under the wagon seat and walked toward the trees. "I'll stand watch," he said.

"Who is he watching for?" asked John.

"He is watching for the slave boat and for trackers," William replied. "The conductor bringing in the slaves will watch for two lanterns, one red and one blue, five feet above the water. That is how the conductor knows he has found the right location. Pappy watches to make sure no one else approaches. They should be here within the hour."

"What's a conductor?"

"Because this is called the Underground Railroad, we use railroad terms to describe what people do. The conductor is the person who transports the slaves. The slaves are called passengers."

A short time later, Mordecai whispered loudly, "They're here."

A large rowboat slowly came from down the river toward the bank next to the wagon. John could see a large man who was rowing the boat, and a number of people seated in the boat with him. The man rowing the boat whispered loudly, "Hey, Mordi, William. Who is that with you?"

"Yo, Tom, this is John, my cousin from North Carolina," Mordecai replied. "He is going to help us transport."

The large man waved at John. "It is good to have the help. We need it."

Tom pulled the boat up to the wagon, where he tied it. "Be careful you don't touch the ground when you get out of the boat," he said to the passengers. William walked into the edge of the water to help the passengers keep their balance as they stepped from the boat into the wagon without touching the ground. A sixteen-year-old first-generation immigrant slave climbed from the boat onto the wagon. He paused before crawling into the space and looked directly at John as if he had something to say but did not know how to put it into words. Perhaps he wanted to tell about the inhumane treatment the slaves had received on their journey across the ocean. The slave then put his head into the small compartment in the floor of the wagon and climbed inside.[31]

After all of the runaways had entered the hidden compartment beneath the floor, William and Mordecai fastened the timbers behind the opening and placed the bales of hay back on the wagon to conceal the hatch to the hidden compartment. They all climbed up on the wagon as Mordecai moved the wagon out of the water and back toward the main road. This night left a lasting impression on John. Later in life he often struggled with issues of slavery, and

---

31 Several years later, the United States Supreme Court ruled in *Dred Scott v. Sanford* 60 US 393 (1857) that an African American was not a human being within the meaning of the Constitution and thus had no right to invoke the jurisdiction of the courts. When the Dred Scott case was published, a young lawyer was deeply disturbed with the opinion. His name was Abraham Lincoln. Because of what he read, Lincoln began creating the Emancipation Proclamation, which was not to be read publicly for the first time until July 22, 1862, when Lincoln presented it to his cabinet. See Lincoln, Abraham, Initial draft of the Emancipation Proclamation, July 22, 1862. Holograph manuscript, Robert Todd Lincoln Papers, Manuscript Division, Library of Congress.

though he eventually became a slave owner, it is said that he did so with uncertainty of the morality of the institution and that he always treated his slaves better than the other slave owners treated theirs.[32]

Eventually John left the Mordecai Duke homestead, married, and moved to Milan, Tennessee, west of the Mordecai's farm, though he did not ever reveal the identities of the conductors of the Underground Railroad about which he had learned while living at the Mordecai Duke homestead. Years later, Washington set out to find his brother John. He was able to locate him and tried to persuade him to return to North Carolina. Despite his best efforts, Washington could not persuade John to return, though two of John's children, Lida and Lillie, moved to Durham, where they lived out the remainder of their lives.[33]

---

32 Years later, Mordecai developed a shoe manufacturing business and made boots for both Union and Confederate soldiers. This was a great risk, given that assisting the enemy was considered treason in the Confederate States. Once criticized for helping the Union Army by providing boots, he replied, "Whether Confederate or Union, they are still our boys who suffer in the pangs of war with frostbite and blistered feet. Anything we can do to ease their discomfort we should do, whether Confederate or Union."

During the Civil War, four of Mordecai's sons were to be conscripted into the Confederate Army. Because conscripted soldiers were treated more poorly than volunteers, they volunteered. Five months later, the four brothers were sent on a mission and found an opportunity to escape. After deserting from the Confederate Army, they found a Union camp, where they surrendered and then enlisted as Union soldiers.

33 Lida married Jonathan Cicero Angier, a prominent businessman in the lumber business in Durham. Lillie did not marry but lived with Lida and Jonathan for the rest of her days.

Reany Duke and Amelia Duke, sisters of Washington Duke and daughters of Taylor Duke, both married local farmers. Kirkland Duke and Doctor Brodie Duke, two of Washington's other brothers, went to Florida, where they developed a shipping business. Neither of them ever married or had children. Washington Duke's younger brother Robert lived with his sister Malinda until the Civil War began. He enlisted in the Confederate Army and died during the war.

Washington was very close to both John and Billy. After John ran away, he became closer to Billy, who later said he regretted his harsh treatment of John. Billy had attempted to use firmness to instill responsibility and discipline in John. Unfortunately, John responded by leaving, which was unexpected by everyone except Washington, whom he had told he was going to leave. Washington did not warn anyone, because he did not believe John would really go. After he left, both Billy and Washington missed John deeply. Over the years their cousins Mordecai and William began to cut back on their wagon making venture and focused more on farming. They continued to travel to Durham to pick up parts for the wagons, though not as frequently as when Washington, William, and John were boys. On numerous occasions they invited John to travel to Durham with them, but he refused, saying he could not face his family after all that had happened. He said that they would not want to have anything to do with him because of the way he had left. When Washington learned this, he was distraught. He did not understand how John could walk away from his family, which had been so close when they were young. Washington tried to understand John's decision to leave, but no matter how hard he tried, it simply did not make sense to him. He finally accepted the fact that his brother was gone, and he felt deep sadness.

As Washington grew into his twenties, he began to think about romance and raising a family. In time he became interested in a young, pretty woman named Mary Clinton, who was the daughter of Jesse and Rachel Clinton. The Clintons owned a farm near Ellerbee Creek just outside of Durham. Washington had helped the Clintons on several occasions when they were having difficulty bringing in their crops as a result of Jesse's health issues. Mary was four years younger than Washington, and they began socializing at

---

Many years later, Washington would need assistance in dealing with an issue involving a slave. He called upon Mordecai and William to help him connect with individuals in the Underground Railroad who would assist him.

church functions. Finally, Washington asked her father if he could court Mary. Her father consented.

Washington and Mary cherished their brief time together. They would often take buggy rides on the trails around Hillsboro and Durham. Washington enjoyed taking her on picnics near Eno River, where he had played as a boy. One day in the spring of 1842, he mustered the courage to ask her to marry him. They were sitting on a blanket in the grass by the Eno River.[34]

"Mary, have I ever told you how much happiness you have brought to me?" Washington asked.

"Yes, and it means a lot to me when you say it."

Mary was looking out over the water when Washington leaned forward and took hold of her hand. She turned her head to meet his gaze.

"I want to spend the rest of my life with you," he said. "I want you to be my wife."

Mary tried to conceal her emotion but was moved to tears.

"I will give you time to think about it," he said.

"G. W., I don't need any time. You already know my answer."

On August 8, 1842, Washington and Mary were married. They settled on several acres of land adjacent to Mary's parents' farm. Washington and Mary's household was full of love and happiness. They found humor in almost every situation. Often they would stay up until late at night laughing at each other's humorous anecdotes. Sometimes they would laugh so hard they struggled to catch their breath. Washington developed a parody of his namesake, President George Washington, and Mary joked that someday a Clinton would be president of the United States. Washington would respond by telling her that a Clinton would never be president before a Duke was president.

Washington and Mary were overjoyed when she became

---

34 The details of Washington's proposal to Mary are not known to this author. This scene is created for enjoyment of the reader.

pregnant with their first child, whom they named Sydney T. Duke. Sydney was born in 1845. In 1846 they had a second child, Brodie Lawrence Duke. In April 1847, less than a year after the birth of Brodie, Mary's father passed away. Mary inherited seventy-three acres and $300. They used the money to purchase an additional ninety-eight acres from the Clinton estate. The death of Jesse Clinton was difficult for both Mary and Washington, who had become close to his father-in-law. But this was only the beginning of tragedies in Washington's life. Mary died a few months after her father in November 1847 from typhoid fever. As Washington was recovering from the grief of the loss of both his father-in-law and his beloved wife, he was again stricken with grief when his own father, Taylor, died in 1849 of natural causes. Although Taylor's exact birthdate is unknown today, it is believed that he was born around 1770. Thus, at the time of his death in 1849, Taylor was nearly eighty years of age. While Taylor's death was not unexpected, it was still devastating for Washington, who struggled to recover from the grief of his losses.[35]

After Mary died, Washington began to concentrate deeply on his Methodist faith. He became very active in the local Hebron church and would frequently accompany Billy on his evangelical missions to local churches. On one of those visits to a church in the neighboring county of Alamance, he saw a woman whose appearance was striking to him. Her name was Artelia Roney, and she was sitting with her two sisters in a pew at the front of the church when she caught his attention. She had turned and was looking at the door when Washington entered the sanctuary.[36]

---

35 The information about Mary's family, her family farm, her father's death, her inheritance and death, and the death of Taylor Duke are all a matter of public record. Mary, her parents, and her son Sydney were buried in a small cemetery near Durham that is today abandoned and has been damaged by vandals.

36 The account of Washington's marriage to Artelia is a matter of public record and the subject of several publications. The account given here is based on an actual event, though some details have been added for dramatization.

Washington walked to the front of the church and sat in the pew immediately behind Artelia. He glanced at her several times during his brother's sermon, and she glanced at him as well. After the service, Washington assisted his brother Billy in greeting the parishioners. The young woman approached Washington, who introduced himself. In reply, she said, "I am Artelia Roney."

"Artelia and her family are going to join us at the parsonage for dinner," Billy said. "You will join us?"

"Of course," Washington replied.

As Billy and Washington arrived in the two-horse buggy at the parsonage, Artelia Roney, her sisters, and her parents, John and Mary, were traveling directly behind them. They turned onto the path leading to the humble but clean home. When the carriages stopped, Washington stepped down, walked to the Roney carriage, and assisted Artelia, her sisters, and her mother from their carriage. Artelia, who was known as the most beautiful woman in Haw River, smiled at Washington.

The parsonage was humble but very clean. A fireplace located between the living room and the dining room provided warmth to both rooms. The dining table was made of mahogany covered with a dark stain. Twelve chairs positioned around the table provided enough space for everyone to sit comfortably. On each end of the dining table rested two candle holders that caught Washington's attention. The silverware was made of fine silver. *The pastor lives pleasantly though humbly*, thought Washington. He wondered if he might someday become a pastor like his brother Billy.

During dinner, Washington noticed that Artelia seemed to be studying him. On one occasion she caught his attention and smiled pleasantly at him. After dinner the families retired to the den, where they discussed plans for the upcoming holiday season. Thanksgiving was just weeks away, and Billy and Washington had decided to spend Thanksgiving in Haw River. The Roneys offered their home as a place to enjoy the Thanksgiving fellowship. During this Sunday afternoon visit, Washington and Artelia had occasion to talk of their personal interests and desires. Washington said, "My goal is to find a matriarch for my family. My wife, Mary, was taken at a very young age. Her time with us provided a taste of the beauty a mother brings to her family. Her absence has caused us to miss this beauty, and we were suddenly very alone."

"I understand," Artelia replied. "I pray that you find the woman who will complete your family."

On Thanksgiving Day, the Dukes, the Roneys, and the Edmunds (the minister's family) enjoyed a delightful Thanksgiving dinner at the Roney homestead. It was there that Washington began to consider, for the first time, that perhaps Artelia could become the matriarch of the Washington Duke household. He watched her move about the room and noticed the gracefulness of her actions. She seemed almost angelic to him. He decided that he must ask her father to allow him to court her or she might slip away as quickly as she had arrived. As they were leaving, Washington had a moment to speak with John Roney alone. "Mr. Roney," he said, "would it be possible for us to meet to speak about a matter sometime within the next week?" Unbeknownst to Washington, Billy Duke and John Roney had actually planned the activities together with the hope that Washington and Artelia would meet and share an attraction. In an effort to continue this concealment of intentions, John replied, "I am quite busy over the next several weeks; could it wait until after Christmas?"

"It could," Washington replied, "but it would be better to meet sooner."

"Very well, why don't you come to my house at noon on Tuesday of next week?"

Washington agreed. When Tuesday arrived, Washington awakened early to ensure that he could arrive at the Roney home well before noon. Although not nervous, he had some concern that Mr. Roney would decline because of Washington's known sympathies with abolitionists or that Washington had not established himself as a successful businessman. Washington's concern proved superfluous, inasmuch as Mr. Roney seemed delighted that Washington sought to court his daughter. "I would be pleased for Artelia to court such a fine young man as you."

Washington was relieved that Mr. Roney agreed to allow him to see Artelia. Now he faced the uncertain task of asking Artelia to agree to see him. As he was leaving, he saw Artelia walking toward the house from the barn where she and her mother had been tending to chores. "There is Artelia now," Mr. Roney said. "Why don't you share the news with her? I need to go chop some firewood."

As Artelia came into the house, Mr. Roney said with a smile, "Artelia, you have a visitor."

"I do?" Artelia asked as she looked inquisitively at Washington.

"Indeed; I will let Washington tell you about our discussion," Mr. Roney said as he gently slapped Washington on the back. This was even more sudden than Washington had expected. He had planned to obtain permission to see Artelia and would then tell her in a few weeks, perhaps in conversation during the Christmas holidays, that he had acquired her father's permission to spend time with her. He was determined not to use the term "court" while informing her of the developments. Now he realized that he had to tell her immediately because Mr. Roney would think poorly of him if he later asked Artelia about the conversation, which he was certain to do, and she told him nothing of the proposed courtship.

"What were you and Father talking about?" Artelia asked after her father had left the house.

"We were discussing the winter freeze and plans to go hunting," Washington replied.

"Oh," Artelia replied, somewhat disappointed, having hoped that Washington would say he had asked to court her.

"Yes," Washington said nervously, attempting to recover from the awkwardness, "we also talked about your participation."

"My participation? Whatever are you talking about? I would not go hunting."

"Oh, not that," Washington said with a laugh. "I meant your

participation in the winter activities. We felt that if you and I were to spend time together, perhaps we would get to know each other and ..." Washington looked awkwardly at the floor as his words drifted off into a mumble.

"Washington, are you trying to tell me that you asked my father for permission to court me?" Artelia asked with a smile.

At first Washington did not respond verbally but nodded slightly. "Well, yes," he finally said.

"And my father agreed—is that right?"

Washington began to laugh as he said, "Well, yes, that is true."

"Washington, that is so sweet," Artelia replied. "But unfortunately I have already given my heart to another whose name also happens to be Duke." A golden retriever entered the room and ran up to Artelia.

"Oh, I am sorry. I didn't know," Washington replied.

"In fact, here he is now. Hi, Duke." Artelia knelt on one knee to pet her golden retriever. Washington and Artelia both began laughing, and he said, "Why don't we have a first date? What if I pick you up on Saturday evening to go to the Haw River Christmas Dance?"

"I think that would be wonderful. By the way, don't be embarrassed that you are shy around women. I like that in a man. It is the best guarantee of faithfulness; a man who is too nervous to talk about romance with unfamiliar women will not be talking about romance with unfamiliar women," Artelia said with a laugh. She then became serious. "Washington, may I ask a personal question?"

"Sure, ask anything you like."

"I could not help noticing that you still wear a wedding ring. It has been four years since your wife passed away. Why do you still wear your ring?"

Washington looked down at the retriever and then at his ring.

"I'm sorry, Washington, I should not have asked a question like that," said Artelia.

"No, it is quite all right," replied Washington as a look of sadness came over his face. "I suppose the reality is that I have never let go of Mary. We had so much fun together. It seems we never stopped laughing. My family always tells me that I need to let go and move on, but it really is not as easy as everyone believes. It is actually quite difficult."

"It's time for you to look forward to a new life, Washington. It's time for you to find someone new who can give you the love you felt before."

"Thank you, Artelia," Washington replied.

Washington married Artelia Roney on December 9, 1852. They moved into a six-room two-story house with pine board walls that Washington had built. Soon they had their first child, a girl they named Mary. In 1855, they had a son named Benjamin Newton, and on December 23, 1856, they had another son named James Buchanan. James, who received the nickname "Buck," would eventually become the primary agent in the formation of the multibillion-dollar Duke empire.

Washington loved Artelia very much. They spent many hours together walking in the forest and enjoying the beauty of nature. They were a very happy family, and their children felt the deep love of both of their parents. Washington had not known if he would ever find a woman he could love after the death of his first wife, but he felt very blessed to have found Artelia.

October 15, 1855, was unusually warm in North Carolina. Thirty-four-year-old Washington was visiting the courthouse to look for a file he thought might someday be of importance to the family. The clerk was unable to locate the file, and Washington left the courthouse disappointed. As he walked out of the front door of the courthouse, he noticed a large number of slaves standing in two groups, males to the right and females to the left. As he walked between the two groups, he heard a woman call his name. He turned and saw a beautiful slave woman who was close to his own age. "Do I know you?" he asked.

She replied, "Don't you recognize me?"

Washington studied her for some time and then finally saw a familiarity that he could not identify. "You look familiar, but I don't recall where I know you from. What is your name?"

"Caroline," she replied.

"How do I know you?"

"When we were very young you helped me move a heavy bag of grain across the muddy street in Hillsboro. I have never forgotten that day, and I have never forgotten you."

Suddenly Washington remembered the young slave girl he had protected from her abusive master during his own teen years. "What are you doing at this auction?"

"I am being sold today. The man who was beating me the day I met you died about three years after that. He was always drunk. I think he drank himself to death. After he died, his son took over the farm. The son was mean, like his father. He would beat us for no reason, especially the girls. He died a few months ago, and now his estate is up for auction to pay his debts."

"I am sorry to hear about your hardship, Caroline." Washington paused for a moment and then asked, "What would you like to have if you could have any wish?"

"I would like to be free," she replied.

Washington nodded as he looked at the ground. "It was good to see you again, Caroline," he replied as he turned and walked away.

When the auction began, Caroline stood in the hot sun as the slaves were sold one at a time. After standing from early morning until late in the afternoon, a man finally came and took ahold of her arm. He led her up the steps onto the platform where each slave was to stand when the bidding began. The auctioneer said, "Look at this fine female specimen. We always save the best for the last. She would be a beautiful showpiece when the boys are over for a drink, a true symbol of a gentleman's prosperity." Prying her lips apart, he said, "See her perfect white teeth."

Because of her beauty, the auctioneer opened the bidding at

$300, nearly twice the price of the average female slave in Hillsboro that summer. Caroline did not look up to see the three or four men who were bidding on her. Tears flowed gently down her cheeks as she cried softly to herself. Soon only two voices competed to purchase her. The bidders competed vigorously, raising the number in small increments each time they bid. Finally the bidding stalled at $600. The auctioneer said, "The highest bid is six hundred dollars. Do I hear six hundred and one?"

Hearing no further bids, the auctioneer said, "Going once, twice ..."

"Six hundred and one," shouted a man from the back of the crowd who had not previously participated in the bidding.

"Six hundred and one," the auctioneer shouted. "Do I hear six hundred two? Six hundred and two ..."

"Going once, going twice ... sold to the highest bidder, the man in the back, for six hundred and one dollars. Come and claim your prize, sir. She is a fine one for sure."

A guard led Caroline down from the platform where she stood waiting for her new master to pay the bill.

"She is all yours," the guard said to her new owner. Caroline looked up to see who had bought her. Washington Duke reached out his hand to her. She was so overcome with emotion that she almost fainted as she put her hand in his and buckled over in tears.

"Caroline," Washington said, "you are now a free woman. You will never be a slave again."[37]

When Caroline finally regained her thoughts, she said, "This is

---

[37] Caroline, a slave, was purchased and freed by Washington Duke for $601 on October 15, 1855. (Orange County Estate Records, Inventories, Sales and Accounts [1853–1856], p. 390, North Carolina Department of Archives and History.) The North Carolina Census of 1860 shows that there were no slaves in the Washington Duke household at that time notwithstanding that a free woman, Caroline Barnes, was living and working there. Caroline remained as an employee in the Duke household for many years.

the happiest day of my life, but I don't have anywhere to go. I don't know where I will live."

"You can come and live with us while you decide what you are going to do," Washington replied. In time it became apparent that Caroline would have no place to live if she left the Duke homestead. Artelia and Washington offered to allow her to live with them and draw a salary in exchange for helping Artelia with household chores. Washington built an extra bedroom on the south side of the house where Caroline lived. Caroline and Artelia became close friends. Artelia taught her to read and write. In a short period of time, she was reading books that Washington would pick up from the traveling library that came to Hillsboro twice per month.

Critics of Washington Duke have learned of this purchase of Caroline and, without knowing the entire story, have assumed that Washington Duke once owned slaves. However, astute historians and genealogists have noticed that the 1860 census shows that, although Caroline was living in his home, he owned no slaves. Thus, she was a free woman at least as early as 1860 and—according to the account provided herein, which is believed accurate—was freed immediately upon her purchase.

The history of tobacco in America dates to a time prior to the formation of the colonies. In concentrated doses, tobacco can be hallucinogenic, and Native Americans used tobacco as an entheogen in religious ceremonies long before the arrival of the first explorers from Europe. Sir Walter Raleigh is said to have been the first to bring American tobacco to Europe.[38] It was commercially cultivated in Virginia as early as 1612. For many years tobacco was considered to have medicinal value as a respiratory enhancer, and it was not until the second decade of the twentieth century that

---

38 "Walter Raleigh" (c. 1552–1618), BBC, accessed September 22, 2013, http://www.bbc.co.uk/history/historic_figures/raleigh_walter.shtml.

widespread opposition to its use began to emerge among physicians in America.

The tobacco grown in America tended to be dark in color and had a strong aroma and taste. In 1839, a slave boy working for tobacco producers known as the Slade brothers was curing tobacco on boards that had become wet, which interfered with the curing process. In an effort to complete the curing process without waiting for the boards to dry, the boy decided to dry them using charcoal. He took the green tobacco leaves off the boards and placed them on the charcoal. The leaves turned a light color, as the charcoal absorbed the moisture in a manner similar to what had happened on the times he had laid them on the grass on a warm summer day. Instead of darkening and taking on the typical strong flavor and aroma, the leaves became a light gold color, resulting in a much softer flavor and aroma. The Slade brothers were impressed with the flavor and shared it with their neighbors along with an explanation of how it occurred.[39] This information came to Washington Duke, and by the mid-1850s he was producing tobacco using this charcoal curing method.

Washington found that customers were very fond of the bright leaf tobacco produced with the charcoal drying process. He realized that he had another marketable crop that could be sold at the market along with the produce he had previously grown. He was able to increase the annual household income significantly with the addition of the tobacco crop. He would often talk to Brodie and Sydney about the benefits of tobacco. They felt that by selling tobacco they were bringing a health benefit to the community. Tobacco smoking and chewing had been known as a rich man's pleasure, but Washington tried to keep his prices sufficiently low that everyone could enjoy the pleasure. Even while keeping the prices low, he discovered that tobacco generated a greater profit

---

39   Patricia P. Marshall and Jo R. Leimenstoll, *Thomas Day, Master Craftsman and Free Man of Color* (Chapel Hill: University of North Carolina Press, 2010), 34.

than any of the other crops grown on the farm. It did not take long for tobacco to become the preferred product of the farm. By the late 1850s, the family had shifted its primary crop from fruits and vegetables to tobacco and was beginning to enjoy a steady income from the sales. For the first time, Washington felt that fortune was beginning to smile on his family—that is, until tragedy struck the family again.

In 1858, Orange County suffered a typhoid epidemic, possibly as a result of heavy rains and sewage overflow into the rivers and waterways. The Duke household was not immune from the reaches of the illness. One day Washington and Brodie went into town to trade some crops and pick up supplies. Sydney stayed home with the family to do his chores. When Washington and Brodie arrived home in the early evening, Washington noticed that the house was quiet and there was no evening meal prepared. He saw Caroline asleep in the rocking chair by the fireplace and could hear a wheezing sound coming from the children's bedroom. "Artelia?" he whispered softly as he saw her silhouette in a rocking chair beside Sydney's bed.

He walked into the room, and Artelia whispered, "Sydney took sick. I am afraid it might be typhoid. It's pretty bad, whatever it is. He slept all day." As she talked, Washington noticed that she seemed tired and her skin seemed flushed. A short time later he noticed that her skin had become pale. "How are you feeling?" he asked Artelia.

"I'm starting to feel a little ill myself, but I believe I'm just tired."

Artelia and Washington sat up all night with Sydney, and Caroline stayed with the other children in a separate room. By morning, Artelia was clearly ill, and Washington made a bed for her in the room with Sydney. Several days later, Sydney passed away. This event was terribly painful for Washington. Artelia remained bedridden with her illness. Caroline had to keep the other children away from Artelia, and Washington had to care for Artelia while taking care of Sydney's remains.

Washington and Alex Weaver[40] went to the barn, where they built a small coffin for Sydney from pine boards. Alex was a former slave whose freedom Washington had purchased several years earlier. Like Caroline, Alex moved onto the farm and worked as a paid laborer for Washington when he had nowhere else to go after obtaining his freedom.

Washington gently placed Sydney's small body into the coffin and read scripture from the Bible as he and Alex sat next to Sydney's body. They chiseled a tombstone and loaded it onto the wagon along with the coffin. They took the wagon into the field, and with Artelia's family, a local minister, some of Washington's brothers and sisters, and a few townspeople, they held a small service. Washington fought back his tears as his brother Billy and Mr. Roney lowered the coffin into the ground. As the coffin came to rest in the bottom of the grave, Washington collapsed onto his knees and cried tearfully aloud, "Sydney!"

Ten days later Washington was sitting next to Artelia, who was still in the bed. Artelia was weak and could barely keep her eyes open. Washington caressed her hair with his fingers as she awoke and smiled. She looked at him quietly for several minutes. "It is time to say good-bye, my love," she whispered.

"Don't give up, Artelia; we need you. You made it this long; you will recover."

"No, G. W.," she said. "A woman knows these things. This will be my last night with you and the children. I love all of you so much. I want you to know that I really tried to save Sydney. I did everything I could. I really tried."

"What you did for Sydney cannot be measured. You eased his

---

40   Alex Weaver was living on the Washington Duke property as a free man according to the 1850 census. Although we do not have much information about him, he is believed to have been one of two slaves whose freedom was purchased by Washington Duke, though no record of his purchase has been located at the time of writing this book.

pain before the end. I love you, Artelia." The tears gently flowed down Washington's cheeks.

Artelia's family, Caroline, and the children all waited in the living room, praying that Artelia would recover. Everyone knew how contagious typhoid was, and they understood the danger of being in the home. Washington asked them to stay out of the bedroom, but Artelia's family took turns visiting with Artelia. Finally, later that night, Washington came out of the bedroom and closed the door gently behind him. He looked weak and defeated.

"How is she?" asked Caroline.

Washington leaned against the wood-burning stove, looked sadly at the floor, and shook his head. "She is gone," he finally said in a whisper.

Artelia had stayed with Sydney day and night in an effort to save his life. She loved the boy as if he were her own biological child, and in the end both Sydney and Artelia lost their lives. Now Washington had lost not only his second wife to death from illness, but his firstborn son as well. After the death of Artelia, Washington, though only thirty-seven years of age at the time, did not remarry. The pain of losing a loved one was too much to bear. He remained the rest of his life a widower devoted to his faith and his children. Artelia's sisters Betty and Anne Roney came to live with Washington and the children for a time. But from that day forward, the most important woman in Washington's life was Caroline. She helped Washington most through the grief of the loss of his loved ones.[41]

---

41   The deaths of Artelia and Sydney are well documented events about which there are several publications. The account given here is based on the actual event. Characters and details have been included for dramatization.

4

Washington's Secret Connection to the Underground Railroad

After Artelia died, Washington and Caroline became close friends. Caroline worked from morning to evening to keep the home beautiful and to provide the best food for Washington and the children. She would also spend several hours per day working in the garden to make sure the family always had fresh vegetables.

On a cool April evening in 1861, while Washington and Caroline were sitting together at the oak dining table near the fireplace, Washington said, "Caroline, you really don't have to work as hard as you do. I want you to enjoy life."

The gentle flames of the fire warmed the room comfortably. Caroline smiled at Washington as she took his hand in hers. "I work because I like to. When I work I feel that I am doing something good for you and the children. I always want you to know how much I appreciate everything you have done for me. I want all of you to know how much I love you."

"You have been such a wonderful addition to this family. You are part of this family."

"I am really blessed to be part of this family, G. W."

Nearly every night, after the children went to bed, Caroline and Washington would sit in wooden chairs at the dining table, drinking tea and conversing with each other until late evening. Sometimes when Artelia's sisters, Betty and Anne Roney, were staying at the home, they would all play table games, and sometimes they would read together. Often they would study the Bible together. In his spare time, Washington was adapting Bible stories into a children's book for his children, and sometimes Caroline, Betty, and Anne would help him.

One day in September 1861, Washington, who was forty years of age at the time, came home from a trip to Hillsboro to find Caroline sitting in the garden reading *Uncle Tom's Cabin* by Harriet Beecher Stowe.[42] Although she had only been reading for about five years, she read well and especially enjoyed novels that Washington would bring from the traveling library. As Washington approached, he was taken by her striking beauty and told her so. She laughed and asked, "Okay, G. W., what do you want? Why are you trying to butter me up?"

Washington laughed. "I'm not trying to butter you up. I'm serious. You really do look very lovely sitting here in the garden reading your book. Do you like *Uncle Tom's Cabin?*"

"I do, but it's a very disturbing book."

"It has caused a great deal of controversy. Because of this book many people, for the first time, are seeing slaves as human beings with emotions and pain, just like white people," Washington replied. "People are beginning to understand that a colored woman loves her child just as much as a white woman loves hers."

"I know. I am really glad you picked up a copy for me. I can only read it a little bit at a time because it brings back too many memories. Thank you for picking it up for me. By the way, I have something special for you tonight," Caroline said.

"What is it?" he asked as he sat on the ground next to her.

"I made your favorite, chicken and dumplings and a strawberry pie. Maybe I can't do everything for you, but I can feed you," she said with a laugh.

---

42 *Uncle Tom's Cabin* was first published in 1852 by John P. Jewett & Company.

"Oh, I love chicken and dumplings," Washington said. "Are we celebrating something?"

"Well, maybe. I remember the stories you told me about your childhood friend named Jim. You have talked about him often over the years. I heard about a slave named Jim on the David Souder plantation, and I thought it might be him. So I went over with your sister Malinda to see if it is him. It is." Caroline smiled.

Washington sat up straight with a start. "You saw Jim? How is he doing?"

"He is doing well. Because Malinda was with me, we were permitted to talk to Jim for a little bit. He said he hopes you can stop by to see him."

"I will visit him. I am so happy you were able to find him. I have thought that if I could ever find Jim, I would barter for his freedom. Maybe I will talk to David about that.

"I think I will try to visit him in a couple of weeks, after I get the rest of the crops planted. I almost tripped over that old plow today. It got stuck on a huge rock. I can tell you that a moose does not make a good plow horse. Joseph Stagg told me he had a moose he had raised since birth and that he taught it to pull a plow. He said it is much stronger than a plow horse or a mule. He let me borrow it to see what I thought. He was thinking of going into business raising meese to pull plows because they are easier to find in the wild than horses. I don't know how to tell him, but that animal did not want to pull a plow. I think maybe Joe was joshin' me." Washington laughed as he put up his hand to block the sun and then looked out over the field. "It will be wonderful seeing old Jim again."

Caroline giggled. "Did you say 'meese,' G. W.?"

Washington laughed. "'Meese,' the plural of 'moose.' Okay, 'mice.'"

Caroline laughed even harder. "Mice are those little animals that run on the ground. The plural of 'moose' is 'moose.'"

Washington and Caroline exchanged glances as they laughed.

Washington picked up Caroline's book and held it in the air for emphasis. "If I didn't have anything to do but read all day, I'd know the plural of 'moose' too."

Caroline picked up a large orange tomato and began tossing it in the air and catching it as if she intended to throw it at him. She smiled. "So you think I don't do anything but read all day?"

Washington laughed and then feigned an expression of fear as he looked at the tomato and held up his hand as if to block a blow. "I was only joking."

"I think it would be really good for you to see Jim again. That's interesting about plowing with a moose. Let's go get supper."

They stood up and then walked toward the house. Washington could smell the wonderful aroma of chicken and dumplings. Upon entering through the kitchen door, the sweet aroma of fresh strawberry pie also caught Washington's attention for a moment. "Oh, that smells so good."

"Hi, Pappy!" shouted five-year-old Buck as he and six-year-old Ben ran into the kitchen and gave their father a hug.

"Hi, boys," said Washington. Brodie walked into the room with a sheepish grin on his face. He waved and said, "Hi, Dad."

"Hey, Bro," said Washington as he nodded his head with a smile. "Are you ready for some fine cuisine?"

"Absolutely," replied Brodie with a smile.

As the family sat down for dinner, the boys talked about the fort they were building that day. Mary, Washington's seven-year-old daughter said, "The fort looks good. They're doing a good job."

"It does," said Caroline. "I went inside. I felt safe."

"Why are you building a fort?" Washington asked.

"So that we will have a place to go if the war gets here," Buck replied.

"I see," Washington said as he nodded.

"Do you think the war will come here?" Caroline asked.

"I hope not," Washington replied. "I am hoping this war will end soon."

"If the war comes here, which side will we be on?" Ben asked.

"We will do everything we can to stay out of it, and we need to pray it doesn't come here." Washington rubbed his chin as he talked. "I support the Union, and I oppose both slavery and secession, but the reality is that both Brodie and I might be conscripted into the Confederate Army or Navy."

"What does that mean?" asked Caroline.

Washington noticed the worried look in her eyes. "It means we might be required to fight for the Confederacy against our will. This is a Confederate state."

"But how can you fight against the North when you believe in everything the North stands for?" Mary asked.

"If we are conscripted, we won't have a choice. We could always try to go north to avoid conscription, but that means we would have to leave everything behind. And we don't even know that we will be conscripted."

"But if we go north, will you be conscripted into the Union Army?" Mary asked.

"We might be; then we would be fighting against the South. How could we fight against our neighbors and friends whom we have known our entire lives? This is a very bad war. Brothers are killing brothers, and fathers are killing sons."

Buck asked, "What is a war, Pappy? Isn't that where people kill each other?"

"Yes, that's what war is."

"Why do they kill each other?" asked Ben with a puzzled expression. "I don't understand. The Ten Commandments say, 'Thou shalt not kill,' don't they?"

"People have wars for different reasons," Washington replied. "The war the nation is in now is happening because the North wants to abolish slavery and the South wants to secede from the Union."

"What is slavery?" Ben asked.

"Slavery is an evil abomination where one person makes another person work for him against his will, without pay."

"Jimmy Smith said that colored folks are slaves. I told him that Auntie Caroline is not a slave, and he said it is wrong that she lives here and is not a slave," Buck said. "He said she is supposed to be a slave but she is really lucky because we like her."

Caroline quietly stood up from the table and walked over to the stove. Overcome with sadness, she looked at the surface of the butcher-block countertop next to the stove for a few moments as she fought back tears. Then she stirred the kettle of chicken and dumplings and said, "Would anyone like some more chicken and dumplings?"

"I would," Buck said.

"Auntie Caroline lives here as part of our family," said Washington. "She was a slave before she came to live here, but now she is free and she will never be a slave again."

"It would be really sad if we didn't have Auntie Caroline," Ben said. "I love Auntie Caroline."

"So do I," said Mary and Buck almost simultaneously.

Caroline laughed as she continued to resist the temptation to cry. "I love all of you too," she said as she poured a ladle of chicken and dumplings into Buck's bowl.

Washington stood up and put his arm around Caroline. She stood quietly leaning against the stove. "Are you okay, Caroline?"

"I will be fine. Sometimes I remember things."

"You will never have to worry about those days again," whispered Washington.

One week later Washington got up early in the morning and saddled Samson, his favorite horse. He named his horse Samson because of his muscular features. In a herd, people would notice Samson as a horse of unusual strength. He climbed on Samson and headed for the Souder plantation. When he arrived, approximately an hour later, he saw Jim sitting by a tree, shucking corn. Next to him was a walking stick with a sharp, pointed end. Washington chuckled because this reminded him of the time he first met Jim on the Mangum plantation near his father's farm in Hillsboro, when Jim said his spear was to kill a lion.

Jim saw Washington approaching but thought his eyes were deceiving him. He could not believe it was actually Washington. As Jim stood, Washington dismounted and tied his horse to the fence. Jim walked toward the fence and said loudly, "Washington, is that you? I thought I would never see you again."

"It's me," Washington replied.

Washington climbed through the wooden rails of the fence and laughed as Jim approached. Washington and Jim embraced and then looked at each other as if trying to refamiliarize themselves with one another's appearances.

"You are much taller than I remember," Washington said.

"Well, we are quite older than we were then. I suppose I have grown a little. You are the same height I remember, but you seem much stockier. You have put on some weight, but it looks good on you. You look strong."

"How are things here?" asked Washington.

"Things are okay," he replied. "I am getting along well."

"How does Mr. Souder treat you?"

"Master Souder treats me well. He is a good man."

Washington replied, "Tell me if things are not good here. I might be able to help you."

"Thank you," replied Jim, "but everything is good here."

"Maybe I could persuade David to allow me to buy your freedom. I did that for Caroline Barnes. She now lives with us at our place. Alex Weaver also lives and works at our place as a freeman. I bought his freedom a good many years ago. I can do that for you too, Jim. Do you remember when we were very young and I promised that I would someday obtain your freedom? I still intend to keep that promise."

"I heard about what you did for Alex Weaver and Caroline Barnes," Jim replied. "That was a really good thing that you did, G. W., but I don't want you to spend money like that for me. I will be okay."

"I really don't mind. In fact, I think I will talk to him about it while I am here." Washington climbed back through the fence and said, "I will talk to you in a little while." Washington walked to the left side of his horse, clutched the saddle horn with both hands, and jumped up onto the horse in a single motion without touching the stirrup with his foot. The horse broke into a canter even before Washington's feet were in the stirrups. As a young man, Washington often rode bareback, and he had become a master rider.[43] He rode quickly to the farmhouse, dismounted, and walked to the front door.

Before he could knock, Souder opened the door. "G. W., what brings you here?"

"I have a proposition for you," Washington replied. "I would like to purchase Jim."

"Why do you want to do that?" asked Souder.

"You know I don't hold to slavery. I knew Jim when he was just a boy. I could use a good farmhand. Jim is loyal and he would be a good worker for me as a freeman."

"I wish I could say yes," replied Souder, "but Jim is just too valuable to me. He does the work of three men."

"I would be willing to pay top dollar," Washington said.

"I just can't afford to let him go. I would have to retrain someone to perform duties that have taken many years for him to learn. He supervises over a dozen workers. They would never listen to anyone else the way they listen to Jim."

"What if I offered you four times what he would bring on the open market? Would you reconsider?"

"Sorry, G. W., I just cannot afford to lose Jim," Souder replied.

Souder's response frustrated Washington who felt that Souder was placing his own luxury above the rights of Jim. Why could he

---

43   According to information provided from Sarah Duke, Washington's riding skills were well-known in the community and he occasionally participated in horse races.

not see that it was wrong to keep Jim against his will? It did not make sense to Washington who resisted the temptation to become angry. His father had always taught him that a gentleman restrains his anger and treats others with dignity. Washington would follow the example his father had set for him, but it was deeply troubling that Souder would not allow Jim to be free.

"Okay," Washington said. "If you change your mind let me know. Do you mind if I stop and talk to him a little bit?"

"No, of course not," Souder replied.

Washington rode back down the lane and stopped at the fence where Jim was working. Jim looked up eagerly from his work to hear what news Washington had to share.

"I'm sorry, Jim," said Washington as he dismounted. "Mr. Souder would not agree today. Maybe in time I can change his mind."

"It's all right," replied Jim. "I didn't believe he would agree."

"Don't give up. I will talk to him again another day."

As Washington rode back to his farm, he thought of his younger days when he would walk the plantation with Jim, looking at the amazing sights of the countryside. As a boy he always wondered what would become of Jim when they became older. He wondered if Jim would someday be a freeman. He always believed that Jim was different from other African Americans he had known, but he believed Jim's difference was only the result of Jim's education. For many days he thought of Jim, often wondering if he could find a way to secure Jim's freedom. It only seemed the right and natural thing to do.

The Fugitive Slave Act of 1850[44] provided states with the authority to deal with slaves, and those who assisted escaping slaves, with severity. By the early 1850s, in some states, helping a

---

44   Fugitive Slave Act of 1850 (9 Stat. 462), enacted as part of the Compromise of 1850.

slave escape could result in imprisonment, loss of property, and severe beatings. Those who worked in the Underground Railroad were well aware that they did so at their own peril. A short time after Washington's visit, Souder, Jim's owner, died suddenly. Notwithstanding Washington's offer to purchase Jim's freedom, the executor of Souder's estate did not believe slaves should ever be free, so instead he sold Jim to a farmer who was also named James, though he was commonly called Shorty. Shorty was not as kind as Mangum or Souder had been. He worked Jim long hours and beat him if he did not believe Jim was sufficiently productive. Like Souder, this farmer also refused to allow Washington to purchase Jim's freedom.

One summer day in 1863, when Washington was in Hillsboro buying supplies, he saw Jim in a livery stable. Jim had been hired out for a few days to the owner of the stable. Washington went in to inquire of Jim's welfare. Jim told him how difficult things had become. Washington then told Jim of an idea. He would hire Jim for a few months and allow him to escape while in his custody; then he would wait several days for Jim to reach a safe house in the North. Once Jim had plenty of time to reach a safe place, Washington would contact Jim's owner saying that he had escaped, but by then Jim would be long gone.

"It's too dangerous, G. W. I can't let you do this," Jim said.

"No one will ever know. I will have a horse for you to ride. We will never be suspected, and by the time anyone knows you are missing, you will be long gone."

Washington leaned against a post and put his hands in his pockets. Then he glanced about the stable to ensure no one had come in. Speaking in a whisper, he said, "I have something to tell you, but you can never tell anyone."

"I promise I won't tell anyone," said Jim.

"We have a carefully guarded secret in the Duke family."

Jim stepped closer to Washington to catch every word.

Washington continued. "My cousin in Tennessee has been

involved in the Underground Railroad for over twenty years. He and his sons have been helping runaways come up from Alabama and Georgia through Tennessee into Ohio. They take them to a place called Oberlin, which is the headquarters for the Railroad. Oberlin is a college in Ohio that is used as a safe house for the Underground Railroad. That is where all of the routes are planned and implemented. From Oberlin the slaves are given documentation as freemen and are taken to their new homes in the North. I will ask my cousin if the Railroad will help us. I am sure they will. If they won't, we will find a way to do it without them, but I know they will help."

"I don't know, G. W.; it seems very risky for both of us," said Jim. "Besides, I can't even ride a horse."

"Don't worry about learning to ride a horse; I will teach you to ride."

"It's a very kind thing you are offering to do for me," Jim said. "You have always been good to me."

"It's settled then. I will talk to Shorty about hiring you for a few months. Then, while you are in my custody, I will help you escape to Ohio."

After his conversation with Jim, Washington paid one of his closest friends to travel to his cousin Mordecai's farm in Tennessee, to tell him that he needed a connection with someone in the Underground Railroad. Washington did not trust the mail because it was known that mail was being opened and read by Confederate officials owing to the war. The friend returned and informed Washington that he would be contacted in a few days by someone from the Underground Railroad who would help him. He also delivered bad news in that Mordecai's health was failing.[45] Washington was saddened to hear about Mordecai's health, but the promise about assistance from the Railroad proved true, and the plan was set in motion.

---

45   Mordecai Duke passed away in 1865 at the approximate age of seventy-two.

Several weeks later, Washington stood on the front porch of the house on the farm where Jim was kept as a slave. He was speaking to Jim's owner. "Shorty, I have some work around the place that I cannot seem to get done. I would be interested in hiring Jim for a few months if you are agreeable. I know that he was on the Souder farm before David Souder passed. David told me that Jim is a good worker."

"Well, things have slowed down a little on the farm. We already got the crops in. I suppose I could hire him out for a few months. How much are you willing to pay?"

"I would pay one hundred and fifty dollars for three months," Washington said. It was Washington's desire to pay the full purchase price for Jim, since for all practical purposes, he was removing Jim from Shorty's custody permanently.

"You must need him bad," replied Shorty.

"I need to get my crops in before the other farmers deliver their crops and the price drops. I have looked everywhere and can't find anyone who will hire out a worker."

"Okay, when do you want to pick him up?"

"I will take him now if that is agreeable," Washington replied. "Here is the payment."

"It's a deal," Shorty said. "You will have him back by November?"

"I will be finished with him by the second week of November," said Washington as he handed Shorty the money.

As Jim and Washington rode in the wagon back to the Duke homestead, Jim said, "I can't thank you enough for helping me this way. You have treated me better than anyone has ever treated me."

"I am just helping a friend and a good man," Washington replied with a smile.

As the wagon pulled up to the Duke homestead, Jim asked, "Is there a stove in the barn where I can start a fire?"

Washington laughed. "Why do you want to start a fire in the barn? You aren't sleeping in the barn. You are sleeping in the house."

"You would let me sleep in your house?"

"Of course, you are my friend."

For several days, Washington had wrestled with a moral dilemma, though he said nothing to Jim. Washington was a deeply spiritual man and always endeavored to tell the truth in all things. He had always believed that a man should be honest and forthright. Now he would commit two acts that he thought might be sins. First he would help free Jim, who, under the law, was property belonging to another man. Secondly he would misrepresent to Jim's owner what had happened to Jim. *Is this any different from destroying another man's property or turning loose his livestock?* he thought. After deliberating for several days, Washington concluded that there are times when lying and even separating someone from his property are justifiable. He could think of times in the Bible when good men did not tell the truth, and when they removed property belonging to another, because they were fighting a greater evil. Most importantly, Washington concluded that he was not separating a man from his property, because a human being is not property to be bought and sold. Washington felt that saving Jim from the evil of slavery and abuse was surely one of the reasons a man must engage in civil disobedience and violate an unjust law.

In order to protect them and to keep them uninformed, Washington sent Caroline and the children to the Roney homestead for several weeks.

The first night in the Duke homestead, Washington and Jim stayed up until the late hours, sitting by the fire, smoking their pipes, and talking about the days when they played together as boys.

"Do you remember the time we put those toads in Mr. Mangum's hat?" Jim asked.

Washington burst into laughter. "He had been drinking. He put the hat on his head and the toads fell onto his lap. He didn't even look surprised. I don't think he even knew what was happening. He acted like it was supposed to happen. Do you remember the time we were swimming at the river and the cottonmouth swam up to your face?"

"Oh, I have never been that scared in my entire life. I thought for sure I was dead. I was looking right at him. He opened his mouth like he was going to strike, then suddenly he turned and swam in a different direction." Jim and Washington both began laughing.

"I think the only thing that saved you was that you opened your mouth and screamed. He swam away because you opened your mouth wider than he could open his. You are lucky he didn't swim into your mouth and bite your tongue."

Jim laughed. "I would have looked really funny running around screaming with a snake hanging out of my mouth."

After a few moments, Jim said, "I have a question for you, G. W. I hear preachers and other good men say that slavery is a good thing and that it says so in the Bible. I know you read the Bible and you live by it, so why are you willing to do this for me?"

Washington replied, "Well, you know, Jim, people understand the Bible in different ways. Not everyone agrees on what the Bible says. That is why there are Methodists and Quakers and Baptists and Presbyterians and Catholics. They all disagree on certain things the Bible says. It just happens that the church I attend, the Methodist Episcopal Church, opposes slavery, but not all churches agree with this. I have looked at this issue, and I have discussed it with a number of ministers. Some do not believe the Bible supports slavery."

"But good people had slaves in the Bible right?"

"In the Bible there were slaves who were treated badly, like the Egyptians treated the Israelites, and then there were slaves who were treated well. If you look at the history of the Israelites, you will see that they did not have a lot of slaves. Usually they got their slaves when there was a war and they had taken prisoners."

"What did they do with their slaves after they had been taken prisoner?" asked Jim.

"Often they were only slaves until their loyalty was proven; then they were given their freedom. The Bible even tells us how to prepare a slave for freedom. And the few who did have slaves treated them more like laborers than slaves. Often they could leave anytime they wanted to. I don't believe the Bible supports slavery; in fact, I think it does the opposite. The Bible requires us to treat all persons with kindness and fairness."

"But what about the fact that I am property of Shorty and Shorty is your friend? Aren't you taking property away from Shorty by helping me escape?"

Washington laughed. "Are you trying to get me to change my mind about helping you escape?"

Jim laughed. "No, G. W. I just want to know that you are sure about what you are doing for me. I don't want you to regret this someday."

"Well, I don't believe that a human being can be property. I don't believe that one man can own another man like he owns a horse or a dog. In fact, that was the point of the entire book of Exodus, which talks about the evil of slavery and the freeing of the Israelites from slavery. The Bible is really opposed to slavery. For that reason, I don't believe that Shorty can own you. If that is true, then what Shorty is doing is wrong, especially when he mistreats you. Maybe I am actually helping Shorty to not do wrong by helping you escape. I will tell you, Jim, that I have thought about this and I have prayed about this for a long time. I am doing what I believe is right."

Jim nodded. "Okay, I just have one more question about this. You told Shorty that you hired me to help you get the crops in, but you are actually helping me escape. And you are going to wait for several days after I am gone to tell Shorty that I escaped that morning. Aren't those lies? The Bible says that we should not lie, doesn't it?"

"Yes, the Bible says we should not lie, but there are times in the Bible when good people say things that are not true in order to do good things. One of the most famous is when the Israelites were going to attack Jericho and Rahab hid the Israelite spies then told the people of Jericho they were not there. She was later honored by the Israelites for this lie. It served a greater purpose that was honored by God. Think of it another way. Suppose a man is a drunk and suppose his son is in a crowd of people when one of them asks him if his father is a drunk. The boy denies that his father is a drunk. Is the boy doing wrong? I believe the man who asked the question is the one doing wrong, because he is trying to cause the boy to dishonor his father by calling him a drunk."

"So you are saying that because Shorty is doing wrong in keeping me as a slave, your false statement to him is not wrong."

"Scholars have debated this for centuries. Some say Rahab sinned because she lied but that she was forgiven because her lie achieved a greater good. Others say her lie was not wrong in the first place, because she was following a higher morality. I am just glad that I don't have to decide the answer to that question. I believe we should always try to tell the truth, but if a situation occurs where it is necessary to say something false for the greater good, then that is what must be done, but only in those very rare situations. This does not mean that we should go around lying all the time, but there are times when it might be necessary."

Washington took a puff of his pipe and then looked at Jim. "Will you promise me something, Jim?"

"Anything," Jim answered.

"Will you promise that when you reach a safe place you will send word letting me know where you have gone and how you are doing?"

"Of course I will. I will always stay in touch with you."

Washington nodded. "Thank you, Jim. I suppose we should turn in. It's late."

"All right," said Jim as he stood.

"You can sleep in the children's room," Washington said. "There are clean sheets and blankets on the beds. Choose whichever bed looks the most comfortable."

"Good night, G. W."

"Good night, Jim," said Washington as he walked into his bedroom.

The next morning Washington awakened to the aroma of cooking food. He walked out of the bedroom and saw Jim preparing a breakfast of eggs, potatoes, and cornbread. He had prepared the food with basil, cilantro, green peppers, tomatoes, and onions. There was coffee in the pot.

"That smells fantastic. Where did you learn to cook like that?" Washington asked.

"Auntie taught me. When I was little she would let me help her cook so I wouldn't have to go into the fields. Mr. Mangum didn't care. He always treated us good."

"Do you miss Auntie and Mr. Mangum?" Washington asked.

"I miss them a lot. I also miss Pappy. I haven't seen him since I was about five. I wonder if he is still alive. I really don't remember him."

"I am sure he remembers you," Washington replied.

After breakfast Washington said soberly, "Let's get you riding a horse. We don't have much time." Jim nodded.

They went outside to the stable, and Washington led a slender but strong horse from the barn over to the hitching post next to the house. "Do you know how to saddle a horse?" Washington asked.

"Yes, I often saddle horses; I just don't know how to ride."

"Why don't you go ahead and saddle that horse?"

Jim took the blanket off the hitching post and approached the horse from the left; then he laid the blanket across the horse's back. He then hoisted the saddle onto the horse and laced the cinch. He tightened the cinch, waited for the horse to exhale, and then gave it a final pull.

"Okay, now place your left foot in the stirrup and lift your right leg over the saddle," Washington said.

Jim complied and began to walk the horse around the yard.

"When you feel you are ready, kick the horse into a trot, then practice riding up and down the road at a quick canter. We are going to have you ride for several hours each day so that riding will be second nature to you by the time you are ready to leave."

Jim held on to the saddle horn and nudged the horse with his heels as the horse began trotting around the yard. After a few minutes, Jim let go of the saddle horn and, holding only the reins, kicked the horse with both feet. The horse quickly moved into a canter, and Jim continued to ride for about an hour. Washington watched curiously as Jim exhibited the riding skills of an experienced rider.

"That is amazing," Washington said as Jim rode up to the hitching post and dismounted even before the horse came to a stop. "You ride like someone who has been riding his whole life."

"I guess it just comes natural for me," Jim replied, "probably because I have been around horses so much."

Washington removed the blanket and saddle from the horse and laid them across the hitching post. "You already ride like an expert. You should be fine."

Washington and Jim entered the house and sat at the table. Jim lit his pipe and smiled. "What now, boss?"

Washington laughed and then became serious. "Now we have to talk about where you are going." He stood up and pulled a map out from under a Bible on the fireplace mantel and laid it on the table.

"This is where we are," said Washington, pointing to a location on the map called Hillsboro. "You are going to follow this trail west. Your first stop is going to be in about thirty miles. Keep your horse at a trot or a slow, steady canter until it tires, then walk until it is rested. You should be there within three hours at most. You will eventually come to a fork in the road here." Washington placed his finger firmly on the map and focused his gaze on Jim. Surviving, after all, for Jim, meant not making a single mistake. Everything needed to be clear and concise.

"There you will see a sign that says 'Salem' and points toward one road, and another sign that says 'Danville' and points to the other road. You will take the road that leads to Danville. The first farmhouse you see after the fork is a safe house. It will be on the left side of the road. You are to go past it. There is a forest next to it, and you will see a trail leading into the forest. You will cut into the forest, then circle back and go straight into the barn. You will wait in the barn until someone comes out to help you. They will give you a fresh horse. Don't stay there longer than fifteen minutes or so. They will give you food and water. They will also tell you the location of the second safe house."

"Where is the second safe house?"

"We are only going to tell you one safe house at a time; that way if you get stopped and they torture you, you won't be able to tell them the location of all the safe houses."

Jim leaned back in his chair. "There is a lot of detail in this plan."

"We have been planning it since the day I saw you in the livery stable in Hillsboro. You are going to leave very early in the morning, even before it is light. Because you will be on a horse, the trackers will not identify you and they won't be able to track you by scent. It is rare to see a colored man on a horse, so we are going to prepare papers saying you are a freeman traveling on business for a plantation owner in Ohio and are returning to the plantation. Even so, it is better that you not be seen or stopped, because many slave hunters do not recognize such documents and will take you into captivity and sell you to another plantation owner, or they may just kill you. All the time you are traveling, you must watch in all directions for any sign of movement. If you see a person on a horse, no matter how far away, immediately find a place to hide. The route you are taking is rural all the way, so you should not see very many people, except for slave hunters. Always watch for wooded areas where you can take your horse if anyone sees you. Be especially watchful for any military patrol. The Union isn't this far south yet, and the Confederates are not in this area right now, but you need to be careful anyway."

"How many people are involved in this project?" Jim asked.

"There are a number of people assisting in getting you to Oberlin."

"Where will I be taken after Oberlin?"

"The only people who know that are the professors and administrators at Oberlin who plan these trips. Many slaves are being relocated to Northern states; some are going out west, where they can obtain work on cattle ranches, and some are going to Canada."

"Why Canada?" asked Jim.

"Canada officially abolished slavery in the 1830s. It is a free nation. For that reason, many slaves are relocated to Canada. The problem with staying in the United States is that even freemen in a nonslave state can still be extradited by slave hunters and taken back to their owners or prosecuted as runaways. Slave hunters have no authority in Canada, and they cannot arrest anyone for activities involving slavery. Canada is probably the safest place to go."

As they walked back into the house, Washington opened a cedar cabinet and took out a three-piece suit, a dress shirt, and a tie. "This is what you will wear when you ride."

"Those are a rich man's clothes. Why would I wear that to ride?"

Washington laughed. "That is the idea. Slave hunters are far less likely to confront a person who appears prosperous. If they believe you are working for a wealthy plantation owner, on business, maybe they will not want to bring trouble on themselves by interfering with your business. We just have to make you appear very convincing. They will never suspect you are a runaway. Where would a runaway get a horse, ride like a master, and wear expensive clothing."

"G. W., I can't afford these clothes."

"Don't worry. I got the whole suit for a fifty-cent piece, but it didn't fit me. I have been holding on to it until I could find someone to give it to. It would fit you. It's yours as a gift."

Jim tried on the suit, and it fit perfectly.

One morning about a week later, while Washington and Jim

were working in the garden, Washington saw two Confederate soldiers approaching from a distance. "Jim, someone is coming," said Washington as he placed his shovel against a fence post.

Washington and Jim stood next to each other as the riders approached. "Washington Duke, I am Captain Bailey. I have conscription papers for you. You are to report to Raleigh in three days for your conscription."

Washington's heart sank. He had anticipated this day but hoped it would never arrive. He did not want to join the war and especially did not want to fight against the North. Of even greater concern was that his plan to free Jim might now be foiled. "It would be difficult for me to go in three days," said Washington. "I have to finish getting my crops in. Is there any way I could have more time?"

"Ordinarily we do not do that. When your time arrives, you have to go. However, in this case, I can see that your crops are not in. Also, we will not be moving on for three more weeks, so I suppose I can make an exception." Captain Bailey changed the date on the conscription papers, allowing Washington extra time. He then gave the papers to Washington.

After the soldiers left, Washington said, "This changes our plans a little bit, Jim. We are going to have to move much quicker than we planned. Also, we need to keep up appearances. I am going to go over to William Walker's plantation and tell him that I have been conscripted, but that I have your services until the second week of November. I will offer to allow him to use your services until your time with me is up. That way if anyone asks, it will seem that everything is legitimate. However, you will not actually go to the Walker place. You will be headed up north long before the day arrives for me to deliver you to Walker."

Jim nodded as he said, "This is getting a little scary. I think we should forget the plan, Washington. It is getting too dangerous for you now."

"Don't worry," replied Washington. "We just need to change our plans a little, but we will proceed with the plan."

Washington made the arrangements with Walker as he had promised Jim. Because Walker could not afford to pay for Jim's services, Washington said he could use Jim's services free of charge since Washington had paid for him until November. After making the arrangement with Walker, Washington met with his contacts in the Underground Railroad to let them know what had occurred, and that the escape was going to have to occur earlier than planned. His contacts in the Railroad assured him that changes in plans were common and that he should not be concerned.

When the morning for Jim to ride finally arrived, Washington was up long before sunrise. He lit the lantern and went to the barn to retrieve the horse. As he was saddling the horse, Jim came into the barn wearing the three-piece suit and carrying the tie. "I guess this is it," Jim said.

"Yes, I guess it is," replied Washington. "I have enjoyed the time we spent together over the last few weeks. It reminded me of when we were boys."

"Me too," replied Jim. "Those were great days." Jim paused for a moment and then said, "Do you mind helping me with this tie?"

"Sure," Washington said as he reached for the tie. "While you are traveling, you can't untie your tie at night, because you won't be able to tie it to put it back on. That means you will have to loosen it and slip it over your head, but don't untie it. It's going to be light soon. I put a hand mirror in your saddlebag so you can see yourself to straighten the tie when you need to. You look good in your suit. I think if I needed a lawyer I would hire you," Washington said with a smile.

Jim laughed. "You must be joking, Washington; there are no colored lawyers."

"Not yet," replied Washington, "but someday there will be."

As they walked out of the barn, Washington said, "Be sure to write to me and let me know where you are."

"I will," Jim said as a tear swelled up in his eye. "Thank you, my friend."

"I would ride with you if I could, but that would make it more dangerous for both of us if anyone recognized us."

"I know," Jim replied.

Jim reached out his hand to shake Washington's hand. Washington ignored Jim's hand and instead embraced his childhood friend.

Jim climbed onto the horse and rode away. Washington watched him ride out of sight long before the morning sun rose in the sky, not knowing if Jim would survive the ordeal or whether he would himself be arrested for assisting in the escape.

For the next two days torrential rains turned the ground into mud, eroding all the tracks leading from the Duke homestead. It was a warm rain. Washington stood outside at night, inhaling the wonderful fragrance of a North Carolina summer rain. He then sat at his table and wrote a letter to Shorty, telling him that Jim the slave had run away. When the rain finally stopped, Washington went to Hillsboro and mailed the letter. Then he decided to tell Shorty in person, so he went to Shorty's home. "Shorty, I have some unfortunate news. I went to the barn to awaken Jim this morning, and he was gone. All of his clothing and other belongings were gone as well. He seemed depressed last night. I had made arrangements for him to go to William Walker's place because I have been conscripted. He must have decided to make a break for it. I have no idea which way he went. I mailed a letter to you from Hillsboro this morning, but then I decided to come to tell you in person."[46]

---

46 Washington Duke sent the following letter to Jim's owner. "Having to brake [sic] up and go into the service, I let Mr. Wm. E. Walker have your boy Jim until his time would be up ... he, Jim, went to sulking last night and is absent this morning, his clothes are gone. I expect therefore he will go to see you ... if he should would you please send him down to Mr. Walker who will take care of him until his time is up ... unless he should run off. Yours Respectfully, Washington Duke." From "W. Duke to James Cox, June 15 and October 27, 1863," James W. Cox Papers, Southern Historical Collection, University of North Carolina at Chapel Hill. See also Robert F. Durden, *The Dukes of Durham, 1865–1929* (Durham: Duke University Press, 1975), 8.

"Jim ran away?" Shorty asked in a surprised manner. "I would never have expected that. If I find him, I am going to nail him to the barn. Do you have any idea which way he went?"

"I don't," Washington replied, "but if I was on the run, I would head northeast toward Boston this time of year. I would want to get there fast, before winter sets in."

"That's a good point," Shorty replied. "I will instruct the trackers to head north along the coast since they probably won't be able to find his tracks after all of this rain."

"If he shows up at my place, I will let you know," said Washington.

"All right, thanks, G. W."

As Washington drove his wagon to the Roneys' to pick up his sons and Caroline, he continued to contemplate the ethics of his actions. "What is right and what is wrong?" he asked himself. "Am I wrong if I honor a law that hurts others? If I uphold the laws of slavery, am I committing a greater evil than if I break the evil law?" Perhaps in the mind of Washington there was no easy answer to these questions. Perhaps, since he did not believe a human being was property that could be bought and sold, the moral dilemma was not as severe as the risk at which he had placed himself and his family. He knew that he was sworn to secrecy and that, with the exception of those who assisted in the escape, and Jim, this was a secret he would take to his grave.[47]

---

47 The story of Jim's escape is based on a synthesis of information consisting of the following. First, there is an account from Sarah T. Duke that Washington had a childhood friend named Jim who was a slave. Secondly, it was also reported by Sarah that Washington later helped a childhood friend escape slavery, though we were not given the name of the slave whom he helped escape. Given the unlikely possibility that Washington had more than one childhood friend who was a slave, it seems logical that the person Washington helped escape was this same Jim. I also learned from Sarah Duke that during the Civil War Mordecai Duke was contacted by Washington through a messenger requesting an introduction to a representative of the Underground Railroad to help a slave escape to Canada. Through research I discovered that right before Washington was

It was almost two years before Washington heard from Jim. For a long time he did not know if Jim had survived the escape attempt, though he had heard that Jim had made it to the free states. One day, after Washington had returned from his service in the military, he went into Hillsboro to obtain supplies and to collect the postal mail. The postmaster gave him three letters. Two of them were bills from a supplier in Durham, and the third was a letter from Canada postmarked almost two years earlier. As Washington opened the third letter, he recognized the handwriting of the man he had taught to read and write many years before when they were just boys. The letter was from Jim. It said that Jim had settled in Canada just across the border from Sault Ste. Marie, Michigan. Jim said he was learning to read and write French. The letter thanked Washington for being such a wonderful friend and said that Jim would forever be indebted to him. That was the last time Washington ever heard from Jim, and he never knew what became of him. Although he answered the letter, he had no way of knowing if Jim ever received it. He remembered Jim's promise that he would stay in touch. From that promise, and the failure to stay in touch, Washington always assumed that some misfortune had befallen Jim that kept him from writing again, but he always hoped that Jim had bought a nice estate with many acres in the province of Ontario.[48]

As in the case of Caroline, critics of Washington have learned

---

conscripted into the Confederate Navy, a hired slave named Jim escaped while in Washington's custody. The account given here is based on the premise that the Jim who escaped while in Washington's custody is the same as Washington's childhood friend and that Washington actually assisted in the escape.

48   The actual outcome of Jim's escape is not known. The account given here is a dramatization based upon the limited information available. There is an account that Jim returned to Shorty's plantation and surrendered. See Durden, *The Dukes of Durham, 1865–1929*, 8. However, this appears to be based solely upon the failure of Shorty to swear out a complaint against Washington or anyone else for the escape, given that no evidence has been offered for this view. It may well be that Shorty believed the story true and felt it would be pointless to pursue damages against anyone.

of the fact that Jim was hired by Washington from a slave owner. Without knowing the entire story, they have assumed that Washington Duke once supported slavery. In reality they did not dig deeply enough, or perhaps simply did not possess access to critical information to determine what actually occurred. Thus, it appears that neither the story of Caroline nor the story of Jim realistically suggests that Washington ever supported slavery; in fact, both stories (if told in full) clearly show that he did not. Perhaps most importantly, Washington's son Benjamin adamantly insisted that his father opposed slavery from the earliest days of Ben's life. So intense was Ben's insistence that his father opposed slavery, that he would become offended if anyone ever suggested otherwise. Though we will probably never know for sure, perhaps Washington had told Ben the story of the slave named Jim but Ben, like his father, was sworn to secrecy.

5

Washington and the Civil War

W ashington Duke stood in formation at Camp Holmes in North Carolina wearing the gray uniform provided by the Confederate officers who commanded him. Despite his opposition to slavery, and the fact that he had voted for Abraham Lincoln for president, in 1863 he was conscripted into the Confederate Army and mustered in on April 4, 1864.[49] His personal views were irrelevant to those in command who ordered him to take up arms against those whose beliefs he supported. Prior to entering the forces, Washington had arranged for his brother Billy to manage his three-hundred-acre farm. With the exception of his son Brodie, who entered the military with Washington, his children went to Alamance County to stay with the Roneys, Artelia's parents. While living at the Roneys', the Duke children attended a one-room log schoolhouse nearby and attended Sunday school every Sunday morning. Brodie, only sixteen years of age and weighing only ninety-six pounds, was underweight. For that reason he was sent to Salisbury, where he served as a junior guard in the military prison.[50] Military life was extremely difficult for Brodie, who had

---

49   Virginia Gray, *Some Obscure Facts About the Military Man Whose Gifts Brought the College to Durham, Duke Alumni Register*, December 1967, III, 23–25; See also Durden, *The Dukes of Durham, 1865–1929*, 9.
50   Durden, *The Dukes of Durham, 1865–1929*, 8–9.

already suffered severe emotional trauma from the death of his mother, Mary, his stepmother, Artelia, and his brother Sydney. These events caused a deep emotional disability from which he never fully recovered.

As Washington stood in formation with the other Confederate soldiers in his regiment, he felt conflicted. He wanted to run as far away as he could to avoid fighting against the North. Despite his abhorrence of the institution of slavery, and notwithstanding his conscription into the Confederate States Militia, Washington believed that attempting to escape would be futile. In the highly populated southeastern states, he would never make it to a northern state without being captured and possibly executed for desertion. In the unlikely event he reached a Union state, he would probably be incarcerated as an enemy combatant and placed in a military prison throughout the duration of the war, where he could succumb to illness and death. Feeling helpless and uncertain, Washington did the only thing he felt he could under the circumstances. He silently followed the orders of those in command. He thought that perhaps he could avoid firing upon the enemy and that, if he did fire, he would only do so in direct defense of his troops. He learned quickly that war is not so kind to the conscientious objector.

Initially placed on guard duty at Camp Holmes, Washington soon transferred to the Confederate Navy, where he served in a gun crew on a ship defending the harbor of Charleston, Virginia.[51] As he walked on the dirt road from Camp Holmes in North Carolina toward Charleston, Washington heard the loud crack of a rifle and saw the soldier immediately in front of him fall to the ground. Suddenly everyone began running and shouting. Union soldiers ran from the trees, firing as rapidly as they could cock their lever-action breech-loading Henry rifles. Washington dropped a ball into the muzzle of his musket, but before he could insert the ramrod, he found himself in close-quarter hand-to-hand combat. He wres-

---

51   Durden, *The Dukes of Durham, 1865–1929*, 9.

tled on the ground with a Union soldier for several minutes, with neither gaining the upper hand. The other Confederate soldiers attempted to defend themselves with single-shot flintlocks, but their efforts were in vain. All around, fellow Confederate soldiers were falling to the ground. Overwhelming in the ambush, the Union soldiers remained unmerciful as they strived to destroy as many Confederate lives as possible within the shortest period of time. Soon all of the soldiers were engaged in hand-to-hand combat as the dirt road became a bloody battlefield. Then, for a reason unknown to Washington, he heard a bugle blast, and the Union soldiers abruptly turned around and ran back into the woods as quickly as they had appeared. Washington looked around the battlefield at the dozens of fellow Confederate soldiers lying on the ground. Once again he had that familiar sick feeling in the pit of his stomach, just as he had experienced in the tavern in Hillsboro when he heard the plantation owner boast of his sexual exploits with slave women. It had become apparent that avoiding the fight was no option for a soldier trapped in the Civil War.

"That's the hit-and-run strategy," said an elderly officer who saw Washington's amazed expression. "It is a form of mental warfare. They hit us hard, then run before we can respond. That way they are able minimize their own casualties and at the same time terrorize us into despair."

"But why didn't they just kill us all?" Washington asked. "We were clearly outnumbered."

"Because they want us to remember to tell other regiments what we saw here. We were the lucky ones who were chosen by the heavens to survive—at least this time anyway," said the elderly officer as he spat a chaw of tobacco on the ground and surveyed the number of bodies lying in the dirt. "The next time, we might not be the lucky ones."

Washington saw for the first time what he would face in this war. He felt as though he were in a dream and could not understand why the evil of this war was not apparent to everyone. *Who cannot see that this is an evil abomination?* he thought to himself. *God did not create mankind for this evil purpose.*

In 1864, Washington transferred again, this time to Drewry's Bluff, near Richmond, Virginia, to defend Richmond, the capital of the Confederate states. In a short time, his expertise as a marksman became widely known and he was promoted to sergeant and received a commendation as an expert gunner. As the war raged on, the Union forces began moving southward into Virginia. In April 1865, Washington and his troops were in Richmond, defending the city from capture by the Union Army. The city had become a bloody battlefield. Everywhere in the streets lay bodies of Confederate soldiers. The troops had fallen into chaos and confusion, with everyone fearing for his life. A rumor spread that orders had been issued to retreat southward toward North Carolina, but Washington could not obtain confirmation from a higher officer. With fifty men under his command, and his own commanding officer missing for days, Washington could not give the instruction to retreat without confirming the order, but he could not locate an officer. As he ran across a street to find cover for his troops, he was nearly run over by a Confederate lieutenant on a horse. The troops were beginning to break rank and run toward the South.

Washington saluted the lieutenant and shouted "Orders, sir." The officer stopped only for a moment and shouted, "Have you not received the orders? Retreat south toward the North Carolina border. Go with God." As the lieutenant turned his horse to ride away, Washington heard the loud crack of a rifle. The officer fell from his horse and died in the street from a bullet wound to his head. Before Washington could grab the reins, the horse ran up the street looking for his own place of cover. The Confederate troops fled southward, and Washington and his men ran down a street to avoid cannon fire. The blasts of the Union cannons were causing the brick buildings around the men to crumble like dirt, showering the men with debris. They turned down an alley only to discover a barricade and no outlet. As they ran past the corner of a building, they found themselves facing a Union infantry battalion on all sides. Surrender was the only option. As Richmond fell to the Union Army, Washington and his men were captured and imprisoned at Libby Prison, which had previously been the Confederate prison in Richmond. There were so many Confederate soldiers imprisoned at Libby that they had to sleep in spoon positions or laid out on the floor next to one another head to toe. The food was contaminated with maggots, and the water unsanitary. After several months, Washington was transported to New Berne, North Carolina, where he was released. At the time of his release he was in poor health, had no food, and possessed only the worn, ragged clothes he was wearing and five dollars in Confederate money, which he traded for a fifty-cent piece with which to buy food until he reached home. He walked 135 miles from New Berne all the way back to the Duke Homestead in Hillsboro.[52]

As Washington walked up the road toward his home, he noticed its abandoned appearance, except that he could see that his brother William had worked the fields as he had promised. His children, with the exception of Brodie, had gone to stay with the Roneys. Although Brodie had gone into the war with his father, they had become separated shortly after their conscription. *I wonder if Brodie survived,* thought Washington sadly to himself. Brodie had been on his mind since the day they were separated. Washington had received no word from him in months and had been wrought with worry. He was right to worry. One in three Confederate soldiers had died during the war.

Walking up to the front door of the homestead, Washington saw that no one was around. The weeds had overgrown the yard, and it appeared that no one had been in the home since he had left

---

52 The dates and locations of Washington's military service are well documented in various publications; however, little information is known about his actual service, and it is a matter he did not like to discuss. This account is based upon the documented information, though details have been added for dramatization.

two years earlier. After opening the door, he walked inside and looked around the room. He saw no sign of Brodie. He felt a tear swell up in his eye as he sensed that Brodie might not have survived the war. Though he barely had the strength to walk, he decided to go directly to the Roneys' to find the other children. As he turned around to leave, he noticed the figure of a small, thin boy standing in the doorway. He recognized his son Brodie, who ran to him and embraced him.

"Bro," said Washington as he embraced his son.

"Pappy," Brodie said. "I didn't think we would ever see you again."

"When did you get out?" Washington asked.

"About two months ago."

"Are you okay? Where are the children?"

"They are still at grandma and grandpa Roney's place."

"Have you been staying here?" asked Washington.

"Yes," Brodie replied. "Why don't you rest for a while, then we will go get the children."

"I'm exhausted, but I can't wait. Let's go now," Washington replied. Washington and his son Brodie went to Alamance County, where they found the other children safe and well at the Roneys'. They were so excited to see Brodie and their father approaching that they ran all the way to the end of the lane to greet them. Ben said, "Pappy, I knew you would come back. Buck said you wouldn't, but I knew you would." Washington embraced his children and his in-laws, and then they all went into the house so Washington could rest.

Recovering from the devastation of war and restoring the farm presented a tremendous challenge, albeit an unavoidable one. Washington and Billy surveyed the property. Billy had maintained the crops as he promised, but the yard required cutting and trimming. The house was in need of paint but would have to wait, given the limited budget with which to rebuild. Buck and Ben were approaching their teen years, and Mary was already a teenager. The significant age gap between Brodie and the other children forced him to assume a parental role when Washington was in the field or away on business. Often Brodie would accompany his father and the task of raising the children would fall to Caroline.

6

The Tobacco Empire Is Established

B efore going into the war, Washington was growing an annual crop of tobacco along with other crops, such as corn, barley, and wheat. He had begun selling the lighter tobacco, which used a charcoal drying process. This had become popular particularly among younger tobacco users. His brother William had continued to maintain the farm when he left to fight in the war. Thus, upon his release, there was a supply of tobacco in the warehouse on the farm. Not far from the Duke farm, near Hillsboro, North Carolina, was a small train stop called Durham Station, which had been named after Bartlett Durham, a small country doctor who had donated the site for a train station. A fortuitous event in 1865 near Durham Station, originally called Durhamville, set into motion a series of events that would ultimately catapult the Duke family into fame and fortune.[53]

While Washington was awaiting his release from Libby Prison in March 1865, two generals from opposing armies were engaged in settlement negotiations near the Duke farm. General William T. Sherman had entered North Carolina with fifty thousand troops and the objective of joining General Ulysses S. Grant in an effort

---

53   Durden, *The Dukes of Durham, 1865–1929*, 12; William K. Boyd, *The Story of Durham*, Durham, 1925.

to take Richmond. However, when General Sherman learned that General Lee had surrendered to General Grant, General Sherman altered his strategy and began pursuit of General Joseph E. Johnston. Knowing that the South had been defeated and he had no reasonable chance of victory, General Johnston retreated to Hillsboro, just a short distance from the Duke farm.

General Sherman arrived by train at Durham Station and then traveled on horseback the additional distance to Hillsboro. At that first meeting, General Sherman showed General Johnston a communication he had received only that morning, announcing the assassination of President Lincoln. On the twenty-sixth of April, General Sherman and General Johnston signed the final surrender papers that ended the Civil War.[54] For two weeks the armies had an agreed armistice, and they stayed in the Hillsboro area. Durham became a popular place of meeting and conversing not only with one's own troops but with opposing troops as well. The bright leaf tobacco was being produced by John R. Green in a factory about one hundred yards from the railroad tracks in Durham. During this two-week armistice, the John R. Green tobacco factory was sacked, and for the first time, the soldiers had the opportunity to sample the mild, sweet bright tobacco, which they had confiscated. It became instantly popular. Given that Washington was experienced in growing this bright tobacco, he saw this opportunity and seized upon it.[55]

Tobacco production relied on labor skilled at drying, chopping, and rolling the tobacco. First the tobacco leaves would be separated and then laid out on the beds of charcoal to dry. This is known as the curing process. The dried tobacco leaves would then be laid out on tables and beaten into pieces small enough to be rolled into cigarettes or used as pipe or chewing tobacco. This is known as

---

54 Editorial, "Johnston's Surrender," *New York Times*, April 30, 1865.
55 For a detailed discussion of Washington Duke's ventures in the tobacco industry, see Robert F. Durden, *The Dukes of Durham, 1865–1929* (Durham: Duke University Press, 1975).

"beating out" the tobacco. Then the tobacco would be placed in small bags and sold for the consumer to either roll himself or to use for pipe smoking or chewing. Alternatively, the tobacco would be rolled into cigarettes for the end consumer, thus eliminating the need for the consumer to roll his own tobacco. This is known as rolling the tobacco. Prerolled cigarettes became very popular because of the convenience, and Washington saw this as yet another advantage he could have over his competitors, most of whom sold the tobacco without rolling it. An experienced roller could roll two thousand cigarettes per day.[56]

After his release from Libby Prison and his long walk back to his home, Washington gathered his family together from the Roneys', where they had been staying, and returned to his farm. A twenty-by-thirty-foot log barn had become the first tobacco factory in the Duke family. Although a substantial part of the tobacco that was being stored had been confiscated by the soldiers, the family was able to retain enough to sell for supplies they needed to develop their tobacco business with an emphasis on smoking tobacco rather than chewing tobacco. Washington struck out across eastern North Carolina with a wagon full of tobacco and two blind mules. The wagon, which he had obtained long before the war, had begun to deteriorate but was sufficient to accomplish the initial objective of a successful sales campaign to merchants, which would lay the foundation for the Duke tobacco company then called Pro Bono Publico.[57] As Washington traveled the distance from Durham to the ocean, he found many locals anxious to try the golden tobacco. While nearly everyone had heard of it, no one was producing it, and for most smokers it was a novel treat.

"What do you call this tobacco?" asked the operator of a trading post near the border of Virginia.

---

56   "Interview with Laura Cox," *Durham Morning Herald*, January 17, 1926.
57   Durden, *The Dukes of Durham, 1865–1929*, 13.

"I call it charcoal flavored because it is cured by charcoal. That's what gives it that unique taste."

"Do you mind if I try some?" asked the prospective purchaser as he rolled some tobacco into a piece of rolling paper.

"Of course not," replied Washington. "Take this pouch with samples to share with your friends. If they like it, let me know and I will sell you one hundred pounds at a very good discount as your first order. In fact, I will sell it to you at my production cost. That way you can sell to your customers at a discount so they will be willing to try it."

"Why would you sell it to me at cost? You won't make a profit," replied the trading post operator.

"Because once your customers try it, they will ask for more. I will earn money off the future sales."

Washington was correct. Several days later, the owner of the trading post asked for a thousand pounds. He said he was going to ship it up north to sell in Virginia. Within weeks Washington had sold nearly his entire crop and had to take backorders. He realized that in order to stay ahead of competitors, he would have to meet the demand with an ongoing supply of this new tobacco. If he did not, others would move into the market and he would lose his competitive edge.

After returning from his successful sales campaign, Washington began manufacturing smoking tobacco on a part-time basis, while maintaining the farm production of wheat, corn, and oats. In 1866 the Duke family was able to grow and manufacture 15,000 pounds of smoking tobacco.[58] However, growing the tobacco crop required the diversion of land and labor from the other farm products. For that reason, Washington began purchasing more tobacco crops from neighboring farmers, after which he would treat it using the charcoal curing process. In 1868, Washington's son Brodie tried to persuade his father to move the family business to Durham, to be

---

58   Durden, *The Dukes of Durham, 1865–1929*, 14.

closer to the local railroad and the end consumer, but Washington was reluctant. One evening, as Washington, Brodie, Mary, Benjamin, and Buck sat around the wooden table in the living room at the Duke homestead, which served as their boardroom, Brodie tapped his quill pen on the table and said, "The biggest advantage to locating in Durham is the proximity to the railroad stop. It would save a great deal of time, and ultimately money, if we were just a few blocks, or even across the street, from the loading dock."

"There is no question it would be closer to the train stop, but it would be farther from the farmers who sell us tobacco. We need to take into consideration the extra time it would take for them to bring their tobacco to us," Washington replied. "Also, we are now employing a few workers in the factory. They would have to travel farther to get to work."

"They would understand and would see the benefit," Brodie said. "It could mean that we could lower the price we charge for all tobacco, because we would have reduced our expenses of getting the product to the railroad for shipping."

"Another factor to consider, though, is that we sell quite a bit of tobacco right here, near the factory. It would inconvenience those who purchase in our warehouse to have to go all the way to Durham," said Buck, who was still only in his teens.

"Maybe there is a compromise here," Benjamin said. Benjamin, who spent as much time studying theology as did his father, was often seen as the negotiator of compromise in any business decision. "Maybe we should build one factory in Durham and keep another one here. That way we could meet the needs of everyone more efficiently."

"That might not be a bad idea," Washington replied. "Brodie, you've talked of living in Durham for several years now. Would you be willing to manage a factory there?"

"I would like to do that," Brodie replied. Brodie, Washington's son by his first wife, was quite a bit older than his younger brothers, Buck and Benjamin. As is natural in families with substantial differences between the children's ages, the younger two boys tended to spend time together, and Brodie spent more time with older children. As they grew into adulthood, the division in interests remained and Brodie tended to pursue more activities away from Benjamin and Buck. As time passed, the sadness of his childhood, the loss of his closest brother, and the loss of both his biological mother and his stepmother took a toll, and Brodie suffered severe bouts of depression. Eventually he grew more and more distant from his family, traveling to other parts of the United States, where he would reside for long periods of time.

Although Washington chose to keep the manufacturing enterprise at the Duke homestead, he provided enough money to Brodie to open his own factory in Durham. The tobacco would be grown on the Duke farm or purchased from other farmers and then transported to the Durham factory for processing. Despite the expenses of the high revenue tax imposed by the federal government, the Duke tobacco enterprise was able to make a hefty profit. Demand for the tobacco was very high. By 1873, there were three factories manufacturing the Duke tobacco products, in addition to Brodie's factory in Durham, and the annual tobacco production had reached 125,000 pounds.[59] In 1871, a warehouse had been opened near the railroad station, and by 1874 it was finally decided to move the entire family business to Durham to be closer to the railroad station.[60] Brodie was given a wing of the factory for his tobacco business, and Benjamin and Buck were given equal partnership interests in their father's business. Washington had begun devoting most of his time to traveling the countryside, looking for new customers.[61]

---

59   Durden, *The Dukes of Durham, 1865–1929*, 14.

60   Ibid., 15.

61   After Mordecai Duke passed away in 1865, William P. Duke concentrated in other businesses in addition to wagon making. The iron wheels had become popular with other wagon makers, and William spent more time making wheels and less time building complete wagons. As a result, he traveled less often to Durham to buy parts than when his father was still alive. In time he rarely traveled

As Buck and Ben grew in age, their curiosity and interest in the world around them grew exponentially. In the early 1870s, barely in their teens, the boys had become handsome. They were considered among the best-looking men in Hillsboro. Ben had dark hair, and when he reached the age where he was able to grow it, he maintained a well-trimmed beard and mustache. Buck had lighter-colored hair and was clean shaven.[62] In school, the girls talked of courting them, but neither of the boys showed interest in local girls until Ben became interested in Sarah Pearson Angier, whom he married in 1875. Instead, Ben and Buck focused on the family business. For recreation they had become avid hunters. Often they would awaken early in the morning, long before sunrise, and head toward Durham to hunt along the tracks. The area around the tracks was owned by the railroad, which provided an easement to local residents along the side of the tracks for foot travel. This allowed the boys to hunt in a broad area along the tracks without trespassing on private property. One morning in August 1873, they were walking along the tracks south of Durham when they noticed an unusual aroma in the air. It was a smell of something cooking, but part of it was a spice they were not familiar with. As they came to a bridge, they noticed that the aroma was coming from a westerly direction far down the river. They decided to investigate, so they walked off the easement of the tracks, down to the river, and began following a path along the river.

As they proceeded along the path on the north side of the river, in a westerly direction, they noticed that the aroma was getting stronger; then they heard a strange sound of someone shouting in a foreign language. When they came around a bend in the path, they saw a tent camp in the distance. They knew that they were near the Carrington property, but they had not been aware of any

---

to Durham. For that reason, fewer stories were passed on to Sarah Duke than prior to Mordecai's death. Most of the information concerning the family after the 1870s is based on research and interviews of persons other than Sarah Duke.

62   Photos of both Ben and Buck appear later in this book.

transients in the area. They had heard that some Chinese railroad workers had left the railroad and established a small community in the wooded area south of Durham, on an abandoned plantation the owners of which had been killed in the war. They wondered if this could be the Chinese community. They decided to go to the camp to see who was living there. As they stepped off the path, they saw an elderly Asian man approaching them. He was wearing clean, white, baggy attire. His clothing was flowing. The sleeves covered his hands, and the pants completely covered his feet. He wore no shoes.

"Good morning, gentlemen," said the elderly man with a strong accent.

The boys had not heard the accent very often, but they recognized it immediately as Asian.

"Good morning, sir," Ben replied, showing the respect he would show if he were speaking to an elder in his church. "Do you live here?" he asked.

"We live here in this camp," the elderly man replied. "We have permission from the owner, who is an absentee landlord in Richmond."

"Oh," Benjamin said, "we live over in Hillsboro. Sometimes we come over here to hunt."

While they talked, Buck and Ben noticed a group of people who appeared to be engaged in some type of ritual exercise. There was a man standing in front of a group of people in loose-fitting clothing. He was facing the group, which was in a standing position facing him. The leader would shout a word in a foreign language, and those in the group would immediately perform an act, such as a punch, kick, or strike. Each motion was explosive and abrupt. "What are they doing?" asked Buck.

The elderly gentleman smiled and said, "They are practicing the fighting techniques of the Chinese Imperial Guard. The teacher is descended from a teacher of the royal family of China, who trained with the Imperial Guard as a child. He came here to help people from our country get established in this land."

"Why do they want to get established in this land?" Benjamin asked.

"It is the way of our people that everywhere we go, we learn the culture and learn to fit in with the community in which we live. In some parts of the world we have greater opportunity, but in other parts of the world, like America, we are limited by laws, and by people, in what we can do. For example, a man from China cannot obtain admission in many academic institutions in America. It would be difficult for a man or a woman from China to become a lawyer, unless he found a lawyer who would teach him the law. Few lawyers in America will teach the law to a person of our nationality. So we are limited in what we can do in this country."

"Why are they studying the fighting technique of the Imperial Guard?" asked Buck.

"It is an important part of the culture of people from China. In much the way people in America enjoy attending a dance, or going to church, we enjoy practicing the ancient art of combat, but for us it is more of a way of life. It is part of everything we are and will become."

"Do they ever teach these fighting techniques to people who are not from China?" Benjamin asked.

"They have not. Why do you ask?"

"I would be interested in learning these techniques if they would teach us," Ben replied.

"So would I," Buck said.

"Do you like tea?" the elderly man asked.

"Yes," said Buck and Ben almost simultaneously. Ben continued. "Tea is difficult to find in this part of the country. Most of it is imported from Britain or India, and it is expensive."

"Come and join me, and I will give you some tea from China."

"What's your name?" Ben asked.

"I'm called Kin Cheung," the elderly man replied. "You may call me Kin if you like. And what do they call you?"

"I am Buck."

"My name is Ben."

Ben, Buck, and Kin went into the camp, where they were introduced to those living in the camp. They were welcomed and were offered food. They learned that Kin was the father of the man who was teaching martial arts and that Kin had also learned the fighting technique of the Imperial Guard. Kin told them many things about the Chinese culture and about his life in China. Buck and Ben noticed that all of the people deferred to Kin, and it was apparent that they revered him. They stayed and talked with the people from the camp until early afternoon. Finally they announced that they needed to go back home. As they stood up to leave, Kin said, "You said earlier that you would like to learn the fighting technique of the Imperial Guard. If you would like to learn this, I will teach you."

"That would be wonderful," Buck replied.

"Come here every Tuesday and Thursday at sunup, and I will teach you all you would like to learn."

Ben and Buck accepted Kin's offer, and for several years they arrived every morning in the camp to study martial arts. In time, however, Buck found that he was busy with other tasks, and it became too time consuming, so he attended less and less as he grew in age. Ben continued to study martial arts with Kin for many years, until the elderly man passed away. Shortly thereafter, the people in the camp decided to move to New York. They felt that they would have more opportunity in the big city. So early in the fall, with no notice and before the cold weather arrived, they harvested their crops, took down their tents, and left for New York. Buck and Ben never saw any of them again, but they had obtained a treasure of culture and knowledge they would never forget. For the remainder of his life, Ben continued to practice the art that he had learned, even after his leg began to trouble him, requiring that he use a cane. In time, he incorporated his cane into his art as he practiced alone in private. Buck always remembered the art, but he did not practice as diligently as did his brother Ben.[63]

Ben would typically practice martial arts in a cleared private area of the woods near Durham. He would begin his exercise with a quick run on a three-and-a-half-mile circular path through the forest. One summer day when Ben was finishing a particularly rigorous exercise program, he jumped into a flowing brook wearing only his running shorts. After relaxing for about five minutes in the cool water, he decided to go home for a nice evening meal. As he climbed out of the water, he noticed a young man and a young woman standing on the bank. He quickly recognized their attire as a style of dress common among the Eno Indians, who had lived in the region until they were driven out by Andrew Jackson's Indian Removal Act of 1830. Under the provisions of this act, four civilized Native American nations—the Cherokee, the Creek, the Seminole, and the Choctaw—were concentrated by the US government and relocated in Oklahoma in an event today known as the Trail of Tears.[64] Many people of the Eno nation were also captured in the

---

63 The story concerning Ben and Buck studying martial arts is based upon a tradition told by Sarah Duke that they had both studied foreign fighting techniques and that Ben had learned to use his cane as a weapon. Through my research I have been unable to find independent verification except an account based on folklore as provided below, wherein Ben was assaulted when returning from a trip to Virginia. The most common form of foreign martial arts in America at that time was Yangshi Taiji Quan Kung Fu, which had been imported by immigrants from China. If they did study a foreign form of martial arts, it would most likely have been Yangshi Taiji Quan Kung Fu.

64 According to "official records" in the 1830s, 15,000 Native Americans, including women and children, were forced to walk more than one thousand miles from their home states in North Carolina, Georgia, South Carolina, Alabama, Missouri, Kentucky, Illinois, Arkansas, and Tennessee to reservations in Oklahoma. (Some Native American historians claim that 130,000 Cherokee walked the Trail of Tears and that 60,000 died. They further assert that the Bureau of Indian Affairs has falsified or manipulated the records to diminish the extent of this concentration and genocide by claiming that the Trail of Tears occurred only during a certain period of time, or involved only certain

Trail of Tears. The Eno people were a Native American tribe that occupied the area around Hillsboro and Durham before they were moved to Oklahoma.

Ben picked up his towel to dry himself as he quietly studied his visitors with a slight smile. "I have seen you in the woods on occasion. My name is Benjamin."

The young Native American man took a few steps forward. "My name is Jacob Bradley, and this is my sister Lana. We have watched you often. You are very a good fighter, but we have never seen the fighting techniques you use. My great-grandfather knew your great-grandfather. They used to hunt together before the Trail of Tears."

"Who was your great-grandfather?"

"His name was Chief Little Hawk. You probably knew of him by the name Robert Bradley."

"Yes, I remember hearing about him. As I recall he was an expert archer. How did you get here?" asked Ben.

"My family came back to the Durham territory about 1870. My father read law with Samuel Fox Mordecai. We live in Durham. We don't dress like this unless we are away from town. In the city we dress as white people. We come to this forest because we can walk the trails of our fathers without being disturbed. What do you call this strange fighting style you use?"

"Yangshi Taiji Quan Kung Fu," replied Ben as he put on his

---

geographical regions, to achieve a less severe appearance of this event.) During the Trail of Tears, many starved to death, and others died of hypothermia and disease. In addition to the Cherokee, other tribes also suffered high numbers of casualties. The Trail of Tears was one of the worst acts of concentration and genocide in the history of the United States and is a shameful blemish on American history. Moreover, today many Native Americans are unable to prove their ethnicity given that their ancestors "went into hiding" during the concentration and thus were not included in the "official records" of the US government. For a discussion of the Trail of Tears see "Trail of Tears, A Journal of Injustice," National Park Service, accessed September 22, 2013, http://www.nps.gov/trte/index.htm.

shirt and rubbed the towel across his head several times. "It is the fighting style used by the Chinese Imperial Guard. Why is this the first time you have shown yourselves?"

"Because we didn't know you and we didn't know if you would look upon us unfavorably for being here."

"Why should I look upon you unfavorably? This land was your land before President Jackson sent your people into Oklahoma in the Trail of Tears. Why should I begrudge you a place on the land of your fathers? I have cleared a small settlement here for physical training, prayer, and meditation. You are welcome to come here anytime."

Jacob and Lana accepted Ben's offer to use the outdoor recreation facility, and over time they became good friends. They would come often and practice martial arts with him. The three became excellent martial artists and were later joined by a small group of others from Durham who came to learn this novel fighting technique commonly known as Kung Fu. Jacob was also an extraordinary pistoleer, having been instructed in the use a Colt .45 by a railroad security officer; and in exchange for the fighting techniques taught by Ben, he taught Ben the art of quick-draw shooting. Ben became so accomplished with the pistol that he could draw his gun after a silver dollar had been tossed into the air, and shoot the dollar before it hit the ground. Ben's friendship with Jacob and Lana lasted for many years, until Jacob and Lana moved to Oklahoma to be with their family on the reservation, where their father had established a practice of law.[65]

In January 1878, Buck had taken up temporary residence in Poughkeepsie, New York, where he was attending a semester of classes at Eastman Business College. When spring arrived, Ben

---

65   The story of Ben's encounter with Jacob and Lana is fictional and is based upon a tradition that Ben had been taught the art of quick-draw shooting and further that he befriended Native American people living in the community.

decided to spend a week in Poughkeepsie to visit his brother. After an enjoyable week of seeing the sights of New York and visiting classes with Buck, Ben headed back to Durham. He had been invited to stop in Richmond to discuss a possible business venture with three men who had been imprisoned Confederate soldiers during the war with Benjamin's father in Libby Prison. After leaving Libby Prison, they had all three stayed in Richmond. One of them, Paul Drake, had become a shopkeeper; another, Michael Johnson, a lawyer; and the third, Gary Mitchell, operated a shipping company. Washington had warned Benjamin that he did not know them well and could not recommend them as business partners, though their credentials seemed to present favorably. Benjamin and the three men were discussing the possibility of a joint venture involving the shipping of tobacco products, by railway, from Durham to Chicago. The meeting took place at Johnson's law office.

Mitchell said, "I would be delighted to provide transportation to Chicago and other cities where I have warehouses."

"What would you be seeking in return?" asked Ben.

Johnson replied, "What we are offering is an opportunity to take your tobacco company national. We have the technical knowledge to handle all aspects of the business. Mitchell can get your products to Chicago and soon all the way to the West Coast. Drake has the knowledge of retail sales, and I have the legal knowledge you need."

"So far you have been a small, struggling tobacco company with great potential. You and your family started the tobacco company as a small family business, but now you need someone to take you to the next level. That is where we come in," Mitchell said.

Feeling slightly insulted at the manner in which the men had characterized Pro Bono Publico as a small family operation, Ben repeated, "What is it you want in return for the services you are offering?"

Johnson stood up and walked around his desk to offer Ben a glass of brandy. "What we are proposing is that Mitchell, Drake, and

I will receive a fifty-one percent interest in the company and you and your family will retain a forty-nine percent interest. We will handle all of the shipping and retail aspects of the business, and you and your family will continue to manage the production end of things."

Upon hearing the proposal, Ben knew immediately that his father would have no interest in entering into business with these men. He would find them rude and self-absorbed. Ben's only concern was to exit the meeting, have a nice dinner and go to bed so he could rise early in the morning for the long journey back to Durham. Not wishing to offend the men he said, "I appreciate the offer, but of course, I will have to discuss it with my father. So I have a clear picture, how much capital would you be putting up for your investment in the company? And also, why would you be given controlling interest?"

"How much capital?" asked Drake as he jumped up from his chair. "You aren't seeing the big picture. What we are offering you is a gold mine. You will be rich beyond your wildest dreams."

Mitchell nodded at the chair as an instruction to Drake to sit down. "What Drake is saying is that we will help you build an empire. Our combined skill and knowledge will allow us to take Pro Bono Publico to new heights—heights you and your father never dreamed possible. It will be an empire the likes of which has never been seen in America. We will expand the business into other products, like alcohol and opium products. There is no end to what we can do together."

Benjamin stood up from his chair. "Gentlemen, I sincerely appreciate what you are offering. And I will discuss it with my father and brothers and sister. But I don't want to mislead you in any way. I can tell you that my father will not be willing to enter into such a venture. He is a firm believer that opium should be used only for medical purposes and should be closely regulated by the government. It is simply too addictive. And while we might be interested in expanding into other businesses someday, we would do that separately from the tobacco venture."

Johnson walked to the door, blocking Ben's exit from his office. "We aren't getting through to you, Ben. Other tobacco companies would give anything for an opportunity like this. You can't afford not to do this. If you pass this up, we will join up with Bull Durham or one of the other companies and will eventually squeeze you out of business."

Although Ben knew the threat lacked merit, hearing the words caused him to feel momentary nervousness, which quickly passed. "Again, gentlemen, thank you for your hospitality and your offer. As I said, I will discuss it with my partners, and if there is an interest, we will contact you. But again, I do not want you to have false hopes. I am sure that we will not be interested in an offer of the nature you have made. That does not mean that there is no possible way we can combine our efforts, but it would not be by surrendering control of the tobacco company to you. I do have to leave now. I need to turn in. I have a long ride ahead of me tomorrow."

"Okay, Ben," said Johnson, extending his hand to Ben. "Thanks for stopping by."

Ben shook hands with Johnson. Drake and Mitchell did not bother to get up or even say good-bye. They glared at Benjamin as he left. As he walked through the door, he heard Drake mumble beneath his breath, "What a pompous little cocker. I have a mind to kick his rear all the way back to Durham."

After Ben left Johnson's office, he sensed that he was being followed by someone in a distance, on horseback. He went back to the hotel where he had dinner, and he then retired for the evening. The following morning, he awoke for the long ride back to Durham. He dreaded the 160-mile ride from Richmond to Durham and wished he had not stopped in Richmond for the meetings. Something about the meeting put him on edge, and his nerves did not calm with sleep. He continued to experience the feeling that someone was following him, so he kept his cane close at hand. After riding for half a day, he came to a fallen tree blocking the road with four men standing next to it. He did not need to see that the tree had been cut clean across to realize that something was wrong. The rocky terrain would not allow him to pass around the tree. He dismounted, lifted his cane from the saddlebag, and exaggerated his limp as he approached the men standing by the trunk.

The four assailants wasted no time pulling out wooden clubs and forming a circle around Ben. Ben did not waste time either and quickly put to use the martial arts training he had learned from Kin. In less time than it would take to explain, all four assailants were lying flat on the ground. After confirming his suspicion that they had been sent by Johnson, the attorney he had met with the night before, he sent the four men back to Richmond, but only after first requiring that they remove their pants. Naked from their waists down, the men climbed on their horses. Before they left, Ben pulled back his trench coat to reveal a Colt .45 revolver that he had not even used in disabling them.

When Benjamin arrived in Durham, he sent a telegram to the US marshal for the Territory of Virginia, who intercepted the four men at the Virginia border. He took them into custody, obtained a sworn declaration from each of them as to the identity of the person who had hired them to assault Benjamin, and then, upon Benjamin's request, released them conditionally on a promise that they would never assault anyone in the future.

Two days later, Ben, Buck, and Washington, accompanied by the US marshal, stormed into Johnson's office. The attorney jumped to his feet in disbelief and fell backward against the wall of his office. Ben threw the four pairs of pants he had taken from the assailants onto the attorney's desk and said, "The next time you send someone to carry out your dirty work, I suggest you send men and not boys. Our business is over, and now you will face whatever consequences your actions have caused." The US marshal stepped forward and said, "You are under arrest for conspiracy and the attempted murder of Benjamin Newton Duke." He put the attorney in handcuffs and escorted him from his office. Washington and his sons thanked the marshal for his assistance, walked out of the building, mounted their horses, and returned to Durham.[66]

In the summer of 1878, Washington hired a young African American man named Lawrence to work in the factory in Durham, processing tobacco. The young man had a unique skill. His uncle had developed the charcoal processing method that had made the Pro Bono Publico tobacco products so famous. Lawrence was very proud of his uncle and took great pride in his own work. He also possessed unique communication skills that made him very effective in working with the employees. Despite the pervasive racism in post–Civil War America, this young man was very well liked by the other employees, both black and white. Often Washington would walk the factory in the early morning, where he would find Lawrence working before anyone else had arrived. Lawrence thoroughly enjoyed his work and would often arrive long before the other employees to make sure the equipment was operating properly; then he would enjoy a cup of coffee in the warehouse while he awaited the arrival of the other employees. It was not long before Washington and Lawrence began enjoying a cup of coffee together several mornings per week.

During their frequent morning conversations, Lawrence would sometimes tell Washington about a dream he had of owning his own tobacco processing factory. He would discuss how the equipment would be arranged and how the employees would be treated fairly, in the same fashion that Washington was fair to his employees.

---

66 The account of Ben's trip to New York and his encounter with the businessmen from Virginia is based upon folklore. The details are scant, and the names of the businessmen are unknown. For that reason, they have been assigned fictional names. The event reportedly occurred at a time when the Dukes had just begun documenting events related to their business, which may account for the lack of written record, if it is a true event. Without the actual names of the four men involved it would be nearly impossible to confirm through public records whether this event occurred, and for that reason no attempt has been made to search arrest records in Richmond.

Washington could have seen this as a threat of competition and fired the young man, rendering him unemployable in the tobacco industry. Instead, Washington was so impressed with the young man's ideas that he allowed him to manage a large production line at the tobacco plant. One morning in early summer, Washington had arrived at the warehouse before Lawrence. He had brewed a pot of coffee and was reading a newspaper.

"Top of the morning to you, sir," said Lawrence as he walked into the warehouse and tossed his saddle on a bench at his work station.

"Good morning, Larry," Washington said with a smile as he gave the young man a cup of warm coffee. After a brief pause, Washington said, "I was wondering, are you still thinking you would like to own your own tobacco production company?"

Lawrence took a sip of his hot coffee. "That is what I would like more than anything, but that is just a fantasy. A colored man can't own a business. We both know that."

"Why not?" asked Washington.

"Because white folks won't allow it. They'd burn me out."

Washington stood up. "Larry, how would you like to go on a short journey with me this morning?"

"Sure, Mr. Duke. Where are we going?"

"There is something on the south side of Durham I would like to show you."

Washington and Lawrence climbed into a delivery wagon that was hitched to two horses. Washington took the reins and shook them slightly as he said, "Heah, cht cht." The horses began a slow trot down the dirt street behind the warehouse. They stayed on this road until they were out of the main part of town. After riding for about twenty minutes, Washington pulled the wagon to the side of the road next to a large new brick building. "Let's go inside," he said to Lawrence.

"What's this?" asked Lawrence as he stepped down from the wagon.

"Lawrence, this is your new tobacco processing plant if you would like it."

"How can it be mine, Mr. Duke? I couldn't afford something like this."

Washington reached under the seat and pulled out a key ring loaded with large skeleton keys. He gave it to Lawrence. "It's yours if you would still like to have your own processing plant. I will purchase at wholesale all of the tobacco you can process. When you get on your feet, you can pay back the loan to buy the plant by selling to me at some percentage lower than wholesale but above cost. If you do well, we might be able to waive interest and even some of the principal on the loan. Are you interested?"

"Absolutely," Lawrence replied. "Why would you do this for me?"

"Because you are a good man who deserves a break, and because you can provide a good product to the Duke tobacco venture."

"Thank you, Mr. Duke, for believing in me. I won't let you down," Lawrence said as they opened the door to the production plant and stepped inside. Lawrence looked around the large curing room and down the hall to his left at the loading dock.

"It's my pleasure," Washington replied. "I asked Mary[67] to deposit one thousand dollars in a bank account for you as soon as you tell her what the company will be called. Our attorney can take care of filing all the business formation documents. We have ordered enough supplies and raw materials to keep you going for six months. By then you should be showing a profit. I know you will do fine, but I remain at your service if you need to call on me. You have been doing this for many years, but now you will be the owner. No one has to know the source of the money to buy the plant unless you want them to."

---

67 Mary Elizabeth Duke Lyon was the only daughter of Washington Duke and Artelia Roney Duke. Mary worked in the office for the tobacco company until her untimely death in 1893.

As they rode back to the Duke warehouse, Lawrence said, "This will no doubt cause an outcry when the townsmen learn that a colored man owns a tobacco processing plant. I hope it doesn't get dangerous."

"No one really has to know," Washington replied. "If you form a corporation, no one will know who actually owns it unless someone takes the trouble to investigate. Tobacco people know that you have been managing a production line at my factory, so they will just assume you are doing the same thing here."

Lawrence was able to build a very successful tobacco processing plant. Many years later it was to become one of the many companies that would form the American Tobacco Trust.[68]

The Duke tobacco business continued to prosper, and by the late 1870s, Washington Duke had become one of the wealthiest men in Orange County. He was very active in the Republican Party, and would later run unsuccessfully for political office on several occasions,[69] but his primary focus was his tobacco enterprise. In 1878, Washington visited with George W. Watts in Baltimore to invite him to join the Duke tobacco enterprise. Watts was one of the few persons Washington ever considered as a possible partner, with the exceptions of his sons. Watts had been exploring the idea of prerolled cigarettes and was convinced that eventually they would dominate the market. Washington, Buck, Ben, and Mary had been producing prerolled cigarettes and felt that Watts would be a good

---

68   The story of Washington assisting Lawrence in establishing his own tobacco company is a fictional dramatization to demonstrate Washington's benevolence toward African Americans who were trying to become established in the post–Civil War years. It is well documented that Washington assisted numerous African Americans build their businesses, such as the Coleman Manufacturing Company in Concord, North Carolina. See Durden, *The Dukes of Durham, 1865–1929*, 145. Another was North Carolina Mutual, an insurance company owned by African Americans. See Durden, *The Dukes of Durham, 1865–1929*, 105.
69   "Coalition in North Carolina, Liberals and Republicans Uniting on a State Ticket," *New York Times*, May 3, 1884.

match as a partner. After negotiating the terms, it was agreed that Watts would join the venture with an investment of $14,000, for which he would receive a one-fifth interest in the company. The name of the tobacco company was changed from Pro Bono Publico to W. Duke, Sons & Company.[70] Watts's investment allowed the company to expand its base of operations and compete more efficiently with other tobacco companies, such as Bull Durham.

It was a fall afternoon in Poughkeepsie, New York. Buck Duke sat in the third row of his business law class in Eastman Business College. Professor Isaac Stevens, a local attorney and adjunct professor of business law, lifted the large hornbook from his desk, opened it to a marked page, and placed it on the lectern. "What was the basis for the court's opinion in *Hadley v. Baxendale*[71] that W. Joyce & Co. was liable only for foreseeable damages incurred by the failure to provide the crankshaft on a timely basis, Mr. Duke?"

Buck replied, "The court found that liability should extend only to damages that the breaching party is aware will occur. Specifically, in this case, the Court of Exchequer Chamber found that since Hadley had not advised Joyce that he would suffer losses during the time the crankshaft was not in operation, Joyce could not be held liable for those damages. The important issue is foreseeability. Here, without Hadley informing Joyce of this fact, Joyce could not be held to have known."

"That is correct," the professor replied. "Suppose a shipper ordered twenty thousand pounds of tobacco from your company, Mr. Duke, but did not tell you that he needed it immediately because he had already secured contracts for the sale. And suppose you promised a time of delivery but you did not know that damages would be incurred if delivery was not timely made. Under the

---

70 Durden, *The Dukes of Durham, 1865–1929*, 18.

71 *Hadley v. Baxendale*, [1854] EWHC J70.

Hadley holding, would you be liable for those damages if you failed to timely deliver?"

"Under Hadley, probably not."

"Do you agree with that holding, Mr. Duke?"

"No, I do not," Buck replied. "If I promise to deliver by a certain date, then I should be bound by my promise and should be liable for all reasonably foreseeable damages sustained by my failure to deliver the tobacco on time. If there is a possibility I cannot deliver it when I promise, then I should not agree to do it. That is the basic concept of right versus wrong."

"So you are saying that reasonable foreseeability should be the determining factor in calculating damages in a case where the defendant doesn't perform timely?"

"Yes, but defined a little more precisely. The court in Hadley was focusing only upon the foreseeability of an event based upon actual knowledge as opposed to constructive knowledge. In other words, actual knowledge of the potential loss is required to find liability for damages under the Hadley holding. But there is another type of foreseeability, which is foreseeability based upon constructive knowledge; where knowledge is imputed to me regardless of actual knowledge, but rather upon the knowledge of circumstances as I know them, or would reasonably believe them to be."

"So you are saying that the factor giving rise to liability in such a case should be damages that are reasonably foreseeable to a person entering into such a contract rather than damages he actually knows will occur?"

"That would be a fair way to say it, though in time I think we will define it even more precisely," Buck replied. "But the trigger of damages should be the reasonable foreseeability of those damages, not just actual knowledge of the potential damages."

After class Buck and Professor Stevens walked across campus to a small café. "So the tobacco business seems to be doing very well, Buck. Is that true?"

"We are profiting. The business is growing and expanding every day."

"Have you ever considered merging with any of the other tobacco companies?" asked Professor Stevens as they sat at a table near the window of the café. "Think of what you could do by the benefit of scale economies. By purchasing equipment and supplies in bulk, and by shipping product in greater quantities, you could substantially reduce your unit costs, thus allowing an increased profit margin, or alternatively you could pass the savings on to the consumer."

"That is true," Buck replied. "I have thought about talking to some of the other producers."

"I know many of them," Professor Stevens said. "Would you like for me to introduce you to some of them?"

"That might be a good idea," Buck replied. "I would appreciate that."

Later that evening, Buck sat at the dinner table with Professor Stevens; his young wife, Mary; and Bill Kimball of William S. Kimball and Co. "Thank you for inviting us to your home this evening, Isaac," Buck said to Professor Stevens. "And thank you for introducing me to Mr. Kimball."

"Indeed," Bill Kimball said. "I see many possibilities here. There are regions where you do not ship and do not have access to markets, and there are many regions where I do not ship or have access to the markets. However, in some of those regions where one of us is not in the market, the other might be. By joining forces we could open the markets for all of our products where we might otherwise not be able to reach."

"That is true," Buck replied. "Also, by joining forces we can substantially reduce our production and advertising costs. I am very open to the possibilities."

Buck and Mr. Kimball developed a friendship that was to last many years. Like Buck, Bill Kimball engaged in activities if he saw a legitimate social benefit in the activity. In the case of tobacco production, both Kimball and Buck believed they were producing a valuable medical product, because in those days tobacco was considered a respiratory enhancer.

When Watts became a partner in W. Duke, Sons & Company, Washington was nearly sixty years of age. He had lived a successful life and had established a business that, if managed properly, would assure that his sons and daughter would never suffer from lack of means. Perhaps at the age of sixty he decided it was time to slow his pace and enjoy life more. Although he never remarried after the death of Artelia, his friends and his philanthropic activities seemed to occupy more and more of his time. For that reason, in 1880, he sold his ownership interest in W. Duke, Sons & Company to a young man named Richard Wright for $23,000,[72] though he did not become completely inactive in the business. He remained available to his sons as an adviser, and they relied on his advice frequently. After Washington sold his interest, the partners in W. Duke, Sons & Company consisted of Buck, Ben, Brodie, George Watts, and Richard Wright.

In 1881, W. Duke, Sons & Company began manufacturing prerolled cigarettes along with smoking tobacco that had to be rolled by the consumer. This provided a major competitive edge for W. Duke, Sons & Company. However, it was largely another development in the tobacco industry that propelled W. Duke, Sons & Company to the forefront when a competitor offered $75,000 to anyone who could produce a cigarette rolling machine. An eighteen-year-old boy named James Bonsack developed the "Bonsack machine" in 1880, but after the purchase, the competitor discarded the machine as unusable. Washington decided to take a chance on the Bonsack machine and sent for a mechanic from the Bonsack Machine Company to help get the machine to operate properly. Eventually they were able to get the machine, which was

---

72   Durden, *The Dukes of Durham, 1865–1929*, 26–55.

the equivalent of forty-eight hand rollers, to work properly and substantially reduce the cost of production.[73]

After selling his interest in W. Duke, Sons & Company, Washington found more time to devote to charitable work. In 1885, he assisted in establishing the Memorial Methodist Church in downtown Durham with a goal of creating an environment where everyone would feel welcome regardless of financial status. The church, today called Duke Memorial Methodist Church, is located on W. Chapel Hill between Gregson and Duke Street. It is known throughout Durham for its outreach services and as a warm, friendly church where all are welcome. Washington also began to take a more active role in the development of several academic institutions, one of which, Trinity College, would later become known as Duke University, and he began using his time to assist African Americans in establishing their own businesses, as noted above.

As Washington became less active in the family business, his sons took a more active role in management and within a short time had assumed control of the enterprise with Washington available to provide advice. Most likely because Buck was a bachelor willing to travel long distances for long period of times, he eventually assumed primary control of W. Duke, Sons & Company. George Watts did not ever intend to become involved in day-to-day management operations, and Ben had his family to which he devoted a substantial amount of time. Richard Wright was a newcomer to the business and within a short period of time became disgruntled and threatened litigation against his partners. The precise reason for Wright's discontent is unclear, though it may have been that Buck called for each partner to make a sizeable investment for expansion.

---

73   Durden, *The Dukes of Durham, 1865–1929*, 26–55; Durden obtained much of his information about the Bonsack rolling machine from letters between the Bonsack Machine Company and W. Duke and Sons—in Box A, property of J. B. Duke—which are today maintained in the Rubenstein Rare Book and Manuscript Library at Duke University.

It has also been suggested that he resented Buck's management leadership, given that Buck was four years his junior.[74] By default, the primary manager of the tobacco enterprise became Buck, and by 1884 he was clearly at the helm. Five years after selling his interest in W. Duke, Sons & Company, Washington repurchased a 20 percent interest in the company.

In 1884, W. Duke, Sons & Company decided to open a factory in New York. The northern market had become vast, and shipping from Durham was inefficient and costly. In addition, money was tight in Durham, which made it difficult to obtain loans. It seemed reasonable that a presence in New York would create more opportunities and increase efficiency of operations. In order to manage the New York facility, Buck moved to New York, which became his primary place of residence.[75] Ben also established residency in New York but continued to maintain his home in Durham, thus having a dual residency.

By 1888, five tobacco companies controlled 90 percent of the tobacco industry. This was primarily the result of technological innovations combined with creative marketing. One of the most important technological innovations was the charcoal processing method that Washington had begun using before the Civil War. Some tobacco companies refused to switch from the traditional curing process, which produced a much harsher product, resulting in a continuously decreasing demand for their product. But the most significant technological change proved to be the Bonsack rolling machine, which allowed the production of far more cigarettes per hour than could be rolled manually. W. Duke, Sons & Company adopted the use of the Bonsack machine as the primary method of rolling the cigarettes in 1884. The Bonsack machine was continuously modified and altered to achieve even greater efficiency, allowing the companies that could afford the technology

---

74   Durden, *The Dukes of Durham, 1865–1929*, 28–29.
75   Ibid., 24–25

to produce far more cigarettes at a much lower price. The greater output allowed these state-of-the-art tobacco companies to make their profit off volume of sales rather than a high profit margin for prerolled cigarettes.

A second factor that allowed the leading tobacco companies to maintain a competitive edge was innovative marketing techniques. For example, small gifts, such as photographs of women, were placed in each pack of cigarettes as an incentive for men to purchase them. In time, some men were collecting the photographs and trading them in the manner that became popular with baseball cards in the twentieth century. The practice of including the photographs in the cigarettes was troubling to Washington and Ben, who felt it was a form of exploitation of the women photographed. Although they discouraged Buck from this practice, they could not dissuade him, and this became a major marketing tool for W. Duke, Sons & Company.

On a summer day in 1889, James Buchanan Duke leaned against the mahogany credenza of a New York hotel room as he smoked a cigar and repeatedly opened and closed his pocket watch as if time would somehow freeze by this gesture. Around a table in the room were representatives of William S. Kimball & Co. of Rochester, the F.S. Kinney Company of New York, the Allen & Ginter Company of Richmond, and the Goodwin Company of New York.[76] These four companies, along with W. Duke, Sons & Company, controlled 90 percent of the tobacco industry. Buck put his cigar in the ashtray, rubbing it firmly in the sand.

"Competition is tougher today than ever before in the tobacco industry. Those of us in this room are destroying the smaller companies. They cannot begin to compete with our prices. Technological

---

76 The first meeting occurred at the Fifth Avenue Hotel in New York City on April 15, 1889. Letter from J. B. Duke to D. B. Strouse, April 20, 1889, J. B. Duke Letterbook no. 1, David M. Rubenstein Rare Book and Manuscript Library, Duke University; Durden, *The Dukes of Durham, 1865–1929*, 48.

innovation and aggressive marketing are causing supply to exceed demand, thus driving prices so low that smaller companies cannot earn enough profit to stay in business. Even so, if we were not in competition with them and with each other, we could actually increase everyone's profit by increasing sales volume."

William Kimball leaned back in his chair. "I think I know what you are saying, Buck. We need to have a tobacco war and totally eliminate the smaller businesses."

"That would be the most logical move," said John Allen. "Now that the smaller guys are at our mercy, let's go ahead and drop prices so low we put them completely out of business."

Lewis Ginter smiled at Buck. "Somehow, I don't really believe that is what Buck has in mind. Am I right, Buck?"

Buck laughed. "You are right, Lou. A long time ago, when my ole Pappy was just a pup, his older brother Billy told him always to be kind to those less fortunate. My dad never forgot that. When I had the same conversation with him a few days ago, he said we should reach out to them by buying them but keeping them in their positions to run their own franchises. We would give them the opportunity to control their own businesses as our managers, we would help them grow their businesses, and we would increase rather than decrease their profits by efficiency. We could even buy them out with shares in the American Tobacco Company so that instead of being owners of the little tobacco companies, they would be owners with us, of the American Tobacco Company."

"That sounds like a great idea, but would it work?" asked Ginter.

"Not only would it work," replied Buck, "but it would also bring a benefit to society. Tobacco has always been a rich man's pleasure. We can make it available to the poor man as well. We would actually be providing a health service. Most doctors believe that tobacco smoke has therapeutic benefits to the smoker.

"Think of it this way," Buck said as he again flipped open his pocket watch to check the time. "There are about two hundred fifty tobacco companies that are not part of our trust, yet we control ninety percent of the tobacco market in the United States. We could do one of two things. We could run them out of business, or bring them into our business and let them enjoy the fruits of our shared labor."

"But how would that reduce costs and increase profits?" asked Allen.

"Well, for one thing, if we join forces and buy the remaining companies, we could buy products and advertise in greater bulk. That means we could negotiate a much better price. Take advertising expenses, for example. Suppose we ran the same ad all over the United States and had to change only a couple of words in each ad, like the name of the entity offering the product, or make no changes at all. We could use the same ad everywhere. A single publisher could provide all the ads throughout the United States, and we would run many more of them, more often, and save thousands of dollars every year in advertising costs."

"That's an amazing idea," Kimball said.

Buck continued. "Because we would be purchasing at such volume, we could obtain much better interest rates on loans needed to cover costs. Everything we do we could do cheaper because the volume of purchases would be much greater. We could all benefit from these savings. This is how the small tobacco companies would wind up spending less than they are now and would actually make more money."

Kimball looked at Buck with a puzzled expression. "But is that legal?"

"Yes, it is," Buck replied. "Though it is true that Senator Sherman, a Republican from Ohio, has proposed a bill called the Sherman Antitrust Act, most attorneys I talk to say it won't pass. It is counterintuitive and actually increases business expenses and thereby raises prices rather than decreasing them. The idea of the bill is to keep businesses small. Realistically, it makes no sense."

"Why would someone propose a bill that advocates inefficiency?" asked Allen.

"The reason for the bill is to keep large amounts of wealth from concentrating into the hands of a few. I believe the fear is that if people become too wealthy they will become too powerful and ultimately become a threat to the US government. In part I think it is fear of another Civil War if too much wealth accumulates in the hands of a few."

"That sounds like pure nonsense to me," replied Allen, "besides, I think such a law would be unconstitutional. I do not believe the framers of the Constitution ever intended something like that."

"Nor do I," Buck replied. "Regardless, I don't think we should allow a possible future law that may never come into existence to prevent us from doing what we know is best for both the business owner and the consumer."

"But what if some of the tobacco companies do not want to join us? What do we do to them?" asked Kimball.

"We don't have to do anything to them; they will be free to compete if they so choose," Buck replied.

After a lengthy discussion, all of the members present agreed to form the American Tobacco Company and to purchase, with shares in the American Tobacco Company, all of the independent tobacco companies that wanted to join the trust. Their idea was that this would reduce overall advertising and marketing costs while at the same time improving organization and increasing productivity. Less than one year later, James Buchanan Duke was on the road, making offers to every tobacco company known to exist. His goal was that every tobacco company would receive an offer. Anything less would be "unfair to the little guy."

In the summer of 1889, Buck rode a horse toward the barn of a tobacco farm in Tennessee. The farm, owned by George Batemen, was about five miles from a little town called Ashland City, in Cheatham County. George had been struggling to keep his tobacco business in operation but was losing customers to the larger tobacco companies that offered prerolled cigarettes at a much lower price. Buck rode up to a hitching post in front of the barn. George was standing just inside the door.

"Can I help you?" asked George, who did not know Buck's identity.

Buck dismounted, tied his horse to the post, and walked over to George, extending his hand. "Yes, my name is James. If you don't mind, I would like to borrow a little bit of your time to talk about a proposition."

"Sure, you can talk," said George as he shook hands with Buck.

Washington said, "I can see that your primary crop is tobacco, and I heard about your tobacco business at the general store in Ashland. How has it been working out for you?"

"I never should have tried to grow tobacco. That is for the big tobacco producers. A little guy like me can't compete with the big boys," George replied as they strolled out of his barn and into the sunlight.

"Have you ever considered joining the big tobacco producers?" Buck asked.

"How could I do that?" George mumbled. "That'd be like takin' down a twelve-point buck with a rock and sling."

"Have you ever talked to any of the big companies to see if they need your services or possibly want you as a partner?" Buck asked as he pulled a cigar from the pocket of his vest pocket and gave it to George.

"Ha, you must be joking. That'd be a waste of time."

"Why do you say that? Maybe you underestimate your worth."

"What could I ever bring to them? What would they want with me?" George looked sadly at the ground. "I can barely feed my own family."

"What would you do if one of the big tobacco companies came to you and asked you to become a partner?" Buck lit George's cigar and then took one out of his pocket for himself. George looked at Buck with a blank expression.

"Let me be direct. I am a representative of the American Tobacco Company, and I would like to offer you one thousand dollars and shares of stock in the American Tobacco Company if you join the American Tobacco Company Trust," Buck said as they started walking slowly toward his horse.

"One thousand dollars!" George thought of his three children—two girls ages three and four and a boy age one. This could mean they would have a solid future.

"Plus, we will guarantee a twenty percent increase over your best annual gross income over the last ten years derived from selling tobacco. The increase will go into effect immediately. All you have to do is continue operating your business as you have, with a little counseling from our production and management teams, and agree to maintain the price for your products that is set by the tobacco trust. It is important to keep the fixed price. If one of the companies operates at a cheaper price, or a greater price, it will disrupt the system. If the offer is not of interest to you, then we will shake hands and go our separate ways as friends."

Buck smiled as he walked back to his horse and opened his saddlebag. "One of my attorneys will be by in four days to see if you are interested in the offer." Buck took a loaf of bread and a block of cheese out of his saddlebag, both wrapped in heavy brown paper, and gave them to George as he said, "Here is a gift from the American Tobacco Company. Thanks for giving your valuable time to talk to me." Embossed on the paper wrapping the block of cheese and loaf of bread was an American Tobacco Company trademark and emblem above the phrase, "Thank you, George Bateman and Family. Please accept this gift from your new friends at The American Tobacco Company. JBD."

"I don't need to think about it," George replied. "If you're telling the truth, I'll sign up immediately. What's your name?"

"Rest assured, I am telling the truth," Buck replied as he climbed on his horse and took a business card out of his vest pocket and gave it to George. "Thanks for taking the time to talk to me. One of my attorneys will be by on Thursday with the documents to sign." Buck waved as he started to ride away.

George could not read, so he gave the business card to his wife, Eliza, who walked up as Buck was leaving. "What does this say?" he asked his wife. "What is it?"

"It is a hard piece of paper with writing on it," she replied.

"What does it say?" George repeated.

Eliza placed her right hand on her forehead to block the sun and took the card with her left hand. "Good heavens, George, that man is James Buchanan Duke? What did he want?"

"He asked if I would become his business partner."

"He asked you to become his partner? Why on earth does he want you?" Eliza stared at George in disbelief.

"I don't know, but I intend to find out." George began running down the road toward Buck. "You got a deal, Mr. Duke," he shouted. "I will join you."

Buck pulled his horse to a tight stop and turned to his rear as he shouted back with a smile and waved his cigar. "Welcome to the family, George."

"Thanks so much, Mr. Duke," George shouted as Buck rode away. "I'll be ready."[77]

Buck and other employees of the American Tobacco Company repeated this conversation many times over the next several years. By the 1890s, Buck controlled the American Tobacco Company, the largest trust in the world, and had purchased over 250 competitor tobacco companies. The American Tobacco Company was listed on the New York Stock Exchange and was one of the original twelve members of the Dow Jones Industrial Average. The success of the tobacco venture exceeded everyone's imagination, but as we will see in the next chapter, the growth was not without challenges. Although the tobacco enterprise thrived, its rapid expansion also caught the attention of President McKinley and subsequently President Roosevelt and eventually became the target of the US Department of Justice in one of most widely celebrated antitrust cases in American history.

---

[77] The account of George Bateman is a fictional dramatization of the manner in which the American Tobacco Company acquired smaller companies.

7

The Duke Family Invests in New Industries and the US Government Takes Aim at Duke Tobacco

Although the Duke family is known primarily for their investments in the tobacco industry, in reality their investments reached deeply into other industries as well. The cotton industry was developing rapidly in the latter part of the nineteenth century, often generating a profit margin as high as 25 percent.[78] The Dukes saw an opportunity not only for investing but also for providing a broad public benefit. Indeed, local demand for textiles in Durham, combined with employment opportunities, fostered a concerted campaign among city leaders and newspaper publishers to encourage industrialists to develop textile mills in Durham. For Ben, textile manufacturing seemed a natural and logical venture for the family interests.[79]

In 1892, Ben Duke and William Erwin met with Durham attorney W. W. Fuller, in his office, to discuss the establishment of

---

78   "Tobacco Plant," Durham, January 25, 1882; Durden, *The Dukes of Durham, 1865–1929*, 123.

79   For a detailed discussion of Duke family business development and expansion, see Durden, *The Dukes of Durham, 1865–1929* (Durham: Duke University Press, 1975).

a textile mill.[80] Erwin was a thirty-six-year-old businessman from Burke County, North Carolina, in whom Ben observed great promise.[81] Erwin possessed experience in the textile industry, given that he was the nephew of Edwin Holt, a prominent owner of a textile firm. Ben first hired Erwin to manage his new textile business in Durham. While watching Erwin manage the enterprise, Ben had opportunity to observe his skills and, even more importantly for Ben, to observe his moral character. He liked what he saw. They developed a friendship and decided to form a joint venture in textiles.[82]

Benjamin explained to Fuller, "I have been planning to expand into textiles for several years now, and as you know, George Watts and I have already invested to a small extent. Now I think it's time to get serious about textiles. That's where everything seems to be moving."

"I think that's a great idea," Fuller replied. "With your knowledge and experience in operating businesses, how could you go wrong?"

"My thought is that I would invest with William here as my partner. We have decided that he will be the secretary-treasurer and the general manager, whereas I will be the president of the company. He has forty thousand dollars he would like to invest, and I will invest the balance of what we need to get started. He will handle the day-to-day operations."

"Have you decided on a name?" asked Fuller.

"Actually, we have not," Erwin replied. "We thought about something along the lines of Durham Textiles, but there is already the Durham Cotton Manufacturing Company, and we think people would get confused."

"William suggested Duke Textiles, but I was thinking it would

80   William K. Boyd, *The Story of Durham* (Durham: Duke University Press, 1925), 122.
81   Durden, *Dukes of Durham, 1865–1929*, 128.
82   Ibid., 128–129.

be good to have a name that honors the Erwin family," Benjamin replied.

"Have you thought about calling it the Erwin Cotton Mill Company?" asked Fuller.

"I think that's a great idea," Ben replied. "That way William would receive recognition for his accomplishments."

"Who are your primary marketing target groups?" asked Fuller.

Ben glanced at Erwin and then replied, "We have given quite a bit of thought about the manner in which we could best serve the community by providing needed products and jobs, and also earn a profit from our venture. Most likely our biggest purchasers will be end-product companies, such as clothing and furniture manufacturers, and we will produce some end-line products ourselves. We would like to help the consumer have a better quality of clothing at a better price. With the production techniques William has learned from his uncle's firm, I believe we could very successfully produce low-priced materials while earning a fair profit. Most importantly, we want to operate our business as good, honest, Christian men with an idea of serving the public to the benefit of everyone. I often think of the children I have seen over the years, many of whom have only one suit of clothing that is so worn out they are ashamed to go off their farm. That just isn't right. The more we can do to help families benefit, the better off we are as a community."

"I have seen that too," said Fuller. "It's heartbreaking. A couple of months back I was visiting a cousin in Charlotte. On the way, I was overcome with thirst. I truly thought that if I didn't get a drink of water, I would choke to death. I reached under the seat of my buggy and discovered I had forgotten my canteen. Up ahead I saw a farm on the side of the road that wasn't much more than a shack. When I pulled the buggy into the yard to ask for water, I saw a group of little children dressed in rags. Their clothes were clean, but they were torn rags. When they saw me they ran behind the house to hide. Finally the mom came out and I asked her for water. She gave it to me from the well and apologized for her unfriendly children. She explained that they were ashamed to be seen because they didn't have respectable clothes to wear. I felt so sorry for them that when I got back to Durham I bought some clothes for the children and had them delivered."

Ben nodded. "Yes, it is very sad."

The room was silent for a few moments, and then Fuller said, "Anyhow, there is another reason for not having the Duke name on the business."

"What is that?" asked Ben.

Fuller tossed a rolled-up local newspaper across his desk to Ben. As Ben unrolled the newspaper, he noticed that the front page talked about a Justice Department investigation of business entities that might be violating the Sherman Antitrust Act, which had gone into effect in 1890 by act of Congress. "The antitrust shriekers,"[83] Fuller replied. "What do you make of them, Ben? Do you think they are a menace to the free-market system?"

"Well, you know," Ben replied, "I have always thought that a society of people needs a good, healthy balance of ideas and political views. I have read the arguments for and against the antitrust legislation. According to Senator Sherman, the act is primarily to protect consumers from arrangements that are designed to artificially control the price of the goods. A second, though less commonly stated goal, is to prevent monopolies. If one person is able to capture an entire market and drive his competitors out of business, then he can set any price he wants at the expense of the consumer. I can't say I oppose the legislation. I know that we will never artificially inflate the price of our goods; in fact, we will do

---

83   During the 1890s there emerged an increasing number of advocates of antitrust legislation and criminal prosecution under the antitrust laws. Some became extreme and began accusing nearly every large corporation of violating antitrust laws. Because of this extreme position, they acquired the name "anti-trust shriekers." When the Department of Justice began prosecuting antitrust cases, the seeming vindication prompted many of them to become even more vocal in their approach and tactics.

the opposite, and we will always try to be fair to everyone, because that's the right thing to do. But we don't know who will control these businesses we create after we are long gone, and we don't know how greedy they might become."

Fuller nodded his head as he reached across his desk to retrieve his newspaper. "Well said, Ben, as always."

"I am curious about one thing, William." Fuller asked, "What does your uncle say about you forming a firm that will be competing against his? Are we going to be facing a possible lawsuit over trade secrets or anything of the sort?"

"Not at all," replied Erwin. "Uncle Edwin was very happy when I told him what I was thinking of doing. He gave me his blessing. In addition, some of what we are going to do involves collaborating with Uncle Edwin's firm on the production of materials. So it's good between us."

As Benjamin and Erwin left Fuller's office, Erwin said, "Thanks so much for this, Ben. It means a great deal to me. I promise that I won't let you down."

"I am very pleased that we are able to work together," Ben replied. "I have seen that you are a very industrious and insightful man. I believe you will make our textile venture very successful."

Ben's belief in Erwin's ability proved accurate. Within a few short years the Erwin Cotton Mill Company had grown into a profitable venture. Erwin marketed the product throughout New England and northward to New York and then began to turn his sights westward. Benjamin was very pleased with Erwin as his partner. Perhaps because of competition, the Erwin Cotton Mill was unsuccessful in finding New England investors and joint venturers, so they relied upon their own resources to build a great textile firm. Soon, however, concern began to develop among some that the textile mill was yet another Duke venture concentrating too much wealth into the hands of very few men. The Sherman Antitrust Act was a common topic of discussion in Durham in those days. Those who opposed Duke financial expansion were often seen as those who would impede growth that results from successful invention, ingenuity, and willingness to accept risk. This was a divisive factor in the Carolinas in the late 1800s. On the one hand were those who felt that the free enterprise system needed to regulate itself, and on the other hand were those who felt that there needed to be some guidance from government to prevent abuse. Ben found himself somewhere in the middle.

Although the Erwin Cotton Mill originally produced muslin cloth for consumer products, soon demand for cotton expanded into products made of denim, such as overalls and jeans. While denim products were not immediately successful in the South, it was not long before the durability of denim made it the product of choice for farmers and other laborers. In a short time, the Erwin Cotton Mill became the largest supplier of denim in the United States. By 1895 the Erwin Cotton Mill was employing over one thousand workers and operating over twenty-five thousand spindles with one thousand looms.[84]

At the same time Benjamin Duke and William Erwin were launching the Erwin Cotton Mill, Ben's brother Brodie was launching the Pearl Cotton Mill, also with William Erwin and his brother J. Harper Erwin as the managers. Brodie, who was often reckless in his endeavors, quickly overextended himself, and it became necessary for Ben and Buck, in cooperation with George Watts, to bail him out. With this assistance, the Pearl Cotton Mill also became a highly successful venture.[85]

An aspect of this industry that does not reflect highly upon the community in those days is the fact that both labor and cotton were

---

84   B. N. Duke to W. A. Erwin, January 30, 1896, B. N. Letterbook, Rubenstein Rare Book and Manuscripts, Duke University; Durham *Daily Globe*, July 18, 1895, August 15, 1895; Durden, *The Dukes of Durham, 1865–1929*, 133.

85   B. N. Duke to W. R. Hall, January 16, 1894; B. N. Duke to W. C. Houston Jr. January 22, 1894, B. N. Duke Letterbook, David M. Rubenstein Rare Book and Manuscript Library, Duke University; Durden, *The Dukes of Durham, 1865–1929*, 133.

very cheap. A skilled male laborer could be hired for as little as one dollar per day, often with twelve to sixteen-hour workdays, and unfortunately many laborers were women, working for forty cents per day, and children, working for as little as twenty cents per day.[86]

In an open town meeting before the North Carolina Child Labor Committee, William Erwin and Ben Duke stated their position on the issue of child labor.

"Those of us at the Erwin Cotton Mill are deeply concerned about the use of child labor in this state. Allowing children to work twelve to sixteen-hour days without the opportunity for an education is not conducive to a healthy state. It is damaging to our children, who should be in school, and it is unhealthy morally for a society to take advantage of its children in this fashion." Erwin glanced at Ben, who nodded slightly in affirmation. "Mr. Duke and I have discussed this at great length. We believe that the minimum working age for children should be raised to sixteen years of age and that education should be mandatory for all children up to the age of sixteen years."[87]

Immediately there occurred murmuring throughout the room. The chairman presiding over the meeting struck his gavel on the table and said loudly, "Order. Everyone will have a chance to speak. Please continue, Mr. Erwin."

"We have been in contact with several legislators to whom we have made our proposal, and we have found them to be in agreement. It is simply wrong to allow children to work in these shops all day long when they should be in school, acquiring an education. And what we have learned, through our studies and investigation, is that many factories in North Carolina have children as young as nine and ten years of age working twelve to sixteen-hour days. In

---

86 Durden, *The Dukes of Durham, 1865–1929*, 134.

87 Erwin had supported statutory changes to increase the working age from fourteen to sixteen years, and Ben agreed with Erwin on this issue. Durden, *The Dukes of Durham, 1865–1929*, 135.

other words, the minimum age requirements currently in existence are not being followed by many companies."

"I fully sympathize with your position, Mr. Erwin," said one of the board members. "But is it really the position of the government to tell families what they can and cannot do with their children? If they choose to allow them to work in a mill, isn't that a decision for the family? Besides, some families need the income to provide the necessary money for the family to make ends meet."

Another business owner stood. "How do we know that this isn't a way for the Erwin Cotton Mill to further strap competitors by diminishing the labor supply? With the development of labor unions, employees are constantly demanding higher wages and good labor is becoming scarce. We have been able to keep up with demand by employing fourteen-year-old workers. What Erwin and Duke are proposing would seriously undermine our ability to compete. My mill is small, and I cannot afford to pay the kind of wages the Erwin Cotton Mill pays. It is only by hiring young labor that I can stay in business. Is this a ploy by Duke and Erwin to drive competitors out of the market?"

Ben stood and addressed the business owner directly. "Let me ask you a question, Sam. What is the youngest age of a worker in your factory today?" The business owner looked at Ben but did not reply.

"Do you know the age of the youngest worker in your factory? I have known you for a long time, Sam, and I want you to be truthful here."

"As far as I know, we have no workers less than fourteen years of age," replied the businessman.

"I know how young the youngest worker in your factory is today. I know his parents, and they told me because they tried to get him a job in one of my businesses, and they later told me you hired him. Do you want me to say how old he is?"

Another business owner shouted, "I know how old he is. He is only nine years of age. Everyone in Durham knows that Sam employees children below the lawful working age."

"This is the problem," continued Ben. "Not only are workers being employed at the age of fourteen years, which I believe is too young, but many children are not even the age of fourteen years."

"You might all judge me for employing younger kids, but I cannot compete if I don't. Everyone is doing it, and they are paying half the wage they pay adults. Some children are working for twenty cents per day. It's not fair that this law is enforced against me and not against everyone else," said the businessman with frustration.

One of the board members said, "This is news to me. I had no idea that any factory in Durham was employing children younger than fourteen years of age. I find this very troubling. How widespread is this practice?"

Erwin turned back to face the board member who was speaking, "It is very widespread. I don't know how much I should say in this open meeting, but I am told that some of your inspectors are taking bribes to look the other way."

The board members looked at each other with expressions of disbelief, and murmuring broke out in the crowd.

"If you don't believe me, all you have to do is investigate. The very persons charged with the responsibility of enforcing our child labor laws are participating in breaking those laws."

The board members agreed that an investigation was warranted, and they assured the community that they would investigate this matter thoroughly. They also assured the community that any investigator found to be taking bribes to allow child labor below the age of fourteen years would be terminated from his position of employment.

Notwithstanding the common use of child labor and excessive workdays, the Erwin Cotton Mill refused to employ underage children and would not allow its employees to work longer than eleven hours per day.[88] Erwin and Duke supported statewide legislation to raise the minimum age requirement for employment of

---

88   Durden, *The Dukes of Durham, 1865–1929*, 134.

children from fourteen years to sixteen years, and they supported mandatory education for children under fourteen years of age.[89] This position on child labor, combined with the fact that the Erwin Cotton Mill was far more successful than other mills in the area, drew resentment from some area mill operators. Nonetheless, the vast majority of mill owners and other businessmen most likely saw the success of the Erwin Cotton Mill as an inspiration and a reason to be more honest and thoughtful in business operations.

While the Erwin Cotton Mill took the high road on the issue of child labor and working conditions, the mill was not as friendly to union organizers who were beginning to appear on the scene. Erwin felt that the Erwin Cotton Mill's employees were paid a fair wage and were treated far better than employees of other employers. It seemed insulting and perhaps downright treacherous to him that they would actually try to form organized unions in the Erwin Cotton Mill. For that reason, he posted a public notice that anyone who joined a union would be terminated with a two-week notice and would be unable to purchase at the company store. Some joined the union, went on strike, and were terminated, while others joined the union but did not strike. In time Erwin permitted nonstriking union members to remain on the job and to purchase from the company store. The forgiveness extended to those who joined the union struck a serious blow to union organizers, who found it difficult to find fault with a company that was already offering more to employees than the unions could negotiate in other mills. In time, the efforts to unionize textile mills in the South began to weaken, in large part because of the devastating failure to unionize the Erwin Cotton Mill.[90]

In the early 1900s, given the success of the Erwin Cotton Mill, Ben and Erwin decided to launch a massive expansion campaign. In time, the Duke and Erwin holdings consisted of numerous textile

---

89   Durden, *The Dukes of Durham, 1865–1929*, 135.
90   Ibid., 136

operations in a variety of locations. A necessary element for the kind of expansion the operations were undergoing was electricity. Yet sources of electric power were quite scarce in those days, and electricity was still relatively unknown to many Americans.[91]

In the late spring of 1904, Buck, W. Gill Wylie, and William States Lee sat on the bank of the Catawba River in South Carolina cooking a meal of largemouth bass they had caught earlier that day. Wylie and Lee had already invested in hydroelectricity in South Carolina. They tried to persuade Ben and Buck to invest. While Ben and Buck had interest, they were still heavily invested in textiles and tobacco, and so they remained hesitant. They also hesitated in investing in South Carolina, owing to the common flooding and high waters that occurred during the rainy seasons. They were not convinced that investing on the Catawba River was a wise decision. Knowing how much Buck enjoyed outdoor activities, Wylie and Lee invited him to go camping and fishing at Great Falls on the Catawba River.

Wylie turned the fish in the skillet and then leaned back against a tree stump. "Hydroelectricity is the Holy Grail of energy for the future of America. Someday the supply of fossil fuels will be depleted and it will be necessary to find safe, clean alternatives.

---

91   In the late 1800s, Thomas Edison invented a number of devices including the phonograph, the lightbulb, and the electric vote recorder to name just a few. Each of these inventions required electrical current for operation. As the demand for these products began to grow, so did the need for a reliable electric power source without which these products were useless. To supply this electricity, Thomas Edison and JP Morgan formed Edison General Electric which sought to provide direct current electricity. A limitation of direct current electricity is that it could travel only short distances. In contrast, Westinghouse and Nikola Tesla, a former apprentice of Edison, promoted alternating current, which could be transported long distances. Edison refused to switch to alternating current and ultimately was forced out of General Electric in the 1892 merger of General Electric and Westinghouse, which then constructed the first major hydroelectric power plant at Niagara Falls utilizing alternating current. This allowed the Niagara Falls facility to provide electricity to distant locations.

'White coal' is what they call hydroelectricity, because it is clean, safe, and renewable. It is incumbent upon those of us who are able to develop this resource for the benefit of current and future generations, to take advantage of this opportunity."

"You are right," Lee said. "Electricity might prove to be the most important contribution we will make to society."

"Your point is well taken. I agree with both of you that clean energy might be the most important contribution we will ever make to society. I feel that I will have achieved good things if in four hundred years historians look back and say, 'James Buchanan Duke did that for society, and it is a good thing that he did.' After everything that has happened in the tobacco industry, I have concluded that my moral compass for the future will always be that in four hundred years from today, when people look back at our time, they will say that we have done a good thing."

Wylie nodded. "I think that is a good compass to direct one's moral decisions. Let the mark we leave on the world be a good one that benefits the greatest number of people."

Buck continued. "Also, someday we will have children, and then they will have children. It is important that we leave a legacy to serve as their moral compass." He paused momentarily. "I want both of you to understand that I am in full agreement that investment in hydroelectricity is sound. I am just not convinced that Great Falls is the best place to build a power plant."

"Let's see how you feel after spending a little time out here on the river. Speaking of families, so what about Lillian McCredy, Buck? Is it going well?" Lee asked.

"Yes, actually I have decided to ask her for marriage," replied Buck.

Wylie laughed. "Hey, congratulations, Buck."

"Indeed," said Lee.

"I was wondering if you would ever settle down and get married," said Wylie. "I think it will be good for you. I also think you are correct about the hydroelectric power. In time this may prove to be our greatest financial venture that provides the greatest benefit to the most people. We need to give sound guidance to our children and their children in the use of the planet's resources."

"I remember a Cherokee saying that my father often repeated and I have never forgotten," said Buck.

"What is it?" asked Lee.

Buck took off his hat and rubbed his forehead with the back of his hand as he tried to recall the exact words. Finally, he said, "Treat the earth well. It was not given to you by your parents; it was loaned to you by your children. We do not inherit the earth from our ancestors; we borrow it from our children."

"That is a great saying," Lee replied.

"I love that," Wylie said.

"I think it is a great thing for us to remember as we make plans for industrial expansion and the development of energy," Buck said.

The men camped that night—under the stars, without tents— at the edge of the river near Great Falls. Throughout the night they could hear the rushing water of the rapids downriver about five hundred feet. "Isn't that a great sound," asked Buck as he rolled over in his bedding. "The sound of rushing water puts me to sleep."

"It keeps me awake," Lee replied.

Wylie laughed. "Think of what these rapids are going to do for our venture in electricity and you will sleep like a baby."

Lee laughed. "Well, when you put it like that, I suppose I can live with it." Lee, who was a talented engineer, proved a tremendous asset to the team. His ability to grasp abstract concepts allowed him to design intricate turbines to handle the available water flow. "I can almost tell you the size of the turbines we will need if we build here, just by listening to the force of the water."

"Hey, what do you get when a man steps in a mud puddle with an electric shaver in his hand," asked Buck.

"I give up," Wylie replied. "What do you get?"

"Well, given that the electric shaver has not been invented yet, I have no idea," said Lee with a chuckle.

"You get a hydroelectric 'damn'!" Buck replied.

"Oh please, Buck, go to sleep." Lee laughed as he threw a pillow at Buck.

The following morning Buck and Lee awakened to fresh coffee, eggs, and biscuits prepared by Wylie.

"Oh, that smells great. Thanks for preparing this," Lee said.

"Are you fellows ready for the time of your life?" asked Wylie. "I have a real surprise for you."

"I am not sure I am ready for this," Buck said with a laugh.

Wylie pointed toward the river. "There is our transportation out of here." Next to the bank of the river was a strange contraption that looked like a wooden boat wrapped in giant black donut-shaped balloons.

"What the heck is that thing?" asked Lee.

"It is called a white-water raft," Wylie replied.

"Where did it come from?" asked Buck as he stood up and began walking toward the raft.

"I built it with the assistance of some engineers," Wylie replied. "It allows us to float down the river at nearly the same speed as the water. This morning I pulled it out of the bushes where I had it hidden."

"What is it made out of?" Lee asked.

"Those are inner tubes, aren't they?" asked Buck as he pointed to the black air-filled rubber tubes that lined the side of the boat.

"Yes, they are. Because they are filled with air, they create a much smoother ride for automobiles. More recently people have experimented with them as wheels for horse-drawn wagons. They are also great flotation devices."

"Are you sure this thing is safe?" asked Lee.

Wylie laughed. "I think so. I did it before, and nothing bad happened."

"You don't sound completely convincing," Lee replied with a laugh.

Within an hour, the team had loaded their supplies into the raft, climbed in, and were floating downriver. Buck was at the bow with a paddle, trying to keep the raft from hitting rocks. Lee was in the middle with another paddle, and Wylie was at the stern, attempting to guide the raft.

"I don't really think this is safe," Buck shouted from the bow of the raft.

"I know it is not safe," shouted Lee from the middle of the raft. "Wylie, I think you have put us in great peril."

"I have put you in what?" Wylie shouted over the roar of the river.

"Great peril," Lee shouted.

Buck turned and shouted "Clarence Darrow?" as he roared with laughter. Wylie could not hear what he said because the sound of the water had become deafening as the raft sped down the rapids. Lee asked, "Isn't he a lawyer for the railroads?"

Buck struck the water on the port side with his paddle. He then swung the paddle into the water on the starboard side. Suddenly the raft shot into the air as it sailed over a four-foot water drop. "Ah!" they all three shouted simultaneously. The men laughed as they struggled to keep the raft upright while riding the rapids.

In time they were being propelled down the river at a high rate of speed. During their course, the boat passed through six sets of rapids. Finally up ahead they could see that there was a calm stretch in the water. Just as they neared the calm stretch, they crashed bow first into a boulder that sat in the center of the rapids, dividing the water. The boat spun around and began floating down the river stern first. As they came to the calm stretch, they paddled over to the bank. The men pulled themselves out of the water laughing as they attempted to catch their breath.

"That was great, Wylie," Buck said. "What a fantastic idea to raft down the river. In a way I feel a little like Tom Sawyer and Huckleberry Finn."

"I don't think Tom Sawyer and Huck Finn ever went that fast," Lee said.

"This water power we have just experienced is the key to the hydroelectric power plant," Wylie said. "That's the reason I asked you to join me in this adventure. I wanted you to feel and see the awesome power that will generate the electricity that will keep the textile mills operating and, in time, will supply electricity to every home and business in the United States."

Lee laughed. "This site for our proposed power plant must be the most valuable real estate in America."

"Indeed," Wylie replied. "There is no question it will prove to be one of the most important pieces of property over the next century. We are right here watching this happen. This is a new era in human history."

Not far from the bank of the river was a dirt road. Next to the road was a 1904 Buick that had been parked there to transport the men back to the city. As they loaded their gear into the automobile, Wylie said, "Gentlemen, what we experienced in these last two days gives us a firsthand look at the white coal. This will be the power source for electricity over the next century. I am pleased that both of you decided to join me in this adventure."

"Thanks for inviting us, Wylie. I had a great time," replied Buck.

"As did I," said Lee.

Seeing the benefits of electricity, and the feasibility of building on the Catawba River, Buck, Ben, Dr. Gill Wylie, and William States Lee established the Southern Power Company in 1905.[92] The Dukes believed that the South was restricted to agriculture because of the lack of industry and that electricity would provide an opportunity for the South to industrialize. Though the original intention was to provide electricity to the textile mills, the demand for electricity became so great that, in time, this hydroelectric power plant was providing electricity for private consumption throughout the region, thereby enhancing economic development of the community.

---

92   Durden, *The Dukes of Durham, 1865–1929*, 183.

In November 1904, James Buchanan Duke married Lillian McCredy. For Buck this seemed an opportunity to finally realize his desire to have a family. Lillian, who had been previously married, apparently did not share Buck's domestic aspirations. Perhaps Ben's happy marriage to Sarah Pearson Angier in 1875, which resulted in two young children, Mary Lillian Duke and Angier Buchanan Duke, had caused Buck to seek the happiness he could have in raising a family. Lillian had been divorced from a former husband with allegations of infidelity against her, and she was a widow of yet another husband. She was known for her flirtatious personality, and her reputation caused concern for Buck's brother Ben. Perhaps to satisfy his father's concern about the morality of his decisions and life choices, particularly since Washington had already expressed disappointment in Buck's decision to place pictures of women in the cigarette packs, and in his failure to settle down and marry, Buck decided to propose to Lillian. Buck was deeply attracted to Lillian and enjoyed her "free spirit." No doubt he believed his romance with Lillian would be different from her past romances, and he felt that their marriage would succeed. Unfortunately Buck's dreams were shattered when rumors of infidelity in her marriage to Buck emerged and even found their way into the newspapers. This was more than Buck could bear, and he filed for divorce in September 1905.[93] Perhaps there was some solace for Buck in that his father, who died in May of that year, did not live to have his heart broken by the demise of Buck's marriage to Lillian.[94] For Washington, who had lost both of his wives to illness, nothing was more important than God and family. He saw the breakup of a family as the worst thing a person could endure. He would never have been able to understand Lillian's infidelity, and he would never have been able to understand Buck's divorce.

After Washington died in 1905, Buck and Ben no longer had

93   "James B. Duke Sues Wife for Divorce," *New York Times*, September 3, 1905.
94   The death of Washington Duke will be discussed more fully in chapter 9.

the sound advice of their father, their mentor.[95] As he neared his final days, the boys were forced to think independently and to make decisions on their own, but they found the transition difficult. They had relied on their father for advice as far back as they could remember. Now they had to manage a rapidly expanding commercial enterprise without their father's counsel. Notwithstanding the absence of their father, Ben and Buck increased the profits in all Duke enterprises, though the success was not without pain. The decade after Washington's death proved to be the greatest challenge they would face in their lifetimes.

While textiles and hydroelectricity proved successful for the Dukes in the first decade of the twentieth century, troubles were just beginning for the Duke tobacco enterprise. The Sherman Antitrust Act was passed by Congress on July 2, 1890.[96] Meanwhile, the American Tobacco Company continued to grow with Buck as president. In the early part of the twentieth century, the US Department of Justice became concerned about the massive amount of wealth under the control of a single man, James Buchanan Duke, and on July 19, 1907, US Attorney General George Wickersham filed a lawsuit against the American Tobacco Company under the Sherman Antitrust Act.[97] The defendants were twenty-nine individuals, sixty-five American corporations, and two English corporations. The suit alleged that the defendants violated the act and that the American Tobacco Company, by virtue of its control over the five accessory corporations and control over subsidiary corporations by stock ownership, had conspired with the other defendants to restrain trade and to monopolize the tobacco industry.

---

95   Durden, *The Dukes of Durham, 1865–1929*, 183.

96   Sherman Antitrust Act (1890), 15 USC Sections 1–7.

97   *United States v. The American Tobacco Company* (1911), 221 US 106. (There were actually multiple suits filed over a period of several years, but the definitive decision resulting in the breakup of the tobacco trust was delivered by the United States Supreme Court on May 29, 1911.)

The antitrust lawsuit threatened to thwart Buck's plans for the American Tobacco Company. He considered this an assault not only on the tobacco company but also on the entire free-market system. He had created an efficiently operating business with little waste and a narrow profit margin. He believed it should be the model for all businesses in America. Profits were earned by sales volume and not by high prices. The benefits to the consumer were lower prices, greater availability, and more choices. Upon learning of the filing of the lawsuit, he met with attorneys W. W. Fuller, William Wallace, and Junius Parker at his office in New York. Buck was seated behind his desk, and the attorneys were seated in three wingback chairs facing the front of the desk.

"We have to do everything we can to defeat this lawsuit," Buck said. "The consequences for the American Tobacco Company will be devastating if Wickersham[98] wins this. We have to find some way to settle this case."

Wallace leaned forward in his chair, resting his elbows on his knees. "Truthfully, I don't believe that is going to happen, Buck. There is a lot of pressure on Wickersham. While President McKinley was in office, I think we had some protection. Although he was advancing the antitrust agenda, he had some loyalty to his Republican friends. Roosevelt has no such loyalty, in my opinion, and he is putting a lot of pressure on Wickersham to take down the monopolies. He sees the American Tobacco Company as a monopoly, and I think he sees this as his own private mission."

"It is really a war on efficiency, in my opinion," replied Buck. "My brother Ben says he can understand the rationale behind the antitrust legislation, but even he thinks the feds are being heavy-handed and arbitrary."

Fuller said, "I had that very conversation with Ben a few weeks back. He doesn't want to be forced to defend a lawsuit but has

---

98   George Wickersham was the attorney general of the United States who prosecuted the case against the American Tobacco Company.

admitted to me that he believes the tobacco trust might be in violation; of course, that was before the suit was filed. I don't know what he thinks about it now."

"I think his biggest frustration, which is the same as mine, is that we are being called criminals. We spent our entire lives trying to be fair and good to others and never violate any law. At no time have we ever attempted to drive competitors out of business as we expanded the tobacco enterprise. In fact, it was just the opposite. We offered good prices and incentives for tobacco companies we purchased, and we never used heavy-handed tactics, like the railroads, when we encountered someone who did not want to join us. I promised Ben and my pappy that we would never use strong-arm tactics to eliminate competitors, and we never have. How can they accuse us of being criminals?"

"It's important to remember, Buck, that violating the Sherman Antitrust Act is not criminal conduct in the traditional sense of the phrase. It is not like committing murder or even theft. It is violating a highly technical set of statutes and rules that many judges do not even fully understand. I wouldn't take it so hard if I were you," Fuller said.

"I understand that," Buck replied, "but I still don't like being called a criminal by the president of the United States for violating some statute that is probably unconstitutional on its face. What chance do we have of winning in the end?"

Wallace replied, "I believe there is a good chance we will lose at the district court level. If that happens we can always appeal, but with this Supreme Court, the adverse judgment potential is high."

Buck said, "I am suspicious that some of this is driven by the new medical reports claiming that tobacco is harmful. I never heard anyone say that until the past couple of years. I think some of those doctors are just trying to make a name for themselves."

"Well, you know there's no proof that tobacco is harmful. It's just a theory," Parker said.

"That's true," replied Buck, "but I'm still troubled. The studies are based upon the number of people with heart and lung disease who smoked for years. Supposedly, these illnesses are disproportionately higher among smokers than nonsmokers. If it turns out someday that this is true, that means we spent our entire lives creating something harmful instead of something good as we intended. So now not only are we being accused of being criminals, but we are also being accused of selling a product that kills people."

"I'm concerned that you might be losing interest in the tobacco venture, Buck," Parker replied.

Buck stood up and began pacing the floor. "Don't worry; I'm not going to abandon the tobacco industry, but I am more serious now than ever about moving into textiles and hydroelectricity. If it turns out that these reports about the harmful effects of tobacco are true, yes, I will divest my tobacco holdings. There is no way we can do anything about the past, but we can avoid doing wrong in the future."[99]

Like his father, Buck always tried to be an honest man and tried to do right in all things. Now he was faced with a devastating lawsuit while simultaneously learning about the potentially harmful effects of tobacco. The loss of his father in 1905 was a loss not only of his advisor but also of his mentor. Who could he turn to now when he needed counsel on such matters?

In May 1911, the US Supreme Court delivered a ruling that resulted in the breakup of the massive American Tobacco Company. After the breakup, four new companies emerged. They were R. J. Reynolds, Liggett and Meyers, P. Lorillard, and the American Tobacco Company. This was a devastating time for Buck and Ben. Quite possibly for the first time in their lives, they began to question the morality of their decisions. If they were wrong in selling a harmful product to the public, and if they were wrong in violating

---

99 The conversation between Buck and the attorneys is a dramatization of conversations likely to have occurred during this time. Parker, Fuller, and Wallace were three of the attorneys hired to defend the American Tobacco Company in the action brought by the US Department of Justice.

the antitrust laws, their wrongness certainly was not willful. Even so, this knowledge did not provide much comfort to them. For the first time, with their father gone and facing these monumental challenges, their confidence began to wane. Buck and Ben decided to drive to Durham to stay at Ben's house for a few weeks. Somehow it seemed that going back to Durham, where they had built everything with their father, would provide comfort and allow them to regain their confidence.

Ben and Buck left for Durham on a Friday morning, stayed at a hotel in Washington, DC, and then drove into Durham on Saturday. When they arrived at Ben's house in the afternoon, Ben's wife, Sarah, was working in the flower garden. Sarah loved flowers and enjoyed tending to them. Known as a pretty woman with a gentle personality, she seemed suited to her affinity with flowers. Ben and Sarah had homes in both Durham and New York. Sarah enjoyed Durham in the summer months and had come back to Durham several weeks earlier. The Durham house, called Four Acres, was located on four acres bounded by W. Chapel Hill Street, Duke Street, Willard Street, and Jackson Street in downtown Durham. Designed by architect C. C. Hook, the house was a Chateauesque revival constructed of granite and brick. The stately mansion had a carport on the right side and a large front porch with a sundeck above the porch.

When Ben and Buck drove into the driveway, Sarah walked over to greet them. As they climbed out of the car, she gave Ben a hug and a kiss on the cheek and then said, "I wasn't expecting you until tomorrow."

"We decided to come back early to relax over the weekend before dealing with business on Monday," said Ben.

"What do you think is going to happen now that the court has found the tobacco trust in violation?" Sarah asked.

Ben replied, "Well, no one will go to jail. Even though we are accused of committing a crime, the end result will be the breakup of the tobacco trust. I don't like the company, or any of us, being accused of a crime, but at the end of the day, I don't know if the actual outcome is such a terrible thing. Buck is the one most concerned about it."

"I am concerned," said Buck. "I don't like this at all. It feels like our world is unraveling."

"Well, come inside and relax a little. You had a long drive," Sarah said.

The following morning they attended church at Memorial Methodist,[100] which was located a short distance from Ben's home on W. Chapel Hill Street. As they entered the church, dozens of parishioners greeted them, not having seen them for several months. They sat in a pew toward the front, on the right side of the sanctuary. During the sermon, the pastor spoke of the anguish one experiences when wrongfully accused, and he provided an illustration using the story of Joseph in the Bible, who was falsely accused of attempted rape by the wife of Potiphar.[101] As he listened to the message, Buck could not help but wonder if this was the pastor's way of offering words of comfort to Ben and Buck, but he concluded that the comments were just coincidence. Nonetheless, he was deeply impacted by those words. As they walked back to Ben's house after the service, he asked, "Do you think the comments about Joseph were for our benefit? I am sure everyone in Durham knows about the antitrust case."

Ben replied, "I don't know that he was thinking of us. What sometimes seems like a coincidence, though, I think is a message from God. Maybe the message here is that regardless of whether we were wrongfully accused, God knows that our intentions were always good. It was never our intention to violate the law or to create a harmful product. And maybe tobacco is not harmful. The case still has not been proven. It is only a theory some doctors have espoused."

---

100 Memorial Methodist Church is today called Duke Memorial Methodist Church.

101 The account of Joseph and Potiphar's wife is found in the thirty-ninth chapter of Genesis.

"Actually, that is a little comforting," said Buck. "I have been feeling like this is the worst time in my life except the time I learned of Lillian's infidelity."

Ben nodded. "It has been a good road and a rough road at the same time."

"The important thing to remember," Sarah said, "is that God knows your heart. He knows that neither one of you ever intended to violate the law or do anything harmful. In the big picture, it really doesn't matter what men believe. It's what God knows that is important."

Buck took off his hat and carried it at his side. "I know that's true, but I can't help but wonder what people think of us now that the US Supreme Court has decided in favor of the Justice Department. And if it turns out that tobacco really is harmful, you know that people are only going to remember us for the tobacco empire we built, and they will never believe that we did not intend to do harm. They will never remember the textile companies and the hydroelectric companies that we built. They will only remember the tobacco, and we will always be known as the tobacco magnates. Let's make a pact. If the studies confirm that tobacco is harmful, let's agree that we will divest all of our interest in tobacco."

Ben put his arm around his younger brother's shoulders and said, "As your slightly older brother, I am really proud of you, and I am really pleased to hear you say that. I agree. If these reports of the harmful effects of tobacco are proven true, we will divest our tobacco holdings and focus on textiles, electricity, and philanthropic activities."[102]

Perhaps the timing of the development of hydroelectricity was fortuitously favorable for the Dukes, given that by 1908 the

---

102 The account of the trip to Ben's house in Durham, and the conversation after church, is a dramatization based upon conversations Ben and Buck are said to have with each other on numerous occasions about these issues. While the actual conversation is fictional, the occurrence of similar conversations between them is probable.

textile industry had become depressed and more studies began to surface concluding that tobacco had harmful effects. Much of the depression in American cotton mills resulted from imported textile products. In an effort to salvage the enterprises, William Erwin and Ben Duke lobbied the federal government to impose higher tariffs on incoming goods. However, the Democratic administration under Wilson was not as protective as the Republican administrations had been. In 1913 the Underwood Tariff (Underwood-Simmons Act) imposed significantly reduced duties on imported goods.[103] While the textile industry eventually rebounded from the slump of the first decade of the new millennium, the Duke investments in hydroelectricity showed the greatest promise for their investments outside of tobacco.

Several years after the breakup of the American Tobacco Company in 1912, as a result of the Supreme Court ruling in *United States v. The American Tobacco Company*, the Dukes divested all of their tobacco holdings in the United States. The decision was based upon several factors that historians have often neglected while focusing solely upon the antitrust impact. The first was that by 1915 many doctors began expressing a belief that tobacco was actually harmful to the health of the smoker and could cause cancer and heart disease. This information was devastating for Ben and Buck, who had always sought to provide a public benefit. A second reason for the divestiture of tobacco holdings was that Buck and Ben learned that, after the breakup of the tobacco trust, in order to compete effectively, many of the spin-off producers of tobacco products had begun enhancing their products with opium to increase both the pleasure from consumption and the addictive effect of the tobacco. Both Ben and Buck found this practice reprehensible and felt that competing in such a market would require serious moral compromises that they were not prepared to make. Lastly, the lawsuit against the American Tobacco Company, of which Buck was

---

103 Durden, *The Dukes of Durham, 1865–1929*, 144.

the president, along with the allegations of criminal conspiracy, was devastating for both Ben and Buck. Throughout their lives they had sought to be model, law-abiding citizens who served as role models for others to follow. Now, after years of success and accolades, they suddenly found themselves on the outside of the law—a position that caused them great discomfort with their involvement in the industry. In response to this combination of factors, the Dukes sold all of their tobacco holdings in the United States and invested their money in other ventures, including philanthropic activities.

Although today the Dukes are known primarily for their developments in the tobacco industry, in reality their most noteworthy commercial enterprise was the development of electric power. However, this achievement did not occur until the last few decades of their lives, and their father, Washington Duke, did not live to see the full fruition of this achievement. Indeed, the first hydroelectric power plant developed by major investments from the Dukes was constructed in 1907, two years after Washington's death. Nonetheless, even though Washington did not survive to see the tremendous success of the Dukes in electric energy, he was fully aware of the intent to launch the enterprise.

The Dukes clearly became the leaders in the development of hydroelectric power with their investments in the Carolinas. They began buying property for sites of hydroelectric power plants. In time the Dukes created a network of electric power companies that supplied electricity to many businesses as well as private homes. This was a new beginning for Ben and Buck. They had officially moved into hydroelectric power. Over the next two decades, they developed the Duke Power Company, now called Duke Energy, which, with its affiliated and subsidiary companies, today provides electricity to millions of households throughout the United States and Canada. Although Ben became ill in 1915, he continued to offer support in the Duke Power Company endeavors, but Buck remained the primary proponent of this venture, until his death in 1925.[104]

---

104 Durden, *The Dukes of Durham, 1865–1929*, 177.

Photograph of Washington Duke
University Archives Photograph Collection,
Duke University Archives, Duke University

Photograph of a young Benjamin Newton Duke
University Archives Photograph Collection,
Duke University Archives, Duke University

Photograph of older Benjamin Newton Duke
University Archives Photograph Collection,
Duke University Archives, Duke University

Photograph of young James Buchanan Duke
University Archives Photograph Collection,
Duke University Archives, Duke University

Photograph of older James Buchanan Duke
University Archives Photograph Collection,
Duke University Archives, Duke University

Photograph of Mary Duke Lyon
University Archives Photograph Collection,
Duke University Archives, Duke University

Photograph of Brodie Duke
University Archives Photograph Collection,
Duke University Archives, Duke University

Photograph of a young Angier Buchanan Duke
University Archives Photograph Collection,
Duke University Archives, Duke University

Photograph of older Angier Buchanan Duke
University Archives Photograph Collection,
Duke University Archives, Duke University

8

The Establishment of Duke University

The origin of Duke University[105] can be traced to a one-room building in Randolph County, North Carolina, called Brown's Schoolhouse. Built by Quakers sometime before 1835 through the financial generosity of a man named John Brown, the building served as a meeting place for several years. Unfortunately the school was operational only when a traveling minister, or other qualified person, passed through the community and agreed to teach. The institution was a boarding school without dormitories, so the children stayed at the homes of local families when the school was in session. While the identity of the original headmaster is unknown, sometime between 1830 and 1835, a pioneer Quaker named Allen Frazier became headmaster. Frazier resigned from his position in 1838 to build another schoolhouse not far from Brown's Schoolhouse, at which time Richard Brantley York assumed the role of headmaster of Brown's Schoolhouse.[106]

---

105 Most of the information in this chapter was derived from information contained in the Duke University Archives, David M. Rubenstein Rare Book and Manuscript Library. See William E. King (Duke University Archivist, 1972–2002), "Duke University, A Brief Narrative History," accessed September 22, 2013, http://library.duke.edu/uarchives/history/narrativehistory.html.

106 "City of Trinity, A City of Vision," website accessed December 6, 2013, http://www.trinity-nc.gov/index.asp?Type=NONE&SEC=%7BC38B6910-9FD7-48C3-9DE7-2B8B18AE8754%7D.

York was a self-taught Methodist minister who, immediately upon assuming the position of headmaster, recognized that a larger facility was necessary to house the sixty-nine schoolchildren then attending Brown Schoolhouse. For that reason he constructed two buildings to house the students and changed the name to Union Institute. The facility then became a Quaker Methodist subscription school.[107]

As Union Institute continued to grow, York realized that his passion lay in teaching and not building academic institutions. For that reason, he decided that he should pass the responsibility of headmaster to another.[108] One day as he walked across the schoolyard to the front entrance of the school, York noticed a small group of students standing by the oak tree in the front schoolyard. They seemed saddened and discouraged. He approached them with a smile.

"What's Braxton Craven like?" one of the students asked.

"Don't worry; you will like him," replied York. "He has great plans for this school."

"Like what?" a student asked.

"He would like to focus efforts on obtaining financial assistance from the North Carolina State Legislature."

"Why do we need financial assistance? Aren't we doing okay now? We have you, and you make enough money to live," said another of the students.

"Yes, the school has been generous to me, and I have lived comfortably here. But there are reasons for additional financial assistance. For one thing, we could hire the best teachers and obtain the best teaching materials. I'm a teacher, not an administrator. Braxton will take this institution to the next level."

---

107 "City of Trinity, A City of Vision," website accessed December 6, 2013, http://www.trinity-nc.gov/index.asp?Type=NONE&SEC=%7BC38B6910-9FD7-48C3-9DE7-2B8B18AE8754%7D.

108 See King, "Duke University, A Brief Narrative History," accessed September 22, 2013, http://library.duke.edu/uarchives/history/narrativehistory.html.

"Will it be the same as it is now?" asked another student.

"There will be changes, but they will be changes for the better. In time we will see this institution become one of the finest schools in the Carolinas. My task was to plant the seed. It is for another to nourish the seed and make it grow."

The words of York proved true in several respects. After leaving Union Institute in 1842, York established six more schools and published a series of language and math books.[109] Braxton Craven[110] assumed the responsibilities of running Union Institute. As time passed, the Quaker families began investing their resources in another Quaker school they had established in Guilford County. For that reason, Braxton Craven sought financial assistance from the state legislature. He was able to successfully obtain a state charter for the school, which became known as Normal College in 1851. Because the state resources were not adequate to build the caliber of institution the supporters sought, Craven went to the Methodist Episcopal Church for assistance, and in exchange for financial support from the church, Methodist ministers were permitted to attend at no cost for tuition. With the backing of the Methodist Episcopal Church, the university began to grow, and in 1859 it was renamed Trinity College.[111]

After Craven passed away in 1882, the school came under the leadership of Marcus Wood and a management committee composed of a number of local businessmen. Wood and the committee managed the school well, but the university changed dramatically

---

109 See William E. King (Duke University Archivist, 1972–2002), *Brantley York, 1805–1891*, edited by Thomas Harkins, David M. Rubenstein Rare Book and Manuscript Library, Duke University, accessed September 22, 2013, http://library.duke.edu/uarchives/history/histnotes/york_b.html.

110 *Inventory of Braxton Craven Record and Papers, 1839–1882*, Rubenstein Rare Book and Manuscript Library, Duke University.

111 See King, "Duke University, A Brief Narrative History," accessed September 22, 2013, http://library.duke.edu/uarchives/history/narrativehistory.html.

in 1887 when John Crowell,[112] a Yale University graduate, became the university's president. Crowell was heavily influenced by the research-oriented teaching institutions of Germany, in contrast to the popular recitation method of learning used in the United States. He brought this learning style to Trinity College through substantial curriculum revision and a campus-wide research library. He also persuaded the trustees that the university should relocate to an urban area in order to attract students, faculty and financial resources.[113] In 1892, after reviewing numerous proposals from various cities, Trinity relocated to Durham, North Carolina, in large part because of the generous financial contributions of Washington Duke and Julian S. Carr.[114]

Washington and Ben walked across the campus at Trinity College in Durham, North Carolina, on a chilly afternoon in January 1894. They were on their way to Trinity president John Crowell's office, where they were planning to meet with Crowell, who was leaving his position, and John Kilgo, who was expected to be the incoming president. Washington had been considering a donation to Trinity but wanted to ensure that it would be used in the most effective way to accomplish the greatest benefit. His daughter, Mary Duke Lyon, died in 1893, and Washington had been reflecting upon her life and upon the reality that she would never have been able to attend Trinity, which only admitted male students. This he found troubling. Walking slowly with one hand in the pocket of his trench coat and the other hand holding a cane he used to keep his balance on the ice, Washington said, "I could just give the money to the

---

112 William E. King (Duke University Archivist, 1972–2002), *John Franklin Crowell, A New Direction for Trinity*, David M. Rubenstein Rare Book and Manuscript Library, Duke University, 1990.

113 See King, "Duke University, A Brief Narrative History," accessed September 22, 2013, http://library.duke.edu/uarchives/history/narrativehistory.html.

114 Carr, like Washington, was a devout Methodist who had earned substantial amounts of money in the tobacco industry.

college and let the trustees decide how to spend it, but somehow it seems that I should make sure it is put to the best possible use, or at least a use that brings the best possible benefit."

"How much are you thinking about giving?" asked Ben.

"I have put aside three hundred thousand dollars that I thought I would donate."

"What would you most like to see accomplished at Trinity?" Ben asked.

"I would like to see Trinity open its doors to women students. It doesn't seem right to me that women cannot attend."

Ben nodded. "A few colleges are admitting women students. Oberlin College in Ohio, Stanford University in California, and Washington University in Missouri all admit women students. There is no reason Trinity should not do the same. Are you going to bring it up with Crowell and Kilgo?"

"I am. What if I make three separate donations to endowments of one hundred thousand dollars each, with one of them conditioned upon Trinity admitting women with the same rights and privileges as men?"

Ben laughed. "Well, I think that would get everyone's attention. Do you think the trustees will go for it?"

"I don't know, but I think I will try. One hundred thousand dollars would be a lot of money for a college to pass up."

"I agree."

Twenty minutes later, Washington, Ben, and John Kilgo sat across the desk from outgoing president John Crowell in his office at Trinity College to discuss Washington's plan to donate to the university. Crowell held up one finger to Washington as he finished his conversation on the candlestick telephone. The fireplace to the left of Crowell warmed the room adequately. Washington looked at the large mahogany desk with the glass doors on the front. Through the glass he could see a several books resting on shelves; then he saw a pamphlet that attracted his attention. It read, "Lucy Webb Training Center." Washington remembered hearing about the Lucy Webb Training Center, an organization managed by women in the Methodist Church, that was involved in charitable activities such as building hospitals. *If women can raise money to build hospitals, why can't they attend college?* he thought. Crowell finished his conversation and hung up the telephone.

"So, gentlemen, what brings you to Trinity today?" he asked with a smile.

Washington laughed. "I came to talk about girls."

The men laughed. "What?" Ben asked. "You didn't tell me that, Dad."

"That's okay for you, G. W., but remember, some of us are married," Kilgo said. "I don't believe my wife Fannie[115] would like this discussion."

"Not like that," said Washington. "I was thinking about the woman's role in education and ministry. Have you ever thought that Trinity should admit female students?"

For a moment the room grew silent. "What happened? Did everyone forget their lines?" Washington said with a laugh, which drew laughter from the others, who knew his unusual sense of humor.

"What would they study?" asked Crowell. "The Methodist-Episcopal church does not ordain women ministers, although some of the alumni at Boston University have advocated it for several years now."

"What do you think about that, John?" asked Ben, looking at Crowell.

"Well, you know John Wesley, the founder of Methodism, allowed women to preach. I have often thought that he would advocate ordaining women if he were alive today," Crowell replied.

Washington said, "I suppose initially I am thinking more about general education. I believe it would be of benefit for women to acquire the kind of education men earn at Trinity. Also, while the Methodist Episcopal Church does not ordain women, someday

---

115 John Kiglo married Fannie Nott Turner on December 20, 1882.

it may, and even if it doesn't, there are other professions, such as medicine, that are not prohibited to women."

Crowell nodded and then asked Kilgo, "What would you think of admitting women to Trinity, John?"

"I haven't really given the idea much thought in the context of Trinity, but in general I believe I would support it," Kilgo replied. "I haven't officially been offered the position of president yet, so I don't know that my opinion really matters that much."

Crowell smiled. "Don't worry; it matters. Why are you asking about admitting women, G. W.? Are you thinking of making a presentation to the trustees on this issue?" Crowell asked.

"Actually, I am thinking of making several contributions to Trinity, but I am troubled that women are not admitted here. I may condition one of the contributions upon Trinity admitting women students. That way Trinity can accept the other two with no strings, but if it wants the third, it would have to admit women."

"I see," replied Crowell. "That could be an effective way of achieving your objective. How much were you planning to donate?"

"Three hundred thousand dollars."

Crowell replied, "That's a substantial amount of money, G. W. The college would be thrilled to receive such a donation. I don't know how all of the trustees would react to admitting women, though. I am fairly certain some of them will resist, but you might actually have a majority in your favor. You know it has been discussed on numerous occasions, and many trustees are in support."

Kilgo said, "If I am offered the presidency, I will support your proposal, G. W. I can't imagine that the trustees would turn it down."

"I will also offer my support as a past president. I think we just might be able to pass this through," Crowell said.[116]

---

116 This conversation is a fictional dramatization of the type of conversation that likely occurred between Washington Duke and members of Trinity College administration.

John C. Kilgo,[117] a well-known orator and Methodist minister, became president of Trinity in 1894, and his Methodist affiliation drew further attention from the Duke family. Trinity accepted the gifts with this condition and for the first time graduated female students in 1898. Thus, Trinity became one of the few colleges in the United States that admitted female students with the same rights and privileges as men, though the men and women's colleges remained separate. These endowments by Washington proved valuable to Trinity, though the aging man began to diminish his personal involvement in the college. As time passed, Ben became the primary liaison between the university and the Duke family.[118]

In 1903, Trinity became a center of controversy when Professor of History John S. Bassett published editorials challenging prevailing views on relations between blacks and whites. In 1902 Bassett had begun publishing the *South Atlantic Quarterly*, in which he frequently challenged prevailing views on race relations. In 1903, while a professor at Trinity, he published an article called "Stirring Up the Fires of Racial Antipathy,"[119] wherein he advocated improving race relations between African Americans and whites. Particularly troubling to many southerners was a comment at the end of the article wherein Bassett stated, "Booker T. Washington is the greatest man, save General Lee, born in the South in a hundred years." The article drew intense criticism from leaders of the Democratic Party, who launched a campaign demanding his termination. President Kilgo, former president Crowell, and many others

---

117 William E. King (Duke University Archivist, 1972–2002), *John C. Kilgo, 1861–1922, A Shirt Sleeve President*, David M. Rubenstein Rare Book and Manuscript Library, Duke University, 1997, reprinted from *If Gargoyles Could Talk, Sketches of Duke University*, by William E. King, Carolina Academic Press, 1997.
118 See King, *Duke University, A Brief Narrative History*, accessed September 22, 2013, http://library.duke.edu/uarchives/history/narrativehistory.html.
119 John Bassett, "Stirring Up the Fires of Racial Antipathy," *The South Atlantic Quarterly* 2, no. 4 (October 1903).

defended Bassett's right to academic freedom. Despite widespread appeals for his termination, the trustees of the university upheld his right to academic freedom, and Trinity became known as an institution of academic thought and scholarship where the free exchange of ideas was encouraged.

The school of engineering, established in 1903, was to become a separate institution in 1939, and in 1904 Trinity opened the law school, which has since become one of the world's foremost institutions of legal study. Trinity's reputation was further enhanced when Trinity became a founding member of the Association of Colleges and Preparatory Schools of the Southern States, and the law school became one of only two southern schools to obtain membership in the Institute of American Law Schools.[120]

When Washington Duke passed away in 1905,[121] his sons Buck and Benjamin took a much more active role in the university. In an effort to establish Trinity as a leading national university, faculty members were recruited from leading northern universities, and by the 1920s, Trinity was a nationally recognized liberal arts college. It was during the presidency of William Preston Few,[122] beginning in 1910, that the plans to build a major Methodist-related institution of higher education were fully realized. From 1910 until 1940, William Few led the university to international recognition and stature. It was largely the result of William Few's leadership and persuasive ability that Buck listened to his older brother Ben and Few's discussions of their vision for a great university.[123]

In 1924, James Buchanan Duke established the Duke

120 See King, *Duke University, A Brief Narrative History*, accessed September 22, 2013, http://library.duke.edu/uarchives/history/narrativehistory.html.
121 The death of Washington Duke will be discussed more fully in chapter 9.
122 William E. King (Duke University Archivist, 1972–2002), *William Preston Few, 1867–1940*, David M. Rubenstein Rare Book and Manuscript Library, Duke University, 1990, reprinted from *If Gargoyles Could Talk, Sketches of Duke University*, by William E. King, Carolina Academic Press, 1997.
123 See King, *Duke University, A Brief Narrative History*, accessed September 22, 2013, http://library.duke.edu/uarchives/history/narrativehistory.html.

Endowment, which consisted of a $40 million trust fund the income from which was to be distributed to hospitals, orphanages, the Methodist Church, three colleges, and Trinity College. William Few convinced Buck that Trinity College should be called Duke University after the great contributions of the Duke family, and because there were already many colleges named Trinity. Initially Buck resisted using the family name in the name of the university, out of concern that it would seem self-glorifying; but he eventually was persuaded, and the university became known as Duke University in 1924.[124] Upon the death of James Buchanan Duke in 1925, the Duke Endowment received an additional $67 million. The Duke Endowment estimates that these two contributions from James Buchanan Duke would be the equivalent of $1.4 billion today, when adjusted for inflation.[125]

In 1926 the School of Religion and the Graduate School began operation, with the Medical School following in 1930, the School of Nursing in 1931, and the School of Forestry in 1938. In 1930 the original campus in Durham became the Women's College, which reunited with Trinity College in 1972 as a liberal arts institution for both men and women. In 1934 Duke became a member of the Association of American Universities, and in 1969 Duke opened the Fuqua School of Business.[126]

In addition to academics, Duke soon became known as a top contender in athletics, with basketball the most widely recognized today. Basketball was introduced to Trinity by Wilbur Wade Card, Trinity's athletic director in 1906. Card was a member of the 1900 class and was known for his creative athletic spirit and willingness

---

124 See King, *Duke University, A Brief Narrative History*, accessed September 22, 2013, http://library.duke.edu/uarchives/history/narrativehistory.html.

125 *Ideas to Impact, 2012 Annual Report*, James B. Duke Endowment, accessed September 22, 2013, http://library.duke.edu/uarchives/history/narrativehistory.html.

126 See King, *Duke University, A Brief Narrative History*, accessed September 22, 2013, http://library.duke.edu/uarchives/history/narrativehistory.html.

to explore new methods of athletic competition. Trinity's first game, a loss to Wake Forest in 1906, was played in the Angier B. Duke Gymnasium, and Duke achieved its first title as state champion in 1920.[127] In 1953 Duke left the Southern Conference to become a charter member of the Atlantic Conference. Duke was a Final Four participant in 1963, and in 1974 Duke won its one thousandth game, a feat achieved by only seven other schools in the history of the NCAA.

Although not as popular as the basketball program today, the Duke University men's football team was once a leader in college football. Duke's football team, then known as the "Iron Dukes," had played the entire season in 1938 without having a single score against them in any game. Despite the great season, Duke suffered a heartbreaking 7-3 loss to USC in the Rose Bowl in Pasadena, California.[128] After the bombing of Pearl Harbor in 1941, the Department of Defense decided that crowds would not be permitted to assemble in large numbers on the West Coast for fear of another attack. For this reason, in 1942 Duke hosted the Rose Bowl at Wallace Wade Stadium at its campus in Durham. The opposing team was Oregon State, who defeated Duke 20–16.[129]

In addition to the football and basketball programs, Duke has enjoyed very successful programs in both men's and women's athletics. In contrast to the administration of some Ivy League universities, such as Harvard University, William Preston Few was a firm believer that mind, body, and soul are all important components of a fully developed individual and should all be part of a college program. For this reason, he supported scholarships for athletes, which many Ivy League universities refuse to do even to

---

127 *Inventory of the William Wade Card Papers, 1876–1943*, David M. Rubenstein Rare Book and Manuscript Library, Duke University.

128 Neal Morgan, "The Iron Dukes, So Close to Perfection in 1938," the *Chronicle*, October 6, 1999.

129 *The Durham Rose Bowl, 1942*, Duke University Archives, David M. Rubenstein Rare Book and Manuscript Library, Duke University.

this day. In large part, it may have been Duke's athletic programs, in combination with the academic programs, that accounted for the extremely rapid ascent of Duke in the world of academia.

It would be inaccurate to say that Duke University was built solely as a result of financial contributions from the Duke family, though clearly those contributions, along with the contributions of others, provided the financial resources that gave the administration the tools necessary to bring Duke to its widely recognized status today. In the final chapter of this book, we will briefly examine Duke University in the modern era. An institution of great pride for students, faculty, and alumni, Duke University is a product of the great dreams of many thoughtful and dedicated individuals. It would be interesting, indeed, to apply James Buchanan Duke's test for success to see what Duke University will become in another three hundred years.

9

The Passing of Washington Duke

As noted in the previous chapters, Washington Duke died on May 8, 1905, at the age of eighty-four. In January of that year he fell and broke his hip.[130] While the fall itself was not the immediate cause of death, it likely portended an issue with equilibrium which in turn was symptomatic of a serious health concern associated with aging.[131] In the years shortly before his death, Washington enjoyed conversations with college students and young professionals. He often visited the campus of Trinity College, where he was welcomed by faculty and students alike. Perhaps socializing with youth reminded him of a time in his own life when he was young and full of vigor. It was not uncommon for Washington to gather with students on campus for conversation, or to invite neighbors and acquaintances to rest on his lawn to read a book or to simply sit in the grass. This may have provided an opportunity for conver-

---

130   Durden, *The Dukes of Durham, 1865–1929*, 162–163.

131   Benign paroxysmal positional vertigo is a common cause of falling among the elderly. Annually, 20 to 40 percent of individuals over the age of sixty fall at home, and annually between 12 and 67 percent of elderly adults who fall and break a hip die within one year. The fall is often the result of a vestibular disorder. While the fall itself may not be the cause of death, the vestibular disorder may be secondary to a deteriorating health condition associated with aging. This is likely the cause of Washington's fall and subsequent death. See http://vestibular.org/node/10, accessed 12/5/13.

sation, which he enjoyed immensely. During this time he took the opportunity to assist the disadvantaged in establishing businesses, and he began to increase charitable giving to various institutions. A particular focus of his assistance and contributions was the African American community, which he believed deserved assistance in overcoming the negative effects of years of slavery. In this respect, he was perhaps one of the first persons in America to offer financial assistance to those disadvantaged by generations of slavery.

As Washington's wealth became widely known, he found himself increasingly contacted by distant relatives and others seeking financial assistance. Many of these solicitations were answered by his son Ben, who like his father, had a tendency to be quite generous. However, as the years wore on, the constant requests for financial assistance became a bit of a nuisance, and unless the request was for a legitimate cause, it would likely receive a polite letter of declination or, in some instances, no response at all. Washington found refreshing the unusual occasion where he would receive a salutation from a relative who was not requesting money but simply offering a word of encouragement or exchanging a greeting.

The entire city of Durham mourned when Washington died. He was liked by nearly everyone who knew him, and those who did not know him personally knew of him. In life he was generous. Perhaps not completely comfortable with testamentary bequests, he gave away the bulk of his estate while still living.[132] His will left most of his estate to charities, his children, and nieces and nephews. But perhaps his greatest bequest was of humility and charity, which he left to everyone who knew him and those who would learn about him.

A well-attended memorial service was held in Washington's honor at Trinity College on June 4, 1905. John C. Kilgo delivered the address.[133] After his death, the family received numerous sugges-

---

132 Durden, *The Dukes of Durham, 1865–1929*, 183.
133 Ibid., 162.

tions of ways to honor Washington, most of which were intended to glorify the proponent, and thus were politely declined. Perhaps if the suggestions had accurately reflected the spirit of Washington as a boy and later as a young man who remained steadfast in his opposition to slavery, and as a person who put human dignity and honor above all things, the suggested memorials would have captured the imaginations of Buck and Ben, who wished their father to be recognized in the most respectable manner. Of the memorials to Washington, several of the most significant were made two decades after his death. One of them was the renaming of Main Street Methodist Church, which Washington cofounded in 1885. In 1907 the church relocated to a property adjacent to Benjamin Duke's mansion on Four Acres in downtown Durham and was renamed Memorial Methodist Church. In 1925 the church was renamed Duke Memorial Methodist Church, more explicitly honoring Washington Duke.[134]

A second memorial to Washington was a statue of Washington sitting in an armchair, which was erected on the campus of Trinity College in 1908.[135] To this day the statue of Washington captures the attention of photographers, students, faculty, and admirers of the campus.

Another important memorial to Washington was the Duke Memorial Chapel, where the remains of Washington, Ben, and Buck rest today in three sarcophagi.[136] The memorial chapel is located within the greater Duke Chapel, also named after Washington and located on the Duke University campus.

Perhaps the most significant memorial to Washington was the renaming of Trinity College to Duke University. The suggestion, originally made by Trinity president William Preston Few, initially faced opposition by both Ben and Buck. However, after hearing

---

134 Durden, *The Dukes of Durham, 1865–1929*, 163.
135 Ibid., 164.
136 Ibid., 259.

the persuasive arguments by President Few, Ben and Buck were persuaded, and Trinity College became known as Duke University in 1924.[137]

The legacy started by Washington nearly two hundred years ago remains a lasting monument to the generosity and kindness of this man. From his humble beginning as an infant on December 18, 1820, twelve miles outside of Hillsboro, North Carolina, Washington grew to become a man whose never-ending goal was to bring fortune and opportunity to others. His life is a testament to the truth that regardless of the obstacles one faces, great achievements are attainable. In that respect, he serves as an inspiration to others that with patience, perseverance, hard work, and integrity, goals are achievable often beyond one's wildest imagination. His life is further evidence that no matter the level of success attained, one can still reach across social and racial barriers and remain a friend to everyone. Throughout his life Washington maintained friendships with people most would have considered beneath his social class, because to Washington social class was immaterial. When Washington passed, the world lost a truly great man, but he left a light shining in Durham—a light that today can be seen throughout the world. Today we call that light the Duke legacy.

---

137 Durden, *The Dukes of Durham, 1865–1929*, 221.

Part 2
The Story of Doris Duke

10

The Richest Little Girl in the World

In 1925, thirteen-year-old Doris Duke inherited $100 million and became known as the "richest little girl in the world."[138] Doris Duke was the only child of James Buchanan Duke, the philanthropist who donated $107 million to the Duke Endowment, which has subsequently given over $3 billion in charitable contributions to various academic institutions and other organizations, and currently has a corpus of nearly $3 billion.[139] Doris Duke died in 1993 without surviving issue, thus ending a very short progeny from her father, James Buchanan Duke.

On November 22, 1912, Doris Duke was born to James Buchanan Duke and his wife Nanaline Holt Inman Duke. Nanaline, a widow from a prior marriage to Will Inman, a successful cotton trader from Atlanta, Georgia, had grown up in a prominent plantation family in the South that had survived the Civil War. She attended Branham School and Wesleyan Female College, where she learned the social graces of young ladies as they existed in the early

---

138 "Reclusive Heiress Doris Duke Dies at Age 80," *Chicago Tribune*, October 28, 1993.

139 "Ideas to Impact, 2012 Annual Report," James B. Duke Endowment, accessed September 22, 2013, http://annualreport.dukeendowment.org/2012/.

twentieth century.[140] The liabilities facing a single woman then, even one with means, presented an uncertain course—particularly for someone in Nanaline's situation; she had a son, Walker Inman, from her prior marriage.

After his unsuccessful marriage to Lillian McCredy, which ended in divorce upon discovery of her infidelity, Buck hoped to find someone with whom he could have a successful marriage. While vacationing at a resort in North Carolina, his brother Ben and his wife, Sarah, met a young widow named Nanaline Holt Inman. They were impressed by her refined presentation—so much so that they believed she might be a respectable prospect for Buck, whom they introduced to her in New York.[141] Unlike his brother Ben, who was known as a man of moderation and discipline, Buck never ceased in his quest for pleasure and seldom paused long enough to develop a meaningful relationship with a woman. In this fashion he spent his youth, such that by the time he opted for a conventional household, he was well along in his years. Yet he longed for a meaningful relationship and a concomitant, successful marriage such as the one he observed in his brother's marriage to Sarah. Buck and Nanaline were married on July 23, 1907, with a private, quiet ceremony.[142] While the marriage was not as blissful as Buck had hoped, he did find a meaningful relationship with their only child, Doris.

Doris Duke, in life, synthesized tragedy and happiness. As a child, her happiness was found in evening conversations with her father and in business trips to various locations with her cousin Angier Duke, Ben's son. Buck, Angier, and Doris spent much time together with Angier acting more in the capacity of an older brother to Doris than a cousin. On a warm late-May afternoon, as they traveled down a gravel road from New York City to Duke Farms

---

140 Pony Duke and Jason Thomas, *Too Rich: The Family Secrets of Doris Duke* (New York: Harper Collins, 1996), 31.

141 Durden, *The Dukes of Durham, 1865–1929*, 170.

142 Ibid., 170–171.

in New Jersey, eight-year-old Doris leaned out the left rear window of her father's 1921 red Cadillac Victoria. Her father, Buck, was driving, and her cousin Angier sat in the right-front passenger seat.

"This has a ninety-degree V-8 L-head engine with cast iron blocks on an aluminum crankcase. This particular vehicle has a one-hundred-thirty-two-inch wheelbase, which I special ordered to achieve greater stability in the turns," Buck said as he gently rocked the vehicle by quickly moving the steering wheel back and forth.

"I like it," Angier replied. "It seems stable and solid."

"I'm glad you both like the car, but I'm getting sick," said Doris, who leaned out of the window in an effort to forget her motion sickness.

"Why don't we pull over and take a short break from driving?" said Angier. "I think Doris is feeling ill."

Buck took his foot off the accelerator. "That would be a good idea."

"So if you were me, you would consider divorce, is that right?" asked Angier. Angier was referring to his marriage with Cordelia Biddle Duke. Cordelia was the daughter of Anthony and Cordelia Biddle, a prominent family from Philadelphia. Angier and Cordelia were said to have enjoyed a fairy-tale romance that later provided the basis for a Disney movie called *The Happiest Millionaire*. Cordelia and Angier were married in April 1915, when Cordelia was seventeen and Angier thirty-one.[143] Angier and Cordelia separated in 1918, though they maintained a close relationship even after the separation.

Buck downshifted the three-speed manual transmission and placed his right foot on the brake as he drove the vehicle over to the right side of the road. "I really can't tell you what you should or shouldn't do. A man has to make his own decisions in such serious matters as marriage and divorce. The only thing I can say is that someday you will look back at your life and you will ask, 'Have I done everything I can to bring happiness to myself and others?'

---

143 Durden, *The Dukes of Durham, 1865–1929*, 175.

When you answer that question, you will know if you have done the right thing today."

"It is a difficult decision for me," Angier replied.

"Why would it be difficult?" asked Buck. "If you don't want to be together anymore then why does it matter?"

"Actually," replied Angier, "getting a divorce is a very difficult and painful thing."

Doris jumped quickly from the vehicle as it came to a stop, and she ran to the side of the road. Motion sickness had troubled her since she was a very young child. Even an elevator ride could cause her to experience nausea. While Buck and Angier sat in the vehicle waiting for Doris to rejoin them, Buck said, "I wish I could divorce Nanaline. Sometimes I believe she stays with me only for my money. How did I ever get stuck with such a woman?"

"Why do you stay with her?"

"I stay with her for Doris. She is not very good to Doris, but even so, I think a broken home would be even worse. I believe she hates me. I think that she would love to see me dead so she could take my estate and find a younger man. I made some changes to my estate plan, though Nanaline doesn't know about it. If I die before Nanaline, she will only get a life estate in several homes and an allowance of one hundred thousand dollars per year. Doris, the Duke Endowment, and Duke University will inherit the bulk of my estate. Don't say anything to Doris. I don't want her to know."

"You have basically disinherited Nanaline," said Angier as he poured a glass of water from the water jug.

"In a manner of speaking, I suppose that is true," Buck replied. "I have employees who earn more than she will earn if I predecease her. I want to make sure she has no control over Doris. I want you to take care of Doris, Angier, if something should happen to me before Doris is grown. That way Nanaline will not dare abuse her. She is harsh with the children. That is the reason I keep Doris with me all day long. Tell me, why do you want to get a divorce from Cordelia? She always seems to treat you well."

"I don't really want to, and she does treat me well. She has done nothing wrong. It is just that I feel that I married too young. There were too many things that I wanted to experience, and I did not have an opportunity before I married. I just want to be free again. We have been separated for three years now. Maybe someday I would come back to Cordelia. It isn't that I don't love her; I just want some space." Angier paused as he looked sadly out of the passenger window. "Why did you talk about something happening to you? Is something wrong?"

"Your father knows about it, but I have told no one else. I have been having chest pain. The doctor believes that I have a heart condition. He said I have to lose weight or I could die from a stroke. A doctor from New York said he believes it could be the result of smoking cigars for so many years."

"Dad mentioned to me that he was concerned about your health, but he didn't say why. Does Nanaline know about your heart condition?"

"No, I have been especially cautious to keep this information from her as well as Doris."

Just as Buck finished his sentence, Doris ran back to the car. "Daddy, I saw a snake. It was scary."

"Did it come toward you?" Angier asked.

"No, but it was big. I only saw it for a second in the grass over there."

"Well, as long as you don't marry him, I think you will be okay," Buck said, winking at Doris as she climbed back into the car.

"Marry him? Why would I marry a snake?" Doris asked with grin. She knew well her father's sense of humor.

Angier laughed and then quickly became serious again. "How long have you been having these chest pains?" he asked quietly as they pulled back out onto the highway.

"About six months."

"What did your doctor do?"

"Oh, he gave me some kind of pill and said that I am to take it whenever my chest starts to hurt. He called it a nitro boost."

"What are you talking about, Daddy?" asked Doris, who had heard only a small portion of the conversation.

"Oh, it's nothing you have to worry about, sweetie."

Doris leaned back in the seat and fell asleep as she watched the orange late-afternoon sun gently caress the grassy fields in the western New Jersey sky over her father's farm—a farm that extended in all directions as far as the eye could see.

The following morning, Doris and her father returned to the Duke mansion on the corner of Fifth Avenue and 1 East Seventy-Eighth Street. As they came into the house, they found Nanaline still asleep in the master bedroom. She did not awaken when Doris said, "Hi, Mommy. Daddy and I had a nice trip with Angier."

Doris and her father went back into the library, where they would often sit and talk for hours. "What were you and Angier saying about your heart when I got back into the car yesterday?" she asked her father.

"Oh, nothing, sweetie," said Buck as he lifted Doris onto his lap.

Doris leaned back and rested her head on his shoulder. "Are you okay, Daddy? I am scared something is wrong."

"Don't worry, baby; Daddy is fine," said Buck as Nanaline walked up to the door, looked into the library at Doris and Buck, and then smiled and waved.

"How was your trip?" asked Nanaline.

"It went well," replied Buck. "We accomplished quite a bit."

"Mommy, I saw a snake," said Doris excitedly.

"You saw a snake?" asked Nanaline.

"Yes, and Daddy said that is okay as long as I don't marry it."

Buck laughed as Nanaline looked at him with an inquisitive expression and then walked away.

In June 1921, Cordelia Biddle Duke filed for divorce after a three-year separation from Angier. Subsequent to the divorce, Angier began spending more time with his friends, often staying out late, especially in the warm months. On September 3, 1923, Angier and his friends were enjoying a late-night party at a yacht club in Connecticut. While playing in a rowboat docked near his yacht, Angier lost his footing. Apparently, in the fall from the boat he struck his head and was rendered unconscious. Despite the efforts of his friends, who were also tossed into the water, Angier could not be located in the darkness and drowned.[144] Doris was only ten years of age at the time. This, her first exposure to loss of life in her close family, and in a peculiar fashion the precursor to the death of her father, James Buchanan Duke, two years later, presented her first experience with severe grief.

After Angier died, Benjamin, Sarah, Buck, and Doris each experienced emotional depression. Buck loved Angier very much and was as close to him as a father would be to a son. The event was deeply troubling for Benjamin and Sarah, Angier's parents, who both cried bitterly upon hearing the news, and it was equally devastating for Doris.[145] She indeed saw Angier as her big brother. She could not imagine life without him. Doris had believed that they would be together like brother and sister for the rest of her life. The reality is that if Angier had survived, things might have turned out differently for Doris. Buck had planned that Angier would become the chief executive officer of the Duke financial empire, but it was unclear who would undertake this task now that Angier was gone.[146] This was a position that Buck felt should pass to his male heir, or an heir of his brother, since women were not afforded the respect and deference men enjoyed in the early twentieth century. While Buck would have been content for Doris to assume the position of control, in the 1920s women were not respected in the business world, which meant that Doris would be facing adversity and confrontation throughout her life. Now neither he nor his

---

144 Duke and Thomas, *Too Rich*, 55–56.
145 Ibid., 56–57.
146 Ibid., 46, 57.

brother Ben had a male heir of sufficient age to whom control of the empire could pass, should Buck die prematurely. This troubled Buck greatly given his fear that Nanaline would somehow manage to acquire the estate and relegate Doris to a position inferior to that of Walker Inman, Nanaline's son by her prior marriage.

One evening as they talked in the library at the Fifth Avenue Duke home, Doris asked her father, "Why did Angier have to die? Why would God allow something like that to happen?"

"I don't know," replied Buck, who felt helpless to answer his daughter's question. "Angier was a good man."

"Uncle Ben says that God loves all of us very much. If that is true, why would he allow Angier to die?"

"We can't really say," replied Buck. "These are the mysteries of God, but it's important to remember that God always knows what's best. It is important to remember that Angier is only gone from us for now. His spirit lives on. He is still with us; we just can't see him and hear him."

"Do you really believe in God, Daddy?"

"Absolutely I do. There are some who say that all that exists in the world today was caused by chance. I believe that is nonsense, and I don't believe that anyone really believes that. It is just a trendy thing to say. In a trillion years, all that exists around us could not possibly have come to be solely by chance. There has to be a divine order to things. This I know. Maybe I do not have the kind of relationship with God that Ben and Sarah have, but I have a different kind of relationship with God, and I know he understands me. I hope and pray that you will have your own relationship with God too." Buck paused for a moment and then continued. "In the past several days, I kept asking myself if I could have been a better role model for Angier. He always looked up to me and emulated all of my actions. I think it was heartbreaking for your Uncle Ben, who wanted Angier to be more like him. In many ways Angier was like Ben, but he was also like me. Ben knew that I have always lived on the wild side a little bit, but he would never say anything, because Ben never criticizes anyone. I just wonder if I could have given Angier a better example of what he could have been. Could I have been a better role model? I hope I am a good role model for you, Doris."

"It isn't your fault that Angier died, Daddy. It was an accident."

"I know I didn't cause the accident, but is there something more I could have done to prevent it?" Buck replied. "If I had been a better role model, maybe he would have stayed married to Cordelia and would have been home with her instead of out on the boat that night."

"I don't understand. Even if he was still married to Cordelia, he still could have had an accident. I think you are just blaming yourself for something that wasn't your fault."

Buck didn't say anything. He looked away toward the window as he fought back his tears. Doris was quiet for a few minutes as she thought about her father's words, and she then asked, "Will we ever see Angier again?"

"We will see him when we get to heaven," replied Buck. Doris began to cry as she fell asleep on her father's lap as she often had in the past. On this night the pain seemed much more severe than usual.

The death of James Buchanan Duke, on October 10, 1925, when Doris was only thirteen years of age, was the second great tragedy in her life. According to some of the servants in the house at the time, Nanaline had caused his death by pulling the covers off his bed on a freezing October afternoon and then ordering the servants to turn off the heat in the house and to open the windows to the bedroom where Buck was recovering from a stroke.[147] She reportedly explained that fresh air was very important for an ill patient and that Buck needed fresh air. Doris later reported that the last thing she ever heard her father say to her, before she was or-

---

147 Duke and Thomas, *Too Rich*, 62–63.

dered out of the room by her mother, was that she should not trust anyone, especially those who say they love her.[148] Believing that Nanaline really wanted only his money, and having faced infidelity with Lillian, Buck was jaded with distrust for every woman who said she loved him. Buck assumed that Doris would have this same problem with men as she matured, and he warned her, perhaps to her detriment, not to trust any man who said he loved her.[149]

On the day of the death of James Buchanan Duke, Nanaline allegedly sat beside his bed wearing a full-length sable coat, covered in several other sable coats, as his body temperature dropped so low that he went into hypothermia and died.[150] The official cause of death was determined to be pneumonia.[151] Nanaline had ordered that Buck have no visitors that night, and Doris waited outside the room while Nanaline sat next to Buck's bed.[152] Who knows what she may have said to Buck in those last hours of his life as he lay paralyzed on the bed, shivering from the cold. It is with ironic tragedy that many years later Doris would suffer a similarly lonely isolated death.

When Buck expired, Nanaline walked out of the room and threw the sable coat at Doris, saying as she walked past her, "Your father is dead."[153] Should Nanaline have been considered a person of interest, or even a suspect, in a homicide investigation? Perhaps today that would be the case; however, in 1925, super-rich families were generally "above the law" and dealt with such issues in their own way. The circumstances surrounding the death of Buck drove a wedge between Doris and Nanaline that would never be removed. Even in death, her mother flung a hurtful message to Doris. The sable coat Nanaline wore while she sat at Buck's deathbed, which

---

148 Duke and Thomas, *Too Rich*, 63.
149 Ibid., 62–64.
150 Ibid., 63.
151 Durden, *The Dukes of Durham, 1865–1929*, 246.
152 Duke and Thomas, *Too Rich*, 63.
153 Ibid.

she subsequently threw at Doris after her father had died, is all she left to Doris in her estate plan.[154] Notwithstanding the allegations made against Nanaline by servants and Duke family members, it is important to recognize that several days before his death, his brother Ben had accepted that Buck would probably not recover from his illness.[155]

Buck's body was returned to Durham for the funeral and burial. The funeral was held at Duke Memorial Methodist Church, which his father had cofounded in 1885.[156] The entire city of Durham mourned. Businesses and schools closed, and thousands of people lined to streets for the funeral procession. Over a thousand Duke University students formed the honor guard, and members of the Duke University men's football team served as pallbearers.[157] Buck was originally buried at Maplewood Cemetery, with his father Washington and his brother Brodie.[158] Both Washington and Buck were later moved to Duke Chapel at Duke University, where they remain today.

When she finally learned of the provisions of James Buchanan Duke's trust, Nanaline was stunned to find that he had only left her a life estate in houses in New York, North Carolina, and Newport, and an income of $100,000 per year.[159] Suddenly, Doris, with a $100 million inheritance, was more powerful than her mother, and it was this power that some believe that may have saved Doris from

---

154 Duke and Thomas, *Too Rich*, 62–63; for an in-depth account of Nanaline Holt Inman Duke and her relationship with James and Doris Duke, see Pony Duke and Jason Thomas, *Too Rich, The Family Secrets of Doris Duke* (New York: Harper Collins, 1996).

155 Letter from Ben Duke to R. L. Flowers, October 7, 1925, Ben Duke Papers, David M. Rubenstein Rare Book and Manuscript Library, Duke University Archives.

156 Durden, *The Dukes of Durham, 1865–1929*, 246.

157 Duke and Thomas, *Too Rich*, 64.

158 Ibid.

159 Last Will and Testament and Codicil of James B. Duke, Inventory of James Buchanan Duke Papers, 1777–1990 and undated, 1924–1925, Box 13, David M. Rubenstein Rare Book and Manuscript Library, Duke University.

physical abuse. But it did not save her from a strained relationship with her mother that was to last until her mother's death in 1962. Shortly after her father's death in 1925, Doris and Nanaline were adversaries in a lawsuit over the proper disposition of Buck's estate.

With Buck's death, Doris lost her father, friend, and mentor. Her mother—whose true focus of attention was Doris's half-brother, Walker Inman—demonstrated an open dislike for Doris. Instead of the love and affection that she had received from her father until his death, Doris suffered the scorn, ridicule, disdain, hurtful comments, and innuendos from her mother. This emotional abuse was far greater than any child should ever endure, and it left emotional scars and a fear of attachment that would last a lifetime.

It was known among the servants and family members that Doris and her father had enjoyed a very close relationship. In her young childhood, Buck would play with her for hours on end. As she got older and became more interested in conversation, Doris would sit with her father in the library of their Fifth Avenue mansion and talk with him until late in the evening hours. Sometimes she would play jazz pieces on the piano and he would sing along, tapping his foot on the floor. It was commonly known that Buck had cautioned her from his deathbed that she should never trust anyone and that many men would love her only for her money. These words of caution, perhaps overstated, impressed deeply upon Doris and became a self-fulfilling prophecy that caused her to build a wall around herself to prevent others from getting close to her.

A third tragedy befell Doris when her uncle Benjamin Newton Duke passed away in January 1929, four years after his younger brother, Buck. Like Buck, Ben was a benefactor of education, donating $3 million[160] to institutions of higher learning from 1926 through 1929. However, while increasing his philanthropic activities, his health deteriorated. In a deep expression of friendship,

---

160 Durden, *The Dukes of Durham, 1865–1929*, 251. The value of $3 million in 1929 would be approximately $30 million today.

Duke University President William Preston Few regularly wrote status reports to Ben, keeping him abreast of the construction of Duke University.[161] By 1927 buildings on East Campus were occupied and construction had begun on the West Campus. These communications from Few about the development brought immeasurable happiness to Ben in his last days.

Ben died in his New York home on January 29, 1929.[162] His last days were spent in the company of his beloved wife Sarah; he recorded many of the events that took place during this time in his diary.[163] After he passed, a memorial in his honor was not immediately constructed, though Duke Chapel became a memorial to Washington and both of his sons, all three of whom were buried in sarcophagi in the chapel. Finally, in 1999, a bronze statue of Ben was constructed on Duke University campus. The statue holds a cane in one hand and a hat in the other.[164] Ben's leadership in the construction and development of the early years of Duke will never be forgotten. After the death of her husband, Sarah continued her support of Duke University. She died in 1936, just seven years after Ben. In her honor, and to signify her love of nature and beauty, the Sarah P. Duke Gardens were established on the Duke University Campus and today remain one of the most cherished features of the campus.

The loss of all of her support family members was devastating for Doris. Perhaps this was the inevitable consequence of being born so late in the life her father. In a span of eleven years she lost Angier, Buck, Ben, and Sarah. These were the only people who had ever given her true family support until that point in her life. Suddenly they were all gone. Given the alienation from her mother, Doris was essentially on her own from the age of twelve. Loyalty for Doris could only be found in those who worked for her. Sadly,

---

161   Durden, *The Dukes of Durham, 1865–1929*, 251.

162   Ibid., 255.

163   Ibid., 256.

164   *Benjamin Newton Duke, Duke University*, Commemorative Landscapes, accessed December 27, 2013, http://docsouth.unc.edu/commland/monument/221/.

the only way Doris could protect herself was to have some form of control over those around her. This was the life she would live from the age of twelve until her last days, from 1991 through 1993, which she spent at Falcon Lair in Beverly Hills, California.

One might think that as Doris reached her dating years, her mother would have shared this happy time with her daughter. Although Doris was a very attractive young woman, her mother constantly informed her that she lacked physical beauty and that she could not expect a man to fall in love with her solely for herself. Thus, Nanaline said, the only man she would ever marry would be one who wanted her for her money. Nanaline appeared to capitalize on the warning Doris's father had given her and used it as a tool of ridicule and abuse. Nanaline did not share in the joy and excitement of Doris coming of age and did not assist Doris in finding eligible young men for dating. She engaged only in the minimal activities expected of the super-rich in assisting her daughter in finding a reasonable suitor, such as hosting a coming-out party of young people the age of Doris. For the most part, Doris was left to her own social skills, as deficient as they were, to find an eligible young man.

Left to her own devices in social relationships, Doris developed an introversion at a young age, which some have mistakenly interpreted as lack of interest. An example of this may be found in a young man named Jason, a college student who worked at Duke Farms in New Jersey during the summer months to earn tuition money. On a warm, breezy summer afternoon Doris sat on the back porch of her New Jersey home at Duke Farms. The seventeen-year-old girl looked up from her book on gardening. Peering through her sunglasses, she saw a young man tending the garden. The servants had told her he was a college student majoring in biology, with a specialty in botany, who was working in the garden for the summer. *He is quite handsome*, thought Doris, quietly hoping he would notice her book on gardening.

As he cut the shrub near her chair, he looked at her with a smile and said, "Excuse me, Miss Duke."

"It's okay," she replied softly with hidden nervousness. *He probably thinks I am unfriendly. I want to talk to him, but I dare not say anything. He would think me forward.*

After seeing each other every day for nearly two weeks, the only communication between Doris and this young man remained simple greetings. In time, Doris had grown to appreciate his physical appearance and became convinced that he was indeed the most handsome young man she had ever seen. One day she mustered the courage to inquire about his interest in gardening. Over the next few days they began having short conversations that seldom lasted more than a few minutes. As Doris hoped, the young student eventually noticed the book about gardening that Doris had been reading for weeks. One day he asked, "I noticed you are reading about gardening. Do you like gardening?"

"I love it," Doris replied. "I think I could spend the rest of my life gardening."

"Miss Duke, do you ever go out to the movies or anything like that? I mean, if you don't mind me asking."

"I don't really. Why do you ask?"

The young college student put down his garden rake and walked over to Doris. "I thought that maybe we could go to a movie sometime."

Doris did not know how to respond. *I'm not ready to date,* she thought to herself. *I am only seventeen years old, and while no one would tell me I can't go out with him, I need to be ready first. I really do want to go out with him.* Doris pulled down her sunglasses and peered at the young man over the top of the frame for a few seconds. She then said, "It is difficult for me to get time away. I have to oversee the businesses. But I appreciate the offer." In reality she wanted to say, "I would love to go out with you," but she was so nervous she could not say the words she wanted to say.

"I understand, Miss Duke; I should have known that. I am sorry for asking."

The truth is that the young man was actually very interested in Doris. He found her very attractive but was intimidated by the substantial difference in their social statuses and their ages. He went home for the weekend and decided to leave his job early in the summer and spend a few weeks at home with his parents. In reality, he was terribly disappointed and embarrassed that he had asked Doris for a date, given that her response caused him to feel that he had violated some sacred unwritten law about social class. In reality, Doris wanted to accept his invitation very much and planned to do so the next time she saw him. That time did not ever arrive. She never saw him again.

Perhaps it was this nervousness and uncertainty in relationships that prevented Doris from befriending the young man who had become the object of her admiration and affection. Perhaps if her father had survived to explain to her the protocol of social interaction with members of the opposite gender, he might have provided insight into methods by which she could develop a relationship with this young man without violating early twentieth-century mores. Perhaps, with his understanding of humility, he would have suggested that she offer him a glass of iced tea on a hot day and then ask about his studies and aspirations. Or Buck might have invited the young man into the house for conversation on an occasion when Doris was present to participate. Unfortunately the young college student, who never learned of her affection, slipped silently out of her life, as so many of her friends and family members would do throughout her life.[165]

Despite allegations by some that Doris Duke was lacking in emotion, accounts of events in her life suggest that she was actually a deeply passionate woman who simply wanted someone who

---

165 The account of the college student is a dramatization of a story that has frequently been told about Doris during the young years of her life. Another account of this story is found in Duke and Thomas, *Too Rich*, 68–69.

would love her unconditionally and not because of her money. Unfortunately, though, it appears that she was so afraid of attachment that she would generally not stay in a relationship long enough to allow unconditional love to develop. One account of this characteristic comes from Washington, DC, attorney Jeffrey Duke Southmayd, whose maternal uncle was named Robert Wilkinson Duke. According to Southmayd, his uncle, a Shakespearian actor living in New York City, met Doris when they were both quite young, at a cocktail party. Doris was intrigued with the idea of a chance meeting with someone in public who shared the surname Duke. They developed a friendship and for months met several times per week at a club for an afternoon of conversation.

As they became more acquainted, Doris asked Robert how they were related. He replied that he did not know. She said, "Tell me your earliest known ancestor, and I will find out for you." He disclosed the information requested and then did not see her for several weeks. One day she entered the club with a disturbed expression on her face. She seemed unusually quiet. When he asked what was troubling her, she said that she had found out how they were related. When he pressed her for the answer, she said that he was part of the family she was forbidden to see.

The young man protested. "What do you mean 'forbidden to see'? You are a grown woman. You can see anyone you want to see."

She turned and looked into his eyes as she replied tearfully, "I am so sorry." With that she abruptly got up from her barstool and left the club. He never saw her again.

Many years later the much older man said to his nephew, "I don't know what it was all about. I simply believe that she couldn't cope with the emotional stress of getting close to someone, and that was her way of ending a relationship that looked like it might develop into a romantic relationship."[166]

---

166 This story was related to me in January 2000 by Washington, DC, attorney Jeffrey Duke Southmayd.

Photograph of Doris Duke
Doris Duke Photograph Collection, David M. Rubenstein
Rare Book and Manuscript Library, Duke University

Left primarily to her own devices to find an eligible bachelor, Doris focused her attention on physical appearance. She seemed attracted to men who shared her fear of emotional attachment. Her boyfriends included such men as Errol Flynn, General George Patton, Alec Cunningham-Reid, Pulitzer Prize–winning fiction writer Louis Bromfield, and Olympic swimmer Duke Kahanamoku.

Doris had two marriages. Her first marriage, in 1935, at the age of twenty-two years, was to Jimmy Cromwell. Previously married to Delphine Dodge, heiress to the automobile fortune and Dodge Motorcar Company, Jimmy's attempt to invest Delphine's money, and the money of their friends, resulted in financial disaster.[167] Delphine eventually divorced Jimmy, whose family fortune was lost shortly thereafter in the stock market crash of 1929.[168] Doris was attracted to Jimmy's handsome appearance, and they were married in 1935. While still on the honeymoon, she discovered that his family had lost their fortune, and it became apparent that his motivation for marrying Doris was solely to obtain financial support for his political career. Jimmy had planned to run for the US Senate and obtain support for the vice presidency and ultimately the presidency. He was far too obvious with his intentions, and as a result, to Doris, he appeared arrogant and foolish. Doris was reminded of the deathbed warning from her father not to trust anyone who says he loves her, because he would only want her money. Jimmy had proved himself untruthful, and Doris saw this as a fulfillment of her father's prophetic warning. He soon became a constant embarrassment to Doris, who was not interested in pretending to be something she was not. Finally, in 1942, Doris received a divorce in Reno, Nevada, despite Jimmy's claim that they were residents of New Jersey. Although the case remained in the appellate courts for several years, ultimately the

---

167 Duke and Thomas, *Too Rich*, 77.
168 Ibid.

judgment was upheld.[169] Doris's second marriage was to come several years later.

In between her two marriages she had several failed relationships, but two that were particularly noteworthy for Doris were her relationships with Olympic swimmer Duke Kahanamoku and fiction writer Louis Bromfield. Of the men with whom Doris developed a romantic relationship, Duke Kahanamoku and Louis Bromfield were the only ones she felt genuinely cared for her and not her money. On July 11, 1940, she gave birth to a premature daughter while living in Hawaii that was said to be the daughter of Duke Kahanamoku.[170] Doris was devastated and blamed herself for the premature delivery, which she felt resulted from surfing while pregnant. Doris named the child Arden. Doris's doctors then informed her that she would never again bear children. Arden lived for only one day. This was another great loss in the life of Doris, and one from which she never recovered.

In 1943, Doris Duke found herself in the Middle East, leaning on a counter at a canteen, looking into the eyes of a man named Douglas. The richest woman in the world was working as a waitress at a canteen for US servicemen in Egypt. Already fluent in nine languages, she said to the young man the familiar Arabic greeting "As-salaam alaikum," which means, "Peace be upon you."

"Ah, salami me likem you too, my beautiful one," chuckled the young sailor, who had only introduced himself as Doug.

"So you are a comedian?" She laughed. "How long have you been in this desert?"

"It seems like forever. I think I will be here for at least three years."

"How did you wind up here at this naval post?" Doris put a piece of salami on a large piece of rye bread and covered it with

---

169 Glenn Fowler, "James HR Cromwell Dies at 93," *New York Times*, March 23, 1990.

170 Duke and Thomas, *Too Rich*, 116.

mayonnaise, tomato, onions, pickles, cheese, lettuce, and mustard, and she then passed it across the counter to Douglas.

Doug slid a dollar bill across the counter to Doris. "I was stationed here temporarily, but now it seems permanent. What is your name?"

"Doris," she replied.

"Well, Doris, I would certainly enjoy taking you to dinner this evening if you can free yourself from this counter."

Doris provided change and laughed. "Well, I could go with you, but I think we would only get into trouble."

"Oh, come on. Who told you that? I am an altar boy." Doug smiled.

That evening they walked into a small restaurant in Giza. As they were shown their table by the waiter, she asked, "Doug, what do you plan to do when you are out of the navy?"

"I don't know if I will ever leave the military. I think the military might be my life."

"Do you know what I would do if I were a military commander in the Far East?" asked Doris.

"What would you do?"

"I would use the navy to secure various islands in the South Pacific. Then I would bring in the army to reinforce the islands and provide military education to the local islanders who seek their freedom from the Japanese military regime."

"Who would provide this military education?"

"It would be some kind of US intelligence agency."

"You know about the Office of Strategic Services, don't you?" asked Doug. Doris did not reply but looked at him with a smile.

"How do you know about that? The information about the OSS is highly classified."

"Don't worry about how I know. I will tell you, though, that I will see you in the Philippines."

Doug laughed. "You are a very intriguing woman. Somehow I think you know what you are talking about."

Doris and Doug saw each other every night for nearly three weeks. One day he stopped by the canteen to visit with Doris during lunch. A young woman came out to the counter he had not seen before. "Who are you?" he asked.

"My name is Mary."

"Where is Doris? She is usually here."

"Doris is gone," Mary replied.

"Gone? Where did she go?"

"You really don't know, do you? I thought she would have told you. She took a job working as a correspondent for the International News Service."

"You're kidding," he replied. "I saw her last night, and she didn't say a word about that. I didn't even know she could write. If she could write well enough to work for the International News Service, why was she working here in this canteen?"

"She was really a volunteer here. Actually, she worked here for one dollar per year."

"One dollar per year? How did she support herself?"

Mary began laughing. "How does she support herself? Don't you know who she is?"

"Yes, she is Doris Duke."

Mary did not reply but instead just looked at Douglas with a smile and nodded.

Douglas laughed. "What? Why are you looking at me like that?"

"Have you never heard of Doris Duke?"

Doug looked at her with a blank expression for a few seconds and then asked, "You don't mean Doris Duke the tobacco heiress?"

Mary just nodded and laughed.

"You mean to tell me that the girl I have been hanging out with over the past three weeks is the richest woman in the world?"

"Yes. She doesn't like people to know, because they treat her differently when they find out."

"She could have at least told me she was leaving."

"She was probably afraid you would ask too many questions and figure out who she is," Mary replied. "Don't worry; I know she likes you. You'll see her again."

Mary was correct. Doris contacted Doug again, and they developed a friendship that lasted for many years.[171]

In 1944, Doris enlisted in the United Seamen's Service and received an assignment of entertaining the troops as a musician.[172] Doris, a talented pianist, felt a deep compassion for the servicemen and found this an opportunity to lift their spirits before they were deployed to the battlefield, from which many of them would never return. However, not fully satisfied with the role of an entertainer, Doris decided to become a spy. She contacted General William Donovan, the director of the Office of Strategic Services, which was the predecessor of the Central Intelligence Agency, who hired her despite protests from a number of military officers.[173] As a female spy she was able to work under the cover of a news correspondent and obtain valuable information that was useful in the war effort. Details of her activities in the OSS are not widely known, owing to the classification of this information.

In 1947, Doris entered into her second marriage, this time to Porfirio Rubirosa, a world-renowned strategic mercenary who had previously worked for Rafael Trujillo, the dictator of the Dominican Republic. Doris seemed to get along very well with Rubirosa. However, because Duke Power Company, owned by Doris Duke, provided the electricity to many US military installations, the State Department was concerned about the threat to security Rubirosa might bring. In an effort to preserve national security, on the evening of his wedding to Doris, Rubirosa was asked by the State Department to sign a prenuptial agreement or be assassinated.

---

171 The account of Doug is a dramatization of the social interaction of Doris in her early adult life. Reportedly, she enjoyed establishing friendships without disclosing her identity or wealth until she felt comfortable with the person.
172 Duke and Thomas, *Too Rich*, 122–123.
173 Ibid., 124–125.

Puzzled and stunned, he reluctantly signed.[174] Doris later became concerned that he was attempting to acquire her estate, so they divorced in 1951.

Louis Bromfield was a mark of a man. In his youth, he generally subscribed to the view that reflective introspection was a juvenile pursuit and that the only opinion of value was the opinion he would form of himself, if any. His important opinions were of morality, of right versus wrong. He wanted no part of the fanciful world of socialites, though most socialites would have jealously pursued an appearance with the world-renowned writer Louis Bromfield. Perhaps his attraction to Doris was her lack of necessity to prove anything, and thus she also cared nothing about socialites, other than the friendship or other attributes they might provide in various forms at various times. In this respect, perhaps, Louis and Doris were celebrated recluses.

Doris Duke was not easily impressed. She found no reason to be. If she chose, she could set the trend for the next sweater design or the next fashionable skirt. She could influence political ideology, and once the evil of Nazism fully reared its ugly brow, she could, and did, influence the formation of government entities. Before, it was not her concern, but once the devastating effects of concentration and genocide were seen on a global scale, she determined that she must direct her resources to the prevention of discrimination on the basis of race, religion, gender, age, ethnicity, national origin, or disability. Governments, after all, like most everything else in this world, can be bought and sold to the highest bidder. Why not finance democracies with an agenda of human rights preservation? Is this not using one's wealth for the positive development of humanity?

It was February 1953. Doris Duke, Louis Bromfield, John F. Kennedy, Robert Kennedy, Robert Sargent Shriver, Eunice Kennedy Shriver, and Jacqueline Lee Bouvier were seated around a dinner

---

174 Duke and Thomas, *Too Rich*, 130–139.

table at an isolated chateau in the Swiss Alps. The chateau was humble yet clean and well decorated with the finest furnishings money could buy. A heavy, black iron chandelier hung above the rustic but elegant dining table. The high, vaulted arched ceilings of the massive oak-paneled dining room necessitated two fireplaces to keep the room heated when the central heating was reduced. The Swiss mountains had enjoyed a heavy blanket of snow, creating the atmosphere of a white Christmas reflective of the Irving Berlin hit by the same name. "I still say he wrote that song in La Quinta," JFK said.

"I think he wrote it in Molgilyov, Russia, as a child," Doris said. She smiled at JFK.

"Wait a minute," said Eunice. "That is interesting, Doris. Why do you say that?"

"I just have a suspicion. I think he spent much of his time as a teenager in that town, where he composed many of his songs."

"It is ironic that you would say that," Eunice replied.

Robert looked at his sister inquisitively. "Why is that ironic?"

"Because he told me that's where he composed that song."

Louis Bromfield smiled at Doris, knowing full well she had also been told that same information by Irving Berlin. He knew because he had been present during the conversation at Rough Point in the summer of 1952.

The room grew silent for a few moments. Jacqueline broke the silence. "Thank you, Doris, for meeting with us to discuss the civil rights issue. Of everyone I could think of, I felt you would be most interested in becoming involved in this cause."

Doris nodded as she looked at the goblet in front of her, listening to the request for support.

Jacqueline continued. "We know of the efforts of your father and grandfather to support the disadvantaged, as well as your own charitable support of the underprivileged. For this reason, we wanted to invite you to participate in this project."

"What is the project?" Doris asked.

Robert replied, "In a nutshell, we believe in equal treatment for all persons regardless of race, ethnicity, religion, national origin, or gender. The playing field needs to have all obstacles removed so that opportunities are equal for everyone. Only in this way can all people be assured of the basic provisions of the Declaration of Independence, which include the right to life, liberty, and the pursuit of happiness. There should be no artificial impediments to anyone's maturity and growth. Not only is this fair to the individual, but it is better for society as a whole in that the most talented will be able to emerge."

Doris nodded. "For many years I have enjoyed the arts and literature of people from many nations and cultures. I have found that when free of the constraints of political ideology or foreign occupation, societies tend to produce the greatest art, literature, and science. But when a society places artificial impediments on a certain group's development, not only do individuals within that group suffer unfairly, but the society also suffers a diminution in creativity, compassion, and empathy."

"That is so true," replied Robert. "Equal access for all persons is the key to a truly blessed and prosperous society."

Doris nodded again. "I agree with everything you say. How can I help in this movement?"

John said, "I think each of us has to look inside to consider how he or she can provide the best support. For some it might mean leading a discussion group; for others it might mean leading a campaign. Still for others, it might mean providing financial contributions, and for some it might mean showing support publicly. I would certainly appreciate your continued support for my position as the US senator from Massachusetts. And though this is strictly confidential, I would be most appreciative of your support for my candidacy for president of the United States, should I decide to run in 1960. President Eisenhower is almost certain for reelection in '56. He was one of the first American political heroes after the war. But in 1960 he will be ineligible to run again. Vice President Richard

Nixon will be the most likely Republican presidential nominee, and I may run against him."

Doris looked at JFK, realizing that he had just announced, albeit discreetly, his candidacy for the US presidency in 1960. The room was silent for a few moments. Doris knew they were waiting for her response. She looked at Louis, who smiled at her. She nodded slightly. "In 1960 you will have my support when you run for the office of president of the United States."

"Thank you, Doris," Jacqueline said.

JFK smiled. "You are appreciated, Doris."

Later that evening, as Louis and Doris walked along the snow-covered deck of the chateau, Doris asked, "So how do you come down, Louie? Are you a Democrat or a Republican? Do you think I made the right decision in throwing my support behind JFK?"

"Truthfully, Doris, I'm not Republican or Democrat."

"How can you not be in one of the two major political parties?" she asked with a smile. "Why don't you like either party?"

Louis laughed. "I am not a Republican nor am I a Democrat because the Republicans don't care about people and the Democrats haven't got a lick of sense."

Doris stopped walking and said, "That is amazing. My father used to say that. I never heard anyone say that before except you and him."

Doris and Louis locked arms as they walked slowly along the deck that wrapped around and completely surrounded the second-floor exterior of the chateau.

"So you don't think my support of JFK was a wise decision?"

Louis reflected for a moment. "No, I think your decision was sound. When I say I am neither Democrat nor Republican, I simply mean that I do not support one party over the other. I support the person or his belief on a particular issue. If that means today I support a Democrat, that means that tomorrow I might equally well support a Republican. In fact, I have often found myself supporting a Democrat for one office and simultaneously a Republican for another office. It's a matter of the character and quality of the candidate in question."

Doris thought it unusual that Louis was not devoted to a single party, but she understood his reason. Besides, he was right. What does the political affiliation matter if the idea is immoral? But what should be the test of morality? Later that evening, sitting in the living room, Doris thought of these matters. "How does someone determine right from wrong?" she asked.

"Before answering that question, one must first identify the question by defining the parameters. Are you talking about a morality independent of any known religious doctrine, or are you talking about morality within a given religion?"

"I don't know. How would they differ?"

Louis took a drink of his brandy as he placed his hand over his abdomen in response to his pain. "Well, in orthodox Judaism, eating pork or mixing meat with milk is immoral. In radical Islam, rape is immoral, though not as much for the person who commits the rape as the victim. And in fundamental Christianity wearing a skirt too short will land you in the time-out pokey."

Doris laughed. "I'm referring to deeper issues of morality. For example, what is a person to do with his life that will benefit society as a whole?"

Louis laughed. "Now you have asked the right question. Unfortunately I won't be around to provide an answer. You will have to get there on your own. I will give you one word of caution: Be very careful of any doctor who tells you that he is on the verge of discovering physical immortality and he wants to share it with you before anyone else. Such a doctor is a self-deluded charlatan. They are worse than the blatant murderer because they come pretending to help while only trying to suck your life from you."

"I haven't met any doctors like that," replied Doris, puzzled at his comment.

"Rest assured you will, and he will probably be tied to a major medical school or a particular branch of the Hollywood elite."

"What you are saying right now is very strange, because it reminds me of what my father told me on his deathbed, but yours is a little more specific. Is this a prophecy of some kind?"

Sadly, numerous physicians would approach Doris throughout her life with such pickup lines.

The following morning at breakfast with John, Doris, Louis, and Jacqueline, Eunice asked, "So how are you feeling, Jackie? Are you nervous about the wedding?"

Jacqueline laughed. "I'm not really nervous. I don't really have that much to do except walk and smile. It is difficult to imagine that anything could go wrong."

"What about the prospect of marriage itself?" Doris asked. "Does that make you nervous?"

Jacqueline laughed. "I suppose with any other man I would be nervous. With John I am terrified." Everyone laughed. She continued. "With John I am terrified because I know that I am the luckiest woman in the world." She looked at John, who leaned over and kissed her on the cheek. John and Jacqueline were married September 12, 1953, at St. Mary's church in Newport, Rhode Island. Watching John and Jacqueline's happiness in marriage caused Doris to again think about the possibility of her own marriage. She so much wanted the happiness they seemed to have.[175]

The relationship between Louis and Doris continued to grow. Their love grew deeper with each passing day. In time they began to discuss the possibility of marriage, and Doris received a confidential proposal, which she accepted. Believing that she had found happiness in a romantic relationship of the kind that would last forever, Doris began to relax the guard she had placed around herself years before upon the death of her father. She relaxed her guard more and more with each passing day as she grew more

---

175 The visit with the Kennedys in the Swiss Alps is a fictional dramatization of a number of such meetings Doris is reported to have had with the Kennedy family.

deeply in love with Louis, whose love grew deeply for her—that is, until the day they learned that Louis had developed a serious life-threatening illness.

It was January 1956. Doris Duke and Louis Bromfield walked across a snow-covered field at Bromfield's Malibar Farm in Ohio. Bromfield, a novelist, had spent his childhood in Ohio with aspirations of becoming a novelist. He released his first novel, *The Green Bay Tree*,[176] in 1924, which was an instant success. He won a Pulitzer Prize for his second novel, *Early Autumn*,[177] in 1927. Over his twenty-two-year career as a novelist, he wrote over thirty books, all of which were successful and some of which were transformed into motion pictures. Bromfield's wife had died in 1951, and thereafter he developed a close relationship with Doris that grew quickly into a romantic relationship.

Doris laughed as she packed some snow together between her white leather gloves, making a snowball, which she threw at Louis. He smiled and then scooped up a handful of snow and tossed it loosely at Doris, allowing it to float to the ground like snow in a snow globe. In her full-length white fur coat and white rabbit hat from Russia, she resembled a Russian princess with the snow falling gently around her.

"Isn't this beautiful," Doris said, looking out over the snow-covered fields toward the woods of the Malibar Farms.[178]

"Indeed," Louis replied. "This is why I love Malibar."

"What are we going to do, Louie?" Doris reached over and took his arm in her arm as they walked toward the barn. "Are you going to tell me?"

Louis looked at the ground. "Tell you what?"

"You know."

Louis said nothing as they walked arm in arm toward the barn. "It's going to chill tonight," he said.

---

176 Bromfield, Louis, *The Green Bay Tree* (Wooster: Wooster Book Company, 1924).

177 Bromfield, Louis, *Early Autumn* (New York: Frederick A. Stokes, 1926).

178 Today Malibar Farms is an Ohio State Park near Lucas, Ohio.

"Do I detect avoidance behavior?" she asked. "You know I want to know what your doctor said."

Louis smiled. "Nothing new. It is what it is."

Doris sighed. "I don't understand life."

Louis suffered liver disease from a life of heavy drinking and in January was told that he had only a few months to live. He said he created his greatest works under the influence of alcohol and would not give up his vice at the cost of his creativity. His doctor had attempted a new treatment he thought might be effective, but it was not.

"What don't you understand?"

"Why it is that everyone I love is taken from me. My daddy told me before he died that I should never believe anyone who says he loves me, because he would only want my money. He never said not to trust anyone who says he loves me because he will be taken away. But that is the way it seems. How much time does he give you now?"

"I don't want to say. We shouldn't talk about that. It does no good."

"But I have to know what I can expect. Please, Louie. Tell me."

"Six months at the outside. Six weeks at the shortest." Louis walked with his head down. "There's nothing we can do. We have to accept it. Will you promise something?"

"What?" Doris asked.

"I don't want you to pay off the mortgage on the farm."

"But I would like to preserve Malabar just as it is," she replied.

"I don't want you to spend your money on the farm."

"Why would you not want me to save Malabar?"

"The local community needs to pay for it. They want to preserve it. I remember when I was trying to become established as a writer locally I received no support from the community. In fact, they were downright rude. The community socialites mocked my writing. Now that I have won the Pulitzer, everyone is my best friend. I think it is only fair that they pay to maintain it. Promise me, Doris."

"I promise that I will not pay the full mortgage, but I will help," Doris replied.

"Okay," he replied with a smile.

Losing Louis was very hard for Doris. Of all of her romances, perhaps it was Louis Bromfield who might have transformed her from a former Secret Service agent in the OSS, living on the edge, into a twentieth-century domesticated housewife. Quite possibly they would have married had he survived. Even when it became apparent that he was dying from his alcohol consumption, he would not give up his vice, and he died in March 1956.[179] Although Doris continued to search endlessly for the one man who would make her happy, and survive to enjoy the happiness, she never found him.

In 1962, Doris's mother, Nanaline, passed away. Doris had been estranged from her mother since childhood, and they never reconciled. Nanaline's funeral took place in Duke Chapel at Duke University. Nanaline left $5 million to Duke University Medical School and the rest of her estate to her grandson, Walker Inman. Sadly, the only item left to Doris in Nanaline's will was the full-length sable coat Nanaline threw at Doris the day her father, Buck, died.[180]

---

179 Duke and Thomas, *Too Rich*, 143–145, 147–155.
180 Ibid., 164.

11

Living on the Edge

By the 1970s, Doris was spending a substantial amount of time with Aristotle Onassis and his wife, Jacqueline Kennedy Onassis, the widow of the late president John F. Kennedy.[181] Aristotle died in 1975, and Doris began to spend most of her time searching for rare and expensive art. By the time of her death in 1993, her art collection and her real estate were valued at more than $1 billion and comprised only part of her vast estate.

Doris never fully recovered emotionally from the loss of her daughter, Arden, in 1940. She spent the rest of her life hoping that she would someday have a mother–daughter relationship. When she met actress Sharon Tate, she believed she had found a daughter, and they developed such a relationship. When the pregnant Sharon was murdered in 1969 by the Charles Manson clan, the similarity between the death of Sharon's unborn child and the death of Arden was overwhelming, and Doris retreated into her own privacy for a time, though she continued in her search for a mother–daughter relationship.[182] By the 1980s she believed that she may have found a daughter in a young woman named Chandi

---

181 Duke and Thomas, *Too Rich*, 187–189.
182 Ibid., 175, 185.

Heffner (Charlene Gail Heffner), and she legally adopted Chandi as her own daughter.[183]

Chandi's father was an attorney, and her mother a surgical nurse. As a child she had attended a Catholic girl's school. Her sister, Claudia, a former model, was married to the wealthy businessman Nelson Peltz, with whom she had eight children.[184] Chandi was an active member of the Hare Krishna movement and a belly dancer. She traveled to India and various exotic places of the world and eventually to Hawaii, where she had an opportunity to meet Doris Duke.[185] Doris later concluded that Chandi had studied her very carefully in order to present herself as a person who could channel to her deceased daughter, Arden. If true, perhaps the plan worked better than Chandi anticipated in that Doris believed not only that Chandi could channel to Arden, but that indeed Chandi *was* Arden.[186]

Chandi had previously developed a relationship with Imelda Marcos, Doris Duke's friend, who also resided in Hawaii. Later Imelda and Chandi would induce Doris to purchase an airplane, from which Chandi and Imelda split a commission of several million dollars. When Doris learned of the commission, she began to suspect that Chandi may have participated in defrauding her. In many respects, her relationship with Chandi was the beginning of her demise. Indeed, Chandi persuaded Doris to hire a butler who had previously been in the employ of Chandi's sister, Claudia. His name was Bernard Lafferty, and he was to become, in the last hours of Doris Duke's life, her "Grim Reaper."

Doris immediately disliked Lafferty, whom she called "Rafferty." Lafferty was a chronic alcoholic who would often disappear in his room for days in a drunken slumber. On more than one occasion the members of the household were concerned that

---

183 Duke and Thomas, *Too Rich*, 240–241.

184 Ibid., 193, 241.

185 Ibid., 193, 203.

186 Ibid., 193, 241.

he may have died, given the length of his absence. Within a short time of obtaining his employment in the Duke household, Lafferty began usurping the authority of the servants who had been with Doris for many years. While Doris disliked Lafferty's arrogance and underhanded tactics, she tolerated him because Chandi seemed to like him. Meanwhile, at the suggestion of Imelda Marcos, who was more of a friend to Chandi than Doris, who actually disliked Imelda, Doris adopted Chandi so she would have an heir. Today some allege that Imelda, who was falsely claiming to Chandi to have more wealth than Doris, saw this as her opportunity of securing a share of the Doris Duke estate. When Imelda and her husband Fernando were indicted for racketeering and their assets frozen, Chandi induced Doris to give Imelda $5 million to cover her bond.[187]

While some believed that Chandi had intended to use Lafferty to get to the estate of Doris, and to speed the process of her demise, in the end it was Lafferty who would have the final influence on the life of Doris. One day Lafferty informed Doris and members of the staff that Chandi, who had been personally preparing and giving Doris her medicine and her meals, was poisoning her. This claim was supported by Dr. Rolando Atiga, who in 1991 prepared a statement setting forth his findings and the reason for his belief.[188] He advised Doris to stay away from Chandi. Doris ordered that Chandi be barred from her properties, and the mother–daughter relationship that Doris had wanted so badly came to an end. In retrospect, it now appears far more likely that Lafferty was poisoning Doris and requested Dr. Atiga to conduct tests that would reveal the poison so he could accuse Chandi in order to move her out of the way of his plans and earn the trust of Doris for himself. Indeed, it is entirely possible that Chandi was innocent of the alleged wrongdoing. We

---

187 Celestine Bohlen, "Doris Duke Offers Mrs. Marcos Bail," *New York Times*, November 3, 1988; Duke and Thomas, *Too Rich*, 196–197.

188 Written statement from Rolando Atiga, MD, December 11, 1991.

will never know, since Chandi's primary accuser, Bernard Lafferty, a man who most likely planned the murder of Doris Duke, is also deceased. While Dr. Atiga had said Doris was being poisoned, he would likely have had no way of knowing how the poison was being administered, and thus he could not have plausibly implicated Chandi over any other person.

After Chandi had been banished from the premises, Lafferty began to assert himself ever more boldly. Previously he had been a very submissive and quiet servant who simply answered the door and offered refreshments while visitors waited for "Miss Duke." Contrary to the claims of Lafferty, after the death of Doris, that he was her close friend and confidant, and that he would accompany her to social events, Doris actually found Lafferty annoying and difficult to tolerate. She thought that he was mentally slow and possessed limited literacy. According to the other household servants, Lafferty would often ridicule Doris when he was out of range of her hearing and sight. When he was in her presence, he acted timid and frightened. However, as her health began to fade, he began to assert an ever more active and eventually dominant role. Lafferty began telling Doris that she needed to implement greater measures of protection given dangers created by Chandi and her fanatical and dangerous Hare Krishna friends. He would constantly tell Doris that people were trying to kill her and otherwise inflict harm upon her. He further explained that, like Doris, he was a victim of Chandi's abuses and that he understood what she was experiencing. These fear techniques allowed Lafferty to assert tremendous influence over Doris. In time he managed to convince her, despite her dislike of him, that he was indispensable to her and that he was the only person she really had left in this life.[189]

---

189 Much of the information concerning events at Falcon Lair come from affidavits and the deposition of Doris Duke's personal chef, Colin Shanley. Housekeeper Ann Bostich also provided substantial information concerning these matters, as did nurse Tammy Payette in sworn statements. See "Did The Butler Do It?" *Newsweek*, February 19, 1995; see also Bill Hewitt, et al., *"Where*

By the winter months of 1991 and the spring of 1992, Lafferty had created a barrier between Doris and the outside world. When friends and family members attempted to call, the calls were intercepted by Lafferty, who always explained that "Miss Duke" was sleeping or not feeling well. In short, he would not allow her to take telephone calls. To family and friends who were attempting to contact Doris, it seemed strange that she would not take their calls and would not return them. Today much of the information about the events behind the closed doors of Falcon Lair comes from depositions later taken by private attorneys and informal discovery conducted by investigators.

In April 1992, Doris underwent a face-lift. Two days later she fell and broke her hip. Thereafter she had very little contact with the outside world, and a year and a half later she was dead. At the time of her death, she was on heavy doses of morphine and other medications. Her body was cremated before an autopsy could be performed to determine the quantities and types of drugs she had been given. No family members were consulted concerning the disposition of her remains. Everything was handled by her butler, Bernard Lafferty. While the circumstances surrounding her death were suspicious to family members, there was no information upon which an investigation could be launched—that is, until employees of Doris began to come forward with information about the circumstances leading up to her death. One of the first to begin providing information about her last days was Colin Shanley.

Shanley was Doris's chef for many years, until Chandi Heffner came to live with her and undertook the task of preparing the food. After Chandi left, in 1991, Shanley resumed his position as the chef until Doris died. According to Shanley, Dr. Rolando Atiga, who had been the doctor of Fernando Marcos, and who alleged in a written statement in 1991 that Doris was being poisoned by Chandi

---

There's a Will," *People* magazine, May 22, 1955; see also Duke and Thomas, *Too Rich*, 190–226.

Heffner, was paid $1 million for caring for Doris. Dr. Atiga began instituting a blood-cleaning procedure involving a large machine similar to that used in dialysis. According to Shanley, this machine had a devastating effect on Doris's condition, and she rapidly deteriorated after this procedure was instituted.[190]

In April 1992, Doris amended her will with a codicil wherein she named Bernard Lafferty as the coexecutor of her estate along with Walker Inman II, the nephew of Doris's half brother, Walker Inman. Thereafter, Lafferty began advising Doris that Inman II was using her for her money and that he was simply waiting for her to die. When Inman II would call, Lafferty would refuse to put his calls through to Doris, claiming that she was either asleep or ill. Shortly thereafter, the will was amended again, and Walker Inman II was removed as coexecutor, leaving Lafferty as the sole executor to the multibillion-dollar estate.

After Doris fell and broke her hip in 1992, she experienced a long and difficult recovery. In fact, she never fully recovered. This created a state of helplessness for Doris, and Lafferty was very eager to step in to "assist" Doris in her time of need. Indeed, the more helpless she became, the more willing he was to assist. The reality is that the more helpless she became, the more control he exercised over her. By the early months of 1993, Lafferty had taken complete control of the multibillion-dollar empire. According to Shanley, Lafferty would routinely brag that he was in control of the entire Duke estate, and the reality is that he probably did possess that control. On February 15, 1993, Doris suffered a stroke and was hospitalized until April. After her discharge, she seemed to suffer from disorientation and confusion.

In his book *Too Rich: The Family Secrets of Doris Duke*, Pony Duke, the son of Angier Biddle Duke, a first cousin of Doris, stated that Doris placed several telephone calls to his father in 1993 asking for assistance in finding legal counsel. In March 1993, Doris called

---

190 Deposition of Colin Shanley.

her cousin Angier, who thought she sounded lucid and oriented. She was again asking his assistance in finding attorneys. Angier sent a facsimile transmission containing the name of an attorney he thought would be good for Doris, but she failed to respond, which slightly offended Angier and his son Pony. It is likely that Lafferty intercepted the faxes the same way he intercepted the telephone calls. Notwithstanding Angier's recommendations to Doris, it appears that Lafferty did not allow her to schedule appointments with those attorneys. In retrospect, Angier and Pony believe that she was crying out for help.[191] As will be discussed below, Don Howarth and Suzelle Smith, who had been her most recent personal attorneys up until that time, had been ousted by Lafferty as he was taking over the estate of Doris and convincing her that everyone around her was working to her detriment.

In March 1993, Ann Bostich, the housekeeper of Falcon Lair, was instructed by Bernard Lafferty to come to the hospital room where Doris was staying. When she arrived, Lafferty and Doris's attorney, William Doyle, were present. Nuku Makasaile[192] and attorney Alan Croll[193] were waiting in the hallway outside of Doris's room. Ann was told that Doris was dying and that Ann was needed to witness a codicil to the will that Doris was about to sign. According to Ann, Doris was not lucid and her voice quavered as she attempted to respond with yes and no answers to questions posed by attorney Doyle. Ann later stated that she told Lafferty at the time that she could never testify that Doris was of sound mind when she signed the codicil.[194]

In her last days, the care Doris received was nothing short of elder abuse. Her hair was not washed, and she was not bathed. According to witnesses, Lafferty physically abused her by throwing

---

191 Duke and Thomas, *Too Rich*, 210–212.
192 Nuku Makasaile was Doris Duke's housemaid.
193 Alan Croll was an attorney in the same firm as William Doyle, Katten, Muchin, and Zavis.
194 Sworn statement of housekeeper Ann Bostitch.

her frail body about and literally jerking her hair out of her head in clumps.[195] At one point Doris asked to be taken to Duke University Medical Center, where she might receive life-saving care; instead she was taken to UCLA Medical Center. Lafferty no doubt was concerned that she would receive extraordinary care at Duke and that the doctors and nurses might become suspicious of his abuse, so she was not taken to Duke. For all practical purposes, Doris had become a prisoner in her own home at Falcon Lair, completely at the mercy of her butler, Bernard Lafferty.

---

195 Sworn statement of housekeeper Ann Bostitch.

12

The Quest to Right the Wrong

The year was 1994, and Doris Duke, the richest woman in the world, was dead. At the time of her death her estate was officially estimated to be in excess of $1.2 billion, though insiders maintain that it exceeded $3 billion, and the full extent of her holdings may never be fully discovered.[196]

In addition to approximately $1 billion in cash held in a checking account in Chemical Bank, an art and real estate collection valued at more than $1 billion, and vast amounts of securities in various corporations and other business entities, Doris had inherited tons of gold that had been placed in vaults in Europe by her father, to avoid the IRS. Quite likely that gold has not been touched since his death in 1925.[197] It is unclear precisely who has knowledge of all of the gold hidden in Europe and whether it has all been identified and assessed. It is impossible to tell how much of this gold may have passed outside of her estate or may have been set aside for some future gift outside of the estate plan. A family member once joked that a person could not spend an average day in any American city without coming in contact with some product or service that was provided by a company in which Doris had an interest. It is believed

---

196 Duke and Thomas, *Too Rich*, 4.
197 Ibid., 62.

that after her death a substantial part of her estate may have been misappropriated and embezzled by some of the very people who were retained to protect it.

By the summer of 1994, the newspaper headlines, which had initially reported that Doris had died of natural causes, were now reporting that she had been murdered. And in a shocking reenactment of the age-old murder mystery plot, the headlines read, "The Butler Did It." Soon to come under investigation, by the Los Angeles County District Attorney's Office, for the murder of the richest woman in the world, was the butler of Doris Duke, Bernard Lafferty.[198] Lafferty had orchestrated a last-minute amendment to her will wherein he placed himself as the executor of the multibillion-dollar estate, with an inheritance of $4.5 million and an annual salary of $500,000.[199] Lafferty had taken control of the estate of Doris Duke, including the Doris Duke Charitable Foundation, with a net worth of $1.4 billion. In order to gain popularity among the social elite and Hollywood celebrities, he had appointed actress Elizabeth Taylor to the board of trustees of the foundation and had begun working his way into elite social circles. Lafferty was attempting to befriend Mary Duke Biddle Trent Semans, the first cousin of Doris Duke, whose holdings exceeded $300 million, and Nannerl Keohane, the president of Duke University, whom Lafferty named as a member of the Board of Trustees of the Doris Duke Charitable Foundation. With great trepidation and caution, these astute individuals began to give Lafferty the benefit of the doubt and a chance to prove his validity—that is, until the allegations by

---

198 "Police to Investigate Death of Heiress," *Los Angeles Times*, January 25, 1995; "Probe of Tobacco Heiress' Death Finds No Evidence of Foul Play," *Chicago Tribune*, July 26, 1996.

199 Technically, Doris Duke had an estate plan consisting of several testamentary instruments, most notably a trust. We use the term "will" generically to refer to her estate plan, since that is the term the attorneys have used in the legal proceedings.

Doris's employees of the alleged murder began to surface in early 1994.[200]

Meanwhile, since Doris had become alienated from her closest family members, and since her peripheral family members did not have access to her greatest secrets, her cousins stood by helplessly, watching in horror, as the greatest crime in history unfolded right before their eyes. Meanwhile, Harry Demopoulos, MD, a personal friend of Doris, had become suspicious of the circumstances surrounding her death. Doris had previously named Dr. Demopoulos, without his knowledge, the executor of her estate, for which he was to be compensated $25 million upon her death and $5 million per year for life. Had it not been for the interference of Bernard Lafferty, this appointment might have materialized. When Dr. Demopoulos attempted to contact Doris, the calls were not put through. Then one day she called him and said she did not ever want to speak to him again. Dr. Demopoulos felt that he needed representation to address his concerns, and he retained Don Howarth and Suzelle Smith, of the law firm of Howarth and Smith. Together they set out to perform the impossible task—to expose and unravel the "perfect crime."

Suzelle was a graduate of the University of Virginia School of Law. After law school she joined the prestigious firm of Gibson, Dunn & Crutcher, where she met Don Howarth. She was ranked among the top ten trial attorneys in the United States by the *National Law Journal* and was a celebrity among attorneys. Suzelle's career had been one successful verdict after another.

Don had enjoyed a legal career equally impressive as Suzelle's. Raised in San Diego, California, Don received his undergraduate degree at Harvard University. He then obtained a master's degree from the Kennedy School of Government, and finally, a law degree from the Harvard University School of Law. Don taught at Harvard and then clerked for a Federal Court of Appeals Justice for several

---

200 Duke and Thomas, *Too Rich*, 236–237.

years before returning to California and accepting a position at Gibson, Dunn & Crutcher, where he was later named a partner. He and Suzelle left Gibson, Dunn & Crutcher to form their own firm in 1985.[201]

After the death of Doris, household employees began coming forward to tell the police what really took place at Falcon Lair before she died, much of which is set forth in the previous chapter. Those accounts made clear that as Lafferty began to emerge as the person in charge of Doris Duke in her last days, members of the Hollywood elite began to encircle him. One person in particular, Elizabeth Taylor, recommended medical professionals who could assist in caring for Doris in her last days. As the investigation by Don and Suzelle revealed, an alliance had been formed among some of these medical professionals and Lafferty. This was an alliance of the strangest cast, for Lafferty, the butler, was at the center of this real-life "reality show." Lafferty began promising members of this circle tremendous rewards, such as admission for their children to Duke University and positions on the board of the Doris Duke Charitable Foundation.

Don and Suzelle learned that Charles Kivowitz, MD, a long-time friend of Elizabeth Taylor, had assumed total responsibility for the medical care of Doris, for which he was compensated $1,000 per day. Then Dr. Kivowitz had arranged for Doris to be placed in an isolated suite at Cedars-Sinai reserved for celebrities and the super-rich. There, in privacy and isolation, Dr. Kivowitz summoned William Doyle, an attorney from Los Angeles who had replaced the attorneys Doris had used throughout her life. William Doyle had been the attorney and a friend of Dr. Kivowitz for many

---

201 Don and Suzelle are no strangers to the courtroom. In addition to a $12 million award within one year of leaving Gibson, Dunn & Crutcher, Don obtained an award in another case of $101 million. Shortly thereafter, Suzelle received an award of $43 million representing rural communities' residents and victims of toxic contamination by Colter Corporation in Colorado. These types of verdicts have become commonplace for attorneys in the Howarth-Smith law firm.

years. Thus, Doyle was also part of the inner circle of Doris in the last days of her life.

On April 5, 1993, Doris Duke signed the final codicil to her will, which named Lafferty as the sole individual executor of her multibillion-dollar estate. The witnesses to the signing were Charles Kivowitz, MD, Jerold Federman, MD,[202] Lidia Rives,[203] and Margaret Underwood.[204] Jerold Federman, MD, testified that he was simply asked by Dr. Kivowitz if he was available to witness the signing of the codicil. He stated yes and was requested to witness the signing.[205]

By the end of 1994 Don and Suzelle had accumulated enough evidence to prosecute their case. They had obtained medical records and witness statements that suggested to them that at the time Doris signed the last amendment to her will on April 5, 1993, she lacked testamentary capacity. They had also obtained evidence that Dr. Kivowitz, who arranged the signing of the will, had received promises from Lafferty that he would benefit once Lafferty became the executor and took control of the foundation. If true, that meant that he was not a disinterested witness.

Don and Suzelle reviewed the medical records with their retained medical expert, who stated that Doris was receiving extraordinarily high doses of Demerol and morphine, which were gradually increased until the time of her death. Additionally it appeared that Doris was given other combinations of medications that were contraindicated. At the same time, Lafferty was giving her large quantities of alcoholic beverages. Those combinations of medications and alcohol did two things. First, they rendered her incapable of understanding the nature of her estate and her bequests, meaning she was deprived of testamentary capacity. But

---

202 Dr. Federman was a friend of Dr. Kivowitz, who had limited involvement in the treatment of Doris near the end of her life.
203 Lidia Rives was a nursing assistant in Dr. Kivowitz's office.
204 Margaret Underwood was a secretary in Dr. Kivowitz's office.
205 Deposition of Dr. Federman.

more importantly, it was this combination of drugs that cost Doris her life. The final step in this apparent conspiracy was to cremate her body so no autopsy could be performed, notwithstanding that throughout her life she adamantly insisted that her body never be cremated. She wanted to be buried at sea but not cremated. After reviewing the evidence with their medical experts, Don and Suzelle concluded that this was a very carefully orchestrated act intended to seize control of the Doris Duke estate and to destroy the evidence.

In order to remove Lafferty as executor, it was necessary to show that he exercised undue influence at the time Doris signed the will, or that she lacked testamentary capacity when he was named executor. Don and Suzelle believed that both conditions existed in this case. They were astounded that something like this could happen with an estate the size of Doris's estate. Ordinarily, people with a large estate take tremendous care to ensure that their last wishes are met and that they are cared for by their loved ones. But the deeper they went with their investigation, the more shocking information they uncovered. For example, they learned that while Doris was on her deathbed, Lafferty went on a spending spree, spending on himself in excess of $60,000 of the money from Doris's estate. This is the man who had become the executor of her estate. For all intents and purposes, Doris disinherited her closest relatives and left the bulk of her estate to charity and appointed her alcoholic butler as her executor.

It was also discovered that when the US Trust Corporation, the institutional coexecutor of the estate, learned about Lafferty's spending spree, they insisted that Lafferty repay the money he spent. But when Lafferty informed them that he was financially destitute, the trust loaned him the money to repay the "embezzled funds." Don and Suzelle felt that a legitimate executor would never have done this. Those funds were undoubtedly loaned from the funds of the estate. In her will, Doris appointed Lafferty as the sole individual executor of her estate. The trust provided the following:

"I direct BERNARD LAFFERTY to appoint as a co-executor such bank or trust company (the "corporate executor") as he, in his absolute discretion, shall select." In the event Lafferty failed to appoint a corporate executor, then the US Trust Company of New York would serve as corporate executor. Because Lafferty had the authority to remove US Trust as the coexecutor, it appears they were determined to keep him happy. This created a conflict for the trust, which Don and Suzelle believed amounted to a breach of fiduciary duty to the estate. The attorneys felt that both Lafferty and the trust should be disqualified for self-dealing and breach of fiduciary duty.

Don and Suzelle scheduled the deposition of Dr. Kivowitz for January 4, 1995, hoping to accomplish several things. First, they hoped to force Kivowitz to admit that a decision had been made to allow Miss Duke to die by instituting a "no code blue" and that he then introduced high levels of morphine to speed her dying process. Additionally they would attempt to show by his testimony that Doris was not of sound mind and lacked testamentary capacity at the time she executed her will on April 5, 1993.

Meanwhile, on the East Coast, another attorney, Marie Lambert, was bitterly fighting to have her client, Irwin Bloom, an executor named in the trust prior to Dr. Demopoulos, reinstated as executor of the estate. Lambert, a former judge in the Surrogate Court of New York, was also convinced that Lafferty had not only exercised undue influence, but had also conspired with numerous other persons to bring about the premature death of Doris in order to seize her estate. Irwin Bloom was an accountant who had previously worked for Nelson Peltz, the husband of Claudia Heffner, the sister of Chandi. He had been brought into the employment of Doris Duke upon the recommendation of Chandi. Like the many other associates brought into the alliance by Chandi, Doris did not trust Irwin Bloom and became uncomfortable with his interest in her finances. Attorneys for Lafferty, and Doris's estate, alleged that Bloom had skimmed millions of dollars from Doris while serving as her accountant by disguising the funds as commissions on investments. Bloom settled with the estate, and in 1999 was charged with failing to report those earnings on his 1992 and 1993 tax returns.[206] He was found guilty in 2001 by a federal court jury in New York.[207]

As the headlines began to expose the misconduct of Lafferty and his team of conspirators, defensive tactics were already underway. Utilizing the public relations team of Elizabeth Taylor, Lafferty began an appointment of members to the Doris Duke Charitable Foundation. Absent from his appointments were any members of the Duke family, Dr. Demopoulos, and Irwin Bloom. Lafferty's appointments included Christine Todd Whitman, the governor of New Jersey; Marion Oates, a close friend of Doris; J. Carter Brown, director of the Newport Restoration Society; Nannerl O. Keohane, the president of Duke University; and, finally, Elizabeth Taylor, the Hollywood actress. Lafferty had hoped to appoint Michael Jackson, but allegations of his molestation of children made such an appointment unfeasible.

It was a true-to-life game of chess. The lines were being drawn, and the defense was preparing its alignment of allies and public-relations strategists. The coup was well underway, but the loyalists were already cornering the usurper, who had violated the cardinal rule of chess by "surrounding himself with himself," leaving no avenue of escape. Suzelle Smith and Don Howarth sat silently for weeks, watching and studying every move of Lafferty the usurper until they knew the right moment was upon them.

---

206 Jerry Capeci, "Heiress Ex-Advisor Charged," *New York Daily News*, August 24, 1999.
207 "Duke Accountant Guilty of Tax Fraud," *New York Times*, January 27, 2001.

13

The Critical Evidence

As Lafferty and Demopoulos squared off for the dynasty battle of the century, Chandi Heffner was approaching the estate for her share of the inheritance. After considering exhaustive and expensive litigation, Chandi decided that settlement was the most reasonable course of action. Knowing that a lengthy court battle could be risky, with great expense and possibly providing nothing in the end, she accepted a settlement of $65 million in exchange for a release of all of her interests in the estate. While the settlement was not looked upon with favor by family members, they all knew that, in the end, it was the most practical course of action.[208]

As the case began to unfold, the Demopoulos team produced a damaging witness, Tammy Payette, a twenty-eight-year-old nurse who had provided care to Doris during the last few weeks of her life. According to Payette, Lafferty had conspired with Dr. Kivowitz to bring an early end to Doris's life by providing excessive doses of morphine and Demerol. Although Payette was a strong witness for the Demopoulos team, her credibility was weakened when she was arrested in Beverly Hills on one count of grand theft for allegedly taking property from the Duke estate. Nonetheless, she

---

208 David Elsner, "Battles Over Duke Harriman Estate Are Settled," *Chicago Tribune*, December 30, 1995; Duke and Thomas, *Too Rich*, 243.

remained one of the most powerful weapons in the arsenal to dethrone Lafferty.

Meanwhile, former Manhattan district attorney Richard Kuh had been appointed by Judge Eve Preminger[209] of the New York Surrogate Court to investigate the strange circumstances surrounding the death of Doris Duke.[210] To assist in the investigation, he retained the services of Dr. Nicholas Macris to conduct a forensic analysis. Based upon his examination of the medical records, Dr. Macris concluded that although Doris was terminally ill in the fall of 1993, Dr. Kivowitz had caused her to stop breathing by administering excessive doses of pain medication, including morphine. This, in turn, caused her death. In his sixty-four-page report released in April 1995, Mr. Kuh concluded that the death had been caused by an overdose of pain medication.

In the last days of her life, there were several peculiar events. Dr. Glassman, a plastic surgeon and a friend of Doris, had received a $500,000 check. Although Glassman stated that the check was authorized by Doris, he did not produce any evidence of that, and Kuh could find no such evidence. Toward the end of her life, Dr. Kivowitz was receiving nearly $50,000 per month. Additionally, Lafferty, who was supposed to be protecting the estate of Doris, went on a spending spree, spending $60,000 on personal items for himself, $50,000 for a new Cadillac (after wrecking another

---

209 Eve Preminger received her LLB from Columbia Law School in 1960, where she was editor of the *Columbia Law Review*. After graduation she went into private practice specializing in complex and commercial litigation. She served as justice of the Supreme Court of New York County from 1987 to 1990 and surrogate for New York from 1991 to 2005. After resigning from the bench she went back into private practice with Kramer, Levin, Naftalis & Frankel, LLP. See Kramer Levin, accessed December 22, 2013, www.kramerlevin.com/epreminger/. During her tenure as surrogate court judge of New York, she presided over the probate proceeding, Will of Doris Duke, File Number: 4440-93.
210 Probate Proceeding, Will of Doris Duke, Ruling of The Honorable Judge Eve Preminger, Surrogates' Court County of New York, File Number: 4440-93, January 20, 1995. See the actual court order in appendix A of this book.

Cadillac), and $320,000 on renovations to Falcon Lair. He borrowed in excess of $800,000 from US Trust to maintain the lifestyle to which he had become accustomed. During this time he suffered four drinking blackouts, one of which resulted in hospitalization, in a period of eighteen months. He was taking multiple prescription medications, including seven different types of antidepressants, three types of sleeping pills, and six antianxiety medications. But the strangest event of all was the law firm of William Doyle, who for a period of eight months was paid over $8 million in attorney fees for representing the estate and Lafferty.[211]

On Wednesday, January 4, 1995, at 12:45 p.m., Don and Suzelle entered the Malibu Room A of the Hyatt Hotel on South Flower Street in downtown Los Angeles to take the deposition of Charles Kivowitz, MD.[212] With Don and Suzelle were attorneys Rodney Houghton and Thomas Vandenburg, also representing Dr. Demopoulos. Dr. Kivowitz was sitting behind the conference table with his attorney, John Barnosky,[213] immediately to his left and the court reporter to his right. Coexecutors Bernard Lafferty and US Trust Company of New York were represented by Lee Ann

---

211 See "Law Firm Defends $8 Million Doris Duke Estate Fee," 'Lectric Law Library, accessed December 22, 2013, http://www.lectlaw.com/files/cur32.htm, last accessed December 22, 2013.

212 A deposition is an out-of-court proceeding wherein the witness is asked a series of questions as if he or she were in a court of law. Although there is no judge or jury present, the testimony is given under oath and has the same force and effect as if it were given in court. The testimony is preserved in a typed document called a transcript, and objections can be made, as if in court, and are also preserved in the written transcript. Depositions are intended to obtain valuable information under oath, which can then be used to impeach a witness if something different is said in trial.

213 John Barnosky, a New York attorney, received his Juris Doctor from St. John's University School of Law and his LLM from New York University School of Law. He specializes in probate litigation. See Farrell Fritz, accessed December 22, 2013, http://www.farrellfritz.com/attorney/john-j-barnosky/.

Watson.[214] Dr. Kivowitz leaned forward on his elbows as Don and Suzelle entered the room and introduced themselves.

"Are we ready to begin?" asked Don as the court reporter finished adjusting the paper in the transcriber and the video technician set the camera. The court reporter nodded. "Let's begin," said Don.

Dr. Kivowitz was sworn, and the attorneys formally introduced themselves on the record. During the first day of deposition, Don elicited important information concerning the role of Dr. Kivowitz in the final days of the life of Doris Duke. The following summarizes some of the important information obtained:[215]

- Dr. Kivowitz identified and authenticated his signature on the will of Doris Duke dated April 5, 1993. He stated that he had never witnessed any patient's will other than Doris Duke's. He testified that Margaret Underwood, one of the witnesses to the will, was a secretary in his office. He further testified that Lidia Rives, who also witnessed the will, was a nursing assistant in his office.

- Dr. Kivowitz first saw Doris Duke in February 1992, at which time she consulted him for a fractured femur.

- On March 8, 1993, Dr. Kivowitz was contacted by Doris Duke's attorney William Doyle at Cedars-Sinai Medical Center and was asked if Doris would be able to sign a codicil to her will that night. Dr. Kivowitz understood that Mr. Doyle was asking about her general health and capacity to sign a codicil. He felt that Doris was perfectly competent

---

214 During the proceedings, Ms. Watson received a letter that claimed that Irwin Bloom, another litigant, had embezzled funds from Doris Duke in the last years of her life. This letter led to an investigation that ultimately resulted in a settlement between the estate and Mr. Bloom.
215 For a more comprehensive compilation of excerpts from the deposition of Charles Kivowitz, MD, see appendix B.

to discuss any affairs with Mr. Doyle and to sign any documents Mr. Doyle felt needed her signature.

- Dr. Kivowitz is the person who referred Doris Duke's attorneys, Alan Croll and William Doyle, to her, and he may have made such referrals with other patients on one or two other occasions.

- On October 27, the day before Doris Duke died, Dr. Kivowitz anticipated that Doris Duke would die the following day.

- Based on discussions with Doris Duke and the content of her living will, Dr. Kivowitz entered a do-not-resuscitate order but did not document those discussions with Doris in the medical records.

- Dr. Kivowitz did not know for certain if he was aware of all the medications Doris had been receiving. He further stated that he did not keep a record or document in the medical records of what drugs he knew she was receiving, because he was concerned that the information would wind up in a publication such as the *National Enquirer*.

- Dr. Kivowtiz was paid $50,000 for the medical treatment he rendered to Doris over a period of four to seven weeks. He estimated that he may have provided one hundred hours of services during that time but was uncertain. He would simply submit the bill to the Doris Duke business office and it would be paid. He did not ever discuss his fee with Doris.

- Dr. Kivowitz had instituted a no code blue for Doris before she died. (A no code blue means there will be no attempt to resuscitate a patient in the event of cardiac arrest.) Dr.

Kivotwitz testified that this is what she requested in her living will.

- Dr. Kivowitz stopped providing therapy to Doris because he had determined that she was dying and the therapy would be of no benefit. He felt that would be consistent with the wish she expressed in discussions with him, though he did not document those discussions with her in the medical records.

The deposition of Dr. Kivowitz took five days to complete over a period of two weeks. Don Howarth had diligently attempted to lay the foundation for the critical testimony concerning the cause of death of Doris Duke. Finally, on the fifth day of Dr. Kivowitz's deposition, Howarth was prepared to lead Dr. Kivowitz into the admission that was needed to prove the case. And finally Dr. Kivowitz provided the critical testimony Don was seeking.

Dr. Kivowitz testified that he ordered that Doris be taken off Demerol and placed on a morphine drip notwithstanding that she was experiencing no discomfort on Demerol. The following testimony is taken directly from the transcript of the final day of the deposition of Dr. Kivowitz on January 12, 1995. The questioning is based upon exhibits ninety-two through ninety-five, which are pages from the medical records recorded at Falcon Lair on October 26, 1993, through October 28, 1993. For clarity and brevity, extraneous testimony and disputes over exhibits and objections are generally omitted.

Questioning of Charles Kivowitz, MD, by Don Howarth on January 12, 1995:

Question: ... Doctor, what were you saying?

Answer: What happened here is we changed her from the Demerol ...

Question: Did you want to change the time or something?

Answer: Yes. I was there at that time, and I believe what
             I did was I changed her from a Demerol drip
             to a morphine drip. And the reason I did that
             is that the amount of fluid that we had given
             the day before was in excess by over a thousand
             cc's of the output, and I changed it to reduce
             the amount of fluid she received.

[Testimony omitted]

Question: And she doesn't wake up, and you start the
             morphine drip; right?

Answer: The morphine drip simply replaced the
             Demerol drip.

Question: Morphine is much more potent than Demerol,
             isn't it?

Answer: On a milligram-for-milligram basis, morphine
             is more potent than Demerol. However, the
             amount of morphine I was giving her was es-
             sentially equivalent to the dose of Demerol.

Question: The 5 milligrams?

Answer: Yeah, the dosage equivalence is roughly ten
             to one, and I changed it from 50 milligrams
             of Demerol to 5 milligrams of morphine and
             ordered titrate for comfort and sedation.

[Testimony omitted]

Question: And when you started the morphine drip, there is no indication of any pain here in the records, is there?

Answer: As I said, I changed the ... I changed from the Demerol drip to an equivalent dose of morphine and titrated it because of the volume involved in administering the Demerol.

Question: When you started the morphine, there is no indication of any pain here in the records, is there?

Ms. Watson: Objection.

Answer: She was pain free from the Demerol.

Question: And in fact the Demerol had been keeping her asleep; right?

Answer: The Demerol had been effective, yes.

[Testimony omitted]

Question: Let's take a look at exhibit 94. Exhibit 94 is 311.

[Exhibit 94 was marked.]

Answer: Okay.

Question: Now, we're on October 27, still at 1930. Right?

Answer: Yes.

Question: Morphine drip goes up to 15 milligrams. Right?

Answer: Yes.

Question: Your order?

Answer: No, I don't believe so, but it was probably on the basis of an earlier order.

Question: Of yours.

Answer: Of mine.

[Testimony omitted]

Question: No sign of pain or discomfort?

Answer: She is not in pain, no.

Question: And then there is a call to you to discuss increasing the drip?

[Testimony omitted]

Answer: I assume that the call occurred about 2100 as it's said here.

[Testimony omitted]

Question: Let's see, where was I? 2100. 2200, you were there; right?

Answer: Yes.

Question:	Ten o'clock at night. "10 milligrams of morphine IVP." What's that?
Answer:	It means I gave her morphine 10 milligrams in the intravenous drip.
Question:	Over and above what was in the drip?
Answer:	I believe it may have been over and above what was in the drip.
Question:	And how did you give her this?
Answer:	As I said, intravenously.
Question:	Did you pump it into her arm?
Answer:	Into her arm.
Question:	Or into wherever the drip was connected?
Answer:	I believe again I answered the question. I gave it to her intravenously.
Question:	Did you pump it in?
Answer:	What do you mean by "pump"?
Question:	Did you push it into her arm?
Mr. Barnosky:	Objection as to form.
Answer:	I put it into an intravenous line into a burette or into the line directly.

Question: Did you just let it drip or did you pump the line?

Answer: "Pump the line." I don't recall.

Question: Did you force it at a faster rate than the drip?

Answer: I don't recall. Probably it went in at a faster rate than the drip; otherwise, I wouldn't have given it that way.

[Testimony omitted]

Question: She is in a deep sleep?

Answer: I think she is moribund.

Question: In a deep sleep?

Answer: More than a deep sleep.

Question: Not arousable?

Answer: Hopefully not arousable.

Question: And then another added 10 milligrams to the burette.

Answer: If it says I did that, I did that.

Question: Do you remember doing that?

Answer: I don't remember it.

Question: And then a 15 milligram dose by the doctor?
                   What was that?

Answer: No. It says here another … it says another 10
                   milligrams added to burette's 15-milligram
                   dose. So that, over a period of time, the rate
                   of the morphine administration would be in-
                   creased. It was not pushed at that point or in-
                   jected directly. It was placed in the burette.

                   At this point in time, I expected and for
                   24 … at least 24 hours before, I expected … my
                   expectation that Miss Duke's condition was ex-
                   pectant, I expected her to die, and at the same
                   time I was treating her with increased doses
                   of morphine, she was fulminant pulmonary
                   edema from which I would not under any cir-
                   cumstances expect her to awaken.

Question: And you expected her to die when you added
                   that extra morphine, didn't you?

Mr. Barnosky: Objection as to form.

Answer: I expected that at some time during the suc-
                   ceeding hours, she would die.

Question: Weren't you surprised that she did not die
                   earlier?

Ms. Watson: Objection.

Answer: Actually, no.

Question: 2300 hours, "Lungs filling up with fluid." Do you see that?

Answer: Yes.

Question: Did you do anything to stop that?

Answer: No. As I said, I was not treating pulmonary edema or the condition that preceded it, which was severe corporal edema or the ... I was not treating what I knew was an overload of fluid in her body.

Question: It says "Additional morphine from doctor hasn't changed patient's assessments, ineffective." Right?

Answer: I don't think that means a thing. And I don't believe that that was true.

Question: Did you tell anybody that was wrong?

Answer: No.

Question: Then "Morphine drip continued, 15 milligrams per hour"?

[Testimony omitted]

Question: I guess we go over to the 28th now on the next entry. 100 hours, "Circulatory status increasingly deteriorating"?

Answer: Yes. This is a description of a woman who is terminally ill dying on a morphine drip. It is a very good description. It is a miserable kind of death, except she was not aware of it. And she was comfortable and she was pain free.

Question: And then the morphine is "continued at 15 milligrams an hour, eyes closed"?

Answer: You're reading this note?

Question: Yes, down at the bottom of the page. "Morphine continued at 15 milligrams per hour, eyes closed."

Answer: Yes.

Question: No signs or symptoms of pain or distress?

Answer: I hope not.

Question: You believe that to be accurate?

Answer: I believe that is accurate at that time.

[Testimony omitted]

Question: Dr. Kivowitz is called, and you increase the morphine drip.

Answer: Yes.

Question: Why was that?

Answer: I wanted to end the agony of these last few
                       hours of life.

Question: She wasn't feeling anything at this time,
                       was she?

Answer: No.

[Question omitted]

Question: Do you agree with me that she is not suffering?

Answer: I agree she is feeling no pain.

[Testimony omitted]

Question: When you say you increased the morphine
                       level so she wouldn't linger, you mean so she
                       would die?

Ms. Watson: Objection.

Mr. Barnosky: Objection as to form. You can answer.

Answer: **The answer is that I increased the morphine
                       so that she would not linger, that she would
                       not suffer, and ultimately that she would die
                       perhaps shortly or sooner than she would
                       have otherwise died from her medical con-
                       ditions, which I judged within a 48-hour pe-
                       riod were of a terminal nature.** [Emphasis
                       added]

At the conclusion of the deposition, Don and Suzelle loaded their notebooks into their briefcases and turned to exit the room. "Thank you, Dr. Kivowitz," said Don.

"You're welcome," said Dr. Kivowitz.

As Don and Suzelle drove back to their office, they talked of the testimony they had obtained from Dr. Kivowitz. Certainly there was an admission that a no code blue had been instituted shortly before the death of Miss Duke, and it was known that she had been receiving high doses of morphine. Dr. Kivowitz admitted that he had increased the dose of morphine from five milligrams per hour to fifteen milligrams per hour, and then he introduced an additional ten milligrams, and he continued to order increased amounts of morphine so that she might die sooner than she would have otherwise died from her medical conditions. There was absolutely no merit to the assertion that he was attempting to ease her suffering, because she was not suffering. She was already under the influence of five milligrams of morphine per hour, which was more than enough to prevent suffering. The clear intent was to terminate her life.

As noted previously, the body of Doris Duke was cremated immediately after her death, before an autopsy could be performed to determine the quantities and types of drugs she had been given just prior to her death. No one was ever charged or indicted in the death of Doris Duke. Eventually Bernard Lafferty and US Trust were removed as coexecutors of her estate. US Trust was criticized by Judge Preminger for failing to control lavish spending by coexecutor Barnard Lafferty and for loaning money to Lafferty to assist him in repaying funds he spent from the estate. Dr. Demopoulos was named as one of the trustees of the Doris Duke Charitable Foundation, a position he holds to this day.

In 1996, Bernard Lafferty, the butler who inherited $4.5 million and a $500,000-per-year salary for life, suffered a heart attack and died at the age of fifty-one years. Although the coroner determined that there was no sign of foul play, many speculated that someone had induced his death as punishment for his mistreatment of Doris. However, no one was ever charged or indicted in his death.

As I reflected upon this case, I wondered why there was no criminal prosecution for the death of Doris. There was not the slightest suggestion by anyone that she ever requested an assisted suicide. Instead there was a doctor who admitted that he increased doses of morphine so the patient might die "sooner than she would have otherwise died from her medical conditions," with absolutely no indication that the patient had expressed this desire. But even if she had, inducing the death would be unlawful under California law. I thought of the affidavit signed by Doris's nurse, Tammy Payette, wherein she stated that Doris Duke would have lived at least an additional five years if her death had not been induced, and that Bernard Lafferty and Dr. Kivowitz had conspired to murder her with an overdose of morphine. I thought of the fact that Dr. Federman, whose deposition was taken after Dr. Kivowitz's, testified that Doris Duke was discharged home from Cedars-Sinai Medical Center though her doctors believed she was going to die. Then I thought of the fact that at the time of her death, the only people around her deathbed were her butler Bernard Lafferty, attorneys, doctors, and nurses, but not one family member. There was not one person to speak up on behalf of Doris Duke, as her death had been induced by morphine.

As I thought of all of these things, I wondered, was there motive for Bernard Lafferty to orchestrate the murder of Doris Duke? Why not simply wait for her to die and then inherit from her estate and become her executor, and why would others assist in this murder? Then it occurred to me. The reason Bernard Lafferty would orchestrate the murder of Doris Duke when he did, in the way he did, is that if her death were postponed she might become lucid and change her mind about allowing Lafferty to serve as her executor and inherit from her estate. In the effort to acquire her multibillion-dollar estate, it was necessary to move quickly while she was incompetent and unable to make decisions concerning her bequests, because when she became lucid, she might change her mind. Thus, there was motive.

Perhaps most peculiar is the fact that Gil Garcetti, the Los Angeles district attorney in 1993, chose not to prosecute this case. Do we value our elderly so little today that we can arbitrarily terminate their lives? Do we value them so little that we will not prosecute those who openly admit to terminating an elder's life? Michael Jackson, who was considered for appointment to the Doris Duke Charitable Foundation, also died from an overdose of medication, and his physician, Conrad Murray, MD, was convicted of involuntary manslaughter in 2011. What possibly could have been Gil Garcetti's rationale for not prosecuting the case involving Doris Duke? As I pondered this question, I remembered that there is no statute of limitations for murder in the State of California.

14

Remembering Doris Duke

I stood with Don and Suzelle next to the fireplace in the living room of their large home on the three-acre estate, high in the mountains overlooking Malibu and the Pacific Ocean. On each side of the fireplace was a life-size statue of a Russian wolfhound. Above the fireplace was a beautiful original Andrew Wyeth painting of a woman leaning on a large anchor, talking to two young boys on an Atlantic beach.

"Is that a painting of Suzelle?" I asked Don.

"Yes, it is," he replied with an affectionate smile. "There is a copy in the Howarth-Smith Conference Room at the University of Virginia Law School. As you know, Suzelle is the youngest member of the Board of Trustees of the University of Virginia. Someday this original will be in the conference room in place of the copy."

On the mantel of the fireplace was a photograph of Doris Duke she had given to them years earlier. In the photograph, Doris appeared to be in her late twenties. It caught my attention. Suzelle picked it up, and we looked at it closely. "She really was a very beautiful woman," said Suzelle. "It is hard to understand why her mother always told her that she was unattractive. I suppose we will never know why Nanaline seemed to have so much hostility and anger toward Miss Duke. Undoubtedly it caused tremendous psychological damage."

Suzelle set the photograph back on the mantel as we turned and walked to the sofa and chairs. After we had taken our seats, Don and Suzelle began to reminisce about the years when they served as Doris's attorneys. It was clear as they talked that they had a great deal of affection for her.

"I think that Miss Duke had learned to keep a wall around her until she decided that she could trust someone. Once that trust was established, she would let them in and could be very gracious and kind," said Suzelle. "I always called her 'Miss Duke.' I grew up in the South, and we always referred to elderly women in that fashion. I think Miss Duke was very comfortable with that. Trust is something that is earned. It can't be faked. While Miss Duke was clear in her thinking, she generally knew who she could trust. I suspect that when she was younger she would sometimes associate with people she didn't really trust, but it didn't matter, because she could control them. But I think her loneliness in her later years caused her to become careless in those she actually trusted. That is what caused her demise."

Don and I were each enjoying a cup of English breakfast tea as we talked. Don leaned back on the sofa, crossing his right ankle over his left knee. An avid surfer, he had the appearance of the perfect contemporary gentleman in his designer jeans and casual shirt. He began to remember stories of their experiences with Doris. He also referred to her as Miss Duke. "Miss Duke would often invite us to spend the night at Shangri La (her mansion in Hawaii). I would explain to her that we were her attorneys and that it was important for us to maintain a professional relationship, and for that reason we needed to stay in a hotel. While that seemed to disappoint her, I think she understood that we were watching out for her best interest. Suzelle had to be careful that Miss Duke did not begin to think of her in the way she thought of Chandi—that is, as her lost daughter, Arden."

*Photograph of Don Howarth, personal attorney of
Doris Duke and Harry Demopoulos, MD*

*Photograph of Suzelle Smith, personal attorney of
Doris Duke and Harry Demopoulos, MD*

"There were a few times when I became concerned that she was developing those ideas about me, and I tried to find ways to discourage it without hurting her," said Suzelle. "Miss Duke was a very vulnerable woman who could become easy prey for the unscrupulous. That is probably how so many dangerous people were able to take advantage of her."

"How did you meet Doris?" I asked Don.

A smile broke on Don's face as he said, "I will never forget the time Miss Duke was introduced to us by Dr. Demopoulos, in 1991, to deal with the problem of Chandi Heffner. She told us that she wanted to 'unadopt' Chandi. I explained to her that although our firm does not practice adoption law, I know that an adoption is like a live birth. It can't be undone, assuming the adoption was done properly. Miss Duke looked exasperated. 'What do you mean it can't be undone? I divorced two men. Why can't I unadopt my adopted daughter?' At Miss Duke's request we later obtained all of the documents from the probate court concerning the adoption. As we expected, every i was dotted and every t was crossed. Chandi's attorneys were very careful to make sure the adoption was legal. We told Miss Duke that while she could disinherit Chandi, she could not unadopt her. My suggestion was that she settle with Chandi by giving her a million dollars or so and getting her to sign a full release of all claims against the estate. For some reason Miss Duke did not want to give her a dime, even though she knew that if she did not do so, Chandi would someday receive much more." As Don spoke, I wondered if subconsciously Doris wanted Chandi to receive more than just the suggested $1 million. I wondered if, although she would never have admitted it, deep down inside she was hoping that Chandi would receive a sizable portion of her estate and later in life remember that Doris had only wanted the love of a daughter. In reality, that is precisely what happened when Chandi settled with the estate for $65 million.

"Despite Miss Duke's tremendous wealth," said Don, "she could be extremely frugal, and sensitive to others' concerns. I remember an occasion wherein Suzelle and I had invited her to dinner at a nice restaurant near Shangri La in Hawaii. She looked at the menu and said that she would like a particular salad, but she went on to say that because it was two dollars more than a less expensive salad, she wanted to choose the lesser salad. It was almost as though she wanted us to reassure her that it was okay with us for her to have the more expensive salad. Of course we invited her to select the salad she really desired. But it was interesting how she thought of others despite her tremendous wealth and how she always remained frugal. On another occasion we were at her home in Hawaii with an artist who was assisting us in creating mosaic artwork. Miss Duke loved her art. While we were working, Miss Duke sent Bernard to a local store to purchase some glue. He returned with a tube of glue that Miss Duke could not get to work properly because the tube was defective. Although the glue had cost only about a dollar twenty-nine per tube, she sent Bernard all the way back to the store to return the defective tube of glue."

Suzelle added, "I think even at that time the seeds were being sown for the later actions of Bernard. I noticed that he really seemed to resent being sent to the store to return the glue. After the death of Miss Duke, when we learned that Bernard had been appointed executor, we were astounded. Bernard is the last person we would have thought would ever be her executor. He generally stayed in the background. She would not let him eat or drink with us. When she wanted something from him, she would summon him with a bell. When we flew on the plane, he was in the back of the plane unless she wanted something, and then he would be summoned. Nothing about their relationship ever suggested that he would ever have any possibility of being her executor. Indeed, when we were discussing possible executors for her estate, his name was never mentioned. It didn't make sense that he would suddenly become her executor."

Don then recalled an occasion when they were flying with Doris on her private jet. "I was sitting next to Miss Duke on the plane when she said she had a dividend she needed to cash. She was afraid that if she didn't give it to me, she would lose it, and she didn't seem to trust Bernard with it. She pulled from her purse a crumpled dividend check in the amount of one hundred thousand dollars and gave it to me to deposit for her."

"Why do you think the New York Surrogate Court ultimately decided to remove Lafferty and to put Dr. Demopoulos on the Board of Trustees of the Doris Duke Foundation?" I asked.

Suzelle leaned forward slightly in her chair. "I believe that as Judge Eve Preminger heard the evidence, she ultimately concluded that Lafferty had, at minimum, engaged in self-dealing and breach of fiduciary duty, which is the reason she removed him as the executor of the estate. I should mention that Judge Preminger did a phenomenal job presiding over this case. At first she just thought that the case was a little unusual, as litigation involving large estates often becomes. But as she began to see more of the evidence, she began to realize that something was seriously amiss. She was under tremendous pressure to leave Lafferty and US Trust in office as the executors. The newspapers were publishing scathing articles about her decisions in the case. Ultimately she ordered Lafferty and the trust removed, and she appointed Dr. Demopoulos as one of the members of the Board of Trustees of the Doris Duke Charitable Foundation. It was an uphill battle all the way. We were very fortunate to have a judge as astute and honest as Judge Preminger. Many judges would have caved under the pressure."

"Do you feel that Doris was murdered?" I asked.

Suzelle said, "According to the deposition testimony of Dr. Kivowitz, he had concluded that she had only thirty-six to forty-eight hours to live. He claimed that as an act of mercy, while she was on Demerol, he administered morphine to speed the dying process. Immediately upon hearing that, I placed a telephone call to Ira Reiner, the former district attorney of Los Angeles County, and asked him his opinion of the admission that had been obtained from Dr. Kivowitz. He said it met the definition of murder. Even so, neither Dr. Kivowtiz nor Bernard Lafferty, nor anyone else for that matter, was ever prosecuted for the death of Miss Duke. This was a case that no one wanted to prosecute. Maybe it was just that no one wanted to be on the wrong side of Lafferty if he prevailed. I just don't know."

Suzelle continued. "Another person who was under tremendous pressure during this process was Tammy Payette. She was Miss Duke's nurse and the person who first came forward with information concerning the events in her last days. She had a tremendous amount of information to share about the incident and claimed quite frankly that there was a conspiracy to murder Miss Duke, and that she had been murdered. Unfortunately, her credibility was damaged when she was charged with petty theft for taking property from Miss Duke's estate. It was known that after Miss Duke died, people began taking small items from her home. Tammy was one who was set up and caught—we believe because she was prepared to testify against the others. What she had taken was petty in comparison to Lafferty's million-dollar spending spree. But she is the one who got prosecuted. It just didn't make sense."

Later that same day we enjoyed lunch at a nice Italian restaurant in Malibu. The owner stopped by our table to say hello to Don and Suzelle, who seemed to know nearly everyone in the community. "Please excuse the construction," he said. "We are expanding." As we enjoyed our Italian cuisine, Don began to recount another amazing incident in the life of Doris.

"One of the strangest events in the last days of Miss Duke," he said, "involved a checking account with Chemical Bank, where she had placed one billion dollars that was collecting the simple interest one would expect in a checking account. Any financial advisor would tell you that would be the last thing one would want to do with his money. Apparently Bernard convinced her that her money wasn't safe there and needed to be moved. As amazing as it sounds, he actually obtained a counter checking account withdrawal slip. He persuaded her to sign it and sent it to the bank. Can you imagine the expression that must have appeared on the poor teller's face when she got a withdrawal slip for one billion dollars?" Don laughed.

He continued. "The bank was so concerned about losing the money, which they no doubt had invested elsewhere, providing a substantial interest income, that they sent a vice president and some other bank officers to try to persuade her not to withdraw the money. They came into her room at Falcon Lair, where Bernard and several employees of the household were with Miss Duke. They asked her a few questions about whether she indeed wanted to withdraw the money. Bernard asked her leading questions that required yes or no answers. She provided the answers she thought Bernard wanted her to say, thereby assuring the bank officers that she did intend to withdraw the money. They left disappointed but believing that she knew what she wanted, which was to withdraw the funds. As they left the room and closed the door behind them, Miss Duke turned to those left in the room and said, 'It sure is lovely here in Paris today.' She didn't know she was in Beverly Hills. If they had heard that, they would have known something was seriously wrong and might have been able to do something about her situation. But they didn't hear her."

Before we parted company that day, I asked Don and Suzelle, "If there were one message that you could convey to of the members of the Duke family, what would that message be?"

Don said, "The story of Miss Duke is so unfortunate. She had become an island unto herself. She had lost contact with all of her family members. If that had not happened, she never would have become alone and vulnerable to the abuses of Bernard Lafferty and his cohorts. If there were one message I could convey to the members of the Duke family, after seeing what happened to Miss Duke, it would be that nothing is as important as family. Anyone, even a distant family member, could have prevented what happened to her. Family can never be replaced. It is the most important institution we possess. Because she had lost contact with her family members, Miss Duke died a tragic, lonely death."

Suzelle said, "I would agree with what Don said. I would encourage the members not only of the Duke family but of all families to reach out to one another and share the family relationships with which we are blessed. I would encourage people to avoid losing contact with one another and remember the importance of love and forgiveness. I would say, 'Don't allow yourselves to become distant and separated.' Once family relations break down and a person is lost, that person is gone forever. You can't go back and undo what has been done, or do what has not been done."

As I drove down Pacific Coast Highway from Malibu toward Santa Monica, with the ocean to my right on this overcast afternoon, I understood the reason Doris had enjoyed the company of Don and Suzelle and wanted them as her attorneys and her friends. I contemplated the tragedy of the circumstances surrounding her death and how her butler had managed to cut her off from everyone who could have helped her, and I thought of Don and Suzelle's message for families everywhere: Family is the most important institution we possess. Once family relations break down and the person is lost, that person is gone forever.

Part 3

The Legacy Continues
(Featured Stories)

Although this book is written in the form of a historical fiction novel, it is based almost entirely on factual events, though events have been dramatized to bring them to life for the enjoyment of the reader and for purposes of illustration. Ordinarily a novel flows from beginning to end in what my editors refer to as a story arc, which is a single theme throughout. When writing a biographical novel that spans several generations, it is difficult to keep a single story arc throughout. The stories in this section do not fit well within the arc that flows loosely through the first two sections. For that reason, I have included these stories in part 3 of this book. While this section is separate from the first two sections, I believe the reader will find it equally of interest.

15

An Amazing Story of a Missing Heir of James Buchanan Duke

B orn on April 11, 1982, at Centinela Medical Center in Inglewood, California, a suburb of Los Angeles, Sean Means entered the world a happy baby boy with little concern about life's difficult issues. Shortly after Sean's birth, his parents, Jack Means and Karen Rich, separated briefly. They reunited when Sean was one year old, only to separate permanently when he was five years old. After the breakup, his mother faced the formidable task of raising Sean as a single mother. Sean's father moved to Arizona in 1990, so Sean knew little about him except that he was a drummer. Yet, for reasons he could not fully understand, he found himself interested in his paternal historical roots, though he knew nothing of his ancestry.[216]

I met with Sean and Karen for lunch on a cold, cloudy afternoon in February 2013 at a popular Mexican restaurant in Manhattan Beach called Ponchos. At a height of six feet four inches, Sean exhibits an appearance of confidence. His smile reveals the genuineness of his character, which is likewise apparent in his pleasant personality. The host seated us at a table on an upper-floor balcony

---

216 For another account of the story of Sean Means, see Maria Wilhelm and Dirk Mathison, "An Unlikely Inheritance," *O* magazine, February 2010.

overlooking the lower level. As the area was surrounded by a large variety of plants, the atmosphere seemed outdoors, though we were inside. Karen sat across the table from me and Sean sat to her left.

"Do you remember your father from your childhood?" I asked Sean.

"I don't have too much memory of him as a child because I was only five when my parents separated."

"You mentioned that he was a drummer; did you ever have an opportunity to play music with him?"

"No, I was really too young to play an instrument," Sean replied. "I remember that he had a music studio in a separate building on our property. That is where the band practiced and recorded. I couldn't even hear them play from the house because the studio was so well insulated. I remember that he loved Yes and Led Zeppelin. He talked about them the most, and their music was always playing in the house."

"Did you hear him play the drums often?"

"I only heard my father play the drums one time. My mother took me to Venice Beach when his band was playing in an outdoors concert. There was a huge crowd. There must have been thousands of people. I was mesmerized by the way he played. The drums seemed to be the prominent instrument in the band."

"At some point you learned that you are descended from Washington Duke, for whom Duke University is named. How did you learn about that?"

"When I was about thirteen, Mom told me that. I don't remember that I had ever heard it before. She said I was his great-great-great-grandson and that Duke University was named after him."

"Did you understand what that meant?"

"At that time I really didn't. I had heard of Duke University and had seen the basketball games on TV, but it really didn't mean too much to me at that time. I was pretty young. Mom didn't really say anything about money. It was more that she was just trying to tell me about my family." Sean laughed. "I remember that my mom told me to look at my toes. She showed me that my second toe was longer than my first and that it was a rare congenital condition called Morton's toe. She said it is a common trait in the Duke family. After that day, Mom didn't mention my heritage again for many years."

As a teenager, Sean would often visit the Duke University website to learn what he could about this amazing university. There he would read about Washington Duke and how he had established W. Duke, Sons & Company, which eventually grew into the American Tobacco Company. He read about the Duke investments in textiles and electricity, and the formation of Duke Energy.

Sean continued. "I often wondered if it really is possible that these people are my family. I have always known Mom to be truthful, but I wondered if she might be mistaken. I wondered if I really was descended from Washington Duke, and I wondered if my cousins would see me as a family member if they knew me. I doubted that they even knew I existed." Sean looked at the table as if he were deep in thought. After a few moments I asked Sean, "What were your favorite activities while you were growing up?"

"I loved art and computer games," he replied. "When I was a teenager I spent most of my time playing computer games. I even got a job working for Nintendo, where I tested their games."

"Did you have an interest in sports?" I asked. "You are tall. Did you consider playing basketball?"

"I did, and I thought about attending college on a scholarship, but I knew the competition would be fierce. Later I was injured in an automobile accident and probably could not have played anyway due to the injury."

"You also mentioned art. Why don't you tell me about that?"

"I remember that I really enjoyed art. Mom would often take me to Venice Beach, where we would spend the day drawing sketches. I enjoyed that as much as computer games. Then I got into graphic art and using computers to create art."

Unbeknownst to Sean, on a number of occasions while he was

growing up, his mother retained attorneys to try to claim Sean's inheritance. The attorneys would contact the Doris Duke Trust and then give up when they were told they would need to submit DNA samples to prove Sean was a descendant of Washington Duke.

As Sean grew into his twenties, he acquired a number of jobs, ranging from working as a clerk at See's Candy to his current job, working in management for Staples. It was a typical day at his job at Staples in 2009 when a fortuitous encounter with a young attorney named Brian Kramer changed his life forever. Brian Kramer had achieved a name for himself in family law by representing celebrities and socialites in divorce and custody cases.[217]

Brian entered Staples to purchase some office equipment. Sean offered to assist, and Brian found him very likable and knowledgeable about office supplies. After they had spent a substantial amount of time looking for a fax machine, Sean learned that Brian was a family law attorney; this seemed to pique Sean's interest. Sean explained that he would like to show Brian something and that he might have a legal matter for Brian to consider. Brian had been impressed with Sean's presentation and professionalism, and he believed Sean to be a likable person. For these reasons, he agreed to stay around the store until Sean's break.

When Sean's break arrived, he took Brian to his car, where he showed him a trunk full of papers and newspaper clippings. "Have you ever heard of the billionaire heiress of James Buchanan Duke, his daughter Doris Duke?"

"Sure," replied Brian.

"Well, I believe I am related to her and that I am an heir to

---

217 Brian received his bachelor of science at the University of Kansas and his doctor of jurisprudence at the University of Michigan Law School and is a certified legal specialist in family law with the California State Bar. His success as an attorney is well-known throughout Southern California, and ironically he has squared off in the courtroom opposite another team of lawyers well-known to the Duke family—Don Howarth and Suzelle Smith, discussed in preceding chapters.

her father's estate," said Sean. As Brian stood looking at this tall, handsome young man standing next to his humble Volkswagen Jetta filled with newspaper clippings and paraphernalia to prove his case, he found it necessary to restrain his desire to chuckle. Yet, while the story seemed so unrealistic, something seemed to give it a kernel of truth.

"Why is it you believe you are related?" asked Brian.

"Many years ago my mother told me that my father was descended from Washington Duke through his daughter Mary Duke Lyon and that I am an heir of the Doris Duke Trust."

"I think we should probably schedule an appointment in my office, where we can discuss this more completely. You have made some very interesting comments. Why don't you try to collect and organize all of the information you can find to show that you are Washington Duke's descendant. We will examine the evidence in my office."

"Thank you for looking at this for me," said Sean.

"I am delighted to help, but I can't promise anything," replied Brian.

Several weeks later Sean and his mother appeared at Brian's Los Angeles office with a box full of documents. Sean set the box on the floor and then began laying the documents out on the desk as he explained his story based on his limited information. The box contained a number of documents of evidentiary significance, none of which was conclusive on its face. Sean and his mother explained that as an heir to the Doris Duke Trust, Sean stood to receive millions of dollars paid out over his lifetime, with a large payout upon the deaths of certain surviving heirs. However, while the money was certainly a matter of interest, the greatest interest for Sean was to know about his family. "I really want to know about my roots, and I hope to meet my family members and possibly become involved in the Duke philanthropic activities."

Brian listened carefully to this intriguing story. The degree of Sean's sincerity somehow made the story seem remotely plausible to Brian. *Either he is correct about what he is saying, or he honestly believes that what he is saying is true, regardless of the accuracy. This cannot be a complete fabrication or imagination,* thought Brian. *It has too many viable moving parts.*

Brian saw documents showing his father's status as a beneficiary of the Doris Duke Trust and a birth certificate that identified him as Sean's father, but perhaps most compelling was documentation showing that his father had paid child support and had had visitation rights while Sean was in his teens. All of these little pieces of evidence could not have been fabricated by Sean or anyone else. There must be something to this story.

Brian asked for the names of any living relatives who could verify the story. Sean gave him the name of his father, Jack Means, and he then explained that he had not had any contact with his father for many years and that his father had not been willing to help previously. Sadly, his paternal grandmother, Marion Means, did not ever see Sean before she died. The only other name Sean could provide was John Sessums, an uncle his father had mentioned. He thought that John Sessums might be able to provide some information for Brian's search.

After the meeting, Brian conducted a person search and was able to locate a deceased John Sessums from Redlands, California, who had been active in the motion picture industry.[218] Further investigation revealed that this John Sessums had a friend named Gerald Sanders, whom Brian was able to locate. Brian contacted Gerald, who confirmed that Sean was indeed descended from Washington Duke and that John Sessums was his father's uncle. Sean's biological paternal grandfather was a Sessums, but his stepgrandfather, who legally adopted his father, was James Means. Brian was able to locate James Means, who was by then in his late seventies, who provided further confirmation of the truthfulness

---

218 Wilhelm and Mathison, "An Unlikely Inheritance," *O* magazine, February 2010, 4.

of Sean's story.[219] By examining court documents concerning Jack's child support and visitation rights, Brian discovered that Sean's father had acknowledged in those proceedings that Sean was his son.[220] The pieces were falling into place. Now Brian had to contact the Doris Duke Trust to assert a claim.

Through his investigation, Brian learned that Sean was descended from Washington through his daughter Mary Duke, who had married Robert Edwin Lyon. Their son Edwin Buchanan Lyon had a daughter named Marion Lyon. Marion's first marriage was to John W. Sessums Jr., and her second was to James Means. Although Jack Means, Sean's father, was John and Marion's son, James Means legally adopted him, which is how Jack and Sean acquired the name Means. Thus, Sean is the great-great-great-grandson of Washington Duke.

The Doris Duke Trust had been established on December 11, 1924, shortly before the death of James Buchanan Duke. Buck had realized that his health was failing and, with the assistance of his legal counsel, had determined that a trust was the best way to ensure the security of his only daughter, Doris, particularly in light of his deteriorating relationship with his wife, Nanaline. The trust provided that two-thirds of its income would be distributed to Doris Duke over her lifetime, with the remaining one-third to be divided among all of the lineal descendants of his father, Washington Duke.[221]

As Brian contemplated the seemingly insurmountable task of obtaining an audience with the trust administrators, he felt that he should first make contact with Jack Means, Sean's father. Previously Sean's father had been unwilling to add Sean's name

219 Wilhelm and Mathison, "An Unlikely Inheritance," *O* magazine, February 2010, 4.

220 Ibid.

221 Last Will and Testament and Codicil of James B. Duke, Inventory of James Buchanan Duke Papers, 1777–1990 and undated, 1924–1925, Box 13, David M. Rubenstein Rare Book and Manuscript Library, Duke University.

as an heir to the trust by executing an affidavit attesting to his relationship to Sean. Eventually Brian contacted him telephonically, hopeful that he would now be prepared to execute such an affidavit. Notwithstanding that Sean had not seen his father in two decades, his father was eager to learn about Sean and his welfare. After confirming to his satisfaction that Sean was Jack's son, and obtaining the affidavit, Brian was finally prepared to contact the trust on Sean's behalf. He presented documentation and a letter to the trust's attorney, Arthur E. Moorehead IV, explaining the relationship between Sean and his father, Jack, who was already a known heir to the trust. While the response from Moorehead was discouraging, it was also anticipated. Because of the unusual circumstances surrounding the matter, the trust required proof by Y-DNA that Jack was Sean's father. This meant that Jack and Sean would have to submit to DNA tests to determine paternity.[222]

Brian again contacted Sean's father, who was eager to assist Sean in obtaining his birthright by submitting to a DNA test. Brian and Sean drove to Phoenix to meet with Jack for their first reunion in twenty years and for the purpose of testing. Upon arriving in Phoenix, they checked into a hotel and notified Jack that they had arrived. Sean anxiously anticipated seeing his father for the first time as an adult. Jack was equally anxious to see his son. Upon meeting, they found an immediate commonality in hobbies and interests, from sports cars to model airplanes. They located a DNA testing facility in a strip mall, where they submitted to the tests. The results, which confirmed the father-and-son relationship, were mailed to the trust, thereby establishing Sean's status as an heir to the Doris Duke Trust.[223]

The question remained, why did Jack let Sean wait so long before disclosing his true identity? I asked Sean that question. Sean

---

222 Wilhelm and Mathison, "An Unlikely Inheritance," *O* magazine, February 2010, 4.
223 Ibid.

replied, "He said that he was concerned that if I came into my inheritance when I was too young, I might not be able to preserve it and it might cause me to be reckless with money and with my life. For that reason he decided to wait until I reached adulthood before helping me claim my inheritance."

Sean paused for a moment then continued. "I am really glad that he did, and I have thought a lot about it. I have decided that I am not going to make any sudden changes in my life. I am going to do everything with a great deal of thought and deliberation."

At the time of the writing of this book, Sean still works at Staples, though he now holds a managerial position. He was determined not to make the common mistake of changing his life too quickly, which often causes heirs of vast fortunes to squander their inheritance. He will inherit millions of dollars over his lifetime, but he still plans to pursue a constructive career as an artist and possibly a professor of art. Sean has completed two years as an art major at Santa Monica City College, where he maintains a 3.7 grade point average on a four-point scale.

"Have you thought about visiting Duke University?" I asked.

"I have, and I think I would like to meet Coach K if I can. I would also like to find a way to become involved in family philanthropic activities."

As we were leaving and waiting for the valet to bring our automobiles around, I heard a sound that reminded me of the roar of engines at the Indianapolis 500 as a boy. I turned around as the valet brought up Sean's famous $60,000 580-horsepower, dual-exhaust burgundy Camaro. "I have heard about that car," I said with a smile. "It's beautiful."

"It's really the only toy I have purchased with the money from my inheritance so far," he replied.

I was amazed at the responsibility of this young man who had first come into his fortune three years earlier. There is no question that Sean will pursue a respectable professional career and will make his family proud. As Sean said good-bye and then climbed into his sports car, it occurred to me that Washington would have been thrilled to meet this young man. He would have been very proud to call Sean his grandson, and Sean would have been very proud to call Washington his grandfather. In some ways it is as though Washington, with that familiar smile on his face, had orchestrated this strange twist of fate from the heavens. Only time will tell what Sean's role in the family will become, but I have no doubt that he will live up to the Duke legacy and carry it forward with a new vision for another great day.

16

A Few Notable Descendants of Washington Duke

Although it is impossible to present all of the notable descendants of Washington Duke in this short discussion, I will highlight some of the best known and ask the indulgence of those not mentioned herein. For clarification of the relationships, please see the Partial Genealogy Chart of Descendants of Washington Duke in appendix D.

Mary Elizabeth Duke Lyon (1853–1893)
Mary Elizabeth Duke Lyon was the only daughter of Washington Duke and is the ancestor of Sean Means discussed in the immediately preceding chapter. She married Robert Edwin Lyon, a businessman from Durham, though she died from pneumonia at a fairly young age along with three of her children. Mary worked in the office of the family business until her death.

Angier Buchanan Duke (1884–1923)
Angier Buchanan Duke was born to Benjamin Newton Duke and Sarah Pearson Angier Duke. He married Cordelia Drexel Biddle, with whom he had two children—Angier Biddle Duke and Anthony Drexel Duke, both discussed below. Angier and Cordelia later

divorced. Angier graduated from Duke University in 1905. It was the plan of both Benjamin Newton Duke and his brother James Buchanan Duke that Angier would become the chief executive officer of the Duke fortune when they retired, but unfortunately he died at a young age in a boating accident in 1923. He served on the Board of Trustees of Duke University and was president of the Duke University Alumni Association. The Disney film *The Happiest Millionaire* was based on his romantic relationship with Cordelia, though the movie provides an ending that differs from the true life story by omitting his divorce and his tragic accidental death. It is said that Angier possessed a deep compassion for others, for which many members of the Duke family were known, and he always tried to bring happiness and fortune to others (hence the title of the movie).

Angier Biddle Duke[224] *(1915–1995)*
Angier Biddle Duke was born in New York City to Angier Buchanan Duke and Cordelia Biddle Duke. In the 1930s, Angier was a skiing editor for *Sports Illustrated*. He enrolled at Yale University but dropped out in 1936. In 1940 he enlisted in the US Air Force, and by the time he was discharged in 1945, he had achieved the rank of major. In 1949 he joined the US Foreign Service, and from 1952 to 1953, at the age of thirty-six years, he served as US ambassador to El Salvador. In 1953 he returned to private life and served as president of the International Rescue Commission. In 1960 he was appointed by President John F. Kennedy as chief of protocol for the US Department of State, where he remained until 1965. In 1965 he was appointed by President Johnson as US ambassador to Spain, where he remained until 1967, when he was appointed US ambassador to Denmark. In 1969 he received an honorary doctor of law from Duke University School

---

224 Richard Severo, "Angier Biddle Duke, 79, An Ambassador and Scion of Tobacco Family Has Died," *New York Times*, May 1, 1995; *Guide to Angier Biddle Duke Papers*, David M. Rubenstein Rare Book and Manuscript Library, Duke University, accessed September 22, 2013, http://library.duke.edu/rubenstein/findingaids/dukeab/.

of Law. From 1979 to 1981 he served as US ambassador to Morocco. Angier Biddle Duke remained athletic and active until his death in 1995, when he was struck by an automobile while rollerblading in Manhattan, New York, at the age of seventy-nine years.

Anthony Drexel Duke[225] (1918–)

Anthony Drexel "Tony" Duke is descended from Washington Duke through his son Benjamin Newton Duke and his wife, Sarah Pearson Duke. Anthony's parents were Angier Buchanan Duke and Cordelia Biddle Duke. After attending Princeton, Tony joined the navy, where he served for five years and was a three-time commander, earning three Battle Stars and a Bronze Star. He is president of the Normandy D-Day National Museum in New Orleans. At the age of nineteen he founded the Boys and Girls Harbor, which is an organization designed to foster academic and cultural achievement among disadvantaged youths and has served over forty thousand young people.[226] Anthony is an author of a book about his life called *Uncharted Course*. He is well-known for his humor and delightfully pleasant personality. Although descended from three prominent North Carolina families—the Dukes, the Biddles, and the Drexels—he has found his own way in life. Like his cousin Mary Duke Biddle Trent Semans, he is known as a compassionate philanthropist who is respectful of all persons regardless of race, religion, gender, or ethnicity.

Mary Duke Biddle Trent Semans[227] (1920–2012)

While Doris Duke, who died without living issue, was the sole descendant of Washington Duke's son James Buchanan Duke, Washington's

---

225 Anthony D. Duke, *Uncharted Course* (Thomaston: The Bayview Press, 2007).
226 Boys & Girls Harbor, accessed December 26, 2013, http://www.theharbor.org/our-people/founder.
227 "Mary Semans, Champion of Duke and Durham, Dies," *Duke Today*, January 25, 2012; Nicole Kyle and Chinmayi Sharma, "Mary Duke Biddle Trent Semans Dies at 91," the *Duke Chronicle*, January 25, 2012; Nicole Kyle, "Mary Duke Biddle

other son Benjamin Newton Duke, and Washington's daughter, Mary Duke Lyon, both had a number of heirs who have achieved notable distinction. One of the most prominent was Mary Duke Biddle Trent Semans, who passed away in January 2012. She was affectionately called the "godmother of Duke University," and her funeral was attended by more than 1,800 friends and family members. Mary Semans was the granddaughter of Benjamin and his wife Sarah. Her father was Anthony Joseph Drexel Biddle, a US ambassador to Spain and Poland, and her mother was Mary Lillian Duke Biddle.

During the early years of her life, Mary Semans lived with her mother at the Benjamin Duke Mansion in Manhattan. At the age of fourteen she moved to Durham to live with her maternal grandmother, Sarah P. Duke. At the age of fifteen years she applied to Duke University Women's College. She was granted admission based upon the provision that she would work hard and maintain at least a C average. Despite her young age at the time of her enrollment, she successfully graduated in 1939 and thereafter chose to continue living in Durham.

Throughout her life Mary was very active at Duke University and became a member of the board of trustees. She was also active in Durham politics with special emphasis on the economically and socially disadvantaged people of that city. She supported minority groups, such as African Americans, long before this was considered acceptable, and is the person considered most responsible for opening Duke University's doors to African American students. She would often post comments under a pseudonym in the Duke University independent student newspaper, the *Duke Chronicle*. She was a close friend of Coach Mike Krzyzewski and a strong supporter of the Blue Devils men's basketball team.

Trent Semans Called the Godmother of Duke," the *Duke Chronicle*, January 29, 2012; "Mary Semans, Heiress, UNSCA Benefactor, Dies at 91," *Winston-Salem Journal*, January 26, 2012; "Philanthropist, Arts Supporter Mary Semans Dies in NC," *Palm Beach Daily News*, January 26, 2012; Bridget Booher, "A Remarkable Life," *Duke Magazine*, April 1, 2012.

During her years as a student at Duke, she met a medical student, Josiah Charles Trent, whom she married and with whom she had four daughters: Mary Duke Trent Jones, Sarah Elizabeth Trent Harris, Rebecca Gray Trent Kirkland, and Barbara Biddle Trent Kimbrell. In 1948, Dr. Trent died of lymphoma at the young age of thirty-four years, and Mary remarried another surgeon at Duke named James Semans, with whom she had three more children: Jenny Lillian Semans Koortbojian, James Duke Biddle Trent Semans, and Beth Gotham Semans Hubbard.

In 1951, Mary Semans was the first female elected to the Durham City Council, and from 1952 to 1955 she served as mayor pro tem of Durham. In 1957, she became a trustee of the Duke Endowment. From 1961 to 1981 Mary served on the Board of Trustees of Duke University and was the first female chair of the Duke Endowment from 1982 until 2001. From 1948 to 1976 she was a trustee of the Lincoln Community Hospital and she also served on the Board of Trustees of the Mary Duke Biddle Foundation. Despite her net worth being in excess of $300 million, Mary Semans chose a simple, humble life. For years she drove about Durham in an old Ford Taurus. Her friends would sometimes joke that she had bought the car secondhand from the Biblical patriarch Moses.

Angier St. George Biddle "Pony" Duke (1938–)
Anthony St. George Biddle "Pony" Duke is a graduate of Duke University who maintains a ranch and a mine in Montana. He is a son of Angier Biddle Duke. He is best known as the coauthor of the book about his cousin Doris Duke entitled *Too Rich, The Family Secrets of Doris Duke*. The book served as the basis for a television movie by the same title.

Mary Duke Trent Jones (1940–)
Mary Duke Trent Jones is a daughter of Mary Duke Biddle Trent Semans and Josiah Trent, MD. Born in 1940, she received a bachelor of arts from Duke University in 1963 and serves on the Board

of Trustees of the Duke Endowment and the Virginia Historical Society. Currently living in Virginia, she is active in the arts and has served on the Virginia State Council of Higher Education, the Virginia Museum of Fine Arts, and the Virginia Arts Commission.

Biddle Duke (1961–)

Biddle Duke is a son of Angier Biddle Duke. He is a graduate of Duke University and New York University and is the owner of the *Stowe Reporter*, a newspaper in Stowe, Vermont. Biddle is known for his generosity, kindness, and delightful sense of humor.

Elizabeth Hubbard (1963–)

Beth Hubbard is a daughter of Mary Duke Biddle Trent Semans and James Semans, MD. Like her mother, she is a graduate of Duke University. With her husband Michael Hubbard, she owns Gotham Entertainment, a motion picture company. Her achievements as a producer so far include such popular titles as *Christmas in Compton*, *You're So Crazy*, *Ritual*, and *Woo*.

Many other descendants of Washington Duke show impressive accomplishments not included in this brief chapter. To those not mentioned here, regrettably this list is not intended to be all-inclusive but is intended to highlight only a few of the activities of descendants of Washington Duke. Perhaps a sequel to this publication will provide a more in-depth discussion of those mentioned here and of those whose achievements have not yet been realized.

17

Duke University and Beyond

Duke University[228] today stands as one of the finest academic institutions in the world. The university's various departments and schools consistently rank among the top ten in the United States in the popular *US News and World Report* university rankings. At the end of fiscal year 2012, the Duke University Endowment totaled $5.6 billion with a goal of raising an additional $3.25 billion by the end of fiscal year 2017.[229] Duke has produced forty-three Rhodes Scholars through the year 2010.[230]

The beautiful campus at Duke University in Durham, consisting of three contiguous campuses—East, West, and Central—encompasses a sprawling 8,600 acres with 220 buildings and includes the 7,200 acres of Duke Forest.[231] The university also owns a 15-acre marine lab in Beaufort, North Carolina. One of the most popular

---

228 Most of the information in this chapter is derived from "Duke University, Campus Overview," accessed December 30, 2013, http://admissions.duke.edu/setting/campus.

229 "Duke University's Endowment," Duke Forward, accessed September 22, 2013, http://dukeforward.duke.edu/ways-to-give/endowment.

230 "Duke Senior Receives Rhodes Scholarship," *Duke Today*, Office of News and Communications, accessed September 22, 2013, http://today.duke.edu/2010/11/rhodes.html.

231 "Duke University, Campus Overview," accessed December 30, 2013, http://admissions.duke.edu/setting/campus.

attractions is the 55-acre Sarah P. Duke Gardens, which consists of five miles of trails and walkways through wooded and landscaped areas divided into four sections: the Historic Core and Terraces, the Doris Duke Center Gardens, the H. L. Blomquist Garden of Native Plants, and the William Louis Culberson Asiatic Arboretum. The gardens are a memorial to Sarah P. Duke, the late wife of Benjamin Newton Duke.[232]

The West Campus buildings are based on a Gothic theme, designed primarily by Julian Abele, for which the West Campus has been ascribed the unofficial title "Gothic Wonderland." The main West Campus, considered the main campus, spans 720 acres and is the location of the administrative and academic buildings. Duke Chapel, sophomore through senior residential quads, academic quads, athletic facilities, the library, science and engineering buildings, the law school, the business school, and the medical school are all located in the West Campus. The center feature of the West campus, with the highest elevation, is Duke Chapel, with a tower 210 feet in height.[233]

The East Campus, the original location of Duke University when it moved to Durham, is the location of all freshmen housing and a number of academic buildings. The architecture is Georgian style, in contrast to the Gothic style of the West Campus. The East Campus encompasses ninety-seven acres and is 1.5 miles from the West Campus. The Literature, Art, History, Music, Philosophy, and Women's Studies Departments are located on the East Campus. In addition, the dance, drama, education, film, and university writing programs are housed on the East Campus. The East Campus also includes facilities to enhance residential living, such as a barber shop, a dining hall, a coffee shop, and similar conveniences. The

---

232 "Quick Facts About Duke," Office of News and Communication, accessed September 22, 2013, http://newsoffice.duke.edu/all-about-duke/quick-facts-about-duke; "Duke University, Campus Overview," accessed December 30, 2013, http://admissions.duke.edu/setting/campus.
233 Ibid.

East Campus was the location of the Women's College from 1930 through 1972.[234]

The Central Campus, consisting of 122 acres, lies between the East Campus and the West Campus and houses sophomores, juniors, and seniors. The Central Campus houses certain administrative offices, a police department, recreational facilities, the Freedom Center for Jewish Life, the Center for Muslim Life, and the Nasher Museum. Plans are underway to provide more of a village atmosphere to the Central Campus over the next fifty years with the objective of transforming the Central Campus into a university centerpiece.[235]

Duke Forest, established in 1931, is one of the most popular attractions at Duke. Consisting of 7,200 acres, it one of the largest private research forests in the world and is the largest in North Carolina. The forest is laced with over thirty miles of trails for public hiking, cycling, and horseback riding. In order to preserve the natural condition and safety of the park, motorized vehicles are prohibited except at two approved picnic sites, and fires are permitted only in approved grills at the two picnic sites.[236] While walking the trails of the forest, one is prudent to remain vigilant for various forms of wildlife, including potentially dangerous bears, mountain lions, rattlesnakes, and copperheads.

A favorite attraction of joggers, and my personal favorite jogging trail, is the Buehler Cross-Country Trail, which starts near Washington Duke Inn and circles through the forest, forming a loop of 2.91 miles. Although not part of Duke Forest, the trail is

---

234 "Quick Facts About Duke," Office of News and Communication, accessed September 22, 2013, http://newsoffice.duke.edu/all-about-duke/quick-facts-about-duke; "Duke University, Campus Overview," accessed December 30, 2013, http://admissions.duke.edu/setting/campus.
235 Ibid.
236 "Duke Forest at Duke University," Nicholas School of the Environment, Duke University, accessed September 22, 2013, http://www.dukeforest.duke.edu/about/index.html.

maintained by the Office of the Duke Forest. On any given day, a runner might suddenly be surrounded by members of the men's or women's cross-country team while jogging the trail; and on an exceptionally good day, he might even keep up with them, at least for a while.

Another significant feature of Duke University is the medical school. Established in 1930, the Duke University Medical Center spans eight million square feet and is one of the highest-ranked medical schools in the world. In 2014, Duke University Medical Center ranked eighth in the nation in research, in the *US News and World Report*.[237]

Duke University School of Law, also on the West Campus near the Fuqua School of Business, ranked eleventh in the 2014 *US News and World Report* law school rankings.[238] Under the leadership of Dean David Levi, the law school has developed numerous cutting-edge programs, such as the LLM in Judicial Studies[239] and programs in literature and the law.

One of the greatest features of Duke University is the Athletic Department. Men's basketball is the most popular sport in the Duke athletic program. The men's basketball team, a member of the Atlantic Coach Conference of the NCAA, Division I, under the direction of Coach Mike Krzyzewski (Coach K), has won four NCAA Championships, has played in ten championship games, and has been in the Final Four fifteen times.[240] Seventy-one of Duke's players have been selected in the NBA draft (more than any other university), and eleven have been named National Player of the Year. Thirty-six of Duke's players have been named All American,

---

237 *US News and World Report*, Medical School Rankings, 2014.
238 *US News and World Report*, Law School Rankings, 2014.
239 Duke Law Center for Judicial Studies, Duke Law, accessed September 22, 2013, http://law.duke.edu/judicialstudies/.
240 "NCAA Basketball Tournament History, Duke Blue Devils," accessed September 22, 2013, http://espn.go.com/mens-college-basketball/tournament/history/_/team1/5847.

and fourteen have been named Academic All American. Duke has been the Atlantic Coast Conference Champion nineteen times, and prior to joining the Atlantic Coast Conference, Duke won the Southern Conference Championship five times. In 2008, Duke Basketball was named by ESPN the most prestigious college basketball program since the 1985–1986 season.

Although not yet as popular as the men's basketball program, the men's football program appears well on its way to a strong return to the national recognition of the early years of the program. In 2007, Coach David Cutcliffe acquired the leadership as the head coach at Duke. Prior to his appointment, Cutcliffe was the head coach at Notre Dame before resigning for health reasons. Prior to that, he was head coach at the University of Mississippi.

Duke has also enjoyed success in a number of other athletic programs in addition to the men's basketball and football teams. The Duke Women's Basketball Team has enjoyed tremendous success over the last two decades under the leadership of Coach Gail Goestenkors and, more recently, Coach Joanne McCallie, with seven ACC Championships through 2011. Other athletic programs at Duke include cross-country, fencing, field hockey, golf, lacrosse, rowing, soccer, swimming and diving, tennis, track and field, volleyball, and wrestling.

Today Duke University is known throughout the world as a leading institution of higher education. Duke has established campuses in foreign locations, such as China, Russia, England, India, and Dubai. Duke Corporate Education, founded in 2000 by Blair Sheppard, former dean of the Duke/Fuqua School of Business and current CEO of Duke CE, is changing the way major universities interact in business and the academic world.

In addition to Duke University, the descendants of Washington Duke have established a number of substantial charities, most notably the James B. Duke Endowment and the Doris Duke Charitable Foundation. Since its inception, the Duke Endowment has contributed billions of dollars to education, child welfare, medicine, religious institutions, academic scholarships, and other charitable entities and activities. Contributions from the Duke Endowment helped to build Duke University, Davidson College, Furman University, and John C. Smith University. Today the Duke Endowment has $3 billion in assets, and since 1925 it has awarded more than $3 billion in grants.[241]

The Doris Duke Charitable Foundation was established in 1996 with $1.6 billion bequeathed to charity by the late Doris Duke. The foundation was the outcome of the litigation discussed in chapters 12 and 13. As of December 31, 2012, the Doris Duke Charitable Foundation has awarded $1.1 billion in grants. The focus of the foundation includes arts, environmental programs, medical research, prevention of child abuse and neglect, historic preservation, Islamic art, and health and welfare of disadvantaged populations.[242]

The Boys and Girls Harbor was established in 1937 by Anthony Drexel Duke, Benjamin Duke's grandson, as a camp for underprivileged boys in New York City. The organization has served over forty thousand boys and girls, many of whom have achieved extraordinary accomplishments in various professional fields.[243]

During his life, James Buchanan Duke often said that the importance of his work will be measured by the view of history from four hundred years in the future. Even after he had taken ill and was bedridden shortly before his death, he spent many hours each day working with architects and engineers on the design of the Duke University campus. Like his father Washington, his brother Benjamin, and his sister Mary, James always thought about the less fortunate and used every possible opportunity to provide benefits for others. The Dukes have always sought to provide tools, whether

241 "Ideas to Impact, 2012 Annual Report," James B. Duke Endowment, accessed September 22, 2013, http://annualreport.dukeendowment.org/2012/.
242 "Foundation Overview," Doris Duke Charitable Foundation, accessed September 22, 2013, http://www.ddcf.org/About-Us/.
243 "History of the Harbor," Boys and Girls Harbor, accessed September 22, 2013, http://www.theharbor.org/our-story/history.

in the form of education, medicine, or quality-of-life opportunities, to other human beings to improve their lives. Washington Duke and his descendants have left a remarkable legacy that will endure for centuries.

18

Afterword

On December 18, 2013, about 9:00 a.m., I was traveling west on Interstate 91, on my way to a deposition in Riverside, California. I pulled my convertible roadster up to a stoplight at the crest of the University Avenue exit ramp in the far left turn lane, where to my immediate left was a Vietnam veteran hoping for financial assistance. He appeared to be in his early sixties with a long, unkempt gray beard and mustache. He was wearing an OG-107 field jacket, probably purchased from an army-navy surplus store. With his vision cast downward, avoiding eye contact, he nodded and said softly, "Hey." On the ground by his feet was a sign that read, "Tough Times; Would Appreciate a Hand." As I stopped my car at the crosswalk, we made eye contact for a brief second. Then he quickly looked away in shame. For that brief second, as I looked into his eyes, I wondered, *What have your eyes seen? What have your ears heard?* I did not see a Vietnam veteran; nor did I see a homeless man. I did not see a beggar or a lazy man. I saw the eyes of all humanity. I saw the soul of life. I gave him a few dollars, and he said repeatedly, "God bless you. God bless you." I thought, *His blessing and gratitude are the most precious gifts he can give, because he is giving everything he has. His words are sincere.*

As I turned left onto University Avenue and proceeded west toward Magnolia Avenue, I continued to ponder the man sitting at the side of the road. *Where will he be tomorrow? Where will he be the next day? How will he live out the remainder of his life?* Most importantly, I wondered, *Do I truly appreciate his expression of gratitude and blessing as I should?*

It seems that we often miss the opportunity to help others due to our preoccupation with our own matters. Rarely do we slow down long enough to empathize with a stranger. Our fast-paced society is not structured to care for the suffering or to accommodate those in need. Our society is structured to reward those who concentrate on their own personal well-being. Perhaps this nature of our society causes us to miss the opportunity to be blessed by the joy of giving.

What I discovered most significant, after twenty years of researching the Duke family, was that helping others find happiness was the passion of the patriarch, Washington Duke. His life was not about amassing a vast fortune; it was not about cheating and selfishly taking advantage of others for his own personal gain. His life was about ending misery and sharing his blessings with humanity. As a means to carry out this noble goal, Washington, and his sons, built a massive fortune. But the fortune was not built for its own sake; it was built in the spirit of their benevolence. From their original misguided belief that tobacco was a medical miracle, to their development of textiles and electricity, bringing a benefit to others was always at the forefront of their planning. This benevolence is the true essence of the Duke legacy. If you are a believer in the existence of God, then like me, by now you have probably asked yourself if Washington was selected for this blessing of fortune and fame because of his infinite spirit of kindness and charity.

It has been my pleasure in this book to share information I have acquired from a variety of sources, beginning with stories my grandmother told me as a child and ranging to public records, interviews, publications, family folklore, legal documents, and the David M. Rubenstein Rare Book and Manuscript Library at Duke University. It is my desire that others will be inspired by these stories to use their gifts and talents for the betterment of humanity. Every time we do an act for the benefit of mankind, we are given a glimpse into the soul of all humanity. In this glimpse, we see that one small act of kindness can neutralize an ocean of cruelty.

For most of us, using one's gifts and talents for the betterment of humanity does not mean becoming a billionaire and establishing great universities and medical centers. It does not necessarily mean becoming a famous writer, actor, or politician who leads a campaign of charity. For most of us, it simply means acquiring a spirit of empathy and allowing the empathy to actualize. It means helping and encouraging others, regardless of their situation in life, in every opportunity one encounters. It means believing and living the words of Mary Duke Biddle Trent Semans, great-granddaughter of Washington Duke, who said, "My feeling is that we are all here for each other. I take this very seriously, this business of treating your neighbor as yourself."[244]

---

244 "Overheard Quotes We Love," North Carolina Community Foundation, accessed December 30, 2013, http://www.nccommunityfoundation.org/section/overheard.

Appendix A
Order of Judge Eve Preminger of the New York Surrogate Court issued on January 20, 1995

The following is the transcript of the order of Judge Eve Preminger of the New York Surrogate Court issued on January 20, 1995.[245] This order is significant because it describes the unique characteristic of the case and sets the stage for the litigation involving the Doris Duke estate, while providing insight into Judge Preminger's thought processes.

> ... Before we get to specific issues, the court has come to a decision with respect to the appropriate manner of proceeding with regard to the allegations of misconduct before the court. The court will decide that aspect of the proceedings before getting into anything else.
>
> As you all know, this is an unusual estate in every way; it involves one of the largest charitable bequests to come before this court. These immense sums have an enormous potential for contributions

---

245 Probate Proceeding, Will of Doris Duke, ruling of the Honorable Judge Eve Preminger, Surrogates' Court County of New York, File Number: 4440-93, January 20, 1995.

to society, and unfortunately a concomitant opportunity for abuse and mismanagement.

There is also a need for prompt resolution of the probate proceedings and its finalization of the transfer of assets. Due to restrictions on investments during the temporary administration period, literally millions of dollars in interest may be lost by each month of delay.

A number of serious and rather sensational allegations from a variety of sources have recently surfaced with respect to both the qualifications of Bernard Lafferty to serve as a fiduciary and the conduct of Mr. Lafferty and his counsel during the period preceding and subsequent to Miss Duke's death. Other charges are made with regard to the co–preliminary executor, US Trust Company. None of these allegations have been proven, and they may turn out to be entirely meritless. However, sufficient questions have been raised and documentation offered to require investigation. The issue is how that investigation can be conducted fairly and swiftly without jeopardizing the estate assets and the interests of the charity beneficiaries.

Counsel for the estate suggests the appointment of an independent referee to hear and report on these issues. The court is concerned with the inevitable delays, squabbles over evidence and witnesses, and time and resources which would be consumed by a formal hearing. A referee sitting in a courtroom is not ideally positioned to conduct a thorough exploration and investigation of the facts.

On the other hand, counsel for Dr. Demopoulos has suggested that the court authorize them to conduct their own immediate investigation. While this procedure might yield results more quickly than a referee, it is devoid of impartiality.

The court rejects the suggestions of both sides.

The protection of the estate requires that limited letters of temporary administration be issued to a person of unquestionable credentials and investigatory and estate experience. The limited temporary cofiduciary shall examine the allegations of the misconduct, examine the affairs of the estate, conduct interviews, to the extent deemed necessary, and report to the court within forty-five days as to the need, if any, for further action.

Accordingly, pursuant to SCPA 6702.8, 9, and 10, the court appoints Richard Kuh, Esq. as limited temporary administrator for the foregoing purposes. Mr. Kuh shall be accorded unlimited access to all documents, books, and records relating to the estate.

The parties and their counsel are directed to cooperate with Mr. Kuh to the fullest extent. Any additional powers necessary to the performance of Mr. Kuh's duties may be proposed by any party in a supplemental order.

Pending further order of the court, Mr. Lafferty and US Trust Company will continue as co–preliminary executors.

This shall constitute the order of the court.

Appendix B
Excerpts from the Deposition of Charles Kivowitz, MD, Taken January 4, 1995, through January 12, 1995

The following is a more comprehensive presentation of key testimony from the deposition of Dr. Kivowitz than in chapter 13. This appendix is included for readers interested in a more comprehensive version of the pertinent testimony, though it is only a small portion of the actual transcript. Extraneous portions of the testimony and discussions concerning objections have been omitted for the sake of clarity. The excerpt in chapter 13 was limited to avoid overburdening the text.

David West, the video technician, recited the introduction of the proceeding. "This is the videotape deposition of Dr. Charles Kivowitz in the matter of a probate proceeding will of Doris Duke, who is deceased. Case number 4440-93. Today's date is January 4, 1995. The time is 1:10 p.m. My name is David West, an associate of Law in Motion, located at 15760 Ventura Boulevard, Suite 1030, Encino, California, 91436. The recording is taking place at 700 South Flower Street, conference room Malibu A, Los Angeles, California, Hyatt Hotel."

Dr. Kivowitz was sworn, and the attorneys formally introduced themselves on the record. The attorneys present included the following:

- For Dr. Harry Demopoulos: Don Howarth, Suzelle Smith, Rodney Houghton, and Thomas Vandenburg
- For Charles Kivowitz, MD: John Barnosky
- For the preliminary coexecutors Bernard Lafferty and US Trust Company of New York: Lee Ann Watson

During the first day of deposition, Don was able to elicit important information concerning Dr. Kivowitz's role in the final days of Doris Duke's life. Dr. Kivowitz identified and authenticated his signature as a witness on the will of Doris Duke dated April 5, 1993. He stated that he had never witnessed any patient's will other than the will of Doris Duke. He testified that Margaret Underwood, one of the witnesses to the will, was a secretary in his office. He further testified that Lidia Rives, who also witnessed the will, was a nursing assistant in his office.

Dr. Kivowitz testified that he first saw Doris Duke in February 1992, when she consulted him for a fractured femur. He testified that on March 8, 1993, he was contacted by Doris Duke's attorney William Doyle at Cedars-Sinai Medical Center and was asked if Doris would be able to sign a codicil to her will that night. Dr. Kivowitz said he understood that Mr. Doyle was asking about her general health and capacity to sign a codicil. Dr. Kivowitz further testified that he felt that Doris was perfectly competent to discuss any affairs with Mr. Doyle and to sign any documents Mr. Doyle felt needed her signature. Dr. Kivowitz stated, "I believe that, on March 8, Miss Duke was a fully competent woman able to discuss her ... whatever affairs she wished to discuss with whomever she wished to discuss with them on whatever basis she wished."

Dr. Kivowitz testified that he was the person who referred Doris Duke's attorneys to her and that he may have made such referrals with other patients on one or two occasions.

The following testimony is taken from the transcript of the deposition of Charles Kivowitz, MD, which began on January 4, 1995:

Questioning by Don Howarth:

Question: Were you present with Miss Duke on the day
        that she died?

Answer: I was present with her on the day prior to her
        death.

Question: What about the day of her death?

Answer: I left the house. I mean the day begins at mid-
        night and I am not precisely certain whether I
        left the house at midnight or before midnight.
        I was present certainly the day before she died.
        I may have been present on the day she died.

Question: Were you consulted in connection with the
        execution of her death certificate?

Answer: I had consulted my associate, Dr. Trabulus,
        prior to the … essentially leaving the city on
        the morning of her death.

Question: Were you consulted by Dr. Trabulus in connec-
        tion with his filling out the certificate of death?

Answer: I just answered the question. I consulted with
        him on the day before. On the day before,
        meaning I believe she died on the 28th of
        October. I consulted with him on the 27th re-
        garding her condition. I turned over the care of
        the patient to him. I did not consult with him
        at the time he executed the death certificate.

Question: Did you discuss with Dr. Trabulus what entries would be made on the death certificate?

Answer: I discussed with him her medical condition and my opinion as to what her problems were.

Question: And you discussed that with him before she died?

Answer: Yes.

Question: Did you anticipate that she would die on the next day?

Answer: Yes.

[Discussion about the admission of exhibits omitted]

Question: Do you recognize exhibit 7 as a copy of the death certificate of Doris Duke?

Answer: Yes.

Question: Have you seen it before?

Answer: Yes.

Question: When did you first see it?

Answer: About a week ago.

Question: Did you ever discuss it after it was executed by your colleague, Dr. Trabulus?

Answer: No.

[Testimony omitted]

Question: And what is the immediate cause of death as
                     described in this document?

Answer: Septicemia urosepsis.

[The witness was asked about a conversation with an attorney
from the law firm of Katten Muchin Zavis concerning the death
certificate.]

Question: What did you say about that immediate cause
                     of death to this attorney from Katten Muchin
                     Zavis?

Answer: What did I say about it?

Question: Yes.

Answer: I mean I didn't ... I didn't ... I'm not sure the
                     conversation ran that way. What I said in the
                     subsequent documents was that the immediate
                     cause of death was acute pulmonary edema,
                     which, in my mind, was the immediate cause
                     of death. I think one has to understand what
                     "cause of death" means. Everyone dies in es-
                     sentially the same way: their heart stops and
                     they stop breathing. As an immediate cause
                     of death, that is somewhat obvious. You can
                     go back a few steps, and one step would be
                     acute pulmonary edema, which is a mecha-
                     nism of death. Another mechanism of death

present in this situation was septicemia urosepsis. Septicemia urosepsis preceded pulmonary edema in Doris Duke. Both would be legitimate immediate causes of death as far as the State of California is concerned.

Question: On the day before her death when you discussed with Dr. Trabulus the fact that you would be away, did you discuss with him what you believed was to be the immediate cause of death?

[Objection omitted]

Answer: I discussed with Dr. Trabulus the fact that she was in acute ... she was in acute and profound pulmonary edema. And we elected not to treat pulmonary edema or any other precipitant cause of death at that time in her medical care, and I told him that I expected that she would die of acute pulmonary edema; namely, that her heart would stop and she would stop breathing.

Question: When you say, "We elected not to treat ..."

Answer: I elected, I elected. I am using the "we" in a general sense. I elected not to treat her.

Question: Did you consult with anyone else in making that decision?

Answer: The decision was made earlier in the course of her ... in the last week of her life or the

314

last two weeks of her life, and was relevant to her wishes—principally her wishes—and the nature of her medical situation, which was judged ... which I judged to be hopeless at that time.

Question: My question is, did you consult with anyone else?

Answer: I discussed this situation with her attorney, Mr. Doyle, and with Mr. Lafferty, her personal executive assistant.

Question: When did you have that discussion?

Answer: I would say ... I would have to ... you would have to show me my ... I would say about a week or ten ... maybe two weeks, within the two weeks prior to her death. A week to two weeks prior to her death.

Question: What is it you would want me to show you to help you fix the date?

Answer: I think there would probably be some record of a discussion. Or if I look through her notes, her ... the nursing notes and the physician's orders, I could probably pinpoint the day within a day.

Question: Did you discuss with Dr. Glassman the making of this decision?

Answer:	Dr. Glassman was … I discussed the decision with Dr. Glassman. Dr. Glassman did not play any part in making the decision.
Question:	What did you say to Dr. Glassman about the decision?
Answer:	Well, her case was hopeless; there was a certain point after which medical care was of no use. And I simply informed Dr. Glassman of this fact, and that's the sum total of my discussion with Dr. Glassman.
Question:	What was the sum total of your discussion with Mr. Lafferty on that point?
Answer:	Mr. Lafferty was concerned only that Miss Duke be kept comfortable at the end of her life, and he was just concerned about her comfort and her being free of pain and that her suffering be limited as best it could by not continuing her care after it was determined that further medical care would be of no use.
Question:	Did you make that determination?
Answer:	Yes.
Question:	Did you consult with Miss Duke in making that determination?
Answer:	Yes.
Question:	When was that?

Answer: At various times during her home care during
               September—late September and early October.

Question: And what record did you make of those consul-
               tations?

Answer: I don't believe I kept a record of consultations
               with Miss Duke in the home. However, there
               are ... there are records that I have read where
               the nurses were aware of Miss Duke's wishes.

Question: I am not talking about the nurses' notes. Is
               there some reason you didn't make some re-
               cord of any consultations you say you had with
               Ms. Duke about this?

Answer: I have never maintained a record of notes on a
               patient in the home.

Question: And with respect to an election not to treat
               and a consultation with the patient, isn't it your
               normal practice to make a note or record of
               that?

Answer: Generally the only note I'll make is that there
               is to be no resuscitation. And that's ... and in
               the case where Miss Duke is concerned, I had
               had several discussions with her at her home
               and in the hospital and earlier, and she had a
               durable ... what is the document called ...

Mr. Barnosky: Living will.

Answer:	She had a living will. And it was my ... I had read the living will, and I was aware of her wishes in this situation, having read of her wishes in this situation, having read of her wishes and having discussed the issue with her several times during the course of her treatment.
Mr. Howarth:	When did you read the living will?
Answer:	Well, I actually read several living wills. I read one sometime in ... I would say in the early part of 1993, which had defined that I would be consulted in matters regarding her health along with Roland Artiga. And I discussed that with her because I had not seen Roland Artiga in nearly a year and I was surprised when I read it to see that Roland Artiga was supposed to consult with me about her ... about her medical care. And I asked her about it. And she said it was an error. I discussed the living will with her attorney, Mr. Doyle, in October of 1993, and I was informed that Mr. Doyle had drawn up that document, and went over it with him ... went over the elements of it, although I am not sure that I actually saw it at that time.
Question:	Did you see any other living wills?
Answer:	No. However, when I first met Miss Duke I was informed by Roland Artiga that he had the ... and I am not certain that this was accurate. I was informed by Mr. ... Dr. Artiga at the time I met him that he, Roland Artiga, had the power

of attorney for medical affairs for Miss Duke, and it was expressed in those ... roughly those terms.

Question: Did you ever see it?

Answer: No.

Question: When did you first meet Miss Duke?

[Discussion omitted]

Answer: April of 1992.

[Discussion omitted]

Question: Where did you meet her?

Answer: I met her in the emergency room at Cedars-Sinai Medical Center.

Question: Was she referred to you?

Answer: Yes.

Question: By whom?

Answer: By Dr. Harry Glassman.

Question: Did Dr. Glassman tell you what his relationship was with Miss Duke?

Answer: He told me only that he had operated on Miss Duke, that he had done a meloplasty, and

319

though I don't ... though I ... and I guess also liposuction. Although my recollection, my only recollection was of the facelift, meloplasty basically. In my review of the ... my admission note, I noted that she also had liposuction, that part of the conversation though.

Question: Did you take a medical history from Miss Duke?

Answer: Yes.

Question: Did you obtain any prior medical records of Miss Duke?

[Discussion omitted]

Answer: In April of 1992 when I met Miss Duke, she was in ... her present physician was present at the time. Dr. Artiga was in the emergency room when I arrived. And he gave me information as to her ... her prior medical history. Dr. Glassman informed me of the procedure he had done. I interviewed Miss Duke and asked her about her medical problems, and I spoke with both Mr. Lafferty and Nuku Makasiale about her medical history.

Question: Did you make notes of those conversations?

Answer: I wrote a medical history and a physical. I made no other notes.

Question:	Did you ever obtain her prior medical records, the actual records?
Answer:	I made an effort to obtain prior medical records as I was given information as to their availability.
Question:	Did you, in fact, ever obtain any?
Answer:	Yes.
Question:	How far back did you obtain medical records?
Answer:	There were some medical records for about, I would say, five to ten years, approximately. They were incomplete; they were not ... they were not, I think, the sum total of her medical records, but they were what I was instructed to obtain.
Question:	Were you ... did you ascertain whether or not Miss Duke was taking any drugs before she consulted with you?
Answer:	"Drugs" meaning what?
Question:	Any medical ...
Answer:	Any medications?
Question:	Yes.
Answer:	Yes.

Question: What drugs or medications was she taking be-
             fore consulting with you in April of '92?

[Discussion between attorneys]

Question: Did you ascertain whether she had taken any
             drugs prior to April of 1990?

Answer: Any medications?

Question: Yes.

Answer: This ... the information I had was from her
             and from Bernard Lafferty and from Roland
             Artiga, and again this is my recollection. I
             wrote down ... I believe I wrote down what
             medications she was taking at the time. She
             was taking Calcidrine, she was taking Lanoxin,
             she was taking Naprosyn, and she was taking
             Halcion and Restoril. She was also being given
             medications by Dr. Artiga intravenously. Dr.
             Artiga explained to me that he was giving her
             vitamins intravenously, but it's not clear to me
             that that is all he was giving her.

Question: Did you make any notes of what prior drugs
             Miss Duke had been taking?

Answer: The only notes I made would be notes in the
             admission history and physical.

Question: And you would refer to those in reference to
             your recollection as to what you learned about
             drugs?

Answer:	I recall also other information regarding a rather extensive history of medication taking, including the extensive use of diazepam ... type tranquilizers, including the use of assorted stimulants, including the extensive ... extensive use of alcohol. But, to the extent that I had any other notes or ... I don't think I had any other notes or ... I wrote down whatever ... I think I wrote down what I have told you.
Question:	Would there be some reason you would not write down all of the drugs you ascertained she had taken before?
Answer:	Yes.
Question:	What reason?
Answer:	Miss Duke is a celebrated person, was a celebrated person, and medical records at Cedars-Sinai Hospital have been known to show up in places like the *National Enquirer.* So any information that I had that might in any way be detrimental to her image as a person, I would not include in the medical record.
Question:	Do you remember having such information?
Answer:	I remember the information about the heavy use of alcohol.
Question:	Any other?
Answer:	At the time, no.

Question:	Who told you that she had a heavy use of alcohol?
Answer:	This was Dr. Artiga.
Question:	Anyone else?
Answer:	It would be very hard for me to say whether anybody else mentioned this because of the nature of the situation. It was an emergency situation. I was obtaining information as quickly as I can ... as I could. And I had objective things to do besides simply getting information.
Question:	Do you recall anyone else telling you that?
Answer:	I would say that I would have asked Bernard Lafferty, I would have asked Nuku Makasiale, I would have asked Dr. Glassman what his recollections were, what his information was, I would have asked all ... and I would have asked her.
Question:	Do you recall any answers?
Answer:	Other than what I have told you, no.

[Testimony omitted]

Question:	What services did you perform for Miss Duke in or around April of 1992 in connection with the time you first met her? What did you do?
Answer:	I interviewed her in the emergency room.

Question:	At Cedars-Sinai?
Answer:	At Cedars-Sinai. I admitted her to the hospital. I attended her during an emergency medical procedure. I attended her in the emergency care unit following that procedure. And I directed complicated medical care until her discharge from the hospital.
Question:	About when was that?
Answer:	I would have to refer ... review the record. I don't know precisely whether that was in ... I think that was in May, but I don't know offhand exactly what ...

[Discussion between attorneys omitted]

Question:	The charges that you made to Miss Duke in connection with that, do you know what they were?
Answer:	In connection with the hospitalization?
Question:	And your treatment.
Answer:	And the treatment and the period shortly after that?
Question:	Your charges.
Answer:	My charges. Yes.
Question:	What were they?

Answer: $50,000.

Question: For what period of time?

Answer: I would have to look at my bill again to specify,
                   but I think it was about a month or maybe a
                   little more, maybe five weeks or seven weeks.

Question: And how did you ... on what did you base a
                   $50,000 charge?

Answer: It was essentially arbitrary. I had put in a great
                   deal of time and effort. I had a very successful
                   outcome, and I felt that this was a deserving
                   fee, if in fact a high fee, for the services per-
                   formed.

Question: How much time had you spent for that $50,000?

Answer: It's very hard to say, but I would say probably
                   in excess of 100 hours during the course of the
                   month.

Question: Do you keep records which would show what
                   time you spent on a particular patient?

Answer: Very crude and very sketchy records.

[Testimony omitted]

Question: To whom did you submit the bill?

Answer: To Doris Duke at the Duke business office.

Question:	When you say "to Doris Duke" you mean you sent it there to Doris Duke?
Answer:	Yes.

[Testimony omitted]

Question:	Did you ever discuss any amounts of any fees with Miss Duke?
Answer:	I don't believe so.
Question:	You did discuss amounts of fees with Mr. Lafferty, didn't you?
Answer:	No, I did not.
Question:	Didn't Mr. Lafferty joke with you about a thousand dollars a day as a fee?
Answer:	Never.
Question:	Didn't Mr. Lafferty hand you checks from time to time?
Answer:	Mr. Lafferty handed me … No, I don't think he ever handed me a check. He was aware of one check that I received from Miss Duke as a gift. Otherwise Mr. Lafferty did not hand me any checks at any time.
Question:	Did you discuss taking a check in Mr. Lafferty's presence and saying now you could go on a vacation?

Answer: Never.

Question: Isn't it true that Mr. Lafferty said to you that Doris Duke would be outraged if she knew you were getting a thousand dollars a day?

Answer: I don't recall.

[Testimony omitted]

Dr. Kivowitz testified that as Doris's condition began to deteriorate, he asked her if he should contact Chandra Heffner, her adopted daughter. She declined. He also testified that Doris refused to talk to Dr. Demopoulos, who had begun calling repeatedly to speak with Doris. He testified that he did not know anything about Dr. Demopoulos except that he was a former doctor of hers. According to the testimony of Dr. Kivowitz, Doris requested Bernard Lafferty to do virtually everything that Doris wanted to be done. Dr. Kivowitz was introduced to Bernard Lafferty by Dr. Harry Glassman, the husband of Victoria Principal. Dr. Kivowitz testified that Bernard Lafferty had a problem with excessive alcohol consumption. He further testified that Doris asked him to provide the name of an attorney. He spoke with Dr. Glassman, who recommended Alan Croll, saying that he had had a long relationship with Alan Croll. Later Dr. Kivowitz introduced both attorney William Doyle and attorney Alan Croll to Doris Duke. Alan Croll, William Doyle, and Michael McCarthy were attorneys at the law firm of Katten Muchin. In response to a question by Mr. Howarth as to whether or not Dr. Kivowitz had a conversation with attorney William Doyle concerning Doris's condition in September or October 1993, Dr. Kivowitz provided the following testimony.

Further questioning by Don Howarth:

Question: All right. Then you said the next time you had a conversation with Mr. Doyle was in September or October of 2003. Do you recall that?

Answer: Yes. I recall saying that to you, yes.

Question: Yes, that's what I mean. Was that the same conversation at which Lee Ann Watson was present?

Answer: Yes.

Question: Where did that take place?

Answer: It took place in Miss Duke's home in Beverly Hills in what was, I believe, a dining room, adjacent to a kitchen.

Question: Miss Duke was downstairs?

Answer: Miss Duke was downstairs.

Question: And did anyone come in or go out of the room during the discussion other than the four people you have identified?

Answer: I believe Nuku Makasiale did.

Question: Anyone else?

Answer: No.

Question: What do you recall saying on that occasion?

Answer: Well, I recall that I was very concerned that we were making no progress where Miss Duke's illness was concerned, that I had a few ideas about how to proceed given the problems that we were facing, and that I believed that we should continue her medical care to see whether or not these measures would be effective to reestablish what I felt was a reasonable chance of bringing her back to a reasonable quality of life.

Question: What was her medical problem at the time?

Answer: At that time?

Question: Yes.

Answer: From top to bottom?

Question: I'm sorry?

Answer: From top to bottom?

Question: What was her medical problem or problems?

Answer: Problems. Okay. She was almost totally blind. She was effectively quadriplegic. She had … in order to breathe effectively and to clear her secretions, she had a tracheotomy. In order to be nourished, she had a gastrostomy. [Testimony omitted] She had a form of refractory anemia that was described variably as a myelodysplastic syndrome, as a preleukemic syndrome, but clearly as a nonnutritional severe anemia. She had either a dependent or an independent arthritic condition which was characterized by some as pseudogout and by others as a reflection of some underlying hematologic process, essentially an arthritic manifestation of an underlying and serious illness. [Testimony omitted] And that doesn't completely describe it. I would have to review her records.

Question: As opposed to the drugs that you were giving her, none of those conditions were life threatening, were they?

Answer: They were all life threatening. All the conditions I described were life threatening.

Question: Where did you write that down, Doctor?

Answer: This was written down throughout her medical record and was essentially a clear understanding of every one of the fifteen or so physicians who saw her.

Question: You wrote down that those things were life threatening, did you, Doctor?

Answer: Did I write them down? This woman was in a medical intensive care unit ...

Question: I didn't ask you where she was, Doctor.

Attorney Watson: Objection …

Dr. Kivowitz: This is pure nonsense …

Attorney Howarth: Did you write down that those were life threatening?

Attorney Watson: Let him finish his answer.

[Discussion between attorneys omitted]

Question: You wrote down that those things were life threatening, did you, Doctor?

Answer: Did I write them down? This woman was in a medical intensive care unit … Let me reanswer the question for you in a nice, sober way. Her medical care at home was designed to be as effectively as equivalent to a medical intensive care unit as we could possibly achieve at home within the parameters that she established.

Question: Sometime you are going to tell me whether you wrote down if these were life threatening, Doctor?

Attorney Watson: Objection to the form and argumentative nature of the question. It's totally unnecessary.

Question: Did you write it down?

Attorney Watson: Same objection.

Answer:	The nature of her … I mean nothing was written down in terms of a progress note when she was at home, except at a point when I felt that she … well, when she went home, that she was not going to be resuscitated, which was a … "resuscitated" meaning if she had a sudden cessation of breathing or a sudden cessation of her heartbeat, she was not to be resuscitated. That was at her specific request. That was a continuum of hospital care. The arrangements were made when she was in the hospital to do, as closely as we could, to duplicate intensive medical care at home.
Question:	Where did you write it down?
Attorney Watson:	I would like to make an objection if I could …
Answer:	I don't know how to answer this question. This is idiotic. This is an idiotic question.

[Objections and discussion omitted]

Question:	Where did you write down, if you did, that the code … "no code blue" was at Miss Duke's request?
Attorney Watson:	Objection to the form of the question.
Answer:	I don't believe I wrote that down.
Question:	Now, you said you had a conversation with Mr. Doyle, Mr. Lafferty, Miss Watson, and Dr. Glassman that you were telling me about.

Answer:	Yes.
Question:	What did you say in that conversation?
Answer:	I think I already described what I said. I said that she had increasing ... we had increasing difficulty maintaining a situation that we had established at home, that there were additional problems evolving that essentially precluded her recovery. I felt that there were other things that one would ... that I wanted to try to assist her in recovering from these problems, and I initiated those measures.
Question:	I am not asking you what you did. Now this is a conversation. Did you tell them that you were going to initiate these measures?
Answer:	Yes.
Question:	Did you say anything else to the assembled group?
Answer:	I don't recall ... I did tell them that I thought that she had a very limited life expectancy, that I felt that she would die within a few weeks at the most if we did nothing different than what we were doing, and that at best she might have a few months to live even if these measures were effective.
Question:	Did you tell them that you wanted to get a second opinion about that?

Answer: Oh, there were multiple opinions rendered throughout this. There were other doctors visiting her.

Question: I'm asking what you told them.

Answer: I didn't ask them about a second opinion in this situation.

Question: Had you gotten a second opinion?

Answer: About ... at this particular time?

Question: Yes.

Answer: Every physician who saw Miss Duke at any point during her medical care—at any point, whether at home or in the hospital or if they saw her during the course of outpatient visits— were asked their opinions about her medical condition, her general medical condition, her specific medical condition. They were asked whether they had any additional suggestions as to what her care was. And this was true of Dr. Federman, Dr. Wolf, Dr. Uman, Dr. Espy, and Dr. Bronstein. It was clear to everyone that this was a dying person. And dying because of ex ... long hospitalization that was ... punctuated by an extended period of respiratory failure.

Question: She had recovered from her hospital problems before you put her on the drugs, hadn't she, Doctor?

Answer: She had not.

Attorney Watson: Objection.

Attorney Barnosky: Objection as to form. You can answer the question.

Answer: She had not. She had not recovered. She was ... in fact, the medications that were administered were administered to treat her problems as they evolved both in the hospital and at home.

Question: You stopped her therapy, didn't you, Doctor?

Answer: What kind of question is that?

Attorney Barnosky: Objection. Let's just ask ...

Question: You stopped her therapy ...

[Objections and discussion omitted]

Answer: In my judgment at the time, in my judgment at the time, continuing therapy both presented problems that were in excess of what could be dealt with and she was clearly dying. She expressed that wish numerous times during the course of her hospitalization, at the very end of her hospitalization, and during her period at home.

Question: That wish is only expressed once in the nurses' notes, isn't it, Doctor?

Answer:	That's …
Attorney Watson:	Objection …
Dr. Kivowitz:	… expressed in the nurses' notes. It did occur more often than once. I believe that the nurses' notes occupy roughly one page per 24 hours. There were two nurses present at all times during a 24 … hour period, and their notes represent only a summary of what transpired.
Question:	And where is the rest of what transpired, Doctor?
Answer:	Presumably in their heads.
Question:	Did you get a second opinion on the "no code blue" decision that you made?
Answer:	No. And I never get a second opinion on a "no code blue" situation.
Question:	Did you discuss it with Miss Duke?
Answer:	Yes.
Question:	And where did you make a note of that?
Answer:	It was not … I didn't make the note … I had discussed "no code blue" with her in June of 1993 in the full presence of Dr. … the orthopedists.
Attorney Barnosky:	From UCLA?

Attorney Watson:	Thomas.
Dr. Kivowitz:	Dr. Bert Thomas. And at the time Dr. Glassman was present, and at the time Mr. Lafferty was present.
Question:	Did you discuss the "no code blue" at the time that you instituted it on October 8?

[Objection omitted]

Answer:	October 8? What is that?
Question:	It's in the reading, but that is a question …

[Objection omitted]

Answer:	I did not discuss the "no code blue" … I didn't write down the … What was the question? I am confused now.
Question:	When you made the "no code blue" entry or order on October 8, 1993, did you discuss that with Miss Duke at the time?

[Objections omitted]

Answer:	I did not discuss … I did not discuss the "no code blue" precisely at that time. I had discussed it with her many times prior to the time I initiated the "no code blue" order. I had discussed her medical situation with multiple other physicians who were involved in her care. I believe that every one of them

338

concurred that no resuscitative measures were appropriate for her. It would have been rather easy for me to attempt to resuscitate her or call the paramedics to resuscitate her. It would have been very easy for me to prolong her misery for a few weeks or a month. That's easy. Very easy. I could do that if, God forbid, any one of us here in this room arrested or had developed a serious and life-threatening and life-ending medical illness. It's not that difficult to do that.

Question: It would have been easy for you to resuscitate her even after you entered the "no code blue"?

Answer: No.

Question: Would it have been easy for you to reverse the "no code blue" entry?

Answer: Yes, I could have reversed the "no code blue" entry.

Question: Then you would have been able to resuscitate her?

Answer: I think that's ... the answer is yes, I'm probably ... I think I would ... had there been ... had we had an order to resuscitate her if and when she ceased to live.

The deposition of Dr. Kivowitz took five days to complete over a period of two weeks. Don Howarth had diligently attempted to lay the foundation for the critical testimony concerning the cause of death of Doris Duke. Finally, on the fifth day of Dr. Kivowitz's deposition, Howarth was prepared to lead Dr. Kivowitz into the admission that was needed to prove the case. And finally Dr. Kivowitz provided the critical testimony Don was seeking. The following is taken from the deposition transcript of Dr. Kivowitz on January 12, 1995. The questioning is based upon exhibits 92 through 95 which are pages from the medical records recorded at Falcon Lair on October 26, 1993, through October 28, 1993.

Further questioning by Don Howarth:

Question: October 27. Tell me when you are ready.

Answer: Okay.

Question: Temperature normal, 98.6?

Answer: Yes.

Question: Demerol at 50 milligrams continued to be given.

Answer: Yes.

Question: The note says she's pain free.

Answer: Yes.

Question: And she had no periods of shortness of breath or not breathing overnight. Right?

Answer: Yes.

Question: Then apparently her eyes opened during suctioning, but she went back into a deep sleep immediately following the procedure. Correct?

Answer: Yes.

Question: She is sleeping soundly and the Demerol is still given?

Answer: Yes.

Question: The respiration is at 14 to 16. Right?

Answer: Where do we see this? Yes, 14 to 16. I see it.

Question: And that's okay.

Answer: Yes.

Question: At seven o'clock, the respiration was nonlabored at 14.

Answer: Yes.

Question: 7:40, her temperature is at 99?

Answer: Yes.

Question: And she opens her eyes at eight o'clock during vital signs. Correct?

Answer: Yes. That's what happened.

Question: Now, were you there at this time, on this page?

Answer: On the page? I am here at 8:50. Excuse me. It says 8:20. I was here at 8:20. "Status report orders reviewed, main objective is to keep patient pain free and comfortable. Recent labs and urine specimen, gram negative rods discussed."

[Discussion among attorneys omitted]

Question: Exhibit 93, 312. Tell me when you're ready to discuss it.

Answer: I've got it. Okay.

Question: This October 27, you're there at 8:20?

[Discussion among attorneys omitted]

Question: Then at ten o'clock here, continuing on October 27, "40 milligrams Demerol given as ordered."

Answer: Yes, that's what it says.

Question: Then the patient opened eyes during blood pressure exam. No overt signs of acute distress, and Bernard is there. Right?

Answer: Yes.

Question: At 1300, "Demerol given as ordered, no signs of acute distress or discomfort." Right?

Answer:	Yes.

Question:	1500, "Patient sleeping soundly, no signs of acute distress or discomfort." Right?

Answer:	Yes.

Question:	1500 also, "Breath sounds clear, no distress, 99.6 temperature, opens eyes to verbal stimulus."

[Testimony omitted]

Question:	I read the rest right?

Answer:	Yeah.

Question:	1600, "Demerol 50 milligrams drip effective." Right?

Answer:	Yes.

Question:	But patient remains easily aroused?

Answer:	Yes.

Question:	You're there at 1630, 4:30?

Answer:	Yes.

Question:	"No new orders implemented, patient ..."

Answer:	No. At the time ... 1630, when I arrived ...

Question:	I read that wrong. Let me start again. "New orders noted and implemented?"
Answer:	Yes. [Testimony omitted] And I examined her. And she was in acute pulmonary edema.
Question:	Did you note that somewhere?

[Testimony omitted]

Ms. Watson:	0616, it's right here, it's right down here.
Question:	I see it. Thank you. I'm sorry. Doctor, what were you saying?
Answer:	What happened here is we changed her from the Demerol …
Question:	Did you want to change the time or something?
Answer:	Yes. I was there at that time, and I believe what I did was I changed her from a Demerol drip to a morphine drip. And the reason I did that is that the amount of fluid that we had given the day before was in excess by over a thousand cc's of the output, and I changed it to reduce the amount of fluid she received.
Question:	So she is …
Answer:	So essentially, the situation at 1600 was the same, but I changed the drip.

Question:	Is a diagnosis of acute pulmonary edema consistent with the nurses' notes that her breath sounds are clear?
Answer:	At the time we're talking about, as I said, the … I did not make the diagnosis of acute pulmonary edema at 1630. I had … I unfortunately anticipated the other sheet, 311, that's out of order. And the events of that particular day. Through this particular time, her condition was the same as it was earlier. I simply changed the drip from the Demerol drip to a morphine drip with no other intention than to maintain the same level of sedation that we had … I had achieved with the … with the Demerol drip. Period.
Question:	Her breath is unlabored, it's noted there; respiration 14.
Answer:	At that time, yes.
Question:	And she doesn't wake up, and you start the morphine drip. Right?
Answer:	The morphine drip simply replaced the Demerol drip.
Question:	Morphine is much more potent than Demerol, isn't it?
Answer:	On a milligram-for-milligram basis, morphine is more potent than Demerol. However, the

amount of morphine I was giving her was essentially equivalent to the dose of Demerol.

Question: The 5 milligrams?

Answer: Yeah, the dosage equivalence is roughly ten to one, and I changed it from 50 milligrams of Demerol to 5 milligrams of morphine and ordered titrate for comfort and sedation.

Question: And then you ordered an increase to 7 milligrams at 1530. Right?

Answer: On the basis of some information I had from the nurse, I must have called or spoken to her, and ... or I was there, and I ... at that time, I can't tell you what from the notes. I was there at 1630. I was there at 1530. I mean there was some discontinuity or reversal of time. And I explained to the nurse that I was going to be out of town and that Dr. Trabulus was going to cover for me and he was going to visit that evening. And at the time, at 1730, at the time the morphine drip was going at 7 milligrams, her eyes were open and she was arousable. And at 10 milligrams, she was effectively pain free and sleeping.

Question: Where were you going?

Answer: I was going to the University of Virginia.

Question:	And when you started the morphine drip, there is no indication of any pain here in the records, is there?
Answer:	As I said, I changed the … I changed from the Demerol drip to an equivalent dose of morphine and titrated it because of the volume involved in administering the Demerol.
Question:	When you started the morphine, there is no indication of any pain here in the records, is there?
Ms. Watson:	Objection.
Answer:	She was pain free from the Demerol.
Question:	And in fact the Demerol had been keeping her asleep. Right?
Answer:	The Demerol had been effective, yes.
Question:	Now, at 1730, it indicates the morphine is flowing?
Answer:	Yes.
Question:	And the patient opens her eyes occasionally?
Answer:	Yes.
Question:	She is still arousable?

Answer: Yes.

Question: The drip is increased "due to patient's arous-
                 able status." Correct?

Answer: That's what it says here, yes.

Question: "Effective" to patient … it's effective.

Answer: Pain free and sleeping, which is what was in-
                 tended at the time.

Question: Respiration goes down to 9 or 10 per minute.
                 Right?

Answer: That's what it says there.

Question: And that was due to the morphine.

Answer: At that time, it may have been.

Question: Let's take a look at exhibit 94. Exhibit 94 is 311.

[Exhibit 94 was marked.]

Answer: Okay.

Question: Now we're on October 27, still at 1930. Right?

Answer: Yes.

Question: Morphine drip goes up to 15 milligrams. Right?

Answer: Yes.

Question:	Your order?
Answer:	No, I don't believe so, but it was probably on the basis of an earlier order.
Question:	Of yours.
Answer:	Of mine.
Question:	And the eyes are "still periodically open but a stare." Right?
Answer:	Yes, I mean Miss Duke was dying. She was on a Demerol drip prior to this. She is now on a morphine drip. And she has … she's heavily sedated with the morphine drip.
Question:	No signs of pain or distress?
Answer:	She is on a morphine drip.
Question:	That's what's noted. Right?
Answer:	Yes.
Question:	And the patient is "comfortable and in no distress," and Bernard is there. Right?
Answer:	I don't see where Bernard is.
Mr. Barnosky:	Right here (indicating).
Answer:	Yes.

Question:	At 2000 hours, "Respiration shallow" and "periods of apnea." Right?
Answer:	That's what it says here.
Question:	She is not breathing for eight to ten second pauses. Right?
Answer:	That's what it says.
Question:	And that's consistent with the morphine that she is on.
Mr. Crofton:	Objection.
Answer:	It's consistent with her ... this situation, yes, and consistent with the use of morphine.
Question:	And she's still responding to physical and verbal stimuli though.
Answer:	Yes.
Question:	At 2100 hours, her respiration is down to 6–7. Right?
Answer:	I don't believe that was the case. But that is what it says.
Question:	You think that is wrong?
Answer:	I think at that time it's probably wrong. But there's no question that she had periods of apnea during that time and I arrived there, I was

called to see her because of the apnea and because of her condition, and she at that point
was in acute pulmonary edema.

Question: And that apnea is indicated as five- to ten-second
               pauses, 2100?

Answer: That's what it says here.

Question: No sign of pain or discomfort?

Answer: She is not in pain, no.

Question: And then there is a call to you to discuss in-
               creasing the drip?

Answer: Where is this?

Question: 2100. Discuss further increase in drip?

Answer: I went to see her at 2200, yes.

Question: At 2100 there is a "Call into Dr. Kivowitz to
               discuss further ..."

Answer: I assume that the call occurred about 2100 as
               it's said here.

Question: And Miss Duke didn't ask for this?

Answer: I think Miss Duke did ask for it.

Question: Not at this time, did she?

Answer: Not at this time, she did not call me and speak
                 to me.

Question: And you never discussed putting Miss Duke on
                 morphine with her, did you?

Ms. Watson: Objection; asked and answered.

Answer: I think I asked the question repeatedly in the
                 past.

Question: Did you discuss morphine specifically with
                 Miss Duke?

Mr. Barnosky: Objection; asked and answered. The witness is
                 directed not to answer. Enough.

Question: Did you discuss … Did Miss Duke know what
                 was happening at this time?

Answer: While she's heavily sedated with morphine?

Question: Yes.

Answer: I don't believe so.

Question: Had you at any time when you had known Miss
                 Duke ever put her on morphine before?

Answer: On morphine?

Question: Right.

Answer:	She may have been on morphine follow … she may have, I don't recall, but she may have been on morphine following one of the surgical procedures.
Question:	Do you recall …
Answer:	Excuse me. She was on morphine at an earlier time.
Question:	When?
Answer:	When she was in the intensive care unit at Cedars-Sinai. I believe she was on morphine when she was intubated.
Question:	Was that your order or the intensive care people?
Answer:	These were by my orders and Dr. Wolfe's orders and carried out by the intensive care people.
Question:	Other than on that occasion, had you discussed putting her on morphine at any time?
Answer:	Discussed putting her on morphine?
Question:	With her?
Answer:	I think I have answered these questions. I discussed keeping her comfortable. It is understood in a hospice situation that one uses whatever medicines one … meaning the physician

uses whatever medicines the physician feels are appropriate to control pain and control agitation. And morphine is a commonly used medicine in this situation at the end of a person's life.

Question: Did you tell Miss Duke that morphine was commonly used?

Mr. Barnosky: Objection; asked and answered.

[Attorney discussion omitted]

Question: Let's see, where was I? 2100. 2200, you were there. Right?

Answer: Yes.

Question: Ten o'clock at night. "10 milligrams of morphine IVP." What's that?

Answer: It means I gave her morphine 10 milligrams in the intravenous drip.

Question: Over and above what was in the drip?

Answer: I believe it may have been over and above what was in the drip.

Question: And how did you give her this?

Answer: As I said, intravenously.

Question: Did you pump it into her arm?

Answer: Into her arm.

Question: Or into wherever the drip was connected?

Answer: I believe again I answered the question. I gave it to her intravenously.

Question: Did you pump it in?

Answer: What do you mean by "pump"?

Question: Did you push it into her arm?

Mr. Barnosky: Objection as to form.

Answer: I put it into an intravenous line, into a burette or into the line directly.

Question: Did you just let it drip, or did you pump the line?

Answer: "Pump the line." I don't recall.

Question: Did you force it at a faster rate than the drip?

Answer: I don't recall. Probably it went in at a faster rate than the drip; otherwise, I wouldn't have given it that way.

Question: After you start morphine, you expected to have increased fluid levels. Right?

Answer: Increased fluid levels?

Question: Yes.

Answer: Where?

Question: In the lungs?

Answer: I don't expect to have increased fluid levels in
                 the lungs. One would expect to have decreased
                 fluid levels in the lungs with morphine, if any-
                 thing.

Question: And the respiration at 2200, 5 to 7 breaths per
                 minute?

Answer: Yes.

Question: Fifteen- to twenty-second pauses?

Answer: Yes.

Question: She is in a deep sleep?

Answer: I think she is moribund.

Question: In a deep sleep?

Answer: More than a deep sleep.

Question: Not arousable?

Answer: Hopefully not arousable.

Question: And then another added 10 milligrams to the
                 burette.

Answer:	If it says I did that, I did that.
Question:	Do you remember doing that?
Answer:	I don't remember it.
Question:	And then a 15-milligram dose by the doctor? What was that?
Answer:	No. It says here another ... it says another 10 milligrams added to burette's 15-milligram dose. So that, over a period of time, the rate of the morphine administration would be increased. It was not pushed at that point or injected directly. It was placed in the burette.
	At this point in time, I expected, and for 24 ... at least 24 hours before, I expected ... my expectation that Miss Duke's condition was expectant, I expected her to die, and at the same time I was treating her with increased doses of morphine, she was fulminant pulmonary edema, from which I would not under any circumstances expect her to awaken.
Question:	And you expected her to die when you added that extra morphine, didn't you?
Mr. Barnosky:	Objection as to form.
Answer:	I expected that at some time during the succeeding hours, she would die.
Question:	Weren't you surprised that she did not die earlier?

Ms. Watson:	Objection.
Answer:	Actually, no.
Question:	2300 hours, "Lungs filling up with fluid." Do you see that?
Answer:	Yes.
Question:	Did you do anything to stop that?
Answer:	No. As I said, I was not treating pulmonary edema or the condition that preceded it, which was severe corporal edema or the ... I was not treating what I knew was an overload of fluid in her body.
Question:	It says "Additional morphine from doctor hasn't changed patient's assessments, ineffective." Right?
Answer:	I don't think that means a thing. And I don't believe that that was true.
Question:	Did you tell anybody that was wrong?
Answer:	No.
Question:	Then "Morphine drip continued, 15 milligrams per hour?"
Answer:	Yes.
Question:	Respiration becomes more shallow, more apnea?

Answer: Yes.

Question: And her skin becomes clammy at 2400 hours?

Answer: Yes.

Question: 20 to 25 seconds of apnea now?

Answer: Yes.

Question: I guess we go over to the 28th now on the next
                 entry. 0100 hours, "Circulatory status increas-
                 ingly deteriorating"?

Answer: Yes. This is a description of a woman who is
                 terminally ill dying on a morphine drip. It is a
                 very good description. It is a miserable kind of
                 death, except she was not aware of it. And she
                 was comfortable and she was pain free.

Question: And then the morphine is "continued at 15 mil-
                 ligrams an hour, eyes closed"?

Answer: You're reading this note?

Question: Yes, down at the bottom of the page. "Morphine
                 continued at 15 milligrams per hour, eyes
                 closed."

Answer: Yes.

Question: No signs or symptoms of pain or distress?

Answer: I hope not.

Question: You believe that to be accurate?

Answer: I believe that is accurate at that time.

Question: Let's go to the next one. 95 is 313. [Exhibit 95
                   was marked.] This is October 28.

Answer: Yes.

Question: At 1:30 her circulatory status is shutting down
                   slowly?

Answer: Yes.

Question: And her kidneys are not putting out?

Answer: Yes.

Question: And her ... "Patient respiratory distress increas-
                   ing." 35 to 40 seconds apnea?

Answer: She is apneic, her respiratory ... and I believe
                   this refers to her respiratory ... This is just a
                   misuse of words. She is progressively apneic,
                   her respiratory rate is slowing, this is ... but she
                   is not in distress. "Distress" is wrong word.

Question: Where do you see the word "distress"?

Answer: It says "Patient respiratory distress increasing."
                   She was not in distress.

Question: Wasn't her respiration rate slowing?

Answer: Her respiration rate was slowing; but as she was completely unaware of this process, she was not in distress.

Question: But that was low ...

Answer: The entire direction of her care from October 7th through this point was to ... was to minimize or eliminate distress during a terminal phase of her life.

Question: Don't you read that as meaning that that's lower than normal?

Answer: What is lower than normal?

Question: The respiratory rate.

Answer: Where does it say that?

Question: "Patient respiratory distress" means it's declining, it's lower. Right? Isn't that the way you read it?

Answer: It doesn't mean that at all. It says "respiratory distress increasing." It could mean that her respiratory rate is increasing.

It says that she's apneic for 35 to 40 seconds. This is an agonal phenomenon. It is a nurse's description of a patient dying of multiple serious conditions while she is receiving morphine intravenously.

Question:	The note does not tell ... does not make a judgment as to what she is dying of, does it, Doctor?
Answer:	It doesn't, no.
Mr. Barnosky:	It speaks for itself.
Question:	That's your judgment. Right?
Answer:	It has been my judgment, it was the judgment of every other physician who saw her, a matter that we have gone over repeatedly in this discussion today and on prior days.
Question:	Nobody else saw her, other physicians, at this time, did they?
Answer:	Dr. Glassman saw her at this time.
Question:	Did he make a judgment of what she was dying of?
Answer:	I think he made numerous judgments about what she was dying of.
Question:	Did he tell you what they were?
Answer:	Did I discuss them at any time?
Question:	Yes.
Answer:	I did discuss them, as I have told you repeatedly in this deposition.

Question:	Did you discuss them on this date.
Answer:	Yes, I did.
Question:	With Dr. Glassman?
Answer:	When Dr. Glassman was at the house, I discussed them with Dr. Glassman. I discussed them with Dr. Trabulus. I am not sure whether or not Dr. Trabulus saw her on that evening. I did not talk to any other physician on that date.
Question:	Did you tell Dr. ... Did you have any discussion with Dr. Glassman other than with regard to what she was dying of, other than what you have already told us on the record?
Answer:	I don't believe so. I said I made this discussion repeatedly ... we have this discussion repeatedly.
Question:	So nothing new.
Answer:	There is nothing new.
Question:	And the morphine is continuing at that time, 1:30? The morphine drip continues.
Answer:	Yes.
Question:	And then down toward the bottom of that page, "Continues to be kept comfortable and sedated." Correct?

Answer: Where are we talking about?

Question: Down at the bottom of that same column?

Answer: Yes.

Question: Bernard, Nuku, Bill Doyle ... There is another
               name there. Lavette?

Answer: Lavette. I don't know who Lavette is.

Question: ... and Bill Doyle are all there at this time. Is
               that right?

Answer: At bedside. Yes.

Question: When did Bill Doyle arrive?

Answer: Sometime earlier ... sometime on the evening
               of the preceding day.

Question: Did you have any discussion with him before
               he came?

Answer: I don't believe so.

Question: Did you have any discussion with him once he
               was there?

Answer: Yes.

Question: What did you say?

Answer:	I said that Miss Duke was dying, that she had been dying, and her condition was expectant from the day before, meaning the day before the 27th, the 26th we're talking about, and that I expected her to die within a very short period of time while she was receiving a morphine drip for sedation and to prevent her from having any pain.
Question:	What did he say?
Answer:	I don't think ... he just responded that this was what was happening, and that's all he said.
Question:	Then she is weaker, 2:30?
Answer:	"Weak" is a subjective note, but it says here ... Where are we talking about, please?
Question:	"Weaker and less strength to breathe."
Mr. Crofton:	It's four o'clock.
Answer:	Well, there is a bit ... That would not be an assessment one would make of a patient who is moribund, but that is what the nurse says at the time.
Question:	Four o'clock.
Answer:	Yes.
Question:	Apnea one- to two-minute duration now?

Answer: Yes.

Question: Dr. Kivowitz is called, and you increase the
                 morphine drip.

Answer: Yes.

Question: Why was that?

Answer: I wanted to end the agony of these last few
                 hours of life.

Question: She wasn't feeling anything at this time,
                 was she?

Answer: No.

Question: "He had instructed PDNs" ... is that what you
                 read? "He had instructed PDNs"? Is that how
                 you read it?

Answer: I read it that way but ...

Question: He had instructed the nurses?

Answer: Yes.

Question: "To keep at 15 milligrams per hour, but the
                 patient is lingering." Do you see that?

Answer: Yes.

Question: That means she's lasting ... she's living longer
                 than you expected?

Mr. Barnosky: Objection as to form. This is the nurse's note.

Answer: I have answered these questions before.

Question: I am asking what the word "lingering" means to you.

Answer: This is just going on for a long period of time.

Question: And therefore, you're going to increase the morphine and "Needs increase the MSO form, new orders obtained"?

Answer: That may be what it means.

Question: You're going to increase the morphine so she won't ...

Answer: This is a standard way of dealing with a terminal patient on a morphine drip. One does not prolong the period of ... the agonal period for longer than is necessary. And there is no necessary period.

Question: You're increasing the morphine so she won't linger?

Answer: I have answered the question.

Question: Is that true?

Answer: I have answered the question.

Mr. Barnosky:	Okay, I think this one might be slightly different. If you can answer it, go ahead.
Answer:	I increased the morphine so she would not linger and suffer in any way at all.
Question:	She is not suffering now, is she?
Mr. Barnosky:	Objection as to form. Argumentative. He already answered that question.
Question:	Do you agree with me that she is not suffering?
Answer:	I agree she is feeling no pain.
Question:	And you increased the morphine level so she would die?
Mr. Barnosky:	Objection as to form.
Ms. Watson:	Objection as to form.
Mr. Barnosky:	And asked and answered as well.
Question:	Is that true?
Answer:	I think I have answered the question.
Question:	Is that a yes?
Mr. Crofton:	Objection.
Answer:	I have answered the question.

Question:	The answer is yes?
Mr. Barnosky:	Yes, he has answered the question.
Answer:	Yes, I have answered the question.
Question:	And yes, you increased the morphine so she would die?
Mr. Barnosky:	Objection as to form. It's been asked and answered. I direct the witness not to answer again.
Ms. Watson:	Objection.
Mr. Howarth:	It has not been answered. Do you want to read the record back?
Mr. Barnosky:	No, I just want you to finish. If indeed any of these—
Mr. Howarth:	No, no, no. This one we're going to get right now. I haven't asked him this before. Let's read the record back. [Record read back as "You're increasing the morphine so she won't linger?"]
Answer:	I have answered the question.
Question:	Is that true?
Answer:	I have answered the question.
Mr. Barnosky:	Okay. I think this one might be slightly different. If you can answer it again, go ahead.

Answer:	I increased the morphine so she would not linger and suffer in any way at all.
Mr. Barnosky:	That is the question and answer I was referring to?
Mr. Howarth:	When you say you increased the morphine so she won't linger ...
Mr. Crofton:	And "suffer" was the word.
Mr. Howarth:	Excuse me, Counsel. I'll ask my questions ... This is not your deposition and you're not to take ... you're not to make objections here. Just one of you ... we've been through this. We've been through this.
Question:	When you say you increased the morphine level so she wouldn't linger, you mean so she would die?
Ms. Watson:	Objection.
Mr. Barnosky:	Objection as to form. You can answer.
Answer:	**The answer is that I increased the morphine so that she would not linger, that she would not suffer, and ultimately that she would die perhaps shortly or sooner than she would have otherwise died from her medical conditions, which I judged within a 48-hour period were of a terminal nature.** [Emphasis added]

Appendix C
A Tribute to the Honorable Retired Judge Elwood Rich, a Notable Duke University Alumnus

It was largely the encouragement of retired Riverside County Superior Court judge, the Honorable Judge Elwood Rich (ret.), that I finally decided to write this book. Over the years I had told him of the stories I had learned of the Duke family as a child, and of my research into family history and genealogy. He would tell me of his years at Duke and of his participation in athletics at the university. He often mentioned that my stories were an invaluable treasure and should be put in writing for others to read. When I saw him at the courthouse, he would often ask with a smile, "When is that book about the Duke family going to be finished?" In recognition of his support, and because it seems fitting to include a tribute to a notable alumnus of Duke University, I decided to include this brief tribute to Judge Rich.

Though he retired from the bench in 1980 after twenty-seven years of service, Judge Rich continued to work as a mediator for the Riverside County Superior Court until 2012, when he finally retired completely from the courts. At the time of the writing of this book, he continues to work in private mediation and manages the law school he founded over forty years ago, California Southern Law School. Judge Rich, who reached his ninety-second birthday on November 20, 2012, graduated from Duke University with a bachelor of arts in 1943 and from the University of Illinois with a doctor of jurisprudence in 1946. While the life of Judge Rich has been fulfilling and worthy of comment, one cannot fully appreciate this fascinating person without understanding the environment in which he works, the Riverside County Old Historic Courthouse in Riverside, California.

Considered by thousands of attorneys to be the most beautiful courthouse in California, the Riverside County Old Historic Courthouse is a stunning example of architecture and tradition. Built in 1903, with donations from the local Masonic lodge, the courthouse today stands as a monument of beauty, equity, and justice. Upon climbing the front steps of this amazing structure, the visitor is immediately humbled by the beautiful architecture and stunning statuette guardians on the roof above the front entrance. As one enters through the tall oak doors, a metal detector obstructs the path as a necessity of the modern world. After passing through security, the visitor encounters the main hall of the courthouse. High on the wall there rests an oil painting of a gentleman whose dignity and graciousness blend seamlessly with the elegant and dignified structure of the building. In the painting, Judge Rich is seated on a bench in the hallway of the courthouse. Immediately to his right stand a young woman and a young girl with a look of peacefulness, as if they have just obtained some long-pursued relief. Throughout Southern California, no member of the California judiciary has elicited a more familiar image than the Honorable Judge Elwood M. Rich as he walked through the great halls of this beautiful courthouse, passing from one attorney to the next, negotiating settlements in their cases.

Judge Elwood Rich is the grandson of University of Michigan School of Law graduate John Wesley Group, who practiced in Rauchtown, Pennsylvania, for many years before retiring to become a full-time farmer. On the father's side of his family, his great-grandfather, John Rich II, was cofounder and owner of Woolrich, the famous clothing manufacturer, whose products are today sold throughout the world. I first met Judge Rich (who was commonly called Judge Woody) in 1987. After graduating from Washington University School of Law in St. Louis, Missouri, I began my practice on Wilshire Boulevard in a Los Angeles firm that was launching a San Bernardino office; I transferred to the San Bernardino office to assist in that launch. The firm's primary areas of practice were professional liability and construction defect litigation. One of my early cases involved a substantial grading project where my client, the grader, was being sued along with the civil and soil engineers because of alleged grading and engineering defects, as a result of which hundreds of homes were sinking into the ground. The claimed damages were $40 million. Approximately a dozen attorneys met with Judge Rich at the Riverside County Old Historic Courthouse on a cloudy fall afternoon. We worked into the evening before finally reaching a tentative settlement. The skill of Judge Rich in finding a settlement became immediately apparent, and over the years, Judge Rich settled many more cases for me at the California Southern Law School, on Elizabeth Street in Riverside, California. The law school, founded by Judge Rich, has become a recognized academic institution in Southern California, with many of its graduates now serving as superior court judges and court commissioners.

On a warm Friday afternoon in April 2012, I met with Judge Rich in the main hall of the Old Historic Riverside County Courthouse. That day the busy court had been disrupted by a bomb threat, and all entrances to the courthouse were closed except the northern entrance. I had just attended a luncheon at the Riverside County Bar Association across the street, where the featured speaker, the Honorable Judge Gloria Trask,[246] moderated a panel discussion concerning a new expedited trial program in California. As I entered the courthouse, I observed Judge Rich at the far end of the hall. He saw

---

246 The Honorable Judge Gloria Trask is a judge in the Riverside County Superior Court.

me enter the building and waved while flashing his always pleasant smile. As I approached, he shook my hand and then motioned for me to sit on a bench immediately next to the front entrance of the building. To our right, high on the wall, was the giant oil painting of Judge Rich described earlier. As we talked, dozens of judges, court clerks, employees, attorneys, and litigants passed, many of them pausing momentarily to say hello. It seems there is no one involved with the Old Historic Riverside County Courthouse whose life has not been touched in some manner by Judge Rich.

"I would like to hear about your childhood—the reason you decided to go to Duke and eventually become a judge," I said.

Judge Rich smiled. "It was really because of baseball that I went to Duke, and it was because of an event at Duke that I became a lawyer and then a judge, but that is getting way ahead in the story. My grandfather on my mother's side of the family, John Wesley Group, was a lawyer and a graduate of the University of Michigan Law School. He had a small practice in Lock Haven, Pennsylvania. He enjoyed law, but he also enjoyed farming. He owned about two hundred acres near Rauchtown and, after many years, gave up the practice of law to become a full-time farmer. I was born on November 20, 1920, in Turbotville, Pennsylvania, to George and Helen Rich." Judge Rich often chuckled with his familiar smile exhibited when contemplating amusing, introspective events. I almost wondered if he actually remembered his birth. "When my mother went into labor, they sent for the doctor, but he did not arrive in time, so I was delivered by a midwife, which was not uncommon in those days.

"In the early years of my life I was raised on the apple farm where my father worked as an apple picker. My father took great pride in being able to harvest more apples that anyone else in the least amount of time. My parents worked hard, and my father saved every penny. In time he saved enough money to start a wholesale candy business with his brother. They would sell candy bars to grocery stores in the community. In those days we didn't have supermarkets.

We had small grocery stores like A&P. So they would take the candy bar samples to the local stores and obtain orders for candy. The samples were free from the candy bar producers. We had Baby Ruth, Mr. Goodbar, Milky Way, Clark bars, and many others. He always had leftover samples, so he gave them to me for free. I would take those samples and sell them door to door for five cents per bar. It was a convenience for the buyer—and a great deal for me. I made a lot of money doing that. During my high school years I also took on the side occupation of selling punches on a punch board. I discovered that the salesmen calling on my father's candy distribution company liked this low-cost gambling. In time I had saved enough money to purchase a 1937 Ford coupe with a sixty-horsepower engine for $650. I traded an old Pontiac for the Ford."

Photograph of the Honorable Judge Elwood Rich (ret.) (left) and author D. W. Duke (right) taken at the Riverside County Bar Association Officer Installation Dinner, September 16, 2013. Michael Elderman, photographer.

Judge Rich leaned back against the wall. "I remember in those days everything was much cheaper than today. You could buy a gallon of gasoline for seventeen cents. Donuts were twenty cents per dozen. Milk was eight cents per quart. We were in the middle of the Great Depression. Many people were out of work, but my family did not have it nearly as bad as some people."

Little League baseball was developing as Judge Rich grew into his teen years. He found the game exciting and interesting, and he played every opportunity that presented. He soon learned that he had unusual talent both at batting, due to his ambidextrous swinging ability, and at playing the position of catcher, due to his keen eye. He developed the ability to recognize where the ball was going as soon as it left the pitcher's hand. In high school, Judge Rich was also on the wrestling team, where he excelled. When looking for a university, he sought a school where he would receive a scholarship for athletic activities. He discovered that Duke offered scholarships for football, so he chose to attend Duke to take advantage of a scholarship. In 1939, the young man enrolled at Duke on a partial football scholarship. Duke's football team, then known as the Iron Dukes, had played the entire season in 1938 without having a single score against them in any game. Despite the great season, Duke suffered a heartbreaking 7–3 loss to USC in the Rose Bowl in Pasadena. After the bombing of Pearl Harbor in 1941, the Department of Defense decided that crowds would not be permitted to assemble in large numbers on the West Coast for fear of another attack. For this reason, in 1942 Duke hosted the Rose Bowl at Wallace Wade Stadium at its campus in Durham. The opposing team was Oregon State, who defeated Duke 20–16.

William Preston Few, the president of Duke University from 1910 to 1940, had received his PhD from Harvard University. Few had been recruited to Trinity College, because Benjamin Newton Duke and the board of trustees believed that the South needed a university of the stature and reputation of a major Ivy League university. They felt that William Preston Few had the credentials and the ability to bring the university to the Ivy League standard. In 1924, President Few persuaded the board of trustees to change the name of Trinity College to Duke University in honor of Washington

Duke, who had been the university's first major benefactor. Initially Benjamin Duke and his brother James opposed the name change, but President Few finally convinced them that the name change would be beneficial to the university. Few recognized the importance of a strong reputation both academically and athletically, and he also recognized that athletics provide a vehicle for national university recognition. For that reason, he supported athletic scholarships, which even to this day are not considered acceptable at Harvard University. The athletic scholarship was beneficial for Rich in that Duke became much more affordable and attractive.

When Rich first arrived at Duke in 1939 and signed on with the football team, George MacAfee, who later played for the Chicago Bears, was playing halfback while also running on the track team. In those days many of the athletes played on several teams within the university simultaneously. Rich played on both the football team and the baseball team. After his first year, he withdrew from the football team, having concluded that it was an imprudent sport except for athletes who possessed large size and great strength, neither of which was an attribute held by Rich. Nonetheless, Rich remained on the baseball team, whose coach was Jacks Coombs. Coombs had retired from pitching in the major leagues to coach baseball at Duke.

In 1939, tuition at Duke was $200 per semester and housing was $50 per semester. The meal book provided three meals for $1. To help defray the expenses, Rich also worked in the dining room as a waiter. The waiters wore white coats with little pockets. The students always asked for extra butter, and Rich discovered that he could carry small packets of butter in his pockets to avoid a trip back to the kitchen. The students always received butter from Rich promptly, which made him quite popular in the dining room. Unfortunately, however, he was so busy with his many activities that he had little time for socializing and dating.

Until his third year of college, athletics remained Rich's primary focus. Academic pursuits were less important than being the best in one's chosen sport, which for Rich had become baseball. He excelled in athletics and ultimately did not place much emphasis on academic pursuits. However, as a student and an athlete, he was required to maintain a certain minimum grade point average, and tutors were provided to assist in this academic endeavor. It was the necessity of maintaining an acceptable grade point average that ultimately caused him to become interested in scholastic pursuits. His tutor was a student in Duke University School of Law named Barry Williams. One of Rich's assignments in his political science class was to brief a number of landmark cases, such as *Marbury v. Madison*. Williams was so impressed with Rich's briefing ability that he encouraged Rich to attend law school. This was the first time Rich had considered this possibility, and he ultimately decided it would be a wise course of action. From that day forward, his legal studies became more important than his athletic pursuits.

Rich applied and was accepted at Duke University School of Law while he still had one year of undergraduate studies remaining. After completing his first year of law school at Duke, and receiving his AB degree, he transferred to USC School of Law because he had heard about the beautiful climate in Southern California. At the time he transferred to USC, the law school was offering three semesters per year, consisting of a fall semester, a winter semester, and a summer semester, which allowed him to proceed at an accelerated pace. After completing his second year at USC, he transferred a third time to the University of Illinois School of Law because USC had stopped offering the summer program. At the University of Illinois he was able to attend in the summer, which allowed him to graduate in September 1946.

While Rich was involved in his academic pursuits, he often thought about romance, though his studies and his heavy workload did not afford much time for romantic interests. Many miles away, on the islands of Hawaii, a young woman named Lorna Smith was experiencing her own difficulties with romance, and though they did not know each other, their lives would someday become intertwined through fate. Lorna lived with her mother and her sister in Hawaii. She knew a young man named Joseph Jirik who was a second lieutenant in the 748th Bomber Squadron of the Army Air Corp. On December 7, 1941, Lorna was living in base housing. As the Japanese planes approached, they were mistaken for US fighter planes. It was not until they began bombing that those on the ground realized that Pearl Harbor was under attack. Lorna lay on the floor under a kitchen table to provide some protection against strafing bullets that were hitting the house. When the bombing and shooting finally stopped, 2,403 men, women, and children had lost their lives and 1,282 were wounded on this tragic day in American history.

In 1944, Joseph Jirik entered pilot training at El Toro, located near Riverside, California. Lorna, her mother, and her sister decided to move to Riverside, California, because it was near March Air Force Base, where there was a commissary they could utilize. Joseph and Lorna were married in 1944. When it was time for him to be deployed, they went together to the East Coast, where Joseph departed for the European Theater. After Joseph left for Europe, Lorna received a few letters from him and then heard nothing further. She did not know what had happened. Finally, it was discovered that he had been killed in an air attack on September 28, 1944, over Germany. He was buried at the Netherlands American Cemetery and Memorial in the Netherlands. For Lorna this was a devastating blow. She had believed that Joseph would return and that she and Joseph would grow old together, but that was not to be.

After graduating from law school, Rich took the 1946 California Bar Examination, passed, and was admitted in 1947 with a bar number of 19335. In 1947, he accepted a position working for the Riverside County District Attorney's Office for $290 per month. His custom was to interview criminal defendants immediately after they were jailed, which was an uncommon way for a deputy to obtain valuable information about a case. As a result of these early interviews, he could often persuade the defendant to enter into a plea bargain. The strategy permitted him to settle more of his cases without going to trial.

Still recovering from the loss of her husband several years earlier, Lorna Smith-Jirik went to a YWCA dance in Riverside, California. Rich had discovered that the dances were a great place to meet interesting people and attractive women. It was on the dance floor that he first saw Lorna. He looked at her with a smile as she came to him from across the dance floor and their journey together began. Lorna and Rich were soon married and shared many years of happiness as spouses and partners in life.

In 1951, Rich decided to run for judge of the municipal court. He was elected and remained a municipal court judge in Riverside until 1971, when he became the eighth sitting superior court judge in Riverside. It was in his capacity of superior court judge that Rich achieved his greatest recognition in California jurisprudence. His keen perception and ability to spot issues, combined with his ability to find a compromise, provided a unique ability to settle cases. He became a strong proponent of mediation and settlements, always maintaining that it was far better to conclude a case by settlement with certainty than to place one's fate in the hands of a jury of unknown peers who lacked the authority to reach a compromise. Rich often says, "With a jury there is only a winner and a loser, and the winner usually does not win nearly as much as he had hoped, and the loser's losses are usually far greater than anticipated."

After many years on the bench, Rich began teaching torts at Riverside University Law School in Riverside. The law school ran into difficulties, and it became necessary to close its doors. As a result, a number of students who had completed a year or two of law school were left with no place to finish their studies. Judge Rich considered this event a misfortune and for that reason decided to open the Citrus Belt Law School in Riverside, California. The Citrus Belt Law School later changed its name to California Southern Law School. Lorna began working in administration at the law school in 1971, where she remained until 1983. Lorna passed away in July

2007. In front of their home in Riverside, California, Judge Rich still keeps a sign that says, "Casa de la Muchacha Dulce" which means "Home of the Sweet Girl." Judge Rich says, "While she was here, she managed the law school. Now she is the manager of the angels."

During his years on the bench and to this day, Judge Rich has been a strong advocate of judicial economy. He has vigorously proposed cost-cutting measures to reduce the expense of operating a court system. He has always believed that if less is spent in maintaining the courts, more is available for other needed services in the community. Many of his ideas of judicial economy have taken root not only in Riverside County but throughout the state as well. Undoubtedly the footprint Judge Rich made in the Riverside County court system will remain for centuries to come.

Judge Rich continued to mediate in the Riverside County courts until the end of 2012, though he still serves as dean of California Southern Law School, where his sons Greg and Brian work in administration. He also maintains a private mediation practice for litigants whose cases do not fall within the perimeters of eligibility for the court mediation system. His unique ability to help litigants and attorneys find resolution in conflict has left a permanent impression on the court system throughout California. Those of us who have the fortune to practice in the Riverside County Superior Courts are grateful for the work of Judge Rich, who over the years has helped many litigants learn the meaning of forgiveness and resolution. Perhaps the concept of mediation and conciliation is something Judge Rich learned at Duke University; but regardless of the source of philosophy, it has clearly impacted the lives of thousands of Californians in a positive and meaningful way.

Appendix D

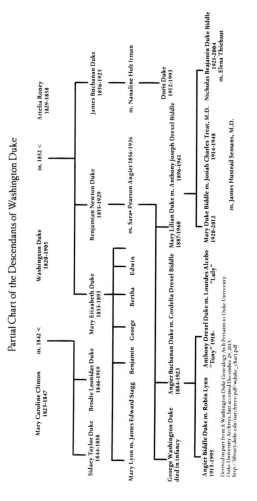

Partial Chart of the Descendants of Washington Duke

Mary Caroline Clinton
1825-1847

m. 1842 <

Washington Duke
1820-1905

m. 1852 <

Artelia Roney
1829-1858

Sidaey Taylor Duke
1844-1858

Brodie Leonidas Duke
1846-1919

Mary Elizabeth Duke
1853-1893

Benjamin Newton Duke
1855-1929

James Buchanan Duke
1856-1925

Mary Lyon m. James Edward Stagg

Benjamin   George   Bertha   Edwin

m. Sarah Pearson Angier 1856-1936

m. Nanaline Holt Inman

George Washington Duke
died in infancy

Angier Buchanan Duke m. Cordelia Drexel Biddle
1884-1923

Mary Lillian Duke m. Anthony Joseph Drexel Biddle
1887-1960   1896-1961

Doris Duke
1912-1993

Angier Biddle Duke m. Robin Lynn
1915-1995

Anthony Drexel Duke m. Lourdes Alcebo
"Tony" 1918-   "Luly"

Mary Duke Biddle m. Josiah Charles Treat, M.D.
1920-2012   1914-1948

Nicholas Benjamin Duke Biddle
1921-2004
m. Elena Thiebaut

m. James Hustead Semans, M.D.

Derived in part from A Washington Duke Genealogy As It Pertains to Duke University.
Duke University Archives, last accessed December 29, 2013.
http://library.duke.edu/uarchives/pdf/wduke_chart.pdf

CPSIA information can be obtained at www.ICGtesting.com
Printed in the USA
LVOW11*1934281014

410968LV00005B/5/P

9 781491 726211